TH DE SERIES
OOK THREE

JANE WASHINGTON

Washington, Jane

Sauter

www.janewashington.com

ISBN: 9798869937513

CONTENTS

ALSO BY JANE WASHINGTON

Ironside Academy

Book 1: Plier

Book 2: Tourner

Book 3: Sauter

Book 4: Relever

A Tempest of Shadows

Book 1: A Tempest of Shadows

Book 2: A City of Whispers

Book 3: Dream of Embers

Book 4: A Castle of Ash

Book 5: A World of Lost Words

Bastan Hollow

Standalone: Charming

Standalone: Disobedience

Standalone Books

I Am Grey

Curse of the Gods

Book 1: Trickery

Book 2: Persuasion

Book 3: Seduction

Book 4: Strength

Novella: Neutral

Book 5: Pain

Seraph Black

Book 1: Charcoal Tears

Book 2: Watercolour Smile

Book 3: Lead Heart

Book 4: A Portrait of Pain

Beatrice Harrow

Book 1: Hereditary

Book 2: The Soulstoy Inheritance

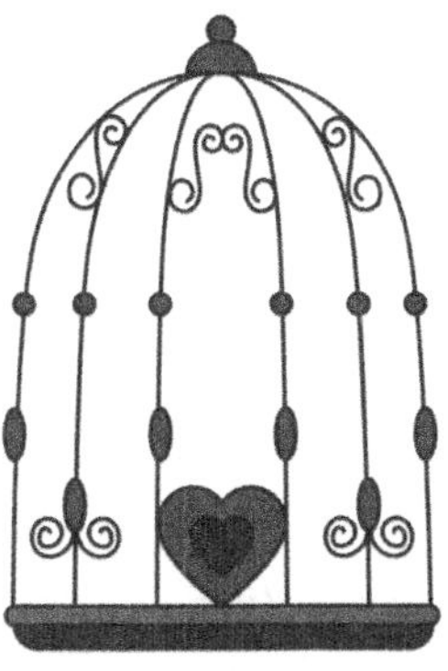

Oh, the irony of this beautiful game,
Where shadows gather, dressed for fame,
Glitter on the brow, a star in the eye,
Iron on all sides, as the insides lie.

TRIGGER WARNINGS

panic attacks/flashbacks
neglect and abuse (not within main group)
sexual harassment (not within main group)
traumatic and violent crime resulting in death *(not within main group)*

If you or anyone you know needs support, please visit lifeline.org.au.

DISCLAIMER

Some crystals dissolve in water.

This will make sense later.

IRONSIDE ACADEMY MAP

To view the map of Ironside, please scan the QR code below.

IRONSIDE ACADEMY PLAYLIST

To listen to the playlist for the Ironside series, please scan the QR code below.

IRONSIDE ACADEMY CHEAT SHEET

To view the character cheat sheet for the Ironside series, please scan the QR code below.

Main Character List

This book has **ELEVEN** main characters, which is a lot! Feel free to bookmark this page if you have trouble keeping track of them all. (In order of age).

Isobel Carter

Moses Kane

Theodore Kane

Elijah Reed

Gabriel Spade

Cian Ashford

Niko Hart

Kilian Gray

Oscar Sato

Mikel Easton

Kalen West

I

SOUL INFRACTION

ISOBEL DRIFTED IN AND OUT OF CONSCIOUSNESS FOR WHAT seemed like an eternity, bobbing up and down like a rag doll tossed into a stream and pulled along with the current. Sometimes she was in free fall, tumbling down a waterfall with no end in sight. She thought she screamed when that happened, but it never amounted to anything. No impact when she landed. No sudden submersion. One minute she was falling, and the next, she was asleep again.

Sometimes she passed through warmer currents where she drifted closer to the surface, sunlight striving to stroke her cheeks. That was when she knew she was herself, and someone was holding her. She was cocooned in a warm, resinous scent. Sweet, like a drop of honey on the tip of her tongue, but deep, earthy and woody. *Amber.* It sank into her nose and mouth, filling her up until there was no room for the water she drifted through to spill into her lungs and drown her. After some time, the stream turned into a cloud and she was no longer bobbing, but floating.

She tried to edge away from the heat when it grew too much, but burning hands always dragged her back, tucking her against muscles that seemed tight and stiff with tension. His voice was the first tangible thing she registered after days of floating. It was as tight and tense as his body, biting out a harsh word to someone else. An unfamiliar voice answered, sounding calm and measured, their tone resonant. It was clearer than the rasped rebuttal from the warm body wrapped behind her.

"You cannot lie to me," the calm stranger stated. It was impossible to tell their gender.

Isobel flinched at the change in the amber scent wrapped around her, that drop of honey against her tongue souring into something acidic that burned her taste buds.

"And *you* still haven't told me how you manage to get in here every damn day." The words were growled out of the warm body behind her.

"We walk from the chapel to the hospital," a third voice supplied. It was droll. Young and feminine with a sharp, sardonic undertone. Another stranger.

Isobel peeled her eyes open, the movement taking far more effort than it should have.

"She's awake," the androgynous voice stated. "You're overheating her, by the way."

"Fuck off." It was Theodore holding her, his gravelled tone ripping through her body. She was curled in his lap in a hospital bed, the back of the bed raised to allow him to sit up while he cradled her.

He was also *very* warm.

"Illy?" His voice softened instantly, his hand supporting her head as she tried to lift it up. His thumb brushed across her cheek. "Welcome back." His eyes narrowed on hers like he had more to say, but he only sucked in a breath, his pupils dilating as they flicked over her features before he turned back to the other voices. "Now isn't a good time."

"Now is the perfect time," the younger voice replied. "That's why we came *now*."

"Hush, Sophia," the androgynous stranger scolded.

Isobel dragged her attention to the speaker. A tall woman with skin like cinnamon baked happily in the sun and elegant, narrow eyes that stared unflinchingly back at her. The deep, gold-ringed, mahogany hue of her stare unsettled Isobel, making her shrink back against Theodore.

The woman was an Alpha. Her grey hair was cut short, the strands flat and straight, and she was wearing plain, threadbare clothes, her grey shirt sporting mismatched buttons, though the cloth was perfectly pressed and probably better cared for than the numerous designer outfits Isobel had been stitched into during ...

The settlement tour.

She shuddered, her teeth mashing together as pain laced through her body and mind.

"Get the nurse!" Theodore barked.

The Alpha with the grey hair stepped closer, peering at Isobel. She towered over the bed, her dark brown eyes shrewd. There was a small pin in her collar, a silver lyre. Her only adornment.

"Both of her eyes have changed," the woman noted. "She's been wearing a contact." Her tone was devoid of shock or curiosity. She was simply making a calm observation. "I suppose the bond specialist wouldn't have thought to check the authenticity of her normal-looking iris."

"You're seeing things," Theodore growled, cuddling Isobel closer, his hand cupping her face, blocking off her view of the woman. And hiding her eyes.

She pulled his hand down with shaking fingers—the Alpha woman had already seen her eyes—and watched as the other woman thrust out her arm, offering Isobel her palm.

"Maya Rosales," she introduced herself. "You can call me Maya, or Guardian Rosales if you like. I keep the chapel."

Isobel's brow furrowed as she stared at the hand, some of her remembered pain slipping away as she was distracted by the very hot, vibrating body curled behind her. Theodore felt like he was seconds away from lunging forward and ripping the older Alpha's entire arm off.

"K-Keep the chapel?" Isobel's voice cracked, the words barely dragged into existence as she slipped her hand weakly into Maya's.

"The academy tries to keep a Guardian on grounds for the students who still follow the Gifted religion." Maya immediately turned Isobel's hand, revealing the deep wounds spidering up her arm. They looked like scattered lightning bolts, raw and puckered, a deep angry red. Stitches knitted her skin back together.

Theodore finally snapped, gripping the other woman's wrist between his thumb and forefinger. He flung it away from Isobel before tucking her arm gently back in against her chest.

"These are my children," Maya continued, without so much as a flinch at Theodore's overreaction. "They came to work as my Soul Keepers." The Guardian stepped out of the way, revealing a girl around Isobel's age and a boy who couldn't have been older than nine. "Sophia and Luis. They don't usually accompany me on my hospital rounds, but Luis is quite the Ironside fan. I hope you don't mind."

"I'm sorry." Isobel glanced between them all. "I don't know much about the Gifted religion."

"Yeah, Icon kid and all that." Sophia cocked her head, watching as Theodore pulled out his phone, angling his screen away from Maya. "Soul Keepers are like chapel assistants. Glorified cleaners and librarians, really."

The girl was stunning. Her skin was golden with a rich olive undertone, her hair cut into a shining dark bob, her features regal and full of grace, just like her mother. Her lips were naturally full, flushed with a pink colour that matched the second-hand shirt her brother was wearing. The boy was also beautiful, with a wary, shy gaze and oversized spectacles that hung down his nose. He pushed them up nervously as Isobel looked at him, but they immediately drooped down again, teetering on the tip of his nose. He had the same curious, narrow stare as his sister and mother.

"I was the one who suggested the chain," Maya said.

"What chain?" Isobel peeked at what Theodore was doing with his phone.

He was texting Kalen.

Theodore: Need help.

Theodore: Isobel is awake.

Theodore: Annoying Guardian lady saw her eyes.

"That one." Maya gestured to Isobel's arm, which was still tucked against her chest, held there protectively by Theodore's free hand.

She wiggled it out of his grip, frowning at the delicate, gold chain wrapped around her wrist. She had been too distracted and disorientated to notice it before. It was looped several times, the other end disappearing into the blanket, reappearing to lead up to Theodore's wrist, where it circled in a firm grip. She didn't recognise it instantly, but the longer she stared, the more peculiar it seemed. Almost like it was glowing slightly from within. And then she realised what it was. It was the chain that had appeared when Sato kissed her.

"By the time they found you, you had already been out there for something like six hours," Maya explained. "They thought you wouldn't survive, so I was called to bless your body when you passed."

"Out where?" she asked, barely above a whisper.

"The hiking trail," Theodore supplied, dropping his phone.

Kalen took her back to the trail. How much did they know? Eve's involvement was fairly obvious by the fact that it had all happened inside her house, and several people had seen her greet Isobel at the door. But did they know *why?* And where was Eve now?

She stared down at her wounds again, frowning even harder. She was full of stitches, which meant Kalen hadn't taken her body back in time. Or maybe he had, but her wounds had been too serious.

Maya spoke up again. "Your father arrived with your possessions, and I was there when the nurses searched your bag. I saw the chain and knew what it was immediately."

"They've been visiting every day," Theodore whispered against the shell of her ear. "Waiting for you to wake up. Sticking their noses into everything."

"And now you have woken up." Maya smiled. She looked like she was waiting for Isobel to thank her.

"What is it, then?" Isobel held up the chain, deciding to act dumb. Her voice cracked again, and she winced, prompting Theodore to reach for a pitcher of water set beside the bed. He pushed a cup into her hand, and she thanked him with a strained smile, sipping the cool liquid.

"It's a soul artefact." It was Sophia—the daughter—who spoke, looking a little bored, or maybe she was just uncomfortable. She seemed to be standing protectively in front of her little brother and shooting Theodore the occasional wary look. "Like from the stories, back when bonding was more common."

At Isobel's baffled expression, the other girl rolled her eyes. "So the gods chose to bind people together, right? Well, they used to bestow gifts on bonded couples to show their blessing. Glowing halos, crowns of flowers, matching wedding cloaks, love birds following them around, red strings and golden chains tying them together." She waved her fingers toward the chain, her blue-painted nails flicking dismissively. Either she didn't believe what she was saying, or she wasn't sure that Isobel was worthy of the god-given gift.

"Well ..." Isobel swallowed. "Okay then. What made you think this was a ... soul artefact?"

"A chain of exquisite design long enough to wrap all the way around two people lit within by a subtle glow?"

Maya returned dryly, before pulling a folded piece of paper from her pocket. It was a photocopied image from a book. "Because of Aphelina," she explained. "In the older texts, she's called The Celestial Enchantress."

The woman in the picture was nothing short of *radiant*. Her appearance hinted at so many different lineages it was impossible to tell which race she belonged to. It should have been confusing or overwhelming, but ... it made sense, somehow. It was as if she had been assembled with the ideals of beauty from each individual race, turning her into a tapestry of humanity so complicated it somehow became simple. She *was* beauty. Her eyes were deep and expressive, a gradient of colour that ran from rich brown to pale gold. Her hair was lustrous, floating around her like a cloud. It was inky black and auburn closer to her skull, but soft pastel shot through with bright white along the ends. Her skin had beautiful patches of ivory and oak, light and dark. Even her full and shapely lips seemed to shift from a soft rose to a warmer peach, to a deeper berry. Her face was a balance of symmetry that exuded a calm, harmonious nature in every line, slope, and curve ... but the most shocking detail about her was the chain.

Despite the extremes of her appearance, she only wore a thin linen dress, the chain looping around and around her like a living, cognisant thing, appearing to glow softly from within.

"Is that one of the Gifted gods?" Isobel asked,

handing the picture back. She didn't comment on the similarities of the chain, even though something hard and fearful lodged in the back of her throat. *They were talking about* gods, *now?*

"One of them, yes." Maya folded the paper and tucked it back into her pocket. "Aphelina inspires both the mortals and the gods toward aesthetic expression. In layman's terms, you could say that she's the goddess of love and beauty. She is always the most liberal with her gifts, though I haven't heard of her bestowing any in some time—"

The door flew open, Kalen striding into the room without a knock, Niko right behind him. They both stopped short when they saw Isobel sitting up in Theodore's lap. Kalen's gaze flicked down to her arms before settling on her face again, his huge chest swelling as he sucked in a breath.

Niko didn't give anything away, but he only tore his eyes from her for a quick moment to do a rapid sweep of the room before settling his attention back on her. It was heavy, watchful, but his expression was blank, his beautiful eyes guarded. He situated himself out of the way, leaning back against the wall and crossing his arms. The lopsided smile he always gave the cameras was thinned into pressed lips, his muscles twitching even as he kept himself still, his broad shoulders hunched inward.

"Guardian Rosales." Kalen greeted the woman

tersely. "I see you returned." His tone suggested that she had been asked not to return.

"I have free rein of the hospital." Maya faced off against the massive Alpha, her backbone apparently made of steel. "The patients find us comforting."

"You've seen her eye." Kalen didn't bother engaging in the pleasantries Maya's tone suggested she was trying to draw him into. "None of us find that comforting. Least of all Carter."

Kalen's power rippled through the room, causing the boy, Luis, to whimper. Sophia tucked him beneath her arm, edging him behind their mother. Both of them were bowed over, their heads lowered in submission. Unlike their Alpha mother, they appeared to both have the rust-coloured Delta rank ring around their irises.

"I'm surprised to learn that you're in on this as well, Professor." Maya flicked her hand to the bed. "I know how Alphas can be, but surely some lines of proprietary remain—"

"And yet, they don't." Kalen sighed, rubbing the side of his face. "I have to protect my Alphas. If you tell anyone about the Sigma's aberration, they're going to resume their search for her mate within Ironside and we both know the very first place they'll turn to. I need my Alphas to stay focussed on narrowing down their specialisations and building their fan bases. I'm already allowing several of them to surrogate for Carter—since it does so well for their ratings—but I have to draw the line somewhere. I need their heads in the game, and there's only so much time until summer break. Who knows how long they'll be gone if the officials bring them in for testing? Screen time is everything, Rosales."

"After the Colorado shooting and the Vermont attack, I'm surprised you're willing to speak so freely against the OGGB." Maya took a small step back like she didn't particularly want to be caught standing too close to Kalen. "They're on the hunt for anti-loyalists, especially *here*."

Here, because of ... Eve?

The Vermont attack?

Isobel recoiled, acid spilling into the back of her throat. Theodore slipped his hand through the ties in the back of her hospital gown. His palm pressed against her bare skin, surprisingly cool despite the absurd heat of his body. The touch gave her something to focus on, and she concentrated on the way he gently drifted his fingertips over the subtle bumps in her spine until some of the panic had subsided. Niko still hadn't taken his eyes off her, and it seemed like he released a short breath when she blinked back into focus.

Kalen stared stoically at Maya, who eventually deflated slightly, withering under his stare, their brief battle of dominance presenting a clear winner.

"I won't tell anyone about her eye—your eye." Maya flicked her attention to Isobel, frowning slightly at the way Isobel's skin had turned ashy, sweat gathering on her forehead. The Guardian paused for a breath before continuing. "But if you aren't going to allow the academy to study her," she turned back to Kalen, "then I would like to—"

"No," Kalen cut across her. "Nobody touches her. Looks at her. *Studies* her."

The room grew quiet, Maya's attention turning immediately assessing. Even Sophia peeked out at Kalen, brows jumping up. Maya looked back to Theodore and Isobel, her eyes dancing between them, her lips pinching. "While it is possible for the soul artefact to feed off a surrogate to heal a soul infraction, this recovery has been quite miraculous." Her attention narrowed on Theodore. "Have you been tested, Mr Kane?"

"Tested, how?" Theodore's voice was silky smooth, his grumbling vibrations under control as he turned his attention to soothing Isobel.

"Have your eyes been tested?" Maya asked sharply.

Kalen stepped forward in a blur, but Isobel quickly sat up and then raised herself onto her knees, fighting off dizziness as Theodore's hand slipped away from her back and everyone in the room turned to look at her. She clutched Theodore's knee to keep herself steady as she held herself up. The situation was seconds away from spinning out of control.

"Don't disrespect my surrogate," Isobel demanded quietly. She fought to keep her tone even despite the shake in her limbs. "If you ... if you keep it quiet that I've been hiding the fact that both my eyes changed, you can have the chain. You can study it or whatever you want to do with it. That's why you keep coming back, right? Because of the soul artefact?"

"And you." It was Sophia who spoke, giving a small shrug. "She's very excited that Aphelina is blessing us again."

"Agreed." Maya eyed the chain. "I won't tell a soul. Not even if they torture me." She assented so fast that Isobel found her mouth popping open, the arguments she had been trying to muster falling away.

Not even if they tortured her?

Who the hell made promises like that?

"I advised your bond specialist to cut the chain away when you woke up," Maya continued like she hadn't just shocked all of them. "They had to add links to close it properly. But if you would permit me to do it now?"

Dread filled Isobel, and she curled a hand protectively around the chain circling her wrist. She looked to Kalen, but he was locked into some sort of silent conversation with Niko. Niko nodded subtly, and Kalen fell back a step, moving away from the Guardian to put his back against the door.

They were allowing this to go ahead.

For a moment there, it almost seemed like Kalen was about to advance on Maya. Maybe he could force her mind to go back in time just like he had forced Isobel's body back in time. Kalen met Isobel's eyes, dipping his chin in a short nod, and she turned back to Maya, swallowing hard.

"Will it hurt?" she asked, staring down at her forearms. *Hurt* didn't even begin to describe how it had felt to have the light torn out of her. Just the thought of it had her fingers curling into fists, wanting to close around her strands of light and hoard them close to her chest.

Where were they now? The thought sent another tingle of panic shooting down the back of her neck.

"Yes," Maya stated plainly. "But your bond specialist will do it either way. You can't go about your life tethered to someone else. You're out of the woods now, so there's no reason to keep the connection ... especially since they only did it to humour me in the first place. If you don't believe in soul artefacts, then you have nothing to worry about, hm? You won't feel a thing. It's just a random chain that appeared completely out of thin air for absolutely no reason whatsoever."

Isobel sank back onto her heels. Theodore caught her hips and pulled her fully back into him again. She crossed her legs, cradling her bound wrist as Maya brushed past a roll of bandages on the table beside the bed, picking up a small pair of pliers. They must have been left by whoever added the links to her chain. She held out her hand, but Theodore pulled Isobel's wrist back, holding out his own hand first.

Maya snapped the chain deftly, and the pain was immediate. Sharp, hot, warm, and wet. It felt like a knife straight to her chest. She gasped, pressing her hands against the hospital gown, surprised that no blood flowed over her fingers. The pain speared all the way through her body, making tears spring to her eyes. Her toes curled, her body hunching inward, trying to curl into a ball.

Maya paused, eyes on Isobel. She didn't look triumphant that she had been right about the chain being some sort of soul artefact, only sympathetic over Isobel's pain. Thin lines bunched between her elegant brows as she waited for Isobel to recover.

"J-Just do it quickly," Isobel chattered out through her teeth, lifting her shaking hand.

Maya quickly cut the chain, but it seemed to come alive suddenly, glowing furiously and immediately wrapping around Isobel's wrist again, digging painfully into her skin. Isobel's breathing turned harsh. Theodore didn't seem to be breathing at all. Kalen and Niko both surged forward a step, Niko's eyes widening in astonishment. Kalen whipped out a hand, holding the other Alpha back from coming any closer.

Maya put the pliers to the chain again but pressed down much slower, her grip experimental. The chains glowed and vibrated in warning, but the further Maya adjusted the tool away from Isobel's hand, the less of a reaction she got. When she was far enough away, she quickly made a cut, and the end of the chain whipped up, striking Maya's hand and leaving behind a welt, blood already welling up to the surface of her skin before it recoiled to wrap contentedly around Isobel's wrist. The end of the chain settled down over the back of her hand, nestling against her skin.

Sophia rushed forward, quickly wrapping her mother's hand in a bandage while Maya just stared at her torn skin, brows pushed high, mouth slightly parted. She seemed to be breathing faster, but she held her composure well.

"It's still alive," Maya eventually stated, turning slowly back to Isobel.

Isobel rocked in Theodore's hold, her arms crossed over her chest as she tried to swallow down the pain. It seemed unbelievable that all this *feeling* had been held back by a chain. A chain that had seemed at least somewhat ordinary until Maya had cut it.

Her fingers shook violently as she gathered up the rest of the metal, holding it out to the Guardian. It felt cold and heavy, like all the magic had escaped from it to burrow into the short length wrapping her wrist, leaving only plain, expired gold behind. Maya took it hesitantly, relaxing only when it did her no harm as she turned and poured it into the small bag that Sophia held open.

"If there's anything you want to know about the soul artefacts or if any more of them appear ..." Maya backed toward the door, arching a brow in an expression resembling surprise as Kalen easily stepped out of her way. "I live in the small residence behind the chapel. You can also find me in the chapel in the mornings."

Isobel nodded. It was all she could manage.

"I will inform the nurses that she is awake. You should have a few minutes," Maya added, aiming the statement at Kalen before she ushered her children out ahead of her.

Sophia popped back into the opening before Kalen could shut the door, her mahogany eyes lighter than her mother's, her Delta rank ring making them appear a tarnished bronze. "Or me," she said to Isobel. "You can come talk to me if you ever get sick of these Ironside posers. See-ya." She gave a weird, dorky salute before disappearing.

Kalen snapped the door shut, leaning against it again as his eyes settled back onto Isobel with a heavy weight. The lighter, translucent hue of his gaze dripped into molten gold, simmering with fierce intelligence. He had the eyes of a predator, always scanning for weaknesses in the flimsy disguises people wore, digging out chinks and dints until all their efforts to appear perfect were in vain, leaving behind only primal fear for what he might do with what he discovered about them.

The only thing was ... he didn't quite have that effect on her.

Everything about him that had made him seem so intimidating now made her feel safe. He was a victim of this situation as much as she was, but he had protected her at every turn. He had saved her life.

"You took me to the trail?" she asked, her voice muted by the pain that still thrummed through her. "Where is my light?"

He dipped his head, nodding once. "Cian told me to put all the strings back inside you. I did what I could and then I took you back to the fire trail. I couldn't heal you completely. Too many people had already seen your wounds. I just healed them enough that the light strings were hidden again. They were already searching the mountain when I got there so I had to leave you pretty far out from the trail. I stayed with you as long as I could. The officials searched the trail and Eve's house for your threads but then decided they must have disappeared when you teleported."

"Thank you," she whispered.

He didn't ask what had happened at Eve's house. None of them did. She glanced at Niko, who was still staring at the chain on her wrist, his expression now arranged into mild curiosity.

"I didn't ... the bond didn't ..." She struggled to put it into words.

"Cian, Oscar, and Kilian were all too far away from you when you were cut," Kalen answered. "You're still only half bonded."

Theodore was keeping himself under control despite the utter turmoil that was trying to hammer into her body from his direction. He was drowning out the emotions of everyone else in the room, and there were too many competing thoughts and feelings for her to even attempt to decipher them with how scattered she already was. One of his hands stroked lightly up and down her spine, as the other wrapped around her legs, keeping her balled up against his chest.

Kalen eventually stepped away from the door, tilting his head like he could hear something on the other side. "You'll want your space to process all of this," he said. A statement, not a question. She wouldn't have thought Kalen knew her that well, but he seemed to understand that she preferred to process things on her own, in her own way. "But we should have a meeting with everyone as soon as possible. Can you manage?" He fished a set of contacts out of his pocket and handed them to her.

She had a feeling he wasn't asking after her health. He was wondering if she was ready to face all of them after finding out that they were *all* her mates.

After kissing Sato, even if she had been under the influence of the glowing chains.

After snuggling all over Kalen in his bed, even though she had been under the influence of the beautiful light patterns beneath his skin.

Especially after she wondered if the bond really was influencing her, or if it simply lowered her inhibitions.

And Eve ... and the strings ...

"I'll come as soon as I'm released," she promised,

extracting one of the contacts and tipping her head back to drop it into her eye.

"They'll likely release you tonight." Kalen held out his hand for the contact case and she dropped it into his palm. He returned it to his pocket and jerked his chin at Niko. "So we'll do dinner, and then nobody will make you sleep in their room. I promise."

An empty laugh bubbled up in her throat, and she easily swallowed it down, nodding as they left the room. Only thirty seconds later, the nurses came in, holding charts and headed by Teak.

"Isobel." Teak sounded relieved and overwhelmed, her smile shaky as she stood beside the bed, her hands fidgeting like she didn't know what to do with them before she settled a palm on Isobel's shoulder.

Theodore shifted so that none of Teak's fingers touched his chest, his nose brushing once against the side of Isobel's neck, sampling what was probably a harried, pained scent.

"Hey," Isobel greeted weakly. "Thanks for giving me all these surrogates."

Teak smirked. "Don't think I could take them away if I tried. You have a very special bond with your friends."

Isobel stiffened, watching as the other woman retreated, quickly consulting with the nurses.

"She didn't mean it like that," Theodore whispered, his breath misting over her ear.

She shivered, turning slightly to face him, but almost

as soon as their eyes connected, he nudged her back to face the front. Something had been off in his expression, but he hadn't given her enough time to examine it.

The nurses didn't seem to want or need Theodore to move as they examined Isobel, though they were careful not to touch him in any way. The more they skirted around him, the more confused Isobel grew, and eventually, Teak seemed to notice.

She gave Isobel an understanding smile. "It's important to treat surrogates like real mates, especially in times like these."

"Oh." Isobel didn't understand at all.

"People hate to have their mate touched in front of them," Teak specified. "Or not in front of them. At all, basically."

"*Oh,*" she repeated.

Theodore scoffed out a soft laugh behind her. "You have upwards of five surrogates and understand exactly zero rules."

"There are rules?" she asked as the nurses took her blood pressure. "Is five too many? It seems too many."

"Just *try* reducing it." Theodore's voice turned gritty. "We aren't just going to let you get sick and die. But yes, five is approximately four more than usual."

"There aren't strict rules, exactly." This came from Teak, who had pulled a seat to the side of the bed, waiting for the nurses to finish their examination. "It's more that surrogates should mirror a proper mate as much as possible, with two notable exceptions. Sex and—"

"Marking," Theodore supplied.

Teak looked impressed.

"The others did some research," he muttered.

"Hmm." Teak crossed one tanned leg over the other, her skirt catching at her knee as she relaxed back into the chair. "The 'others' are correct. While only a permanent marking can complete a bond, sex will bring a half-bonded pair much closer together. If a surrogate permanently marks a bonded or half-bonded person or has sex with them, it is considered an egregious disrespect to the bond, and could result in a minor tear."

"Tear," Isobel echoed, peering down at the arms the nurses were now lightly bandaging.

"A soul infraction," Teak specified. "They happen in varying degrees of severity. Some soul infractions can kill a person. It's very important to avoid them. If a soul infraction kills an Anchor, the Tether will also die. Being intimate with someone outside of your bond isn't likely to cause you much damage, but if you have a strong emotional connection with that person, the bond may see it as a defilement. Accidental markings might have no effect at all, but deliberate markings can have very serious consequences. In your case, since you haven't even met your mate and you're only half-bonded, it's highly unlikely that sex will cause any sort of soul infraction, but permanent markings and ..." She motioned to Isobel's arms. "Direct assaults on the bond magic are a different story, no matter how close to your mate you are."

When Isobel looked back up, Teak's eyes had filled with tears, but the bond specialist managed to blink them away so fast that Isobel started to doubt she had seen anything at all.

"I'm sorry for what happened to you," Teak whispered, her voice cracking before she cleared her throat delicately. Her next words were smooth and even. "Most people don't survive such a serious soul infraction. Some believe it's a rupture of the soul itself, and if the body doesn't shut down from the abuse, the mind will. But you seem ..." She shook her head, a small smile trembling on her lips. "You must have an incredibly strong mate to sustain you through such an event, and to continue to sustain you even without being by your side as you heal. I bet they're an Alpha."

"Yeah," Isobel agreed hollowly. "Maybe." *Or there were ten of them.*

"I should caution you, though." Teak straightened in her chair, flicking her eyes to Theodore briefly, though the Alpha behind Isobel was keeping quiet. He seemed to be monitoring what the nurses did to her very closely. "With your bond still unformed, your mind and soul will take longer to heal than your body. There will be side effects."

"I love side effects," Isobel said dryly, but the joke

didn't really land. Not when her voice was so raspy and her mouth was still pinched in pain.

Theodore was the only one who reacted, his soft exhalation against the back of her neck sounding like the beginning of a laugh.

"Would you like to discuss everything later?" Teak asked, surveying Isobel with concern.

"Am I getting out of here tonight?"

"If you're cleared," Teak hedged.

Isobel sighed, sinking back against Theodore, most of the strength sapping out of her. "Might as well get it over with, then."

"I'm sorry." Teak patted her hand. "You probably just want to sleep."

"I've been asleep for ... days?"

"Over a week," Theodore corrected her.

"Over a week," she repeated numbly. "So ... actually I *am* tired. Why am I so tired?"

"One of the side effects," Teak explained. "You're going to sleep a lot, and you'll be weak. Your appetite will disappear, but you need to force yourself to eat. A man suffering from a soul infraction once died of thirst without even realising he hadn't been eating or drinking. So, sip water regularly and eat at your usual mealtimes even if it's only a little. Do light exercise regularly—"

"Can I dance?" she interrupted, her heart jumping into her throat and pounding there viciously.

Teak swallowed, looking down at her lap for a

moment. "No strenuous exercise. I'm sorry. Walking and stretching only for now. Your body might appear fine, but you need to very carefully monitor yourself for a little while to make sure your symptoms are getting better instead of worse. Of course, if we knew who your mate was, you could simply complete the bond and you would heal much faster."

"What if I don't want to complete a bond?"

The nurses all stiffened, glancing at each other. One of them diverted his attention to Teak. "She's clear to go tonight. Should we inform her father?"

Teak waved her hand. "I've been in touch with him. I'll inform him."

The nurses quickly scrambled out of the room, and Isobel sighed, sitting up straight and crossing her legs, examining the bandages on her arms. She was so dizzy, so *tired* already. "What did my father say?" She fiddled with the bandages, not having the heart to look up at Teak as she asked the question.

She wasn't surprised to wake up and find her father missing.

"He asked if you were fit to return to a full filming schedule," Teak replied firmly, a hint of emotion catching in her voice, which she cleared her throat to cover. "He was called away for work, but he wants you up and running as soon as possible. He's asked for me to arrange extensive physiotherapy and counselling to minimise the damage."

Isobel scoffed, glancing back up. “And my other question?”

Teak stiffened, shifting in her chair. “What if you don’t want to complete a bond?”

Isobel nodded, waiting.

“Well …” Teak blew out a heavy breath. “I’m not sure you’ll have a choice. That’s the storyline Ironside is chasing. They’re very impatient to find your mate, though the Alphas are, admittedly, providing plenty of entertainment in the interim.”

“We’re very entertaining,” Theodore agreed, but his usual charming tone was dulled, his voice carrying a subtle strain of some kind.

“But you aren’t her mate,” Teak said, digging into the inside pocket of her jacket.

Isobel watched the other woman’s hand, throwing her walls down with a wince and reaching out carefully to test Teak’s emotion. *Suspicion*. She sipped at it, drawing it in as slowly as she could. It was painful. The effort to use her ability and the concentration required for her to wield it with so much control was almost too much. She could feel her energy slipping away with every second, but she refused to go any faster. If Teak felt her intrusion, she would do far more harm than good.

Teak pulled out a little torch and Isobel pretended not to notice it. Even Theodore seemed to be pretending not to notice it. She could feel most of his muscles against her back, shoulders and arms, and he kept his entire body deliberately relaxed, curved around her in a calm, loose way. Apparently, both of them had been thinking of the possibility that Teak might try to test Theodore's eyes at some point. They were both prepared ... but a few minutes of preparation didn't really amount to much.

"If Isobel was my mate, she would be wearing my mark all over her body," Theodore drawled, tightening his arms around her.

She kept siphoning off Teak's suspicion, one tiny drop at a time, hoping the other woman wouldn't notice ... but it was hard to concentrate because Theodore was once again proving himself a phenomenal actor. He had inserted just enough gravelly possession into his voice, twisting it with the right amount of torment and longing. And then he gave a small, self-aware laugh, making Teak blink at him. He was probably giving her a beautiful, perfect, heartbreaking smile. She was probably questioning everything she thought she knew about the world and falling under his spell just like everyone else did.

Her grip on the torch loosened, and she smiled back at him, mirroring whatever heartbreaking expression he wore, her eyes flitting over his face. "She'll never forget what you're doing for her." She tried to console him gently. "What all of you are doing for her. Right, Isobel?"

Theodore brushed his cheek against Isobel's, folding his legs and wrapping strong arms around her middle until she was lifted fully onto his lap. "But especially *me*, right, Isobel?" He nuzzled near her ear. "I'm your favourite, aren't I?"

He was probably trying to remind Teak that there were four other Alphas all acting as surrogates, so Theodore couldn't possibly be her mate. Apparently, a true mate couldn't stand other people touching the person that belonged to them. But whatever his game was, it was short-circuiting her brain. She melted in his arms, the tremble easing from her limbs.

"You're very good at that," Teak noticed, watching Isobel turn into a puddle.

"But not good enough to be the real deal," he returned with a forced casual tone, trying—and failing—to mask the hint of agony that rode his voice.

Jeez. Talk about laying it on thick.

And ... Teak was eating it right up. She surreptitiously slid the torch away, her other hand twitching like she wanted to reach out to him. The woman was one big, bleeding heart. Isobel very carefully, very slowly slid her wall back up, cutting herself off from Teak before she could pass out.

"Um ..." Isobel interrupted before they could devolve into sobbing and wiping each other's tears. "Is there anything else, or would it be okay if I go now? I want to walk out of here while I can still walk."

2

SIGMA SPONGE

ISOBEL WIPED HER SWEATY HANDS ON HER SHORTS, STARING AT the door to Dorm A. Kilian had left clothes and toiletries in her hospital room—she knew it was him, because they carried his earthy bergamot and bark scent. After showering, washing her hair, and dressing in small cotton shorts and a long-sleeved sweatshirt, she felt much more like herself. Even if the sweatshirt was Kilian's.

There was a light sheen of perspiration dotting her skin from the slow, easy walk to Dorm A, even though Theodore had ambled along beside her slower than she had ever seen him walk before. Whenever she tried to speed up, he had touched her elbow to slow her down again, completely ignoring the students who stopped in their tracks at the sight of them, phones whipping up to snap pictures. She didn't catch any of their whispered words, but the Vermont attack—as Teak had put it—was probably big news. Bonded people were important to the Gifted, and Isobel had never even heard of a bond infraction or soul infraction before, let alone known of it happening in the time she had been alive. Granted, her only source of gossip had been the human news, and they didn't particularly bother with what happened in the settlements, only what happened at Ironside.

Theodore looked down at her, not pushing her to enter the dorm. "Doing okay, Illy?"

She turned her head up to him, her lips curving, her smile tremulous. "Nope."

His expression was drawn, his Alpha ring shrinking to a thin, gold line. He was holding back so much emotion and he was so good at it, but now that they were alone and there were no cameras watching, she could see the cracks. She could feel them, too. His energy was sneaking out like a whip to crack lightly against her skin. It was sharp, electric, and restless. She rarely felt Theodore's power like a physical force, likely because he had spent his entire life trying to escape it.

"Say the word and I'll take you back to your dorm instead," he offered.

"I want to be alone for a while, but I don't know ... if I can."

"Say the word and I'll crash on the floor with you."

"It's a bed," she defended.

"It's a floor. With blankets."

She scowled at him, and his attention snapped to her lips, the storm in his eyes darkening, roiling, as he watched her nose scrunch and her lip curl. Despite the intensity in his eyes, his smile threatened to appear.

"Isobel ..." He rumbled out her name, the hint of his smile dropping away. He scrubbed both hands over his face, wiping away all traces of joy. "I'm so fucking sorry."

"I know," she said, kicking the toe of her sneaker against the rocky ground.

"For hiding it from you," he pressed.

"I know."

"It's not enough." He sounded frustrated. "You should slap me. Call me names. Never speak to me again. For a day," he quickly tacked on.

She snorted. "Two days."

"Day and a half."

"A week," she said. "Final offer."

"You're negotiating in the wrong direction." He backed her into the door before she realised what was happening, his hands on her hips. His body was trembling suddenly, his eyes full of turmoil. "Don't speak to me for thirty seconds." His voice had lowered to something resembling a warning, something that begged her to back away ... but he had her cornered.

And he was warm.

And he was Theodore.

She lifted her chin, accepting the challenge, and his eyes flitted to her lips again. A short groan tore its way out of his throat. "I should be giving you physical intimacy to help ease the bond," he said.

He hadn't stopped touching her since she woke up. She furrowed her brow, showing her confusion. *Twenty-three seconds and counting.* The grip around her hips pinched tighter, his expression suddenly torn.

"We can't push it too far. In either direction." He sounded so agonised, the words guttural. One of his hands released her hip to lift her chin, tilting her face up. She could feel his breath against her lips, choppy and harsh. "I'm going to help you get through your first night alone, okay?"

She had already forgotten that she was supposed to not be talking to him, but she didn't have any words anyway. Her mouth was dry, her throat tight, her hands shaking. Her whole body was tingling in fear and anticipation. Fear, because Theodore was untouchable. He was the most approachable, the most personable, the one with all the friends, the one people gravitated toward and championed. But Isobel suspected it was all an act, and that would make him the opposite of all the things he pretended. It would mean she didn't really know him at all.

He waited for something, his thumb brushing along her lower lip from one corner of her mouth to the other, dragging the flesh slightly as he increased the pressure.

Every slow, measuring caress sparked something to life low in the pit of her stomach, eventually making her squirm. He hovered closer when she moved, every plane of his body pushing up against hers. She could feel how hard he was just from touching her mouth and everything suddenly seemed connected, their bodies triggering a cycle of responses in each other. His thumb pressed between her lips, catching on her bottom teeth, tugging her mouth open only slightly. Her stomach clenched hard. His erection pulsed, and he lowered his mouth over hers, not releasing her or making any move to kiss her. Some of his sharp, crackling power eased from her skin, but the goosebumps along her arms remained.

"Do you want help? Or do you want to do it on your own?" he whispered. "Should I tide you over? Fill you up enough that you can last the night?"

She made a small, begging sound. It was all she could do with his thumb in her mouth. It seemed like a strings-free offer ... like he really was a surrogate instead of her actual mate, and that allowed her to be in the moment, to not think too hard about what he was offering.

It didn't really *mean* anything.

He slipped his thumb out of her mouth, replacing it with his lips, and she melted, just like she did every time he touched her. He controlled the kiss right from the start, using his grip on her chin to angle her face, tasting her slowly and sweetly until she felt like she was drowning and only his strong body anchoring her against the door was keeping her upright.

She grew restless, but he kept the same maddening pace, scrambling her brain. She tried to move, to push against him, to tug his shirt and quicken the kiss, but he only nipped at her lips for the effort. She half expected his skin to start glowing or another chain to magically appear, but something didn't feel right inside her. Something deep within her was hurting, and while Theodore's touch was tunnelling her into a nerve-wracking cloud of lust, there was something deep down that was still *broken*.

She was on her own with this. No magic to siphon away her inhibitions and make her brave.

So when his hand brushed over her stomach, pushing her back just far enough to draw the oversized shirt up, bundling it above the hem of her shorts, she suddenly found that she couldn't breathe. He paused, his breath rough against her lips, and she realised he was debating whether to stop.

"More," she whispered. He was holding back too much. She was burning up from the inside and he was far too controlled. She hated it.

He issued a throaty growl, inching his face back as he considered her.

"You sure?"

"M-more." She tugged on his wrist to try and bring him closer, or to pull his arm around her, but instead, his fingers pushed into her shorts.

She hadn't been prepared for that. She just wanted

him to feel as out of control as she did, but as soon as his fingertips slid into her panties and brushed her clit, she realised it was *exactly* where she needed him. Anyone else might have tried to ease her into having their hands down her pants ... but not Theodore. He liked to shock her. He applied a little bit of pressure, watching the colour flood into her face as she clutched nervously at his arms.

"Stop pushing my arms, Illy. I can't risk feeling how wet you are." He groaned the words, nipping at her chin before kissing her. His lips pressed harder this time, his tongue demanding more from her as his fingers gently circled the bundle of nerves, increasing the pressure until she was squirming. It was like he already knew her body inside and out. Like she was an instrument and he had been practising her studiously for years and had already been awarded some kind of diploma.

What she wouldn't pay to see him *not* automatically succeed at something.

He watched her every reaction, changing the pressure and position and cadence of his touch with every shift in her expression or hitch in her breathing. He took her right to the edge and then suddenly stopped, cupping her sex gently and leaving her there to float and pant into his lips.

"Okay?" he rumbled, even though she was soaking the pads of his fingers and clutching his shirt so tightly she was almost tearing it off his wide chest.

It gave her a moment to level out the emotions raging through her, the furnace burning beneath her skin. She swallowed, tears burning behind her eyes, her nerves frayed.

Everything was frayed.

Her heart felt like it was in a tattered mess, unravelling all over the place and Theodore was letting her use him to overwhelm her senses, to ignore the clutter and fill her mind and body with a heat so scorching it barely mattered if she was unravelling or whole ... but he wouldn't let her escape entirely. He was bringing her back just far enough that she was still there, still with him.

He nuzzled her cheek, inhaling her scent, and she nodded.

"Fuck. My perfect girl," he praised, low and rumbling, his wet fingers drifting back up to where she needed them, massaging her swollen bud until she was lost again, teetering on that same edge. "You've never looked so beautiful, Illy."

The drop on the other side wasn't so scary, this time.

Which was a good thing because he didn't give her a chance to catch her breath again. As soon as she reached the precipice, he pushed her right off the edge without a warning, sending her into a dizzying, delicious wave of stuttered heartbeats, unsteady fluttering, and the pain-pleasure of her whole body clenching.

She wanted to scream, or cry, or pull him as close to

her body as she could get him, but she didn't have the strength. His whole body was vibrating when she blinked the black spots from her eyes, her throat hoarse even though she was sure that she hadn't uttered a single word. He pulled his hand out of her shorts and gently adjusted them again on her hips, letting her oversized sweatshirt fall. She was limp against the door, a gentle hum taking up residence beneath her skin.

"How do you feel now?" he rasped, his hand disappearing beneath the waistband of his pants. He adjusted himself, his jaw clenching, his eyes flashing. When he dragged his fingers out, they were no longer glistening with her dampness.

For some reason, her body clenched again, really liking the fact that he had smeared her essence over his cock; it made a sharp, possessive feeling spear through her chest. It was just *right*. She was almost panicked at the thought that he could have walked away *without* doing that.

"I feel ..." She swallowed, trying to stand straight again and trying to shove away her strange and intrusive thoughts. "Steadier and unsteadier." She laughed softly. "More grounded and more freaked out."

"Don't be embarrassed." The words seemed to slip out in accidental Alpha voice, and he winced, quickly amending, "Shit. I mean ... please, don't be embarrassed. You suffered a soul infraction. You need a little extra soothing. It's natural."

She nodded, chewing on her lip. It felt puffy and tender. "And you're ... I mean ... you're okay with—"

"Seriously. Don't." He grinned at her, his smile stretching wide and disarming, his perfect teeth flashing brilliantly. "I offered to be a surrogate. I knew you would need me to touch you."

"I didn't know."

He scoffed. "Give me the signal and I'll make sure you only have to suffer through one of us." He narrowed his eyes on her. "I'm talking about me, by the way."

"And have the rest of you accuse me of tearing the group apart and picking favourites?" She frowned at him, the pleasant buzz inside her not abating in the slightest. "You saw what happened when I asked Cian to continue surrogating for me."

"Mhm. A conversation for another time, I think." He carefully arranged his expression. "Ready to go inside? They can't fuck with the cameras this time. It would be too suspicious."

"So how are we going to talk?" she asked, confused. "Why would Kalen call for a group meeting?"

"Because five of his Alphas are actively stepping in to nurture your bond while the officials scour the countryside for your true mate, and because you're about to be moved into Dorm A, which makes you one of his charges. A little Sigma-Alpha."

She scoffed, the laugh leaving her unwillingly.

"Right. I thought we were going to talk about ..." She swallowed, unable to continue.

"We'll talk about the attack." He brushed her cheek lightly. "Just remember to be careful with what you say, that's all."

It should have been weird and humiliating to continue a normal conversation after what he had just done, but instead, it felt natural. Theodore made her feel comfortable, easily side-stepping between the role of "surrogate," and friend.

They entered the common room quietly, glancing around the empty space before Theodore took her hand and tugged her toward the stairs. The Alphas had dragged two of the seating areas together on the rooftop, forming one long table with enough chairs for all of them. Moses was in the kitchen, holding a glass pitcher of water when they reached the top of the stairs.

His nostrils flared, flicking between Theodore and Isobel, and then his grip loosened on the pitcher, leaving it to shatter against the floor. Theodore ignored him, steering her toward one of the free chairs. The rest of the Alphas seemed confused by Moses—who stood as still as a statue—until she reached the table, and then they all reacted at once.

Easton pounced to his feet, backing away from the table and swearing under his breath. Kalen was gripping the edge of the table so hard she heard the groan of stone cracking. Reed and Spade both twitched, their eyes slamming into her, their nostrils flaring. Niko shoved his chair back, muttering about the broken glass as he escaped to the kitchen. Sato, who sat at the far end of the table, arched a dark brow at her, a heavy question in his onyx eyes. Cian rubbed his mouth like he was swallowing back a laugh.

Kilian was the only one who didn't do anything weird.

He strode over to her and captured her into a tight hug that pulled her feet from the ground. When he set her down again, he suddenly whirled on Theodore, snatching his wrist and pulling Theodore's hand up between them.

"Wash your hands before you eat," he said silkily, his tone hiding an undercurrent of sharpness.

Isobel went white, finally realising what everyone was reacting to, but as mortified as she was, the comfortable feeling of her blood singing happily through her veins pushed her to shrug off their stares and sit down. Kilian immediately claimed the seat beside her, tucking her beneath his arm, his nose brushing her hair.

"You smell happy to see us," he said.

"Shut the hell up." She elbowed him.

He chuckled, dragging her closer. The others stared at the two of them like they were speaking a foreign language.

"Well." Easton cleared his throat, glaring at Theodore for several awkward and prolonged seconds before pulling out a seat opposite Isobel. "It's good to see you awake."

"*So* awake," Cian drawled, flashing her a wry grin. "Super switched on."

"You can also shut the hell up." She glared at him, before shyly flicking her eyes to Easton's tie. "And um, thank you, Professor."

There was a light scoffing sound from the other side of the table. She wasn't sure who it came from, because the others were still moving around. Niko and Moses brought over half a dozen dishes from the kitchen before Moses picked up Theodore's chair, dragging it—and Theodore—away from Isobel. He inserted a chair between them and sank into it, shaking his head at his brother.

Theodore wasn't even paying attention. He was loading his plate up with food like he hadn't eaten in a week.

"I'm sure you have a lot of questions," Easton continued, ignoring the Kane twins.

"What happened to them?" The question almost exploded out of her. She had been waiting to ask it since she opened her eyes in the hospital.

"*Them*?" Kalen demanded. The whole table stilled. Moses dropped something else. More glass shattered.

"Someone else was there?" Sato snarled. "Nobody else entered the house. We were watching. Eve didn't mention a second person in her confession and her confession was enough to get her ki—" He paused, his eyes flicking to the side, almost like he was seeking out one of the cameras. "Enough to get her into trouble," he revised. "So we assumed she wasn't lying."

Isobel curled her fingers around her fork, her stomach suddenly churning as she gazed at the food laid out before her. "There was a boy. I can't remember his name. He was leaving the house when I came in, then he must have looped around and entered through the back."

"I remember him," Cian said. "Tall, dark hair, had a look on his face like he was smarter than everyone else. Wore an old motorcycle jacket—"

"Aron," Kilian croaked.

Another glass exploded, Easton cursing as he shook out his hand.

"Aron?" Cian's voice was heavy with dread. "As in—"

"Yes." Kilian swallowed, all of the animation suddenly seeping out of him, his eyes taking on a vacant look. "My ex."

"He's not even a student ..." Moses trailed off as Kalen stood from the table, pulling out his phone and searching for a number before raising it to his ear and walking away.

"And now he's as good as dead," Kilian said, still staring blankly at the table.

"Eve already confessed." Moses frowned over at Kilian. "Why was Aron even there?"

Isobel swallowed, peeking at Kilian. He didn't just

look emotionless. She couldn't feel anything from him. Nothing at all. Somehow, that seemed worse than feeling a terrible, heavy pressure against her chest.

"They were both convinced that Kilian was my mate," she said carefully.

"Why would they think that?" Niko asked, his eyes razor-focussed on her. She had never seen them so clear, the earthy green and rich brown hue blending together, binding her attention so well that she forgot to blink, tears springing up at the strain it took to hold his gaze.

I told her. I broke my promise. This is all my fault.

"I ... messed up. I thought she was my friend."

Niko leaned forward, drawing her further into that forest-green oasis, his power wrapping around her so subtly that she barely realised he was exerting his influence until it draped her like a second skin. "Why would she think that Kilian is your mate?" he repeated, his voice soft.

It would be too easy to lie. To claim that she had nothing to do with it. She could even use the cameras as an excuse.

But *they* were the liars. Not her.

"Because I told her everything," she said evenly. She let that hang in the air for a moment before she warped the rest of the story for the cameras. "Everything I wanted to believe, anyway. I told her Kilian was my mate because I wished he was. I don't want my real mate. I don't know who he is. But Kilian is *nice* to me.

He cares about me. And he probably wouldn't ever make me complete the bond because he isn't into girls."

She sagged back against her chair, dropping her fork and crossing her arms. They were quiet. Kilian didn't even act like he had heard her. He was still staring at the same spot on the table.

"That ... wasn't wise," Easton finally said, as Kalen returned to the table.

"That was really fucking *unwise*," Moses growled, always the first to rip away a sugar-coating.

"I'm aware," she gritted, before tamping down on her defensiveness. They had warned her not to tell anyone, and she had promised she wouldn't. But knowing that she was technically in the wrong didn't make apologising any easier. "I'm sorry."

Kilian pushed away from the table, avoiding looking at anybody. "I'll ... be ... I'm just— I need a minute."

She pushed her chair back to follow him, but Moses dropped his fingers to her thigh, barely even touching her as he shook his head, his frown deep and frightening.

Cian stood, his expression troubled as he swept his eyes quickly over the table. He looked like he was about to say something before he changed his mind, striding off after Kilian.

"You should eat." Easton assessed Isobel as the silence around the table grew deeper, more unsettling.

She stared at the food piled onto the table that

nobody else was reaching for, hearing the words Easton *didn't* say.

He wanted her to eat so that she could leave.

She moved to push back her chair again, but Moses repeated the same motion as before, his fingers tapping her thigh, pulling her up short.

"Eat something," he suggested.

No Alpha voice.

She pushed her chair the rest of the way back and slipped away from the table.

THEODORE FOUGHT BACK THE URGE TO STOP ISOBEL AS SHE took several steps away from the table, and then several more, just to make sure she was out of arm's reach of anyone. The tantalising, syrupy scent that he had managed to foster into a heady perfume only ten minutes ago was already gaining a bitter edge, shrinking back into her veins until he was no longer beating back the need to do something incredibly stupid in front of nine of his closest friends.

It was bad enough that he had covered his fingers in her syrup and spread it over his dick. *That* was a completely unhinged thing to do, and it was the reason he was still half hard. Even now. Probably forever. Despite everything.

He noticed Niko relaxing slightly and Elijah's shoulders inching down. Kalen and Mikel no longer looked like they wanted to throw themselves off the rooftop ... but a different kind of tension had descended, and none of them seemed to know exactly what to do with it. The situation was bad—Isobel might have just blown their cover entirely—but none of them were angry at her. At the situation, yes, but not at her.

Unfortunately, she didn't seem to realise that.

"I'm really sorry," Isobel repeated, staring at the ground with a frown. There was only so much she could say, even though she had moved away from the cameras.

She was struggling, fighting for the words, but it didn't matter. They knew what she was apologising for.

"Did you tell anyone else these ... stories?" Kalen asked.

Well now Theodore wanted to *shove* him off the rooftop.

Except Kalen would only say that this was Theodore's fault. They had all told him right from the start that they couldn't trust her with their secrets when they barely even knew her. There was too much on the line. But they were also the ones who had lied to her first, and there were ten of them. There was only one of her. They all had each other and she had no one.

Were they really going to be dicks just because she wanted *one* friend on her side?

For the love of all things holy, keep your damn mouths shut.

He glared at them one by one.

"No. I didn't tell anyone else." Isobel's scent was a cherry tree shoved through a woodchopper, splinters and dust flying everywhere, ripe juice running through the gears until it was oily and tainted.

Kalen was treating her like one of his Alphas. Asking the questions necessary to do damage control before he focussed on the emotional side of things—or let Niko or Kilian focus on the emotional side of things. Theodore just hoped Isobel wouldn't think he was angry at her. Kalen seemed like he was angry all the time, but she would only need to see him truly angry once to know the difference.

Isobel straightened slightly, her eyes flashing up to Kalen's before flicking around to the other faces. "The assault wasn't my fault. They had it planned. They had their suspicions, and they were going to torture me no matter what I said. Eve has been torturing me since I came here. I was just too stupid to see it because she's right. I'm gullible. I believe everything you tell me."

Her eyes flicked to Theodore, her stare landing harder than the slap he had told her she should give him.

There it is.

Despite the hollow pain he felt at her disappointed expression, he was glad she had said it. He nodded slightly, showing that he understood what she was saying, and some of the lines digging into her forehead eased.

"You're right." Gabriel stood from the table, tossing

down his napkin. He wasn't going to eat the food anyway. Not with how many glasses had shattered and the possibility that a shard might have landed on his plate. "Eve was already targeting you. All the students named by her in the attack before spring break are all on camera in different locations. They have solid alibis. She lied to you and the officials. I don't know who attacked you, but it wasn't her usual group of Delta friends. The only person at Ironside with a recorded ability to create darkness and shadow is a second-year Beta, Kiki Rayne. As for the other thing ... ignore Moses. He's just worried about Kilian."

Isobel sat up a little straighter, shocked at Spade's defence of her. She watched as he grabbed a bread roll and began to walk off, thinking that he was following Cian and Kilian ... except he paused at the stairs, looking at her. "Come on, puppy."

She hurried over to him, so grateful for the escape that she could have hugged him, but he probably wouldn't have liked that. So instead, she just followed him quietly.

"Are you making sure I don't try to talk to Kilian?" she asked, as they passed by the door to his room.

Spade didn't answer, just handed her the bread roll and kept walking.

"Eat," he suggested as they rounded the lake.

The bread tasted like cardboard and her hands were shaking again, but she obeyed, nibbling it slowly as they walked.

When they were halfway back to Dorm O, he finally sucked in a short breath, slipping her a quick, sideways look. "How are you feeling?"

She shrugged. "Honestly? Not too bad right now."

"Orgasms will do that. Sex will do more—but I would have to very strongly advise against that."

She choked on her own saliva and almost tripped over her own feet but at least they were outside and the cameras likely couldn't hear what they were saying. The students passing on either side of the path, however ...

Isobel glanced back at them wildly, but they seemed to be too busy trying to snap pictures of her and Spade—as he caught her elbow to steady her—to have been paying attention to what he said.

"I'm not even going to touch that," she eventually said. "But thanks for the advice."

"Anytime." He kicked a rock out of his way, slowing his pace when she grew tired. "You're inexperienced. You might misconstrue things."

"I haven't misconstrued anything. Theo told me why he was doing it."

"Oh?" Spade seemed to smile a little. "Good for him."

"Spade? This is weird."

"Gabriel."

"Yeah, I reckon he's weird too."

His smile twitched a little wider, but then he licked his lips, and it was gone in a flash. "Let's be friends, Isobel. I want to keep an eye on you."

"That's a terrible reason to propose friendship with someone."

"It's not my only reason." He slowed further and then turned suddenly to the right, forcing her to turn with him so that he wouldn't collide with her shoulder. He steered her toward the edge of the lake, where there were fewer people, and then took a seat on the solitary bench overlooking the water, his gaze turned toward the dock that she was uncomfortably familiar with.

He tapped the bench beside him, and she sat, tucking her cold hands between her thighs and rolling her lips together, choosing to look anywhere except the dock.

"Why are we stopping?" she asked.

"Because you need to catch your breath. Your heart rate is too high. I can see your pulse jumping in your neck. Even with Theo's ... assistance, this is still your first night out of the hospital and you went immediately into a high-stress situation instead of the bond-soothing activity with several of your surrogates as Elijah had planned."

"Okay." She kicked her shoes, enjoying the brush of her soles against the wooden planks. "So what's the other reason you want to be friends if it's not just to keep an eye on me?"

"I have two best friends who share a single defining

quality. They have sacrificed greatly for me. You exhibited the same quality. By my definition, we're already close friends. I'm just making it known."

She stopped kicking her legs, her brow furrowing. "Um ... I don't think I—"

He dropped his head to the side, suddenly giving her his full attention, and the sentence died on her lips.

"You have sacrificed," he assured her. "Deliberately, though not mindfully."

"Yes." She studied his face, trying not to wither under that much attention. "I deliberately but not mindfully sacrifice myself for people all the time. It's my thing."

"You're supposed to use a different tone of voice when expressing sarcasm."

"Are you a dictionary?"

"Try a mocking intonation. If you forget to make it obvious in the moment, you could add a chuckle at the end."

"Oh my god." She gazed at him. "You're malfunctioning."

He scoffed, shaking his head. A blond strand of hair fell into his eyes, and he brushed it back, patting the side of his head to make sure all the other strands were in place before he let his attention drift back to the lake. He stretched his legs out, crossing them at the ankle, his arms wrapped over his chest, his hands tucked in on the opposite sides.

"It's just a theory ..." He lowered his voice until it was

almost inaudible. "But I think you're absorbing most of the side effects that we should be getting. I think it's an extension of your Sigma power."

"Sounds about right," she muttered, not nearly as surprised as she should have been. "Did you feel it, when …?"

When they tore out my light.

She didn't want to say it out loud, but Gabriel seemed to understand. His mouth immediately tightened, his arms bunching like he had suddenly formed fists.

"Yes," he gritted quietly. "But nowhere near what you would have felt. That's not normal. We should have been incapacitated like you. You took more than your fair share. If anyone suspected any of us were your mates before, that suspicion has now decreased dramatically. We should have been hospitalised right alongside you. Elijah thinks we're sharing the Anchor side effects evenly amongst ourselves, spreading it thin. I think it's more than that. I think we're sharing it with you, and I think you're taking more than us."

She shivered, and he surveyed her slowly.

"Let's go. You need to rest." He stood, stretching out his neck to the left, and then the right, that same lock of hair falling out of place again. He tucked it back into line with an annoyed flick of his fingers and started to walk in the direction of her dorm, expecting her to follow.

. . .

Oscar sat on the very edge of the rooftop—one long leg hanging and the other notched on the stone edge—long after Gabriel returned home. Mikel came up to find him after checking on everyone else. He could be like an ill-tempered mother hen with a mauled face sometimes.

"Need a session?" Mikel asked, hands shoved into his pockets, eyes trained steadily on Oscar.

"Those aren't for me," Oscar shot back. "Remember the part where we get paid at the end of them?"

Mikel rolled his eyes. "I'd prefer you try to beat me up, rather than the alternative."

"What alternative?" Oscar challenged, swinging back over the ledge, and walking toward the professor.

Mikel scrubbed a scarred hand over his face, obviously frustrated at not being able to speak his mind. The camera trained on them was too close, now that Oscar had approached him.

"You hurting someone else," Mikel finally gritted out lowly, before turning on his heel and stalking back to the stairs. "Go to bed, Oscar."

Alpha voice.

Oscar grunted, falling still as he fought off Mikel's influence. It was heavy and solid, like iron. It took him a good few minutes and a deal of discomfort, but then he was free to do as he liked, shedding the heavy power that had tried to wrap around him.

And he quite liked the idea of hurting somebody.

A very particular somebody.

His tread was light, silent, as he prowled downstairs, opening the door to Theodore's room. He reached the sleeping Alpha in a few easy strides, launching onto his torso and capturing his right hand. Oscar slammed the captured hand down onto the pillow beside Theodore's head, whipping a tactical pen knife from his back pocket and extending the blade to rest against the fingers that still faintly carried Isobel's scent.

The memory of sticky cherry syrup thick in the air had black spots dancing before his eyes, and he wrested for control over himself.

The Sigma was fucking *his.*

Theodore had woken up at some point, but had quickly stopped fighting, and now kept himself very still, his breathing measured, his eyes narrowed and watchful.

"Oscar." He sounded miraculously calm, his voice raspy with sleep. "Didn't realise you felt that way about her."

"She's *mine,*" Oscar snarled, pressing the blade harder against Theodore's skin.

He didn't mean to say that out loud.

Theodore didn't even flinch. "You want her? Want to date her? Want to take her to the movies on Ironside Row? Want to shake her asshole daddy's hand and fetch her coffee in the morning just the way she likes it?"

"I kissed her first," Oscar growled, his voice sounding foreign to his own ears. Something wasn't right. He felt unhinged—more than usual.

Theodore's words were registering, but barely.

Fuck no, he didn't want to do those things.

Shake her daddy's hand? More like rip her daddy's arm off and use it to backhand him until his face turned purple and blue.

"You resuscitated her," Theodore corrected. "Moses kissed her first. But I saw her first."

The door flew open, the light switching on. Moses stood in the opening, his sharp nose probably picking up the hint of blood in the air.

"Fucking hell," he muttered, getting an eyeful of whatever deranged look was on Oscar's face and the blood dribbling down Theodore's hand to soak into his pillow before he backed out of the room.

Oscar dismissed the open doorway, turning back to Theodore. "Touch her again and I *will* cut off your fingers."

"Then I'll touch her with fucking stumps," Theodore growled back. "I didn't ..." He gritted his teeth, flicking his eyes to the doorway and lowering his voice. "I didn't *bond* her, asshole. I just helped ease the side effects."

"Oscar," Elijah snapped, striding into the room, Moses and Gabriel close behind him. "Look at me." The door clicked shut behind them.

"Piss off," Oscar snarled. "I'm busy."

"You need to level out," Elijah said. "You're surging. Focus, Oscar. Get your head in the game."

Surging.

Dammit.

Surging was bad. Surging meant he had to stop whatever he was doing.

But he *really* wanted to cut Theodore's fingers off.

"Theo isn't a threat," Elijah continued, his voice calm, deep and resonant. The know-it-all fuck. "He's one of us. Part of the group, part of the pack. Family. Look at him, Oscar. He's family."

"He can be family without his fingers," Oscar grunted, the feral, ragged edges of his mind smoothing over slightly. He pulled back, retracting the blade and recapping it.

Theodore finally winced in pain, clenching his fingers into a fist. "You've got a screw loose, Oscar."

"What triggered you?" Elijah asked, pulling out his phone, ready to take notes.

Oscar breathed in deeply, resisting the urge to snatch Elijah's phone out of his hand and punch it through Theodore's teeth.

"I think that part is obvious," Theodore grumbled, waving his bloodied fist before turning his glare back to Oscar. "Dude, get off me."

Oscar shoved against Theodore's chest, finding his feet, and running his fingers agitatedly through his hair.

"It might be obvious, but I need to hear it from him," Elijah countered. "And I need to hear it in detail."

"He touched her." Oscar jerked his thumb back at

Theodore, who was now reaching under his bed for a first aid kit.

"In detail," Elijah repeated irritably, tapping away at his phone screen.

"I could give you details," Theodore offered, slapping the kit between his legs, and rummaging through it. Despite his mocking tone, he didn't expand on the offer.

Smart move.

"Not those details." Elijah glared at them both through the lenses of his reading glasses. "What *exactly* triggered you, Oscar? And what did the surge feel like?"

"You know what?" Oscar gripped the top of Elijah's phone, pulling it down from his face. "It felt just like how I always feel like."

"So ... significantly unbalanced." Gabriel pulled his own phone out, making notes while Elijah stared back at Oscar with an infuriatingly patient expression.

"Yeah." Oscar smirked at him. "Like that, but with less of the usual nonsense holding me back."

"How different was it from your surge in Isobel's hotel room during the break?" Elijah asked.

"Well, I didn't want to fuck Theodore," Oscar admitted, completely deadpan.

"Wait, what?" Moses frowned, looking between them all. Theodore was making a low, grumbling sound. "You surged around Isobel?"

"Yes," Gabriel answered for Oscar. "When the chain appeared."

"Why don't I know about this?" Theodore demanded, springing from his bed, the first aid kit forgotten.

"Because you're not her nanny," Moses shot back, annoyed, before he shifted his attention to Elijah and Gabriel, who both seemed to be perfectly aware of everything. They had probably written half a research paper on it and were waiting on further data to finalise their hypothesis.

"The surge in the hotel room was because you found out Isobel was hurt," Elijah said, reading from—*yep, his notes*. "And this time, because someone else touched her."

"Proprietary aggression." Gabriel sighed.

"Should have known it would be a problem with him," Elijah agreed. "He doesn't have a lot to his name."

"Don't fucking need this." Oscar began striding for the door, but Elijah quickly stepped in his way, holding up his palms.

"None of us need this." Elijah gentled his tone as he took off his glasses and shoved them into his pocket. "But I warned you all what would happen with so many Alphas living together in such close quarters. It was manageable before ..."

"Isobel," Gabriel supplied.

Elijah shot him a narrow look. "I know her name."

"Then use it."

"Trouble in paradise?" Oscar interjected, making his

tone sound bored when it was actually highly entertaining to watch the wonder twins split their shared brain cell in half to trade barbs.

"It was manageable before Isobel," Elijah ground out. "We need to get this under control before we all spiral. You." He jammed a finger into Oscar's chest. "Up your training time. Up your sparring time. Don't back down until someone's bleeding. We need to get your aggression under control."

"Was planning on it anyway," Oscar responded in the least aggressive tone he could be bothered to muster. So ... his normal tone, really.

"I'll write up a new schedule for everyone." Elijah sighed, nudging his reading glasses back on and moving around Oscar to reach for the door. "I think we're going to need to add an extra small group session with Mikki."

"Fine by me." Oscar shrugged, shoving his hands into his pockets and rocking back on his heels.

Elijah gave him a narrow-eyed look before opening the door and waving at the hallway. "After you."

"No, after you." Oscar gave his best imitation of a smile.

Gabriel snorted. "We aren't leaving you alone in here, Oscar."

"Fine," Oscar snapped. "I was hoping to spare all your delicate sensibilities, but ..." He strode back to the bed, snatched up Theodore's hand, and snapped two fingers back as the younger Alpha tried to get away.

The break was nice and clean.

Hardly aggressive.

"Sweet dreams, everyone." Oscar grinned around the room, striding for the door.

The violence eased something inside him, and he couldn't help but feel a spark of admiration for Theodore, who managed to not make a single sound and was still holding onto an ominous silence.

Hopefully, he was planning revenge.

That could be fun.

3
Chains and Choke-Holds

Isobel didn't see Kilian for weeks. He seemed to disappear entirely. Even Theodore was distant, spending more and more time training or practising ... though he was still at every one of the small group sessions with Easton every morning. The Alphas were very careful to keep her surrounded, while still somehow maintaining their distance. She saw them all daily, and at least one of them had transferred into all of her classes, but they avoided the topic of Kilian, and she was too scared to push for more information.

Reed was as distant as the professors during their piano lessons, and Easton had upped the ferocity of their small group sessions—for everyone except Isobel. The others weren't even pretending to do vocal training anymore and were simply beating each other up.

Brutally.

They dragged themselves out of each session panting and bruised, completely sapped of energy. She was too intimidated by Easton to ask what was going on, and Theodore artfully evaded the question whenever she dared to bring it up.

Ironically, the only Alpha she felt any normalcy with anymore was Niko. He called her out of her dorm room for training sessions a few times a week—eventually taking the place of her physiotherapy sessions at the medical centre—and she was really starting to enjoy his company. Especially after seeing him let loose on the other Alphas during Easton's sessions. It was now painfully obvious just how drastically he was holding back on her.

Like now.

"Again," he said, hauling her up. There wasn't even a drop of sweat on his brow.

Her shirt was already sticking to her skin. She groaned, planting her hands on her knees. "Just a minute."

She had gone back to her full academy schedule only a week ago, after several weeks of being banned from dance classes and practises. Her body was struggling with the increased amount of exercise.

"Take a break." Niko reached over the ropes, grabbing two water bottles, and tossing one to her. He sank to the mat, stretching his legs out and draining half the bottle before recapping it and rolling it away.

She gulped the cool water, collapsing opposite him and trying to rub out the cramp in her calf with her free hand. He rolled his striking eyes at her, gripping her ankle and hauling her closer so that her leg landed over his lap. She almost sloshed water all over herself.

"You aren't one of my surrogates," she said. "You don't need to do that."

He gave her a flat, bemused look. "No, I'm not. I'm your trainer."

"I'm too sweaty." She tried to pull her leg away again, but he held firm, his brows dropping lower.

"Stop it," he ordered. "Let me check the muscle and then you're free."

She wiggled uncomfortably. Niko didn't touch her unless it was to sweep her onto her ass and pull her up again so that he could knock her straight back down with a bored look on his handsome face. That was the extent of their physical contact.

It wasn't that *he* made her uncomfortable, the problem was that his touch felt ... good, and she had no right feeling like that. Niko was as detached and cold toward her as the professors, always stringently maintaining boundaries and keeping their relationship black and white.

Still, her body wasn't getting the message.

Her skin warmed when his fingers dug into her muscles, pulling a strained moan of relief from her throat. His gaze shot straight to hers, but his fingers didn't still, deftly working the cramp out of the muscle.

"It's my birthday," he said conversationally.

"What?" This time she did dribble water over herself. She quickly wiped her chin and set the bottle away.

"Today." His well-formed brows arced up as if to ask: "Are you going to do anything about it?"

"Ah ... happy birthday," she managed. "Why didn't you say anything earlier?"

"I was debating inviting you to hang out tonight." His talented fingers brushed the full length of her calf, drawing a shiver out of her body that she tried to hide by shifting on her butt in a pretence of getting more comfortable. "We're going to do a movie night."

"We?" she croaked, even though she knew the answer.

Niko gave her an exasperated look and then stood, sweeping her up again. He never let her take long breaks and he didn't hang around with her after their sessions. She suspected it was because of the cameras. After airing their first few sessions and making as big a deal out of it as possible, the production team seemed to get bored, and they moved on when Niko didn't give the show anything interesting to air. Either that, or they had decided to stock up on footage for some diabolical future episode, which was always possible.

"I share a birthday with Kilian," he said as he effortlessly swept her onto her ass again, except this time, the breath was knocked out of her from his words as well as his actions. "He'll be there."

"Is he okay?" She bounced back to her feet, dropping into the defensive position Niko had taught her. She gripped the opportunity to talk about Kilian like a lifeline, her blood buzzing frantically. They all refused to talk about him, and she didn't want to text him in case he needed space from her.

"They removed him from Ironside for a little while," Niko answered, his tone casual but his eyes guarded. "Just to make sure he didn't know anything about Aron's involvement in the Vermont attack."

The Vermont attack. It was the first time anyone had said those words to her since the night of their disastrous dinner. Even Teak and Charlie were careful to skirt around the topic during their sessions, since Isobel had declared that she didn't want to talk about it. Hearing it mentioned so casually was like a physical kick to the stomach. The air whooshed out of her, and she winced.

The chain around her wrist warmed, constricting tightly. She jumped a few inches, staring down at it. It had been acting up lately—warming or buzzing when her emotions went haywire—but never anything like this.

It vibrated so hard it looked like it was moving.

No ... it *was* moving.

It uncoiled like it was stiff from holding its shape for so long, stretching out languidly before darting up her arm, the metal warm and smooth against her skin. She shrieked, but Niko quickly snatched her wrist before she could pull it off.

"Don't ever mess with a soul artefact," he whispered, his eyes hard as the chain snuck beneath the sleeve of her shirt and crawled across the centre of her chest, dipping into her cleavage. It grew prickly, like the links were sprouting little metallic caterpillar legs, and Niko gripped her other hand when it tried to fly up to her chest. The chain settled along her sternum and then it pinched in, those little metallic legs piercing her skin.

Niko swore, his expression torn as she yelped.

"What the fuck is it doing?" he groused, his usually controlled tone unsteady.

A shrill ring sounded through the room. At first, she thought it was a phone, but then she realised it was echoing all around her. *An alarm.*

"I d-don't know," she stuttered, as Niko's eyes flashed with unease, his grip on her tightening to the point of pain. "What's that alarm? I've never heard it before."

"What alarm?" he asked, as the sound dwindled into something softer, almost like a twinkle.

He released her wrists and her hands immediately tunnelled into her shirt, her fingertips coming away wet with blood.

"It's embedded itself into my skin," she breathed out unsteadily. "But it's ... finished. I think."

She gripped Niko's forearm, using him to keep herself upright as a small whine of pain slipped from between her lips. The chain felt *alive* again, like it had been resting up and healing right alongside her these past few weeks, but now it desperately wanted to be a part of her again.

Niko pulled her out of the ring without warning, tugging her in the direction of the bathroom. "Let's get you cleaned up." The statement was tight-lipped, his voice rigid with restraint.

As soon as they passed through the door, he suddenly changed, his touch gentling, his eyes sparking with frantic energy.

"It's glowing," he hissed, pushing her up against the counter, his body tight behind hers.

They both stared into the mirror at the subtle light peeking through her shirt, and she pulled down the neckline with shaking fingers, staring at the links nestled into her cleavage.

It was thinner than before, the most delicate gold chain spouting little beads of blood that had smudged against her skin. She leaned forward, entranced, the pain falling away as that tinkling sound turned into a warm, happy hum before fading away into nothing. She could make out the tiny links arching from the chain to the skin on either side: little metallic hooks to secure the jewellery in place.

The brighter it glowed, the less it hurt, until the

wounds from those little hooks were completely healed. Niko was breathing hard against the top of her head, his hands braced either side of her, gripping the counter tightly.

"Are you okay?" she asked him, watching his face warily.

He twitched, his gaze sweeping up to hers in the mirror.

His energy was off.

His usual warm and inviting whiskey scent was curdling, bubbling, and boiling until he smelled more like gasoline, the green sinking out of his eyes until the more dusky, tawny hue took over, darkening his entire expression.

"Dammit." The word was spoken through his teeth, more a hiss than anything else. "Give me a minute, Sigma." His voice sounded completely different.

A sense of danger skittered across her skin, his power suddenly swelling into the room like an ominous cloud, closing in against her mind like a metal compress. Her breath turned shallow, her thoughts tripping over themselves. It was eerily similar to what had happened to Sato in the hotel room in Nevada, and just like that time, her mind snapped back to her father.

To when he would lose control.

Sato hadn't acted like her father, but faced with that dangerous roll of influence again, Isobel's mind was suddenly blank, filled with the trauma of her childhood.

There was no room for her to kneel on the ground, to stretch out her back for her father's belt, to turn her head to the side against the ground where the carpet fibres would tickle her nostrils.

And she was too scared to reach for her phone, to call Reed.

She let out a low sound of distress, turning around with her shirt still tugged down to show him that she was fine. She wasn't bleeding any more. It was instinctual, and it seemed to work. Niko's eyes narrowed in on her pale skin. His hands switched from the counter to her hips, drawing her up onto her toes. It didn't seem to be enough because he pulled her up further, higher and higher.

She scrambled to draw her legs up, needing to feel something beneath her, and he sat her on the counter, her legs tucked beneath her. It put her a little higher than him, his face level with her chest. Niko was wearing a completely alien expression, like the real him had stepped out for a while, allowing some kind of Alpha predator to take his place. It terrified her, but he was the last person who would hurt her—outside the wrestling ring—and she repeated that fact inside her head. Niko stood up for her. He was doing all of this so she could protect herself. And he had helped her through a panic attack with all the patience and kindness of a person who was used to caring for victims of violence—not like he was a perpetrator of it himself.

It didn't matter that there was a dangerous rattle emanating from his chest.

His strong hands drifted up her sides, uncaring that her shirt was still damp with sweat, his focus narrowing in on the few spots of blood showing through the material. She watched warily, both of them ignoring the trembling of her body as his hands drifted back down, gathering the hem of her shirt and pulling it up.

His eyes flicked up to hers once, his Alpha ring so swollen it almost seemed to be merging with his pupil, the black and gold meld of colour turning him into a stranger for a brief moment, and then he was ducking, his warm breath scattered low across her belly. He pressed his face against her skin, breathing deeply, like he was trying to regain control of himself, but his attention was dragged up higher, past her belly button, to the bottom of the chain. He pushed her shirt up further, and a low growl vibrated out of his mouth, teasing along her skin.

He flattened his tongue to the base of the chain, causing Isobel to jump in shock, but he didn't stop there. He dragged his tongue up the length of the chain, pushing her shirt higher and higher, until the material was at her chin, bunched there, blocking his path. He buried his face in her shirt, his whole body vibrating, and she hesitantly tunnelled her fingers into his hair, feeling the sweep of panicked violence that emanated off him.

She tried to focus all of her energy on him—to ignore

the fluttering in her stomach, the coolness of his saliva striking a line all the way up her sternum. His quiet rumbles were making her squirm and she fought back the *insane* urge to pull her shirt the rest of the way off and see where else he licked.

Christ.

Maybe she should have been spending a little more time with her surrogates.

Or *any* time with her surrogates.

Niko suddenly pulled back from her with a shudder, releasing her shirt. "How did you know what to do?" he demanded in a roughened tone. "Why the fuck does it feel like you've had experience with this?"

She couldn't make sense of his tone, or the muddled press of emotions battering against her chest.

Fury, possession, disquiet.

"With Alphas?" she dared to ask, the words barely more than a squeak. "My father is an Alpha."

"He's *one* Alpha." Niko's perfect brows pulled down, his lips pressing tightly together as he frowned. "And he lived outside the settlements. He's practically human."

She chewed on her lip, wondering if they were even talking about the same thing.

"How did you know what to do?" he asked again. He wasn't moving back or releasing her, but at least his eyes were only focussed on her face and her shirt had mostly fallen back into place.

"My father has rages. My mother taught me to always submit when he's angry."

Niko breathed in deeply, his nostrils flaring.

Rage.

The sweep of his emotion lashed out at her, but his face remained impassive, his eyes burning. "It's not the same thing," he whispered. "We don't have rages. We have ... well, according to Elijah, it's our hindbrain. Your father is an abuser. It's different. We don't want to hurt you. The *last* thing we want is to hurt you ..."

He trailed off, easing back slightly, his face dipping at the last second like he was quickly scenting her skin before he lifted her from the counter. "Your skin broke. I tasted blood." He set her on her feet, and then backed several paces away, running his hands down the front of his wrinkled shirt. "It must not have been deep enough to scar you."

She froze, realising what could have happened, before quickly shaking her head. "The chain healed the skin right after it pierced it. How is what just happened to you different to what happens to my father?"

"Surging only happens in Alpha formations. Our hindbrain can be triggered to take control, turning us into ... well, our base instincts. While we struggle to hold onto our humanity, the trigger usually needs to be remedied. You were hurt. It triggered me. You offered up your skin for me to taste and scent, which allowed me to reassure myself that you were okay."

She stared at him, a slow realisation dawning. "You weren't supposed to tell me that, were you?"

He smiled slightly, shaking his head. "I just ... um." He motioned to her chest. "I figured I owed you an explanation."

She snorted out a shaky laugh. "Yeah, maybe. You were a gentleman about it, though."

He looked like he was blushing. "We shouldn't linger in here. I'll see you at the dorm in an hour. Don't come in smelling like blood unless you want a riot on your hands and ... go easy on Kilian."

"Go easy on him?"

"One more thing." He stepped up to her, ignoring her question. "If it's about Alphas and it isn't common knowledge, best you don't repeat it. The whole base instincts thing in Alpha formations? The officials don't need to know. I really can't emphasise that enough."

She nodded, watching as he walked out before wetting a paper towel and cleaning the remaining smudges of blood from her chest. The chain now looked completely innocent, the glow dying away.

NIKO ESCAPED THE GYM AND WALKED ALL THE WAY BACK TO THE dorm without a flicker of emotion for the cameras, but as soon as he was enclosed safely inside his own room, he quickly sank to the floor, his eyes staring blankly through the window, a tremor taking up residence in his hands.

He could still taste her blood on the back of his tongue and there was a burning, overwhelming urge exploding somewhere in the back of his brain, trying to convince him to run back there and lick up her quivering torso again and again until the metallic taste of her blood mixed with the thick, sweet scent that had tried to creep out of her when his head was buried in her shirt and he was trying to wrestle himself under control.

This should have been easier.

He liked the girl, but he wasn't desperately in love with her *or* desperate for a mate. He just liked her, as a person. It should have been easy to brush off this incident, to hunt down Elijah and record it the way they were supposed to be doing. But selfishly, he wanted to keep this to himself. Elijah didn't have fucking boundaries. He might ask if Niko got turned on. He was worse than the goddamned officials.

Niko groaned, scrubbing a hand down his face. It was getting harder not to touch her ... and worse than that, he knew it wasn't the bond. She was small and sweet and vulnerable and also none of those things at all, and he was struggling to keep his thoughts under control when his hands were *always* on her and her scent, heavy with sweat, was always clinging to his clothes.

And now her blood was in his mouth.

She was *invading* him ... and he didn't like it.

• • •

Isobel had an hour. She should probably run back to her room and get changed, but instead, she found herself walking toward the chapel, her fingers running over the chain now fused to her skin. It wasn't even sore anymore, and it hummed happily beneath her touch, sitting almost flush with her skin, like a tattoo made of metal.

She checked the chapel first, but when she only found a first year huddled before a candle, she skipped around to the back, where there was a small residence surrounded by an enclosed courtyard. She pressed the button on the outside of the gate and rocked back on her heels, waiting.

It was Sophia who came out, Luis' head appearing in the opening of the door his sister had left hanging open. He peered at Isobel with big eyes, his spectacles hanging off his nose again. Sophia tucked her black hair behind her ear, flashing a wrist stacked with shining, beaded bracelets.

"Was expecting you sooner, to be honest." Sophia unlatched the gate, standing to the side and waving Isobel in.

"I don't have long," Isobel said, her eyes darting around what appeared to be a haphazard herb garden overgrown with weeds as Sophia flicked the gate shut and led the way back to the house.

Luis skittered away, hiding in the next room, his owlish eyes blinking out from another shadowy doorway as Sophia led her into a pokey kitchen. "Tea?"

"Ah, sure." Isobel glanced around. "Where's the Guardian?"

"Mom is sleeping. She gets these awful migraines that knock her right out. But let's be honest, you came here to talk to me."

"I did?" Isobel furrowed her brow at the other girl.

Sophia's lips twitched. "You want information. But do you want it from the *obviously* super cool and super pretty Soul Keeper with the world's most adorable little helper, or from the Guardian who cut your soul artefact off and bargained to keep it?" She didn't wait for an answer. Her light mahogany gaze caught on the top of the chain peeking out from Isobel's now-stretched neckline and she dropped the kettle she had picked up, the sound of it clattering back to the stovetop, making Luis flick back into the shadows.

"Is that ..." Sophia drifted forward, eyes wide in wonder.

"It just happened." Isobel covered it with her hand, feeling oddly protective. "It's ... kind of embedded into my skin."

Sophia whistled, taking in Isobel's body language before backing off and spinning to the kettle. She pulled down three mugs and dropped teabags into each of them, glancing furtively to the doorway her brother was hiding in. "You have any idea what it means?" she asked.

"I don't know what anything means anymore," Isobel said. "And I ... don't trust anyone."

"Understandable." Sophia leaned against the counter, folding her arms. "After what that bitch did to you. We heard the officials talking about it in the hospital. They didn't bother much with your friendship on the show, but the officials said you guys were close and that she was always the first person there to comfort you after she orchestrated an attack against you."

"Well ..." Isobel scoffed. *She could have done without the knowledge that the officials were gossiping about the attacks they allowed to happen.* "Yeah. It was pretty messed up. I really thought she was on my side."

"Maybe she was?" Sophia shrugged. "For a little while, anyway. I mean, it makes sense to pretend to be your friend while they haze you, in a sadistic sort of way. But when you gained some popularity on the show, maybe she tried to switch things up to get some screen time with you. Until she thought you were bonded to her crush, that is. Then I supposed she had to weigh up whether the screen time was worth it."

"You know the game pretty well for someone who isn't even playing it."

"Girl." She laughed. "Everyone knows how this game works. At Ironside, you're predator or you're prey. There's no in between. And the prey? Well ... they never make it very far, do they? I'm surprised you're still kicking."

"I'm not prey."

Sophia poured hot water into the mugs, setting one

on the far edge of the counter before carrying the others to the small, circular dining table. Luis ducked out from the hallway, grabbing the third mug and hovering by the counter indecisively.

"Those Alphas are definitely trying to push you into the predator category, especially with all that 'initiation' crap Sato started a little while ago," Sophia allowed, pulling out a chair and plopping into it, folding her legs as she blew on her tea. "It's pretty obvious what he was trying to do. But you aren't there yet. Maybe the Vermont attack was just the push you needed."

Isobel sat, pulling her mug closer, fiddling with the tag from the teabag as Luis approached his sister's side, eyes fixed on Isobel as he nervously fiddled with his overlong sleeves.

"Anyway"—Sophia waved a hand as though to disperse the topic—"you said you didn't have long. What is it you wanted to ask?"

"These soul artefacts." Isobel touched the links through her shirt. "What do they do?"

Sophia grinned like she approved of the question. "Literally anything. It entirely depends on the god who gifted it to you. If you believe that kind of thing."

"Which we do," Luis squeaked. "It's really real."

"I thought the Guardian said it was from the woman in the picture?" Isobel asked, switching her gaze between them.

"Aphelina?" Sophia clicked her tongue. "I find that

hard to believe. You were gifted the chain before you even knew who your mate was. Her gifts are usually preoccupied with love and desire, so if you were gifted the chain when you were alone, then there's no reason for it to be from her."

Well, that answered that question. If it was all real, then Aphelina had been trying to matchmake her and Sato. Which could only mean one thing.

The Gifted goddess of love was a terrible matchmaker.

"And now?" Isobel dropped her hand. "What does it mean that it's doing *this*?"

"May I?" Sophia brushed her hand through her brother's inky mop of hair before she stood, rifling through the kitchen drawers to pull out a magnifying glass.

Isobel hesitated.

"It's okay," Luis said shyly, slipping into a third chair. "Sophie—" He pronounced it like *Sof-ee*. "—is really good at this. Even better than Mama."

"I'm just a Soul Keeper," Sophia quickly inserted, shaking her head at Luis. "I've got a long way to go to be a Guardian."

She hovered until Isobel finally sighed and nodded, turning in her chair, and pulling the neckline of her shirt down. Sophia hovered the magnifying glass over the chain, making thoughtful sounds every now and then as she examined it. She was more thorough than Isobel expected.

"It doesn't like *me,*" she noted with a laugh, pulling her hand back quickly like the metal had given her a little zap. She fell back into her chair, placing the magnifying glass on the table and folding her arms over her chest to stare narrowly at a spot just below Isobel's collarbone, apparently deep in thought.

Luis watched her, waiting expectantly, some of his shyness melting away to be replaced by a bashful eagerness. Isobel wasn't sure how to feel about all of this. Her father was scathing when he spoke about the Gifted religion and the "stupid fanatics" who still followed it. But on the other hand, a lot had been happening recently that she couldn't explain. She was seeing ghosts. She had *ten* mates.

And now her body was producing light and gold ... which seemed to have a mind of its own.

It was all a bit too much.

"I don't know." Sophia sighed, but the look on her face told a different story.

"You have an idea," Isobel prompted.

Sophia winced. "It's not any of the nice gods, let's put it that way."

"The only god I know is ... Artos? Artus?"

"Arterus," she corrected easily. "The King of Gods. It could be from him, but there's no historical record of him giving gifts to mortals, so I doubt it. And it wouldn't make sense for him to give a gift so strongly associated with Aphelina, like the chain."

"Historical record?" Isobel asked doubtfully.

Sophia smirked, surveying her metallic blue nails. Some of the blue beads on her bracelets were the exact same shade. "They can't ban books or art from any of the Guardians' collections. They're classified as religious artefacts. You know, because it's a dead religion and all that."

Something sparked inside Isobel, a feverish need to get her hands on some of those artefacts, but she didn't trust Sophia enough to ask. Especially since Isobel's main research interests were focussed on Alphas going feral and Sigmas seeing dead people.

"Stygian!" Luis suddenly exclaimed, slapping his hands onto the table with an excited gasp. "It's Stygian, isn't it?"

Sophia winced again. "Yeah, I think it is."

"Which god is that?" Isobel asked nervously.

Sophia pulled up from her chair, disappearing into the other room for a moment and returning with a huge tome. It had a thick spine and faded gold edges, but it was clearly very well used. She found the page she was looking for and set it onto the table in front of Isobel, tapping the image of an hourglass on the first page. It was half filled with twinkling, airy light and half filled with twisting, menacing shadow, the two mixing at the waist of the hourglass like coloured smoke.

“Stygian,” Sophia announced. “The Duskfall Warden. He maintains the balance between dark and light. He’s very powerful, and ... terrifying. People who don’t understand how the Gifted religion works sometimes call him the God of Mysteries.”

Isobel scanned the paragraphs detailing Stygian’s power, skipping over to the next page, where it showed an illustration of a man with eyes like stars—a bright galaxy of light twinkling through his stare, though it wasn’t a peaceful expression. It was hard and fierce, most of his delicate face cast into heavy shadow, his skin a meld of deep ebony and shadowed dusk. He wore strings of stars around his neck and held an apple in each hand. One was rotten, with worms crawling through the brown flesh. The other sparkled with vibrant colour, its skin flawless, a fuzzy green leaf unfurling from its stem.

“Why would a god of mystery make my chain turn into some sort of ... piercing?” Isobel sat back from the page, her stomach churning, her head feeling heavy.

“That’s exactly why I think it’s him,” Sophia emphasised. “Because there’s no plausible reason. If this has anything to do with Stygian, then all you can do is wait for him to reveal its purpose.”

“He’s scary,” Luis said to the table. His excitement over guessing the right answer dying off. “He fixes good luck.”

Isobel quickly took a few hasty gulps of the tea before

taking the mug to the sink. "Maybe he'll be nice to me." She forced out a faint laugh. "I've had pretty shitty luck."

"Maybe not," Sophia said carefully, standing to walk Isobel back to the gate, her arm winding around the narrow shoulders of her brother. "Your mate is exceedingly strong. Stygian might think you've been given too much."

Ten mates was definitely too much.

Damn.

Isobel's hands shook when she opened the gate and stepped through, but she paused to look back at the siblings. "Thanks," she said softly. "It's nice to talk to people who aren't ... you know."

"Fighting to the death for a spot of fame?" Sophia chuckled, an accent that Isobel hadn't taken much note of the first time she had met the girl becoming more obvious the more at ease she became. There was the slightest lilt to her words, the *s* sound softer and the consonants crisper. They might have been from Mexico or another Spanish-speaking country.

"Yeah, I knew I was right about you," Sophia seemed to decide out loud. "You're exactly how you appear on screen. You should work on that. Be more like Kane. Be a better actor. Be a predator."

Sophia saw it too.

The *real* Theodore.

For some reason, that made Isobel like her just a little bit more. Most people didn't see through Theodore's golden boy mask. She kept her mouth shut instead of commenting on Theodore, but her lips curled into a smile.

"You can come back," Luis offered, answering her smile with a toothy grin. "You can finish your tea next time."

"Maybe I will." Isobel waved at them and then started off toward Dorm A.

4
THE COLD EMOJI

ISOBEL WALKED HALFWAY TO DORM A BEFORE HER NERVES GOT the better of her and she redirected herself to Dorm O. She couldn't turn up in sweaty exercise clothes spotted with blood and without birthday gifts. Niko never invited her to anything, and she hadn't seen Kilian in weeks.

She agonised over what to wear, her stomach flip-flopping sickeningly. Her fingers itched to snatch one of Kilian's shirts from the shelf, but they didn't smell like him anymore. She considered wearing the dress he had bought her, but it reminded her of Eve ... and the fact that nobody had attacked her since Eve was expelled.

The news about Aron had broken to the public the same night she told the guys, but none of the officials had reached out to her to hear what she had to say. Not even her father had asked her what had happened in

Vermont. He had given her an exhaustive lecture about wasting her time on Omegas and then ignored her for two weeks for ruining his settlement tour, abandoning his apartment in the family centre until she was well enough to start playing the game again.

She had no idea what had happened to Eve.

Nobody would tell her, and the news was only focussing on Aron, keeping the details just vague enough that it almost seemed like they were blaming him for the attack ... and him alone. None of it made sense, but that was Ironside. The officials didn't have to explain themselves. They decided what narrative to play, and the rest of the world never questioned what they saw. The only thing that remained to be determined was *why*, exactly, they had chosen this narrative.

Isobel settled on a pale slip dress—one of the pieces her father had brought to their last dinner. He had one of his assistants analysing the latest fashion trends and purchasing designer pieces for Isobel to wear. A post had gone viral of Isobel recycling the same five oversized T-shirts, always tucked into black tights or shorts, and some of the comments had linked her apparently limited wardrobe to the less-than-stellar box office numbers for her father's latest movie.

One of his team had decided to bring the comments to his attention, and now Isobel had more clothes than she knew what to do with.

He didn't care that the T-shirts were Kilian's, or that

she spent most of her day exercising. He had told her to get changed between every single class so that she was never anything less than absolutely presentable.

The slip dress skimmed her body gracefully, the fabric silky smooth, gliding against her thighs as she slipped her feet into sandals. The neckline was subtle, the spaghetti straps accentuating her pale collarbones. She quickly moisturised and brushed her hair, twisting it into a ponytail when it flared out, a little too wild after all her activity for the day.

She picked two ribbons carefully off one of the more extravagant dresses she would likely never wear and hurried outside, almost running straight into a harassed-looking Theodore.

"Good. You're here," he said. "Already checked everywhere else." He cast a quick, uncomfortable look at the door. "Can we please leave, like now? I've been accidentally groped twice."

It had been weeks, and it was still hard to look at Theodore without thinking about his hand pushing into her panties. Most nights when she flopped onto her makeshift bed, that intense look in his eyes as he eased her toward orgasm was the first thing she saw. The way his arm had shuddered with restraint as she came on his fingers. The way he had bitten his lip so hard it had drawn all of her focus. The way his eyes had burned hotter than they ever had before was seared onto the backs of her eyelids.

“Ah.” She cleared her throat. “Hello.”

“Hello back at you, cutie.” He grabbed her hand and began dragging her away from the dorm. He clearly wasn’t as affected as her. “What are the ribbons for?”

“I’m going to pick some flowers for Niko and Kilian.”

“What for?”

“For their birthday.”

“I don’t get it.”

She was jogging to keep up with his long strides, but she didn’t care at all because the warmth from his hand was tunnelling through her body, easing away her exhaustion and calming the feeling of her stomach turning over and over like a carnival ride—the same uncomfortable feeling she had been dealing with for weeks.

“To give them as presents?” she tried again.

“Oh.” He cast her a tight smile. “Of course. How … *you.*”

“I can’t tell if you’re insulting me or not,” she grumbled.

“I would never insult you …”

She dug her heels in, forcing him to slow down before she continued walking, analysing him with her eyes narrowed. “Why did that sound like there was a but?”

“Well … I don’t have the highest opinion of your innermost survival mechanisms,” he admitted gently.

She flinched, thinking he was talking about Eve, but he quickly added, “Because of Oscar.”

“Sato?” She frowned up at him, but he avoided her eyes, both of them silent as they walked around the lake.

She broke away from him when they got to Jasmine Field, and quickly gathered up two floppy bouquets of flowers before they approached Alpha Hill. It wasn’t until she was halfway up the steps that it finally hit her.

“The kiss,” she whispered, almost tripping over the next step.

Theodore caught her and then quickly released her. “Mhmm.”

“The chain made me do it,” she muttered the words lowly even though the cameras were too far away to catch any words spoken on the stairs.

He glanced immediately to her chest, which wasn’t surprising. Niko had likely told them everything in a group message as soon as he walked away from her.

Well … almost everything.

She doubted he said anything about licking her. They seemed to share a lot with each other … except their more intimate moments with her. Theodore must have only just recently found out about the kiss with Sato, or she was sure he would have brought it up earlier.

“Does it hurt?” he asked, glancing away.

“Not anymore.” She shrugged. “It healed straight away. Now it just feels … comfortable, I guess. I visited Sophia—the Guardian’s daughter. She thinks it’s a gift from one of the gods. Something about 'if it's a mystery, then it's probably from the god of mystery.'"

"That would check out." Theodore smirked. "I'm glad Niko was there."

"Where have *you* been?" She winced the second the words were out of her mouth, but she didn't try to take them back. She understood that she had broken his trust, but he broke hers first and she only ignored him for a short amount of time. Not that he had *ignored* her, exactly. But he had definitely stepped back.

"Kalen's orders," he uttered quietly. "A Tether in pain, healing from a soul infraction ... you shouldn't be able to tear that person away from their mate with a towline and a tank. Since I didn't leave your side at the hospital, he wanted to make it seem like it would be easy for us to be away from each other. I didn't want to tell you because you struggle to ask for help as it is, so adding a reason you shouldn't contact me seemed like a bad idea. I wanted to still be here for you if you needed me."

"Oh." She halted again, wanting to prolong their conversation.

She turned back like she was pausing to survey the view from halfway up Alpha Hill. The breeze drifted through her hair, the desert flowers vivid in the afternoon light, the academy appearing calm, though she could hear music playing over outdoor speakers in the direction of Dorm A. He paused with her, his fingers dancing lightly up her forearm before sliding back down to her wrist. He seemed to want to take her hand, to fit his fingers through hers, but he didn't.

"If you needed me, all you had to do was say so, Illy." His voice was gruff, but soft, like he was trying not to speak too loudly. "Or you could just come to the dorm. You're always welcome."

"Not always." She forced a laugh. "What if you were with Wallis?"

"She's not allowed inside the dorm. Mikel said her scent is too strong."

Isobel blinked, taken aback. "Seriously? What does she smell like?"

"A would-be rapist."

Isobel winced. "What does she actually smell like?"

"A group of kids having a craft day. Loud and messy." He gave her a sideways look as they started climbing the stairs again.

She laughed hollowly. "How can someone smell loud? Or messy?"

He shrugged. "Same way you can smell messy ... but in a good way."

"What's the good way?"

"Forget I said that."

"Okay, so ... the other ... um, girlfriends? What do they smell like?" she asked, avoiding his eyes. "James and Ellis?"

"Newspapers, and popcorn."

"Newspapers aren't so bad," she said. "Gabriel could be into that."

"Musty newspapers," he corrected.

"And popcorn? What's wrong with that?"

"Burnt popcorn."

She rolled her eyes. "I find that hard to believe. You all smell ... amazing. Not to mention Wallis has already been inside Dorm A. I was there."

"You were more than there. You were the one who invited them to stay. And people's scents change depending on your feelings toward them. If a person disgusts you, their scent will evolve into something that disgusts you."

They had reached the top of the stairs and Isobel was saved from answering as she kicked the last stair in shock, her eyes widening at the number of students who had gathered around Alpha Lake. They were spread out on picnic chairs or blankets, all of them facing a giant projection screen that had been rolled from the rooftop of Dorm A to cover a portion of the front of the building.

Ironside staff were manning snack booths off to the side, and there was a small, roped-off area right in the prime position directly across from the screen, a wooden platform set up to house eight cosy bucket chairs, several cameras on tripods facing the seating area to catch even the slightest whisper.

"What ... the heck?" Isobel muttered, trying to take it all in. "Who *organised* this?"

"The officials." Theodore shrugged casually, disinterested in the whole scene ... which for Theodore, could have meant absolutely anything.

"They're hoping for a show," Isobel whispered, raising her brows at the platform in the middle of it all. There were even dimmed spotlights set up, a soft glow haloing each individual chair.

Moses pushed through the crowd, stopping before them. His nose crinkled in a way that would have been adorable if his expression wasn't painted thickly in aggravation ... and if it wasn't Moses.

"You're both late," he snapped, his darkening eyes drifting over her figure in the shift dress like he couldn't help himself before he noticed the two haphazard bundles of flowers in her arms. "I thought Sigmas were supposed to be generous."

"I thought Alphas were supposed to be cool," she said stiffly.

His lips twisted, flashing the briefest shadow of a smile before he took the flowers off her. "Relax, Carter." He rolled his eyes at her sound of protest. "I'm just leaving them on the platform." He turned away, striding off toward the roped-off area.

Theodore's grip wound softly above her elbow, tugging her toward the snack booths. Isobel spotted Wallis making a beeline for Theodore, her attention fixed on him, her mouth a tight line of determination. He let out a soft sound of frustration and plastered on a welcoming smile—which was several inches more than anything Isobel could muster—before he released Isobel.

"There you are!" Wallis looped her arms around his neck and tried to kiss him, but he turned so that her lips landed on his cheek instead.

Isobel busied herself with the containers of different candy laid out before her, scooping little squares of caramel-coated chocolate into a paper cone and pretending she wasn't listening to the fake couple an arm's length away.

"I've been waiting here for an hour," Wallis complained. "We're wasting valuable camera time."

If Isobel didn't know that Wallis had sexually assaulted Sato, she might have thought that Wallis' voice sounded husky and alluring. Instead, it made her skin crawl.

"The chairs are just for ... the birthday group," Theodore returned gently. "They actually have our names on them."

"I'll sit in your lap," she purred.

Isobel peeked at him from beneath her lashes. He did a good job of looking adoring and at ease, but his sweet scent had soured, and his discomfort was reaching out to her, hammering away on her chest and asking for acknowledgment.

She was just about to open her mouth and say something stupid when Reed appeared, wrapping his arm around Theodore's shoulders and leaning down to stage-whisper to Wallis.

"How much do you really want to piss off Theo's adoring fans, hm? They've waited years to have an hours-long live session of his disgustingly handsome face at close range, and you want to *block their view*?" He shook his head, whistling a tone of warning. "Way to get yourself cancelled, Wally."

"It's Wallis," she said, appearing shocked that Reed was talking to her, and even sort of knew her name.

"Right. Enjoy your night." He dragged Theodore off, and Isobel quickly stepped away, just in case Wallis decided to latch onto her instead.

She looped around, keeping an eye out for Kilian or Niko before stopping before the candy booth again and filling up her paper cone with more chocolate caramels.

"Um ... Carter?" the woman behind the candy stall asked nervously.

Isobel quickly focussed her attention on the woman. "I'm allowed to eat these, right? Shit, I didn't even ask. Sorr—"

"No, no! It's all free!" The woman was waving her hands like mad, red colouring her cheeks. "I was just going to suggest these, since you like the caramels so much." She held out another paper cone, already filled, looking nervous as hell. "I'm a huge fan, by the way. I know we're not really supposed to talk to the students, but ..." She trailed off as the man in the booth beside her cleared his throat, shooting her a quick warning look. "Big fan," she repeated in a whisper as Isobel took the second cone.

"Me too," a familiar voice spoke behind her, making the woman's eyes go wide with shock.

Isobel also froze, her skin prickling.

What the fuck?

What the absolute fucking fuck?

She turned slowly, both cones dropping out of her grip, chocolates scattering over the ground.

Eve Indie was thinner, with dark circles under her eyes, but she was *there*. Dressed in loose, high-waisted jeans and a tight tank, a row of gold necklaces dangling brightly around her neck.

"Good to see you again, Iz—"

"Get away from me." Isobel stumbled back, her hip butting against one of the plastic candy containers.

"It wasn't me." Eve's lower lip was wobbling, her hand reaching out for Isobel. "That guy—Aron. It was all him, he forced me, threatened me ... He has this power that drugs people ..." She took another step closer, and Isobel shot to the side, backing rapidly away. "You really think they'd let me back in here if I was guilty? He demonstrated it in front of all the officials!" Eve called after her, the shout drawing the attention of the students around them. "I'm just an Omega with no abilities!"

Isobel's head was spinning, her vision growing blurry, panic clawing up the back of her neck and filling her vision with an unsteady haze. She stumbled toward the dorm, unsure where else to go.

Maybe she could barricade herself in Theodore's room or—

A strong hand wrapped around her bicep before she could get far, and she swayed toward the familiar scent of crushed petals and spilling sap. Even Moses was a beacon in her current state of panic.

"Come with me," he muttered. "Keep breathing, Carter."

Breathing.

Right. She was supposed to be breathing.

She pulled in shaky breath after shaky breath.

"Not so fast," Moses gritted out as he manoeuvred her through the crowd of people. "Take them slowly."

She focussed on doing what he told her until she found her voice again. "Eve—"

"I know." His voice was a growl. "Kalen just texted us. They cleared her of all charges and delayed the news until now so the fucking *surprise* wouldn't be ruined."

"What?" she cried, an echoing bolt of pain shooting up her arms. She looked down, but there were no new wounds, only the long, puckered pink scars.

He stopped walking suddenly, causing her to collide with his back. They had reached the stage with the eight chairs, the cameras only a few steps ahead. He turned, fixing her with a dark look before ducking to whisper in her ear, his words barely audible.

"You're an *actor* to them, Carter. And they want to make you the victim over and over again because they think you're good at it. You don't want to play out the script they just handed you? Then don't. Don't react. Don't give them the satisfaction."

She choked back whatever she might have replied as he lifted away, grabbing her hand and dragging her onto the platform. The seat with his name on it was in the middle, Theodore's name tag beside it. He released her hand just before the line of cameras and dropped into his spot, arching a heavy brow at her. She sucked in a deep, unsteady breath, her mind turning over and over in shock and disbelief.

Eve had *tortured* her. Almost *killed* her. And they let her back into the academy for ... *a surprise episode?*

For views?

For a plot twist?

Moses was right.

There was no way she was going to play along with this script. She stepped onto the platform and sank into Theodore's seat, crossing her arms and legs. She let her head fall back, her body slumping slightly like she didn't have a care in the world before she tilted her chin up to Moses, trying to thank him without words.

His lips tilted up at the side, then fell back into place again. "Dammit," he muttered. "I forgot snacks."

"There's no way in hell I'm getting them for you," she grumbled. *She wasn't* that *grateful.* "I stand no chance of

wrestling Theo out of this chair if I leave it unattended."
And she was pretty sure her legs weren't working.

Moses dug into his pocket, pulling out his phone, and as his fingers flew across the screen, Isobel's own phone began to vibrate. She extracted it from her small cross-body bag, tapping on the group chat.

Moses: I've got Carter.

Moses: Someone bring us snacks.

Theodore: What's the damage?

Elijah: Who has eyes on Eve?

Mikel (admin): I do. She's with her friends, trying to find a spot near the stage. I don't think she's going to try anything. The story they're pushing now is that Eve was forced by Aron. They're saying he's the one with the illegal drugging power. Apparently, it slipped out of him when the officials were questioning him, but Eve was also in the room.

Isobel: It's not true. I felt her power while I was here in the academy. She's used it on me before.

Mikel (admin): We know.

Kalen (admin): We won't take our eyes off her until the movie night is over. Keep acting unaffected. You're doing perfectly.

Isobel: Okay.

Theodore: What snacks do you want?

Moses: Whatever you're getting.

Moses suddenly looked up. "What were those chocolates you were inhaling?"

"Something with caramel. I don't know."

Moses: And caramel chocolate, whatever types they have.

Theodore: They have like seven types.

Moses: It's for Carter.

Theodore: I'll get them all.

Oscar: Get some for me.

Theodore: No.

Oscar: Why the fuck not?

Cian: You aren't cute enough.

Isobel smirked at her screen, casting a quick look around to make sure Sato wasn't anywhere near her.

Isobel: It's true. You aren't.

"It's all fun and games until someone gets hurt," Moses singsonged, a note of warning in his voice.

"Why is everyone so terrified of Sato anyway?" Isobel seized the opportunity to get more information on him from the Alpha who seemed to spend the most time with him, and to take her panicked mind off Eve. The guys were remarkably good at keeping cool heads in stressful situations ... unless ferality was involved, and then all hell broke loose.

It was easier to mimic their forced ease—to distract herself with their interactions—than it was to confront what had just happened and what it meant for her moving forward.

Moses smirked, shaking his head. "I'm sure the fans appreciate your subtle attempt at gossiping for the cameras, but you're going to have to try a *little* harder if it's Oscar you want to gossip about."

Her phone announced a new message, and she returned her attention to the screen.

Theodore: Oscar took the fucking snacks. I have to go back and get more.

Oscar: Flattery will get you everywhere.

Isobel: We're sorry about before. You're incredibly cute, Sato.

Moses: Incredibly.

Theodore: Gag.

Isobel: Can we have the snacks?

Oscar: Say please.

Isobel: Please.

Oscar: One more time.

Isobel: Please?

Oscar: Again.

Elijah: Stop it.

Gabriel: Are you two flirting?

Isobel: No.

Oscar: Yes.

Isobel: NO. Why would you even ask that?

Oscar: Because he doesn't know what flirting looks like.

Elijah: What does flirting look like, Oscar?

Elijah: Here's a hint: it doesn't begin with "tor" and end in "ment".

Moses: From here on out, I will be calling Oscar "kettle" and Elijah "pot".

Gabriel: Moses has a point there.

Elijah: All three of you can shut up.

Isobel glanced up to find Moses biting back a smirk, his dark grey eyes swimming with humour as he read the messages. Cian stepped onto the platform before Isobel could glance back down at her phone, and he gave her a slight smile. His dusky golden skin was a little paler than usual, his hair pulled into a messy knot, his mouth tightening back into a hard line after attempting to smile at her.

"All good?" he asked her, dropping into the seat on her other side, even though it had Kilian's name on it. His fingers played across her forearm, a gentle brush along the outside of her scar before his hand dropped to rest on his own thigh. It was almost like he wanted her to know that everything was normal with them, that all the tension in his expression wasn't aimed at her.

She nodded, darting her attention over his shoulder for a brief moment, trying to catch sight of where Eve had situated herself. Instead, she saw Kilian and Niko trying to make their way through the crowd.

"It's not that big of a deal," Isobel lied, her eyes darting back to Cian's sharp, sapphire gaze. "She's back. Whatever."

"Let's not waste any time on her," he agreed, a spark of satisfaction flashing across his angular features. "I'm sure the officials punished her suitably." His eyes narrowed just slightly, several of the micro muscles in his face twitching before he wrestled his expression into something calm and unbothered. Despite all the effort, he couldn't smooth out the deep dimple etched into his cheek, showcasing his displeasure. "And how about your bond? You haven't been asking us to surrogate lately."

She reared back an inch, wondering why he would bring that up with a camera staring at them head-on and microphones taped to the chairs.

"I'm surviving," she hedged.

"You're paler than usual, skinnier than usual, and Gabriel and Elijah both said you aren't fulfilling all of your practice time. You keep leaving early like you don't have the energy to keep going."

She frowned at him. "I haven't had much of an appetite and I'm a little weak at the moment. It's no big deal."

"What's in your bag?" he asked, his tone combative.

What the heck?

"Stuff." She frowned harder, and he tipped toward her, quickly tugging on the zipper until he could pull open her bag to peer inside.

"Tissues," he noted. "Cough drops, pills—"

"Allergy medication and anti-inflammatories," she corrected. "Not *pills*."

"Who prescribed them?"

"Someone on my father's team."

"Exactly." He zipped her bag back up, leaning away from her again, though he kept her trapped in his gaze.

"But your *bond specialist* prescribed you something else, didn't she?"

Isobel wanted to hit him.

He waited, and when she didn't answer, his stern expression melted into a soft, wry smile. "We only have a bit over a week left until summer break. Have you thought about who you're going to take home with you?"

She stilled. He was right.

They were almost at the end of the final term, and she had two impossible deadlines looming—deadlines she had conveniently forgotten about while she was getting over what Eve and Aron had done to her.

There was still the anonymous texter who had ordered her to find out how to get into the Icon club, and there was Wallis, whose life she was supposed to somehow ruin.

At first, she had naively hoped that Eve had been the texter, but despite Eve's absence, the messages had continued. Usually, the texter just sent a number of days until the end of term, sometimes accompanied by an assurance not to fuck with them. Sometimes it was just a picture of her walking to class with her head tucked down. It was a constant effort to keep the pressure on her, to make sure she couldn't forget.

"Wait." She blinked away the heavy thoughts. "I can take someone home with me?"

"How else will you survive summer break?" Cian raised dark gold brows, his teeth flashing in a lazy smile.

"I hadn't thought that far ahead," she admitted. She *couldn't* think past the impossible tasks ahead of her. "I'll have to talk to my father about it." Time was slipping away. She seemed to be stuck in the trauma of what Eve had done, unable to think too many steps into the future before the memories dragged her right back again, phantom pain shooting through her arms.

"Still hoping Prince Charming is going to walk into one of the settlements and report a funky eye colour?" Cian asked knowingly.

She rolled her eyes, trying to elbow him, but he only grabbed her elbow and then used it to pull her up to her feet. He tugged her onto his lap, his free hand quickly looping her legs to the side so she wouldn't flash the cameras. She found herself sitting sideways, staring at Moses, who had glanced up from his phone at all the movement.

"Is that necessary?" Moses asked, sounding annoyed.

"She has a bag full of medication and she's lost weight," Cian snapped back. "So I'm guessing it is."

Moses rolled his eyes, slumping back in his chair and tapping his phone distractedly against his thigh. "Where the hell are the chocolates? Chocolate will help."

"Chocolate?" Cian asked, scanning the crowd.

His hand was still on her leg, just above her knee, that touch alone flooding her body with warmth as his tattooed thumb brushed back and forth, the contrast of his dark, tattooed skin against her fair, unadorned skin drawing her eyes again and again.

"Well, food in general," Moses muttered like he suddenly didn't want to be involved in the conversation. "You're supposed to be reminding her to eat."

Niko stepped up to the stage and Moses pointed to the flowers at the base of the camera stand. "Those are for you."

Niko looked from the flowers, to Moses, and back to the flowers, confusion descending over his features.

Isobel quickly jumped up, hurrying over to him, and picking up both bouquets. She pushed one of them into his arms. "Just one of them." She wanted to fret over the already-wilting petals but pulled her hand back, forcing herself not to fidget. "Sorry ... I didn't have much time to prepare."

Niko gave her a lopsided smile—the brilliant, beautiful flash of teeth that he shared with the camera, and never her.

"Thanks, Carter." His attention flicked to her chest for a second, his eyes darkening briefly before clearing so fast she could have easily imagined the shadow of emotion. "You good?"

She nodded, her throat tight.

He surveyed her for a second more before passing her and finding his seat, leaving her to face Kilian. She froze, waiting as Kilian stepped up to her, his pale eyes brushing over the flowers in her arms. "Those for me, Illy?"

He had used her nickname. That seemed significant, somehow. Like he was secretly telling her that everything was fine. Theodore was the only one who used her nickname, the rest of them choosing to call her by her first name, her last name, her rank, or a random—sometimes disparaging—pet name. And sometimes the name of a literal *pet*.

She nodded, holding the bundle of flowers out silently.

His eyes lightened, crinkling at the corners, his lush lips quirking up. Her heart threatened to tear out of her chest. *Holy crap she was nervous.*

Theodore brushed past, arms overflowing with snacks, dark brows shifting up slightly at the way they were just standing there, trying to find words to speak to each other. "Little help?" he grumbled, palming half the paper cones off to Kilian.

"No flowers for the other two?" Elijah asked, striding across the platform and taking a seat, his attention shifting around distractedly. He seemed agitated to have a close-up lens focussed on him. His eyes came to a rest on Isobel, cataloguing her confused expression. "You didn't know," he concluded before she could say anything. "It's Moses and Theo's birthday tomorrow. That's why it's such a big party, we're doing all the birthdays at once."

Isobel whacked Theodore across the chest. "Why wouldn't you tell me!"

He shrugged, smirking at her as he took his seat, reminding her that she never should have vacated it. Cian had moved to the seat with his name tag on it, Kilian settling beside Theodore, offering him a single daisy from the bunch he held. Theodore tucked it behind his ear, still smirking at Isobel. Moses stared at Niko's bouquet, waiting for a pity flower, but Niko only moved it to his other side, out of Moses' reach, pretending not to notice.

Gabriel stepped up onto the platform, finding his own seat quietly, and then Oscar stalked over to the last free seat as most of the spotlights around the lake suddenly dimmed, the projection screen flickering to life, sound booming from speakers all around them. Soft lights remained focussed on the eight chairs, highlighting them in a gentle golden glow.

Kilian crooked his finger at her, and she cast a quick look over the crowd. Her closeness to Kilian was exactly what had gotten her into so much trouble in the first place ... but *fuck* Eve. And Aron.

And all the rest of them.

Kilian was the only Alpha she could safely be close to without it having to mean anything. He was the first person she was really comfortable with since her mother, and that wasn't something she could ignore.

She began walking over to him, but Theodore caught

her attention before she got there, holding out several paper cones full of chocolate. She bit down on her lip as she gathered them up, thanking him quietly and casting a quick look to the far seat on the right. Sato was lounged back, as lazily as he possibly could in the bucket chair, the hood of his jacket pulled up around his face, casting most of it into shadow now that the lights weren't as bright. He still had all the paper cones he had apparently confiscated off Theodore, and he didn't look like he was about to share them anytime soon.

He held one out to her, wiggling it a little before passing it to Cian and muttering something in the other Alpha's ear. Cian passed it along to Kilian, his face completely blank. Kilian was sitting cross-legged, having already kicked his shoes off, the chairs almost wide enough to fit two people in them.

"I think this is for you," he said, as she reached him.

The cone was full of baby carrots.

"For variety," Sato explained, somehow forcing his gritty voice to sound almost friendly.

"Thanks," she bit out, trying not to glare at him.

He only smiled back. Or at least she thought he was smiling. He might have been leering. It was hard to tell because she wasn't sure how far his lips were capable of stretching.

Kilian pulled her into his lap, and she settled back against him, cuddling all her snacks to her chest as the movie started. It was a cult classic, one she had already seen a few times before.

Kilian looped an arm around her middle, his other hand dipping into one of her cones to steal a chocolate. “Are we supposed to watch the movie?” he asked lightly. “Why all the cameras? It’s like they expect us to do something else.”

“We could do something else.” Niko leaned around Theodore to speak to Kilian. “I’m not attached to the movie.”

“It *is* our birthday,” Kilian mused, his voice brushing against her ear, making her want to squirm.

“What do you want to do?” Cian asked, sounding bored.

“Let’s play a game.” Theodore whipped out his phone. “We’ll let the fans pick.” His fingers flew across the screen. “This whole thing is live, so ...”

“They’re already asking us to play confessions, aren’t they?” Elijah asked.

“Literally fifty comments saying exactly that,” Theodore answered.

“This is live?” Isobel whispered.

“Didn’t you look at the camera?” Kilian spoke the words against her temple this time, lowly enough that the microphone might not have picked them up.

She shrugged. She absolutely hadn’t, but she did now, staring directly into the lens and noticing the small sign on top of the camera, stating that they were being recorded live.

"All right," Cian drawled. "Let's play confessions. Everyone gets three passes. We need a punishment for the first person out and a reward for the last person standing."

Kilian pulled his phone out, resting it on Isobel's thigh as he pulled her tighter back against him, notching his chin on her shoulder to look at his screen. He brought up the live broadcast and scrolled to the chat, where the comments were flooding in. Isobel pretended to be reading them as well, but her mind was already wandering.

Maybe Moses wouldn't make her go through with trying to ruin Wallis' life?

She cut her eyes past Theodore, taking in Moses' lounging posture and dark, brooding expression. He sighed out an unhappy sound, diverting his attention from the movie and tipping his head forward to peer down the line of chairs. He seemed to be looking at Sato, but then his eyes slid to her. She quickly looked away.

"Hands off snacks, people. Pile them in the middle," Moses suddenly ordered, unfurling from his chair, and setting down the food he had brought over.

The others followed suit without question, and Kilian put his phone down, releasing Isobel. She added her paper cones to the growing pile, Kilian dropped the one, small cardboard box he had brought over, and then he scooped her up again. The movement was so effortless, making her feel light as air as he sat down and cuddled her into his lap again.

"Okay, so winner gets all the snacks," Cian said, reading his phone. "Loser has to give everyone massages through the second half of the movie." He glanced up at Moses' scoff. "That one came from the comments, not me. Who wants to MC?"

"We'll do it." Kilian pulled up his phone again, tapping back into the comments section. "First confession is for Kane." He lifted his eyes to Theodore. "When are you going to sing again?"

"I didn't realise anyone wanted me to sing again," Theodore answered, smiling right at the camera aimed at his face.

Kilian scrolled back up to the live video, and Isobel swallowed at the image of Theodore on the screen. He looked *beyond* flattered. Touched. Ecstatic. His wide, perfect smile and twinkling eyes had her stomach flipping all over the place, his stormy gaze so beautiful she wasn't even surprised to see links to the Gifted contact store popping up in the comments. They had released a special edition contact called *Kane – A Perfect Storm (Light Edition)*. She guessed Moses would be the "dark edition."

"Crushing much?" Kilian whispered, the words stirring her hair gently.

She tunnelled her elbow into his gut, making him

grunt and almost drop the phone. He chuckled, skipping through the comment section as it flowed with overenthusiastic responses to Theodore's answer. Several of them mentioned Consolidation Day, which marked the end of their final term and the start of the summer break. They were begging him to give them a concert even though the Consolidation Day concert was always hosted by the fifth-year Icon contestants.

It was also in ten days. Another reminder that her time was running out.

"Your turn," Kilian muttered.

She picked a question at random, seeing Kilian's last name. "Gray: Is physical touch your love language?"

Kilian chuckled, his arm wrapping even tighter around her. It was actually kind of ... adorable.

"Is it that obvious?" he asked his camera. Isobel kept her attention on the phone but scrolled up to see that her and Kilian had replaced the image of Theodore. Kilian was pouting at the camera, his beautifully curved lips making her heart skip a few frantic beats before melting into a pathetic pile of goo.

"He's a clingy motherf—uh ... guy," Cian said. "I'm surprised he didn't immediately pass on the question just so that he can lose and give us all massages."

A few of the other Alphas chuckled, but Isobel was too distracted by the comment section, and just how many people were saying that Kilian was the most precious, most adorable man in the world, that he had to be protected at all costs, and that all the other Alphas must secretly love when he clings to them, because you would have to be dead inside to not love Kilian.

Wow.

"Okay, next." Kilian flicked past all the comments, uncaring of the overwhelming praise aimed at him, weeding out the questions in between the compliments. "Sato: Do you have a Gifted ability?"

"Pass." Sato stared his camera head-on, and the comment section filled up with emojis.

Isobel laughed before she could help herself because everyone was using the same emoji. The blue frozen face with ice dripping from it. It must have been some kind of inside joke that the Ironside fans had started, because suddenly, the comment section was a wall of blue. The Sato on screen was looking to the right, and the screen was split to also show herself and Kilian ... who were sitting to his right, with only Cian separating them.

She could feel Sato's attention like a physical caress against her cheek. It was hot. Searing. Kilian hid a smirk against her hair, but she could still see his eyes smiling on screen.

"Okay, next." She cleared her throat, ignoring Sato. "Ashford: How many tattoos do you have now, and do you plan on getting more?"

Cian lifted his shirt, revealing ink covering his side, stretching so far that she couldn't see the top of it, the base of the design disappearing beneath the waistband of his pants. The slightest hint of his nipple piercing glinted at her before he covered it with his knuckle. She could make out geometric patterns and other designs woven between, with random objects hidden in the details—like falling bullets, twisting snakes, a hanging birdcage, or a constellation of stars—but she was too shocked at the sheer amount of ink on display that she barely even categorised a single one of them in detail.

"I added a few over the break," he said. "The officials gave me special permission to have the rest done at the parlour on Ironside Row. It was a reward for agreeing to become Carter's main surrogate."

Moses scoffed loudly. "Her *main* surrogate?"

"That's not a thing," Theodore said, sounding calm. Mildly amused. "What about everyone else?"

"Not all of us are her surrogates." Niko cleared his throat, sounding uncomfortable. "Better clear that up."

Isobel hadn't looked away from Cian, and he noticed. He also hadn't dropped his shirt. He wasn't even sitting up straight or trying to flex, and she couldn't make out an inch of softness. It made sense now that she had seen what Easton liked to put them through.

His skin almost looked gold-brushed in the soft spotlight, smooth and taut. He bit into his lower lip and then released it, forcing a flush to rush to the lush curve, reddening the flesh. His bright eyes became hooded the longer she stared at him, and Kilian's smirk against the back of her head melted into an outright laugh, shaking through his body and into hers, jolting her out of the spell Cian had cast over her.

Cian dropped his shirt, but his tattooed fingers brushed his muscles on the way down, making her focus narrow on the rings littering his fingers as she wondered what the cold metal would feel like if he gripped her skin.

Properly.

Not the small brushes he usually gave her.

She shook her head, trying to dislodge the thought, but it burrowed in deeper, digging claws into her and making her press her thighs together tightly. Kilian stopped laughing immediately, tugging her back until she was flush with his warm chest, his chin notching onto her shoulder again.

“Spade,” he said, his tone deeper than usual as he fixated on one of the comments. Gabriel tilted forward in his chair to listen to Kilian. “When are you going to debut a dance? We’ve been watching you and Reed practise for two years. Why are the Alphas being so secretive about their specialisations?”

“Pass.” Gabriel sat back, looking at the camera in a disapproving way. The comment section filled with immediate scoldings for whoever had asked such a “pushy” question. They were protective of Gabriel for some reason. Or maybe it was just the Alphas in general.

“Hart.” Isobel spotted Niko’s last name, holding her finger on the screen to keep her place since the comments were now flowing in much faster than she could keep up with. “Are you planning on specialising in tennis next year?”

“Nah.” Niko shook his head, tossing the platinum locks that slipped over his vision. He brushed both hands through his hair, pulling the bleached waves back as he shared a warm, secretive smile with the camera. “Next question.”

The comment section exploded.

@reed’s_rhapsody: NIKO HART HAS A SECRET SPECIALISATION? WHAT IS GOING ON?

@kannoisseur: Why does Sato look like the only snack he’s playing for is sitting in Gray’s lap? Can’t tell if I’m turned on or terrified.

@wildestdreamer: Not Niko Hart over here playing 3D chess and making even the fifth-year Icon contestants look unprepared.

@tune_tracker: Niko Hart can specialise in me if he has nothing else going on.

“Carter.” Kilian found a question for her amidst the chaos. “Are you being bullied by the Omegas?”

“No.” Isobel forced a light laugh, wishing she was half as good of an actor as Theodore, or Niko, who seemed able to turn his charm off and on just as easily. “It’s all just normal, healthy competition.”

The comments immediately turned to questions about Eve and Aron, and what happened in Vermont, but

Kilian quickly flicked past them all, pausing on one that seemed to be addressed to Reed instead.

"Reed." She cleared her throat. "Why do you think they let Eve Indie back into Ironside? Wasn't she there when Carter—when I was attacked in Vermont?"

Elijah blinked, looking down at the camera over the rim of his glasses. He hadn't been wearing them when he sat down. Maybe he hoped they would be an extra barrier against the camera. "What does that have to do with me?"

"I think that's a pass," Kilian mumbled as the "cold" emoji started to pepper the comment section again, the rest of the comments admonishing the poster for such a triggering question. "Moses, what did you think of your kiss with Carter? People are saying you've never had a girlfriend before. Is that true?"

"My brother dated every girl in our year group back in the settlement," Moses said blandly. "And I'm not into sharing." His image on screen cocked a challenging brow. "Did I kiss Carter? When?"

Cue another onslaught of cold emojis.

"Answer or pass," Reed inserted, his tone droll.

Instead of snapping at Reed, Moses relaxed further back into his chair, lifting a tanned hand to stroke his scarred chin. His stormy eyes narrowed in thought, one of his legs kicking up to notch against the edge of the chair, his knee swinging distractedly back and forth.

"Pass," he eventually said, the shadow of a smile

ghosting his lips, like he knew he had just driven everyone into a frenzy thinking he might actually answer the question.

Isobel squirmed on Kilian's lap, realising the screen had switched to a split view again, showing her own face. "Sato," she said quickly, picking a question and then pausing ... wishing she had proofed it first. "Why did you ..." She cleared her throat awkwardly. "Did you offer to be Carter's—I mean my surrogate?"

"Pass." He answered instantly, giving the camera the same deadpan stare, his hood still up, his eyes slitted. He was going to lose the game at this point.

Isobel knew her face was bleeding red, but Kilian was already moving on.

"Theodore, who's your favourite Alpha?"

"Moses." Theodore rolled his eyes, and the mood began to lighten immediately, with Cian and Niko both jumping on Theodore and demanding he change his answer.

Isobel and Kilian tried to pick light-hearted questions after that, but Sato still refused to answer any of them, earning himself last place, while Isobel, Kilian, and Theodore tied in first place.

"How should we settle this?" Theodore asked, his competitive streak rearing its head, as he swept his eyes over Isobel and Kilian cuddled up in a chair before turning his attention back to the camera.

Sato suddenly started laughing, and then he stood.

"This one," he said, flashing his phone screen before tucking it into his pocket. "I like this idea. Whoever lasts the longest locked alone with me in a dark room, wins. Except we'll do the garden shed, instead. If any of you break before three minutes is up, I get top spot and you all have to share last place." He started to stride off but paused at the edge of the platform. "Kilian, you're up."

KILIAN DIDN'T EXACTLY HAVE TIME TO ARGUE BEFORE OSCAR strode away, and he was left sitting there in silence with everyone else. Locking himself in a cramped, dark space with Oscar was *very* far down his list of priorities, especially with Isobel snuggled into his lap, but there was suddenly a staff member with a camera notched onto his shoulder and a timer pulled up on his phone rushing to the platform, and everyone else had turned to see what he would do.

He lifted Isobel and plopped her back into his seat before striding off without a word. The cameraman followed him, so he tried to relax his expression, but it soon became glaringly obvious that all the students gathered on top of Alpha Hill for movie night had their screens lighting up their faces and were watching the live stream with rapt attention.

He pushed into the garden shed and slammed the door behind him, turning on his phone's flashlight and dropping it onto one of the workbenches.

"What's got your panties in a twist?" Oscar asked, sitting on the bench, and examining his nails.

"I was comfortable where I was," Kilian sulked, crossing his arms.

Oscar smirked. "You know someone has already stolen her, right? Probably Cian. Maybe even Gabe, just to fuck with Theo."

Kilian itched to check the live broadcast to see if it was true, but forced his arms to wind back in an exaggerated stretch instead. "Are we gonna make out or what?"

Oscar laughed, his eyes glittering darkly. "Nice deflection. How about I describe what it was like to make out with the person you *actually* want to get your hands on?"

"When did you make out with Cian?"

"When did you get so funny?" Oscar's smile suddenly disappeared, and all the glitter twinkled right out of his stare, rendering it blacker than black. "I don't want to hand out massages so here it is, Kili. She tasted exactly like how I knew she would. Like fear, and sweat, and fistfuls of crushed cherries leaking all over her skin. Her little whimpers and moans and the way she pressed against my dick—"

"Yep, I'm out. This was great. Let's never do it again." Kilian stormed out of the shed, ignoring the cameraman checking the timer on his phone as he rushed back to the stage.

The worst part was ... Oscar wasn't lying. That *was* what Isobel tasted like, at least partly. But Oscar hadn't said a thing about the rich, heady syrup scent she gave off, and how her skin tasted like that when she clenched her thighs together and sucked on her lip like she was trying to savour the aftertaste of her favourite candy.

Kilian found himself clinging onto that fact, but then quickly grew irritated that Oscar had managed to turn it into some sort of fucked-up competition in his head.

Isobel didn't belong to any of them, and she never would.

It was impossible.

There was no competition. Whether Oscar tasted her or whether Kilian did, she would always be unattainable. More so now than ever, because Kilian's ex was the one who helped to cut her open and defile their bond.

5
Seven Minutes in Hell

Theodore wasn't expecting much, but he definitely expected longer than Kilian lasted, and he sighed as he got up to take his turn next. Isobel stole his seat as soon as he stood, as though she needed to give Kilian a break, and he tried to tamp down on the rush of satisfaction it gave him.

Not because Kilian would be disappointed—he couldn't begrudge Kilian needing physical contact all the time, that was just who he was, even if Theodore found it endlessly infuriating to have his bergamot and bark scent saturating Isobel.

It was more to do with the illogical urge to *claim* and *possess*. Isobel belonged in his chair because she belonged to him.

Stop. Fucking hell, just stop.

He stalked off and burst into the garden shed ready

for a fight. Oscar chuckled as he closed the door behind him, throwing them into darkness.

"You make it too easy, Theo." Oscar turned on his phone's flashlight, setting it beside his thigh. He was sitting on one of the workbenches, looking like he had already won the game.

"Don't know what you're talking about." Theodore plastered on a wide smile. "You didn't try to make out with Kilian, did you? He practically ran back."

"If I had, he'd be running for a cold shower. Why do you ask? Jealous I might have seduced *both* of your best friends?"

"You didn't seduce Isobel. The chains hypnotised her."

OSCAR DIDN'T FEEL LIKE ANTAGONISING THEODORE. THE younger Alpha was just too ... *amenable*. He kept a cool head with Oscar seconds away from stealing two of his fingers and hadn't even let out a squeak when Oscar had broken them. Or tried to come after him.

Theodore didn't sulk the next day or try to take the issue to Kalen or Mikel. He continued like nothing had happened, smiling and joking around like the infuriatingly good-natured person he was.

Oscar sighed, pinching his nose. This was why he preferred Moses. The moody fuck was always up for a fight.

"Leave now," he expelled on a short breath, "and I won't unleash chaos the second she steps through that door."

"Deal." Theodore spun on his heel and yanked the door open, disappearing immediately.

Oscar leaned back, his head thumping against the wall, his fingers tapping agitatedly against his thigh. He would have just left and refused to play the game at all, but movie night was non-negotiable. Kalen had made that clear.

He wanted to get them in front of a camera. It was time they started stepping things up so that the fans had them firmly in their thoughts over the break.

Isobel walked into the shed, closing the door behind her and leaning back against it with her arms folded tightly across her chest, her eyes skirting all around him but refusing to actually look at him.

"What did you do to the others?" she asked, finally lifting her gaze to his.

He licked his lips, shifting forward to notch his forearms against his thighs. "I sat here and didn't move a muscle. Come closer."

"No."

"Why not?" He smirked at her. "I just want to see your chain."

She took deliberately slow steps toward him, probably trying to drag out the three minutes. "Why is everyone so scared of you, Sato?"

"Because they know what's good for them." He coiled forward when she was close enough, catching the neckline of her dress and dragging her between his legs until she was pressed up against the bench, dirtying the pale fabric that drifted against her skin like the lightest, softest tease.

Her rich-girl clothes did his head in.

He hated that he could sell one of her dresses and fill up his sister's account at the commissary for the next three months, and he hated how beautiful she looked draped in small fortunes. He still remembered the slide of her silky, rich-girl pyjamas beneath his rough hands.

He quickly released her, gripping the edge of the bench to control the urge to rip and tear until she was just as poor and filthy as he was.

"Show it to me." He tried to frame it as a suggestion, but it rolled off his tongue as a husky command, and his gut tightened at the way her hands lifted instinctively, tugging down her neckline as much as she could, revealing only the top of the chain.

"What did Niko tell you?" she asked quietly.

He wanted to touch the chain. It was *his* chain, after all, but he couldn't trust himself. The Sigma was slowly driving him insane, and he had yet to figure out if he had been obsessed with her since his first taste on the rooftop of the chapel, or if he was secretly wishing he had never saved her in the first place.

"He said it happened suddenly," he grunted, staring

at the tiny gold links embedded smoothly into her skin, looking like they had always been a part of her. "It made its way to your chest, hooking into your skin, and then healed you. You're lucky the bond didn't complete."

"I've been thinking about that," she whispered. "Maybe it doesn't count because it's a soul artefact? I mean Teak said the bond can't *force* me, and if an artefact marks me and completes the bond for me, well ... that's forcing ..."

She nibbled on her lip, her mind drifting away. It was only a moment when her attention wasn't on him, but it was enough to snap his control, to draw his hands from the bench.

Except she wasn't there anymore.

She had disappeared and reappeared against the shed door, her arms folded tightly across her chest, her face painted in confusion, her breath a rasp through her pink lips.

ISOBEL GASPED AS A PINPRICK OF HEAT DUG INTO HER CHEST. Sato was already off the bench, already standing before her, his brows heavy with confusion. "Did you just teleport?"

"I ... don't know. It didn't feel like a teleport." She tugged down the top of her dress again, staring at the chain—or more specifically, at the tiny little gemstone that had materialised half an inch from the top of the chain. It was yellowed amber, a light, leering gold that reminded her of the winking eye of a prowling beast.

"What does that mean?" Sato's voice was quiet and rough, spilling over her temple as he leaned over her, staring down her dress.

"I don't know," she muttered distractedly, trying to figure out what had just happened. "Everything just ... blurred. Like time turned backwards, and then I was back here again." She spread her arms, looking at the door.

Sato reached past her, yanking the door open and calling for the cameraman who stood nearby. "How much time is left?"

"Uh ..." The confused reply drifted over. "I mean ... she just walked in there? I only just started the timer—"

Sato closed the door, cutting off the man's response. He drew her away from the door before releasing her and sucking in a sharp breath, his eyes drifting back to the front of her dress.

"Kalen," he breathed. "That's Kalen's power."

Isobel blanched. "What?"

"It's a side effect. You're borrowing power—*fuck*, you could get Theo's, or Moses', or mine, or—"

"I knew you had an illegal ability. What is it?" It was easier to cling to facts than to let the panic sink in.

She could go feral.

His attention snapped to her face, his expression darkening. "You want something from me, Isobel?" His hand landed on her neck suddenly, his thumb stroking up the column of her throat. "Give me something first."

His touch reminded her of when he had gripped her neck while thrusting his tongue viciously into her mouth.

"And then you'll tell me?" She couldn't help swallowing.

He felt it. His lips twitched, his grip tightening slightly. "If it's worth it."

"I ... don't have any secrets."

"Well at least you're getting better at lying." His grin curved a little further, his canines catching on his bottom lip like he was trying to bite it back. "Let's start with what else happened with Niko."

"What are you talking about?"

"You wanted to know what he said. That means there was more he could have said."

She considered him, realising she was leaning into his hold ... but Sato had already offered to surrogate for her, so at least he wouldn't be insulted by her body's reaction to him.

"I think I learned my lesson spilling secrets," she finally said.

He was already shaking his head. "That's not how it works. Secrets suffocate and die in Dorm A. Spilling them to *outsiders* is what will get you killed."

"Fine." She shrugged. "But only because you obviously know all about it. Whatever happened to you in the hotel, it happened to Niko in the bathroom when the chain dug into my skin."

Sato grew very still, his voice lowering to a low, grating timbre. "*Niko* surged? What did he do?"

"Nothing really." She looked down, busying herself by trying to brush off the line of dust along the front of her dress. "Just got really still ... and licked, um ... the chain."

"Have you showered?" he asked, his tone suddenly neutral.

"No?" She pulled her head back a little, trying to read his expression.

"I don't want his fucking saliva on your skin." His casual tone broke, a growl riding his words. "I'll tell you what my ability is if you let me erase it."

"Why?" She was shivering, goosebumps popping up all over her skin at the feel of his influence pushing through her.

His oleander scent was smoking and burning, his emotion a slow crawl of poisonous mist, seeping possessive fury into her pores until she was wearing him like a cloak.

"Because either you let me erase him, or I go back to the stage and cut out his tongue on live television," Sato whispered in his broken, husky voice, his eyes pools of soft darkness.

She swallowed, but it was painful, her throat

threatening to close up in panic. "That's not funny, Sato."

"Isobel," he breathed, leaning down until his face was an inch from hers. "I'm not joking."

"You're scaring me." She tried to side-step him, but he followed, backing her into the workbench.

"You're lying," he returned quietly. "I know what you smell like when you're scared of me. I even know what you *taste* like when you're scared of me."

She pushed against his chest, but instead of it shifting him, it shifted her, the world blurring around her again as her back suddenly hit the door.

Sato turned, still standing by the workbench, a slow, dangerous smirk lifting the corner of his lips. "You aren't reversing time for me," he said, wiping a hand over his mouth to erase the emotion on his face, leaving his expression carefully thoughtful. "Only everyone else."

"Kalen is that powerful?" she squeaked, her heartbeat thundering. *She* was holding that power inside her? *Why couldn't she feel it?* Other than the warm prickle against her chest where the gemstone had appeared, she couldn't feel anything at all.

In fact ... even the prickle seemed to have faded.

She pulled her neckline down again, realising that the yellow gemstone was no longer glinting and leering, the colour fading to a normal, dulled amber.

"Time's up," Sato suddenly said, appearing before

her, his eyes on the gemstone. "No more rewinds. Turn around, Carter."

She obeyed before she could really think it through, and by then, it was too late. The second she bared her back to him, he was working on the concealed zipper of her dress, tugging it all the way down to her waist. He spun her around again, the dress still in place, though it hung awkwardly off her shoulders now.

He seemed restless all of a sudden, his hands disappearing into his pockets, the material bunching as he formed tight fists and shifted his weight, teetering on some kind of action that he ultimately held himself back from, rocking back as his dark eyes swept over her.

"What is this?" she asked, curling her fists around the thin straps of the dress. "Why do you need to do this?"

"Cian told us you're seeing dead people." He sucked in a deep breath, his restless gaze finally settling on her face. "And I know you saw my dad. What did he tell you, hm? Did he tell you nice things? Good things?"

"He told me you would hurt me. He said that other Alphas try to hide their animal side, but he taught you to embrace yours."

Sato's expression tightened, and his shock pierced her chest before he managed to rein in the emotion.

"That's right." He brushed a finger down her clenched knuckles, almost teasing them into relaxing and releasing her grip on the straps. His influence was confusing, his oleander scent cloying, so sweet and seductive. She had to clear away the fog of it all and remind herself quite forcefully that Sato was dangerous.

"I'm not all there." He tapped against the side of his own head. "I have impulses, and they're difficult to control. You're supposed to belong to me, and my impulse is to claim you in every way possible, even though I don't want you. I refuse to share. I refuse to be told who to mate with, who to belong to. But the *impulse* ..." He gripped her hands, guiding them away, and then he slipped his fingers beneath the straps of her dress and tugged them down over her arms. "You didn't get lucky with me, Carter. I'm your curse now. You're going to have to learn to live with me the same way I'm learning to live with you."

"How exactly are you learning to live with me?" She sounded breathless as the top half of her dress fell away, catching at her waist. It revealed her thin, lacy bralette and the entire length of the gold chain embedded into her skin.

"I'm compromising," he said, his eyes still fixed on hers, even as his hand drifted to the chain, the back of his fist pressing against the bottom of it, just below her bra, forcing her to lean more heavily into the door. "I gave you options, didn't I? A peaceful one, and a fun one."

"Why bother if this isn't fun?" She hadn't meant to sound snarky, but something in her tone carried a hint of sharpness, and his eyes glittered in a brief flash of humour before dropping from her face to survey the chain.

Or her boobs.

It was hard to tell.

"You're right." He bent down and grabbed her hips. "I only consider options I like."

He curled his fingers into her bralette as he pressed the flat of his tongue against her skin, right at the bottom of the chain. He lifted, dragging his tongue to the middle of her chest as he yanked his fist back, tearing her bralette so that his journey to her clavicle would be unbroken. He shoved her into the door as he licked all the way up to her neck, pausing at her ear as he pressed the length of his body into hers.

He was breathing heavily, and she wasn't breathing at all.

She had gripped fistfuls of his jacket sleeves, trying to pull him in tighter, her body soaking up the heat and comfort of him being so deliciously close. Sato wasn't someone she thought she could ever find comfort in, but her half-formed bond didn't care. It was reminding her that she had felt hollow for weeks, starved of all the love and devotion her mates should have been showering her with—

Hold up, what the heck?

"You bled." He growled the words against her throat, his body vibrating. "He tasted your blood, didn't he?"

Before she could react, his teeth were grazing the

skin of her neck, just below her ear. She froze, her breath a raw scrape. "Don't."

"You're mine," he muttered against her skin.

"I can't let you."

"Why, baby?" He purred the words in her ear, so un-Sato-like that her eyes fluttered closed and a rush of heat pooled low in her belly, forcing her to clamp her legs together.

Holy crap, he needed to never do that again.

"I can't belong to any of you," she squeaked as he pulled back slightly, his Alpha ring swollen, his expression tight as his nostrils flared. "There are ten of you. It'll never work."

He gripped her hips, drawing her tight to his body. "I can smell how much you want me to do something."

"It's the bond."

"Lie," he snarled, pushing her back into the door. "Time's almost up, little rabbit. My ability is chaos. I cause it. Thrive off it. Can't live without it. Stay if you want a taste. Leave if you're scared."

She surveyed his face, her mind turning over at his admission. Chaos suited him. So did the glint in the darkness of his gaze, telling her that he *wanted* her to leave.

He wanted her scared of him.

And suddenly, her connection to Sato made sense. She *did* want a taste of chaos, but she didn't want to admit it. And he wanted to chase, to hunt, to force it out of her.

He couldn't hide the need even if he tried. It was in every line of his expression. It was in his cloying perfume as it both warned her away and tried to cajole her closer. It was in the dark thump of his emotion against her chest.

She had never felt an Alpha's need before, because need wasn't usually a negative thing, a dark thing.

Until Sato.

His need was pushing against her like all the other dark, dirty sentiments people didn't want to keep.

They complimented each other, in that way.

Her breath hitched, her head suddenly dizzy with the realisation, but she was no closer to having any idea what to do about it. Sato stirred up something dark and *wrong* inside her, a kind of morbid curiosity that made her want to cover her eyes and bare her neck, hoping for the best.

But that was suicidal.

She looked down at the torn lace still covering her chest. "What do I do?"

"Go without," he suggested, knowing she wasn't talking about the scraps of lace that were barely covering her nipples. "Take the rest off. I couldn't give a fuck about movie night."

She gave him a wry smile, even though it didn't look like he was joking. "You're terrifying."

"And you're quite literally tempting fate." He tugged on the frayed edges of her bralette, hastily tying them in the smallest knot before he sucked in a deep breath and took several steps back from her. "How much did that cost?"

"I don't know. My father's team has been organising my wardrobe."

He wiped a hand over his mouth. "Sleep in my room tonight."

She laughed hollowly. "What would be left of me in the morning?"

His eyes flared, like he thought she meant something different, and his voice was husky when he spoke again.

"You've slept with me before. I'm one of your surrogates. You clearly need a surrogate right now."

"I haven't slept with you alone, and nobody knows that we shared a bed on tour except Cian."

"Bring a friend." His grin was humourless. Lethal. "We'll call it a sleepover."

"Is this some kind of ploy? You guys don't want to leave me in Dorm O with Eve back?"

"Don't speak the name of the dead girl," he growled roughly.

"That's not an answer."

He ran a hand along the back of his neck, and then shrugged. "Yes, it's a ploy. It was supposed to be Theodore's ploy. I just don't want to break his fingers again, so I'm asking you first."

"What?" She peered at his face, trying to find even the slightest spark of humour. There was nothing. "What the hell?"

"He had his fingers inside what was mine."

"I'm not yours!" She advanced on him but held herself back right before she could shove against his chest.

"You smell like mine. You taste like mine. You even sound like mine when you're trying to insist you aren't mine." He leaned down, planting his cold expression a few inches from hers, his attention on her dishevelled clothes. "You definitely look like mine right now."

She quickly pulled her dress back into position, twisting her arm behind her back to yank up her zipper. He watched, cool and calm, and then he brushed past her, pulling open the door.

"Glad we sorted that out," he said, before striding out.

She gave a shaky smile to the cameraman who flashed his phone screen at her enthusiastically, probably trying to show her that she had lasted more than three minutes, but she couldn't focus on him as she made her way back to the stage. The second she saw Kilian, she felt her whole body relaxing, and she wanted to hurry right over to him, but then Theodore caught her attention, a question in his stormy eyes as he ran them over her, checking that she was okay. She wondered if she could cuddle up in his lap the way she did with

Kilian.

Of course not, she immediately chided herself. He might have privately offered to help her ease her bond, but publicly, he had a girlfriend. Even though people probably guessed that he was surrogating for her, it would likely become a problem if they started *flaunting* it.

She tried to give him a reassuring smile as she approached Kilian's seat, his hand already held out for her. He pulled her back into his lap, and she fought the urge to melt back into him completely, wary of the camera.

"Well?" Moses leaned forward in his chair, his eyes dancing between Sato and her. "That was definitely more than three minutes. How'd you do it, Carter?"

"He just really wanted to talk about his feelings," she said, forcing her expression to appear unbothered. "Literally wouldn't shut up. He's a real chatterbox when you get him alone."

Most of the Alphas laughed and she shrank back against Kilian, avoiding the heat of Sato's stare. Kilian pulled his phone out in front of them, navigating to a blank message screen.

Okay? he typed out.

She pulled the phone closer to reply. *Will you stay with me tonight?*

"Mhmm," he rumbled against the side of her head, dipping his head in a nod.

In Sato's room, she added.

He stiffened behind her, a short, astounded laugh falling out of him. "Ah, okay ..."

"Hey, you two?" Cian nudged Kilian. "Care to share with the class?"

"She's just making arrangements for tonight," Sato stated calmly. And loudly. In front of the cameras.

"What?" Theodore looked down the line of chairs.

"She's getting sick again. She needs a surrogate ... but she's worried about rumours." He flipped his hood up again, leaning back with his arms crossed like that was all the explaining he needed to do.

In a way, it was ... a smart approach. Explaining things up front for the cameras. "Um, yeah." She cleared her throat nervously. "I thought ... I thought if it was Sato and Kilian, the fans would know it's not anything romantic, right?"

"Because Oscar's idea of romance is—" Theodore cut himself off, smirking before apparently revising his statement. "—not a discussion for polite society."

Sato scoffed quietly.

Gabriel sucked in breath through his teeth, waving his phone. "The fans are asking if you have your pick of the Alphas to surrogate because it really looks like you have your pick of the Alphas to surrogate."

Isobel didn't have to force her laugh. It tumbled out naturally. "No," she said, another chuckle passing her lips. "Sato's offer to surrogate was terrifying and there's no way it was genuine. I asked the Alphas because their energy is the most potent. I was rejected by several of them. Quite brutally, in some cases. I absolutely do *not* have 'my pick' of Alphas. They're just ... decent guys, and they've offered to help. Just a few of them."

"There you have it." Theodore tossed his hands up like the matter was settled. "We're a bunch of saints, just as I always suspected. Pity the movie finished already." He pointed to the credits now rolling on the big screen. "You're going to have to wait until the next movie night for us to prove it."

6
BOUNDARIES AND BONDS

"NEED A MOMENT?" THEODORE ASKED AS THEY WALKED OFF the stage.

Isobel peered sideways at him, wondering if it was that obvious, or if he just knew her that well.

"Just feeling a bit overwhelmed," she admitted quietly. The bond was making her feel things, or maybe the Alphas were making her feel things, but she didn't have any room inside her to entertain conflicting emotions. She still had two intimidating deadlines looming on the horizon and now to top it all off, the officials had let Eve back into the academy.

She had always known they were just pawns to the officials, just puppets in a play to be dangled this way and that way, but seeing such brutal, indisputable evidence of it right in front of her eyes was a whole other thing.

Moses had been right the day he told her to ruin Wallis' life. There was no justice for the Gifted, and especially no justice for Sigmas. She had to make it herself.

Theodore watched her closely, his face sombre, concerned. "They haven't aired any footage of you sleeping in my room or Kilian's room."

"Not yet," she grumbled.

He nodded, still considering her. "What are you worried about, exactly?"

"Blowback." She let him pull her off to the side, closer to the lake as people swirled around them, tidying up their picnic blankets and chairs. She hugged her arms around herself, peeking up at him briefly. "What people will say. I think it would make my father happy but appeasing him is like standing on a razor's edge. He could just as quickly turn around and slap me for being a slut."

Theodore sucked in a deep, shuddering breath, turning his face away for a moment. "Too many cameras," he murmured. "Come inside."

He marched off, and she hurried to catch up with him, spotting Wallis trying to zigzag through the dwindling crowd to get to him. Wallis started running when she saw that Theodore was heading to the dorm, and Isobel quickly stepped into her path. The tall Beta tried to side-step her, but she planted herself in the way again.

"Wallis," she said. "Stop."

The other girl looked down at Isobel, a tight frown pinching her features. She was still beautiful, but the expression showed a flash of something ugly in her eyes. A vicious spark that Isobel had seen reflected in so many people since she had come to Ironside.

At first, it was just her father.

But it turned out Braun Carter wasn't that unique after all.

The academy was full of Brauns ... he was just lucky enough to be an Alpha: to be bigger and stronger and more powerful than all the rest of them.

"Seriously, *what*?" Wallis demanded. "Why are you *always* getting in the way?"

"Because you're the kind of person who shouldn't be left unsupervised," Isobel shot back. "And you should take that as a warning."

"I've been nice to you, Sigma." Wallis leaned down, planting her lips right by Isobel's ear. "Sato made me promise. But Sato made me promise a lot of things, and I'm starting to realise his conditions are a little too constricting. So get the fuck out of my way before I make sure Ironside gets a nice little Vermont sequel—on camera this time, since the officials apparently want to see you get beat so badly."

Isobel reared back, surprised by the venom in Wallis' hissing voice. Wallis took advantage of her surprise, flicking her hair over her shoulder and pushing past, striding toward Dorm A, even though Theodore had already disappeared inside.

"Going to have to do better than that." Moses also brushed past her, turning to deliver her a challenging look. "Should have slapped her as hard as you slapped me," he added, loud enough to capture the attention of most of the people around them.

Isobel shook her head, trailing after him as he followed Wallis—who had knocked on the door and received no response. Moses pulled it open, completely ignoring Wallis as he slammed it again in her face.

Isobel opened it again, but before she could step through, Wallis grabbed the back of her dress.

"You don't go inside Dorm A unless you're *invited*." Wallis somehow made her voice saccharine sweet, like she was doing Isobel a favour as she dragged her back a step. The door fell closed.

Isobel wrenched away. "Don't touch me."

"Why? You let everyone else touch you." Wallis suddenly looked hurt, and Isobel suddenly itched to slap her just like Moses suggested she should.

There weren't even cameras watching the dorm entrance, so the act was all for nothing. Maybe Wallis spent so much time pretending it was hard to turn it off.

Instead of reacting, Isobel flung open the door again and walked inside, pausing at the threshold to the living room, with Wallis holding open the door and peering after her.

Reed and Gabriel were standing at the other end of the hallway, heads bent together as they looked at Gabriel's phone. Niko and Cian were lounging about the common room, game controllers in their laps. Both of them looked up at her, but Niko dismissed her almost instantly.

"Wallis wants to come in," Isobel announced, her tone wiped of emotion.

"Tell her to kindly fuck off," Niko muttered, eyes still on the TV screen.

He had said it lowly enough that it was more like he was talking to himself rather than giving her an actual instruction, so she glanced to the other side of the hallway, to where Reed and Gabriel had looked up from the phone.

"No," Reed said. "Theo is busy."

"Theo is busy," Isobel relayed to the girl still hovering in the doorway, who could hear Reed just fine. "Sorry."

"Busy with what?" Wallis pressed, managing a pout and a pleading blink of her pretty, glitter-outlined eyes.

"Busy with what?" Isobel asked, glancing back to Reed, her fingers twitching into fists.

Reed's lips twisted in a smirk. "Go ask him yourself, Carter. He's in his room."

"I guess I'll go check," she muttered, barely even directing the words to Wallis.

She slipped into Theodore's room after knocking

softly on the door. He was sitting on his bed, kicking off his shoes and looking as annoyed as she felt.

"She's getting pushier," he growled, his eyes flashing dark as they dipped over her, his nose wrinkling. "Did she seriously touch you?"

"Barely." Isobel leaned back against the door, crossing her arms.

Theodore had already lost his sweatshirt, his clothes tossed haphazardly around the room. He tore off his socks, and then jumped up, pacing toward her, the muscles in his chest and neck twitching and pulsing like he was seconds away from tackling her to the ground like Niko did in their training sessions.

As soon as he reached her, he stopped, holding out an arm, his expression unhappy.

"Hug, and then we discuss what to do about the sleepover," he said.

She swallowed. "You took half your clothes off."

"Illy." His voice was gravelled, his expression lit by a troubled darkness. "Hug."

She swallowed, stepping into him, her arms lifting hesitantly to wind around his waist. The rigidness in his posture softened, but he didn't hug her back. He brushed his cheek against the top of her head, and she fisted her hands against his muscled back to hide the sudden tremble in her fingers. His skin was molten, his heat digging into her muscles and making her sag against him with a thin whimper.

"You should stay," he whispered. "For the bond, and because we won't actually let you leave."

"I can't hide from Eve in Dorm A forever," she muttered against his sternum, her lips brushing his skin. He tasted like sweat and sweetness and she licked her lips to savour the combination. It was weirdly addicting. "She's back for good, isn't she?"

"That's what Mikki said," he grunted, his hands finally winding around her, brushing up and down her spine, smoothing over invisible wrinkles in her dress.

His grip settled in the dip of her waist, dragging her tight against his body, and then he was quickly stepping away, shaking his arms out agitatedly. "I'll go deal with Wallis. Want to lock yourself in my bathroom for a while?"

"Literally more than anything," she admitted. "Is that okay?"

"Steal whatever clothes you need and take as long as you want. I'll sort out a way for you to stay here tonight that won't cause any bullshit rumours, okay?"

"You're my hero." She grinned at him, marvelling at the tinge of colour that popped up in his cheeks before he yanked his sweatshirt back on, ignoring the rest of his clothes as he left the room.

She swiped a T-shirt and pair of boxers from his wardrobe, ducking into his bathroom. She just stood there for a small, private moment, marvelling over the beautiful, flowing design and the curved shower with the multiple sprays. Luxury had never really impressed her. It had always been her normal. But for two years now, she had been sleeping on the floor and sharing a bathroom with a clique of Omegas who all hated her. It was strange how quickly her "normal" had become something else.

She pulled off her clothes and turned the shower on full blast, stepping beneath the spray and running her fingers across the glittering tiled wall. She felt safe in there ... which was stupid.

She wasn't safe anywhere.

Her eyes closed against the tears that threatened to spill over, blocking out the view of her scars.

"I wish I knew how to help," a soft voice whispered, forcing her head to jerk up.

The apparition of her mother was back, leaning against the bathroom counter.

Isobel quickly shut off the water, stepping out and wrapping a towel around herself. She opened and closed her mouth a few times before falling back against the wall opposite, simply staring into the familiar, beautiful eyes of Caran Carter.

"My baby girl is changing," her mother noted, a sad smile curving her lips. "I'm here, so you must be scared, but you're wearing it so calmly."

"Yeah, well." Isobel laughed humourlessly. "I've been practising." Her short laugh died, and she sucked in a deep breath. "Mom, what the heck are you?"

Caran looked down at herself, holding up the sleeve of her dressing gown. "A remnant," she said, still with that gentle smile. "I'm sorry, Illy. I can't be anything more."

Isobel swallowed, fighting back tears again. "What happened to you, Mama?"

For a moment, the apparition wavered, Caran's face flinching so violently that it seemed she was about to wink out of existence, but then she settled, her expression smoothing out. "What did you say, Illy?"

Isobel frowned, hugging her still-damp arms around herself. "I asked what happened—"

Her mother was shaking her head, pulling a finger to her lips. "He doesn't like people to upset us. You can't ask us that."

"What? Who are you talking about?"

"Illy." Caran's hands hovered over Isobel's shoulders, but they didn't feel like anything, not even a change of temperature or a whisper of air. "I'm safe now. I'm okay. Just like all the other remnants."

"But how are you *here*? How am I *seeing* you?"

There was a soft knock on the door behind Isobel, but she ignored it, imploring her mother, trying to lay her touch over the ghostly hands that covered her shoulders.

"I'm not." Caran smiled again, pointing to Isobel's forehead. "I'm here."

"Isobel?" Kilian was knocking louder, and after a second, he tried the handle, finding it unlocked. He propped the door open and as soon as he saw her standing there hugging herself, he stepped into the room and nudged the door closed behind him.

Her mother disappeared.

"What's wrong?" Kilian's hands landed on her shoulders, and she almost sagged in relief at the tangible sensation, her eyes drifting shut as she swayed forward, butting her head against his chest.

"Nothing," she lied.

He chuckled, tucking a few wet locks of hair behind her ears. "Clearly. Did you shower? I can still smell Oscar all over you."

"Sort of. Not really. Are you offering to help again?"

KILIAN FORCED OUT A LAUGH JUST TO DISSIPATE SOME OF THE tension, but there was a tight constriction in his chest. *She wasn't okay*. She had been through a lot, and he had seen it all knock her down, peg by peg, so slowly that her decline was almost unnoticeable.

But this Isobel wasn't the same Isobel from before the settlement tour.

"They took my phone," he murmured against the top of her head. "I had a bit of a breakdown the night you told us about Aron ... and a few hours later, the officials arrived to remove me from the academy. I'm sorry I wasn't there for you."

"I don't need you to be there for me." She sniffed

against his chest and the stubbornness in her voice was adorable.

He eased her back again, examining the pink flush in her cheeks. It was hard to tell if she was embarrassed or feverish.

"You have five surrogates," he chided gently. "Why have you been ignoring the others if you needed them so badly?"

She sniffed again, and the colour flushed brighter. "I don't understand why they offered." She side-stepped him, reaching into the shower to turn the water back on.

His eyes dropped to her towel before he forced them back up again. "Blindfold me," he blurted.

She turned, a surprised sound somewhere between a gasp and a laugh falling out of those beautiful, lush lips, her eyes widening. "What?"

"I don't want to leave. You need to shower. We need to talk away from the cameras. The others are only going to leave us alone in here for so long. So blindfold me."

"Kili." She made that shocked laughing sound again. Almost a scoff. "I don't carry blindfolds around."

His heart warmed at the way she shortened his name, heat cracking into the massive gouges the last few weeks had left in the organ. He rolled his eyes, flicking off the light instead.

She giggled. "Okay, now I also can't see."

"Good." He wasn't in a laughing mood, but he still liked the sound of hers. It was light, airy, clear as a bell.

Stunning. It astounded him that she could possibly sound so pure and innocent after everything that had been done to her.

"Why good?" She was unwinding her towel, turning toward him to feel for the rack.

Fuck. Shit.

If he suddenly left the room, he might have to explain to her that his Alpha sight was a *little* better than hers.

"Because I'm not getting in there with all my clothes on." The words expelled from him on a sharp breath, a little too fast, but she was too busy groping for the towel rack to notice.

He fixed his attention to her face, refusing to look lower as he kicked off his shoes and removed all of his layers except his boxers. He slipped past her as she felt her way into the shower, ducking beneath the spray just to clear his head before he retreated to the tiled bench set into the alcove, sitting down, and focussing on the spray that washed over his legs as Isobel stepped beneath the stream.

"I'm sorry," he murmured. "It's not enough, I know, but I ..."

She spun around, her arms tucked over her chest, her hands cupping around her neck. She was covered enough for him to drag his eyes up, but he still got an eyeful of the swell of cleavage pressed between her arms and the way she was pouting in his direction.

That thin gold chain was barely visible, except the very top and bottom of it.

He genuinely just didn't have the willpower to leave her side and desperately needed a moment to talk to her and clear the air ... but now he just felt like a pervert because *that* image was going to stick in his brain for a while.

Or maybe he did orchestrate this.

Now he was questioning everything.

"You didn't do anything wrong," she said, reaching for his shoulder. He quickly looked away, back down to her legs as she stepped forward, her knuckles brushing his chest before feeling up to his shoulder and squeezing.

He licked his lips, narrowing his eyes. "I know. I'm sorry anyway. I'm sorry all this shit lands on you. It isn't fair."

"I can handle it." Her voice was sad, and the warmth her touch tunnelled through his body suddenly cooled again.

"Gabriel said you're stealing most of the side effects and all the shittiness of prolonging the bond," he said numbly. "The least we can do is make it easier. You should be using us."

"It's *awkward!*" she suddenly exclaimed, releasing his shoulder, and feeling around for the bottles of product. "I mean it isn't awkward when we're touching, but *asking* for it is awkward. And weird. And I don't think I can."

"Did Theo help?"

She went still, dropping the shampoo bottle. She had to crouch down to find it again. "Don't know what you're talking about," she muttered, popping up again.

There was *way* too much movement going on, but he managed to keep his eyes on the floor, counting the tiny sapphire tiles to stay focussed.

"Isobel." He chuckled.

She huffed. "Yes, it helped."

"How much?"

"A lot. I felt warm for days."

He hummed deep in his throat, frustration eating away at him. He could offer ... but he wasn't fucking stupid. Isobel thought he was gay and that made him the *only* safe place for her to turn to in Dorm A. Part of him wanted to come clean and tell her that it wasn't all black and white, that he resented some machination of fate telling him that he was suddenly restricted to one person, one gender ... but that it had nothing to do with *her*.

She was stunning, no matter the situation. He had always thought so.

But he was her only safe place. Her only easy option for the physical contact she desperately needed.

He couldn't cut her off from that.

He stood and ducked out of the shower, snatching the boxers she had brought in from the counter, and her bra from the floor, stalking back toward her. She squeaked when she felt him behind her, spinning her around. He knelt before her, gripping her thighs.

"Step," he grunted, holding the boxers against her legs.

She stepped into one of the legs, and then the other. He dragged them up her perfect calves, over her soft thighs, and he closed his eyes as he stood, settling them at her hips.

"You can see," she accused, narrowing her eyes on his chin.

"Yep." He slipped one of her arms into the bra, and then the other, tugging it up against her chest. "I didn't look. Until now." He swallowed, realising he was staring at her tits. Her nipples were covered, but the lace clung desperately to the pale swell of flesh as she twisted her arms behind her back to secure the garment.

Goddamn.

"What happened?" he asked, touching the knot between her breasts where the lace had been tied hastily together.

"Sato," she clipped. "Dude is unhinged. Niko licked my chain so then apparently Sato had to lick my chain. You want to give it a go as well?"

His mouth immediately pooled with saliva and his cock twitched desperately. "No. But Theo will. So don't tell him." He stepped out of the shower, giving the chain the barest brush of his knuckles before he yanked the door open enough to eye the Alpha sitting on his bed, fiddling with his phone, a tight expression pinching his features.

"Well?" Kilian asked as Theodore's eyes widened, flicking over his wet chest, and narrowing on his boxers before darting back up to his face. He tried to see past Kilian's shoulder, his eyes darkening at the lack of light in the room. "The offer won't stay open forever," Kilian grumbled.

They glared at each other for a moment, an understanding passing between them. Isobel needed someone to tend to the bond, and Kilian wasn't going to blur those lines.

Theodore got up and walked to the door of his room, flicking the lock.

ISOBEL HUGGED HER ARMS OVER HER CHEST, WONDERING WHAT the heck Kilian was doing until he stepped back ... and Theodore appeared in the lit doorway. His eyes swept over her huddled in the shower for the briefest moment before he stepped fully into the room, closing the door behind him.

"Um," she said, as the room was swamped in darkness again. "I didn't mean ... Uh ..."

"Doesn't have to mean anything, Illy." Theodore's voice was close, but she had no idea what he was doing.

A wide chest brushed against hers, but it was rich with Kilian's scent, so she didn't jump.

"Let him help," Kilian suggested. "I'll be right here. You're okay."

"I ... I'm still washing my hair," she said lamely.

Theodore's chuckle was deep and *close*, but he only brushed past her, his bulky shadow settling somewhere near Kilian's. It seemed like they were both sitting on the tiled bench cut into the shower alcove. She stood there stupidly, not even feeling the water as it pounded against her back.

Kilian spoke up, his voice silky, "You said it was awkward to ask—"

"I've never had a boyfriend," she quickly cut across him. "Never."

"This isn't a date, baby." There was a smirk in Kilian's voice this time, and she stepped toward it, flinging out her hand in the hopes that she swatted somewhere near his chest. Fingers wrapped tightly around her wrist before she could make contact.

"Shower," Theodore suggested—close enough to convince her he was the one who had caught her—a soft, cajoling rumble in his voice as he released her. "You shower, we talk."

"What do you want to talk about?" she asked, robotically returning to the task of washing her hair.

"I didn't plan what happened the night you got out of the hospital," Theodore admitted, "but did it help?"

"Yes," she gritted.

"Would you like me to do it again, Illy?"

"Do what?" She lost her courage completely, deciding to play dumb. Both of the Alphas chuckled.

"Whatever you like," Theodore said. "We can just cuddle, if you want. You could come here, sit on my lap, and I could hold you until our phones start blowing up, and maybe that would be enough."

"Kilian could have done that." It came out as an accusation, and she hoped their Alpha eyesight wasn't good enough to catch her sulky expression.

"But you would never ask Kilian to do more than that. Maybe a kiss would make you feel better."

"Or I could tell Theo to fuck off and we can cuddle," Kilian offered huskily, before clearing his throat. "If that's really what you wanted. We just want to help, Illy."

"Why now, suddenly?" She frowned in their direction as she rinsed out the conditioner from her hair—or at least she hoped she had shampooed and conditioned in the right order. They didn't answer immediately. She took a step toward them until she bumped against Theodore's knee. "Does this have something to do with Eve turning up? You've been letting me deal with the bond my own way for weeks."

"Maybe it does a little bit," Theodore rumbled softly, his fingers trailing along the outside of her thigh. "I'm feeling very protective right now, but it might have a little more to do with the way you melted into Kilian tonight. You're so good at hiding it, so we didn't realise until tonight."

Theodore suddenly dipped forward, one arm winding beneath her knees and knocking her legs out from under her, the other wrapping securely around her waist. He lifted her onto his lap and Kilian caught her legs, pulling them across his own lap, his hands shackling her ankles.

"Tell us what happened with the chain." Theodore drew her wet hair over her shoulder, his nose brushing along her temple. She relaxed against him, realising he actually meant what he said about just letting her sit on his lap when he continued to stroke her hair, waiting for her to speak.

She fumbled through a retelling of everything that had happened, beginning with the chain appearing. They listened quietly as she told them about Niko surging and how he had tasted her skin, reassuring himself that she was okay. She told them about Sophia's theories, about the big book of gods and the image of Stygian. She even told them everything that had happened in the garden shed with Sato, and about the gemstone that had appeared on her chain as she briefly borrowed Kalen's power.

Theodore kept his emotions tightly leashed the whole time, only a steady thrum of caution nudging her chest as he held her close, his hand passing up and down the length of her spine in hypnotising patterns. When

Kilian began rubbing her calves, his touch graduating from light strokes to a deeper massage, she groaned and flopped her head to rest on Theodore's shoulder.

"What else?" Theodore purred, his strokes lulling her half to sleep as she finished rambling.

There *was* more. There was so much more. And she was sick of having no one to lean on, no one to help her.

"Someone's been threatening me," she whispered against Theodore's sweet-tasting skin. "They know about Mikel's ability and they know I entered my Death Phase on the rooftop. They have pictures and videos. They said if I told any of you, they would hand in all the evidence."

Somehow, neither of them so much as flinched in their calming strokes against her skin.

"Good girl," Theodore whispered, his lips moving over her temple. He tilted her chin up, and she was so sleepy she barely even registered the soft kiss until he was pulling away, his thumbs brushing over her temples again. "Thank you for telling us."

"I'm running out of time," she breathed out softly, wondering at the huge weight that had just lifted off her chest, at the silky, warm river of feeling that wound its way through her. "I'm sick of secrets."

He kissed her temples, their combined scents wrapping around her like a fuzzy blanket, warm and earthy and sweet. Her eyelids began to droop.

"Do you mind if I take your phone tonight?"

She barely registered Theodore's voice and nodded just to make him go back to stroking and kissing her temples, but he gripped her chin gently, demanding her attention.

"Can I take your phone, Illy?"

"Will they find out I told you?" she asked, hating the tremble in her voice.

"Never." He kissed her lips again, another soft, drugging brush before pulling back, a groan building in his chest. "I think it's time for bed. Kili? Can you bring Oscar in without anyone seeing?"

"On it." Kilian gently set her legs down and she could hear him drying off before slipping out of the room.

Theodore bundled her in tighter, a shudder passing through his chest as he kissed the side of her mouth again. "He'll make sure it looks like you're sleeping in my room alone. Why did Oscar want to stay with you tonight?"

"I forget." She nuzzled against his chest, her hands winding around his neck, her sigh spilling out over his wet skin. He seemed to be almost naked, but she could feel material beneath her thighs, where her borrowed boxers had ridden up.

The door opened again, and she turned further against Theodore's chest squeezing her eyes shut at the brief flash of light.

"I have clothes," Kilian said.

Theodore stood, still holding her with one arm as he

turned off the shower, and then set her down on the fluffy bathmat, holding her by the hips as she continued to lean on him.

"Why do I feel so funny?" she mumbled against his skin. "So sleepy."

"I think the bond is a little overloaded, baby." Kilian squeezed most of the moisture from the long length of her hair with a thick towel. "We're going to take off these clothes now, okay? Theo will close his eyes."

"Like fuck—" Theodore started to growl, his fingers pinching in against her hips, before he cut himself off on a rough vibration of sound, which quickly faded to something more comforting, like a gentle rumble. "They're closed."

Kilian slipped the wet boxers down her legs wordlessly, Theodore holding her steady as Kilian lifted each leg clear. She felt drugged, or drunk. Like her soul had been slowly dying of thirst and then suddenly it had been tossed into a swimming pool of the sweetest wine, and it had just soaked all of it up, desperate gulp by desperate gulp.

Kilian dried her legs and she sighed contentedly against Theodore's skin, which was heating up to an almost uncomfortable level. Kilian stood again, his towel-covered hand pushing between her legs. She flinched as a bolt of heat speared from her clit to her chest, burning a straight path of fire through her body, a moan slipping from her lips.

"What," Theodore grated, "the fuck."

Kilian moved the towel to her hips and stomach like nothing had happened.

"Bra," he muttered quietly. "It's already torn."

Theodore's hand flashed up so quickly she didn't even feel his touch against her chest. One minute, her breasts were contained by the tied-together lace, the next, the garment was ripped clean off her body.

"Fucking hell," Kilian swore. "You good?"

Theodore was still behind her, stiff as a statue, his breathing ragged. He didn't answer, and Isobel was too drunk on all their touches to care about who Kilian was talking to. She turned in Theodore's arms, whining as she clutched his neck.

"Tired of standing," she complained, tugging on his shoulders.

Theodore was big and strong and warm. She should just make him pick her up so she could go to sleep.

"Fuck. The shirt," Theodore grunted.

A second later, a shirt was being dragged over her head, and then Theodore was gathering her up.

7

Mikel is Just an Innocent Bystander

Mikel paced across the polished floorboards, agitation rushing through his veins as he listened to the shower turning off in the other room. He eyed Oscar, who was reclined on Theodore's bed, his arm bent up over his eyes like he didn't even want to be there.

"You really don't need to chaperone," Oscar murmured, his gravelly voice amused. "I've slept with her before."

"Kilian said she's acting drugged." Mikel fought to keep his voice even, knowing perfectly well that his words were about to get a reaction.

Oscar lowered his arm, dark eyes flashing. "And you think I'd take advantage of that?"

"No." Mikel stopped pacing, giving him an exasperated look. "But I can't have you breaking fingers or threatening to cut off limbs if she does something stupid with someone else. Not within the group. You know the group is off limits."

"Bah." Oscar covered his eyes again. "I'll be a good boy. You can go."

"I'm here to check on her."

The arm lowered again, just a little. "Why?"

"Same reason you demanded to sleep with her tonight." Mikel folded his arms, his muscles twitching, his entire body vibrating with the need to *do* something. "Because of—"

"Don't speak the dead girl's name," Oscar rushed out on a snarl, half-rising from the bed before deliberately, and slowly, laying back down again, and forcing his arm back up over his eyes.

The door to the bathroom opened and Kilian stepped out. This time, Theodore was behind him, the Sigma wrapped up in his arms. She was dwarfed by an oversized T-shirt, her head pushed into Theodore's neck, her eyes closed.

Kilian put a finger to his lips, and Mikel watched, a little shocked, as Theodore laid the sleeping girl down in the middle of the bed. She whimpered, but Oscar shifted to his side, drawing her into the curve of his body, and she settled back down immediately, brushing her nose against his arm.

It was the first time Mikel had seen Oscar hug anybody other than his sister—and even then, it was more like he endured his sister's hugs more than he initiated them.

Oscar would *kill* for his sister.

What the hell was this supposed to mean?

Kilian, who had already borrowed a pair of Theodore's sweatpants, slipped into the bed on Isobel's other side.

Theodore ducked back into the bathroom and emerged again with a phone, disappearing into his closet to switch out the towel he had wrapped around his hips.

Mikel jerked his head toward the door when Theodore emerged again in dry clothes, and the younger Alpha nodded, casting a quick glance to the bed before tearing his attention away. Mikel began leading him to his office, but Theodore shook his head and strode toward Elijah's room. He opened the door without knocking, Mikel following him in and closing the door behind them.

Elijah was sitting at his desk, frowning at one of his monitors. He didn't even look up when he asked, "What happened?"

"I did everything you said to do." Theodore's voice wasn't right. Too tight. Too short, like he wasn't taking in air at the normal rate. "And you were right. She was completely overloaded. Practically passed out."

"Good." Elijah pushed back his chair and ripped off his glasses, tossing them onto his desk. "But it only worked because she's been ignoring the bond. We can't do this every night. We need to figure out another way to keep her here and keep her safe until the end of term. Eve has already searched her room—apparently, she has a key. She didn't mess with anything, but she seemed to be looking for something. Possibly the glowing strings."

Mikel slumped onto Elijah's window seat, pulling out his phone and glancing at the message they had all received in the group chat at some point during movie night.

Elijah: Carter is in a bad way. Luckily, those dark circles under her eyes make it look like she hasn't been sleeping, or we might have to explain why she's melting into Kilian like he's a damn cloud right now. She's obviously not going back to her dorm alone tonight, so whoever decides to bodyguard while pretending to surrogate, listen up.

Elijah: Getting her in a smaller space with minimal clothes so your scent can properly bake into her is a good idea. Sex is a very bad idea. Lots of skin contact is a good idea. Sex is a bad idea. Touching her pressure points and where her veins are closest to the skin is a good idea. Sex is a bad idea. Speaking to her softly and gently is a good idea. Sex is a bad idea. Keeping her in a harmonious, low-conflict environment is a good idea. Sex is a bad idea.

Mikel skimmed the message again, trying to figure out how any of that would knock the Sigma out. He pocketed his phone again and fixed Theodore with a look. "What did you do, exactly? I'd prefer to know that she's passed out in a good way and not from shock."

"We rubbed her in all the right places." Theodore rolled his eyes before realising what he had said and quickly amended: "Like her temples, her neck, her ankles. She relaxed very quickly and passed out even faster."

Elijah was nodding along while Theodore spoke like he already knew that was exactly how Carter would react. He was also scrolling through the phone Theodore had handed him, simultaneously reading whatever was on screen.

"It's bad," Elijah said, glancing up at Mikel and holding out the phone.

Mikel got up and scanned the messages, the photos ... the video.

"Well." He handed the phone back, his entire body growing still, and calm, like it always did before a fight. "She's even better at keeping secrets than I thought. Pity the one person she chose to confide in was a backstabbing little cunt. She could have used a friend."

"What happened?" Cian pushed into the room, his bright, intelligent gaze darting between them. "Who's guarding her?"

"Oscar and Kilian." Theodore didn't look up from the phone as he surveyed the messages with a thunderous expression on his face, but when Cian drew closer, he sucked in a breath, closed his eyes, and handed the phone over.

"We have limited options here," Elijah said, sitting

back in his chair and folding his arms. "And we have to consider that the *club*"—he rolled his eyes as he said the word—"might be behind all of this to begin with. This might be an initiation task."

"It suits their MO," Mikel agreed, voice tight with annoyance. "You haven't heard any of them mentioning her?"

"No," Elijah confirmed, mouth thinning further. "You and Kalen?"

"Nothing." Mikel stood, beginning to pace. "If they wanted to recruit her, why wouldn't they use us to get to her?"

"Same reason they didn't use you to get to me." Elijah shrugged. "Same reason they haven't used me, Gabriel, or Oscar to get to any of these guys." He waved his hand at Theodore and Cian. "The Track Team doesn't *owe* favours; they collect them."

"This is a lot of dirt," Mikel growled, shooting a glare at the phone. But then again ... they hadn't held back in their recruitment attempts with him either.

Those secrets were worse.

If this was the Track Team, then they were actually going easy on Carter. Elijah didn't respond to him, instead choosing to watch as he came to the realisation himself.

"We have to do something." Theodore was bouncing on the balls of his feet, his eyes growing dark and cloudy.

"Go work out." Mikel's order came out as a bark. "We've got this."

Theodore didn't even pause to argue—despite the slitting of his eyes indicating that he wanted to. He spun and stalked out of the room, his movements jerky and sharp.

Despite everything, Mikel had to quietly admire the younger Alpha. Theodore was completely enamoured with Isobel. Obsessed, possessive, and territorial in the way Alphas could get. But he was holding himself remarkably in check.

Mikel wouldn't have been able to hold himself back.

When a woman was *his*—no.

Nope.

None of that.

"Were they in the shower?" Elijah asked, the second Theodore was out of earshot, raising his brows at Mikel.

Maybe he was echoing Mikel's thoughts.

"Mhmm." Mikel pulled out his phone, hovering over Tilda's contact, pausing there and turning over all the scenarios in his mind.

"Would you?" Elijah asked quietly, watching him. "I know it's a big ask."

"I can handle her," Mikel promised, before punching the button.

She picked up on the third ring, her tone curious. "Why are you calling me from Reed's room?"

He immediately strode for the door, sharing a quick

look with Elijah before slipping into the hallway and walking back toward his office. "Was just leaving. You free later?" he asked, closing himself into his office.

"I'm not available at your beck and call," she snipped.

Usually, he played this game with her. Tonight, he had neither the time nor the patience ... so he let that darker part of him take over.

All of them had a demon of some kind. It was what had drawn them all together, and it was what bound them, still. It was why several of them were drawn to Isobel like they couldn't help themselves.

It wasn't the bond. It was the darkness ... because she was just as damaged.

They all had monsters living beneath their skin: proverbial cloaks they could shrug on and off when the mood struck, the material woven with obscure malevolence. They could use it to do unmentionable things, or they could use it to do the impossible. Isobel didn't wear her darkness the same way. She couldn't seem to control it or demand it serve her.

Maybe that was what drew her to them. She needed someone to bring it out of her.

Enough about the Sigma.

He dropped his carefully walled composure and welcomed that caged beast into his skin with practised ease. He felt the change in his stance, and when he spoke, he could even hear the silken cadence that edged his usually guarded tone.

"It's time to leave work," he said. "Go back to your apartment, Tilda." A calm, cool emotion drifted over him. *Control.* Beautiful, sweet *fucking* control. "I want you waiting on your knees four steps from the door. You'll be punished for every article of clothing left on your body. You have twenty minutes." He hung up, pausing a moment to give her enough time to leave her desk as he had ordered before he made his way back toward Theodore's room.

He didn't need to question whether or not Tilda would obey him. She would. Despite everything, she would. Despite her own nature, even. This was what she wanted, what she was always begging for, always trying to push him to give to her.

The one piece of him he wasn't always willing to share.

Theodore's room was dark as he closed the door, the figures on the bed tensing. All of them except Carter. Even in the darkness, he could clearly see her curled up in a rumpled mess of blankets, her cheek resting on Oscar's arm, her fists curled in Kilian's shirt, pulling it close to her face.

"What is it?" Kilian asked.

Oscar didn't say anything.

"I need her scent." Mikel stopped at the end of the bed, holding out both hands. It wasn't a request.

Oscar lifted to his knees, bundling Carter into his arms. "The fuck for?" he asked quietly, his chest rumbling with a warning.

"Kilian filled you in." Mikel crooked his fingers, fixing Oscar with a cold, steady, demanding gaze. He wasn't asking a question, but Oscar nodded anyway. "I need information from Tilda."

The two of them stared at him for a moment, Kilian's pale eyes widening, Oscar's dark eyes narrowing tightly.

"Now." Mikel's tone turned low and velvety, almost a whisper, his power flexing out and expanding across the room. He didn't bother with Alpha voice.

Oscar knee-walked to the edge of the bed and Mikel reached out, carefully taking the sleeping girl from his arms.

"I don't think that will work," Kilian said gently. Hesitantly. "Mikki, I don't think you can just trick your system like that."

"We'll see," Mikel rumbled out, keeping his voice soft so as not to stir the Sigma.

He held his breath, carefully rearranging her to drape across his front, held up by his arms banded across her thighs and back, her head falling into the crook of his neck.

"You can't get hard with Tilda anymore?" Oscar asked, confused. He was scratching his neck, his attention roaming over Mikel and Isobel.

Kilian shot out a leg, kicking Oscar in the thigh. Oscar ignored him, staring hard at Mikel's arm.

Mikel tried to keep his breath short—when he was forced to draw one—and he blocked out the scent that tried to curve cloyingly around him, just like he was blocking out the sensation of the soft body pressed up against his. She had lost weight. He didn't like that.

It also had nothing to do with him.

"She's desperate for me to Dom her," he said quietly.

"So Dom her." Oscar shrugged.

Kilian rolled his eyes. "I'm sure it isn't that simple."

"It's not." Mikel gave Oscar a disparaging look. Isobel shifted like she was waking up, her nose brushing against his neck. Her hands drifted up his chest, resting at his collarbones, her fingers curling in against the collar of his shirt. Her legs shifted up, like she was trying to cling on to him, and he considered quickly handing her off, but then her legs parted, twisting around his waist, her thighs squeezing with a contented sigh. He could feel the warmth of her everywhere, suddenly, and he forgot to resume his shallow breathing, accidentally pulling in a lungful of her contented scent.

Warm, wet, sticky cherry. It was like she had turned to syrup to drip over his skin. It was simultaneously exactly what he needed and everything he didn't want. He closed his eyes, forcing all the sensations down. When she settled again, her breathing returning to soft little puffs against his neck, he opened his eyes.

Kilian was wrong.

He could *definitely* trick his system.

"Tilda is inherently unhappy." He resumed speaking like nothing had happened, his voice perfectly composed. "That's why she was such a good target in the first place. She was vulnerable enough for me to slip right in and give her everything she needed, but that was last year. I should have cut her off and moved on to someone else, but I got lazy and nobody else caught my interest, so we're stuck with her. I'm not a sadist." He let his eyes rest on Oscar for the briefest moment. "I'm an experienced Dom. I don't like lording my power over people and seeing them suffer. I enjoy women submitting to me."

"Are you asking me to subdue her for you?" Oscar asked, relaxing back against the headboard, ignoring the second kick Kilian aimed at his legs.

"Stop it," Kilian grumbled.

Oscar smirked—he *loved* to tease Kalen and Mikel for their lifestyle. It was a pity. They could probably teach him to harness and control some of his more savage urges, but he wasn't interested in rules and structure, and the kink community was all about rules and structure.

Mikel snorted, his lips lifting into half a smile. "Tilda doesn't enjoy fear. She enjoys control, and that's the problem. Even bound and blindfolded she still never hands over control, and I'm finding it harder and harder to convince my dick that we still need her."

"Why bother playing, then?" Kilian asked. "Just have normal sex. Think about something else." He managed to keep a straight face and not look at Isobel as he said it. Barely.

"She gets it when I need something from her. It's transactional, and we're both aware of that. I ask for something of her, and she gets something of me that she knows I don't want to share with her. It's how she feels in control." Mikel's skin wanted to crawl with disgust, but it seemed to be an impossible endeavour with his little mate curled around him like a kitten.

And he meant that in a purely scientific way. She *was* his mate. She was genetically predisposed to soothe him, to calm him, to make him hard enough to bend other women over pieces of furniture in exchange for information. He hadn't slept with Tilda since finding out about Carter, but that couldn't last forever. There were only so many ways he could please her and appease her ego without fucking her before she started to get suspicious, and he could never admit to *why* he wasn't fucking her. He wasn't fully bonded to Carter and he had no emotional connection to Tilda, so sex wasn't likely to harm the bond in any way, but he owed Carter some consideration. He was certain that if there were any repercussions through the bond, they would likely skip him and flow straight to the Sigma.

"Dump her," Oscar grunted, perhaps reading something on Mikel's face. "It's not worth it, Mikki."

"I've been in here too long," Mikel muttered, gently peeling Carter away and passing her into Kilian's arms.

Kilian took her gently, but his attention scoured Mikel's face, taking in his body language. "I agree with Oscar," he ventured. "You're clearly not enjoying yourself anymore. You shouldn't be doing this if you don't want to."

Mikel ignored them. He *did* have to.

He owed them.

He owed Kalen.

He wasn't contributing to the game the same way they were.

He needed to do this.

Grabbing Theodore's laptop from the desk, he left the room and dropped it off in Elijah's room, delivering them a distracted excuse about needing a reason to go into Theodore's room to speak to the others, and then he made his way out of the dorm.

He should have known that Kilian wouldn't leave it alone.

That boy was a bleeding fucking heart.

"Time to end it," Kalen grunted, appearing out of no-fucking-where with those silent footsteps of his. He fell in beside Mikel as they approached the stairs leading down Alpha Hill.

"No." Mikel didn't break stride.

Kalen caught his shoulder, fingers digging in, forcefully spinning him around. "Go and see her, but break it off, Mikki." His yellow-amber eyes assessed Mikel slowly, carefully, reaching some sort of conclusion as his lips hardened. "You're done."

Mikel shrugged the other man's hand off, and with it, his influence. Kalen rarely tried to overpower or outrank him, but he could already see in the older Alpha's eyes that this would be one of those rare situations, if Mikel resisted. "I can't. You don't know what we're dealing with. Go see Elijah—"

"Elijah already called me and told me everything." Kalen folded his arms, his dark button-down stretching tight across his chest and biceps. "And I'm making the call. You're done. We'll find another way to deal with the Track Team."

"Tilda is our way to deal with *everything* inside the control room," Mikel snarled back, before pushing his hands through his hair, his fingers shaking.

He didn't want to do it.

He had been putting it off since finding out about Carter: stopping short of fucking Tilda, distracting her with her own pleasure, and keeping his distance in general. Elijah had informed them all that different forms of intimacy outside of the bond could come with consequences, and he really wanted to believe that it was part of the reason ...

But he had hit some sort of limit.

He couldn't pretend to care anymore. He couldn't play that game anymore. He needed to switch tactics.

Kalen just waited quietly, a spark of sympathy in his expression.

"Okay, shit." Mikel shook his head. "Yeah, I'm done."

"Good." Kalen turned on his heel, but paused, glancing back at Mikel. "I know you're mad at yourself, but you need to find another way to funnel it out. You need to find another way to punish yourself or you need to deal with your shit. After what happened to Elijah and Gabriel, this is the last example you should be setting."

Mikel nodded, his jaw clenching as he gritted his teeth too tightly. Forcing it to loosen, he muttered. "I know."

"Don't take too long, we need to strategise." Kalen walked off without another word and Mikel fought his way through the emotions to the cool, calm well inside him.

He had completely recovered by the time he arrived at the building neighbouring the family centre, where the on-site officials were housed, and he was focussed as he stepped out of the elevator and opened the door to Tilda's apartment.

She was kneeling, as he had told her to, but wearing a set of lacy lingerie—always trying to push him into punishing her. She always *thought* she wanted to be hurt, pushed, disciplined ... but Mikel knew her. She wasn't made of the kind of material he could work with.

He needed someone who would bend, but not break.

If he ever truly punished Tilda the way she begged for—*his* way—the woman would shatter into a thousand jagged pieces, and Mikel really didn't have a kink for ruining people's lives.

"We're done here," he said calmly, watching as her head snapped up, her eyes narrowing.

Expectation.

Tilda was many things, but she wasn't an idiot.

"That's not very wise," she warned him immediately, jumping up to her feet and reaching for the dressing gown she had tossed over the back of a bar stool. She knotted it tightly, a familiar tremble of fury shaking her full lower lip. "You'll lose all your special little privileges, *Professor Easton*."

"I'll survive." He stood there, waiting. Because there was bound to be more.

She rounded her small kitchen counter, uncorking the bottle of wine she had left out, two glasses already waiting.

"Sit?" She didn't look at him as she poured out two glasses. "You owe me that much."

He moved to one of the stools on the other side of the counter, accepting the glass she handed him, though he didn't take a sip. He was already saturated in Carter's scent and doing his level best to ignore it. He didn't need to add alcohol to the equation.

"You're fucked up, Mikel." Tilda looked down her

slender nose at him. As though she had just read his mind.

He smirked, deciding to take a sip of the wine after all. He levelled her with a cool stare as he waited for whatever else she wanted to throw at him. It was only fair that he stuck around as a punching bag for a few minutes. He *had* just dumped her without explanation.

"We could still play, you know." She set her glass down, toying with the stem, the fingers of other hand tangling playfully with the sash of her gown, her mood shifting abruptly.

Tilda was the kind of woman to beg him to mark her, before turning around to the officials the next day to claim he had forced her.

She had a mind for devious strategy.

They wouldn't give just *anyone* the Creative Director position for the entire Ironside project. She had a big-picture mind and a very small compartment reserved for feelings and emotions—most of which were her own.

He had been telling himself for months that he was just too *lazy* to end it, but the real reason was ... he was concerned about the repercussions.

He needed to tie this up in the right way.

Put a pretty bow on it.

"Come here," he said lowly, snapping his glass back onto the counter.

She moved toward him immediately, stopping between his legs, her hands on his thighs, her tongue running across her lips. She was a pretty woman, sharp-tongued and intelligent. A good decade older than him, but fit and lively. She had a wry smile and eyes that cut through all the bullshit. A thin, stiff upper lip and a full, sensual lower one.

Pity she was disintegrating on the inside.

She could have made some big-shot human director a very terrified man one day.

He coaxed the strap of her dressing gown out of her grip and then yanked it from the loops, tearing one of them and forcing her to stumble forward, eyes wide.

He flicked the silky material up over her eyes, slapping her hands down when they jumped up in protest.

"Do you want this or not?" he growled, ignoring the bile in the back of his throat.

Her hands fell again, and he looped the strap twice, three times, tying it off above her nose.

There, a pretty bow. He could tick that off his to-do list.

He slid off the stool, forcing her back a few steps as he pulled his phone out of his pocket and pulled it up to start a video of her bow-tied face. He deliberately pressed his finger over the microphone, keeping his voice low as he spoke.

"You want this, Tilda? Tell me how much."

He uncovered the microphone, and she made a low,

whining sound in her throat. Part frustration, part annoyance. She wasn't good at begging.

"Just fuck me already," she rasped, and he set his phone down for a moment, blinding the camera. He hoisted her up onto the counter, moved the glasses out of the way, and set the half-full wine bottle between her thighs.

"Show me," he whispered in her ear. "Prove it, and I'll mark you up nice and good."

She should have realised that he was onto her then and there, but instead, she thought she was miles ahead. Running laps around him.

She had no idea.

He had been running laps around *everyone* at Ironside long before he even arrived.

He picked up his phone again, moving back several steps and lifting the camera to focus on her. She shrugged her dressing gown off and shimmied out of the lacy lingerie, kicking the pieces onto the floor, her breaths coming in short pants. As he was recording, a group message notification popped up on his screen, and he clicked on it, leaving the camera to continue recording in the background.

Cian: Any news, Mikki?

Kalen (admin): Mikel is currently ending his arrangement. There won't be news tonight.

Mikel watched as Cian and Theodore both began typing, before they stopped again. It wasn't the best timing, but neither of them would question Kalen or him.

Mikel: I'll be getting the information one way or another, but maybe not tonight.

Kalen started typing, and Mikel rolled his eyes, quickly tapping out a message before Kalen could lose his shit.

Mikel (admin): I still ended it.

Kalen also stopped typing, and then Mikel returned his attention briefly to the woman on the kitchen counter. She was pouring the wine delicately onto her chest, her fingers following the stream down to her hip, where the drips teetered and spilled off to the side of her waist. Her fingers continued down, tunnelling into her pussy. It wasn't hot, those painted claws disappearing between pink lips. He needed more than that.

He covered the microphone. "Drink the wine, Tilda, don't play with it. Empty the bottle."

His phone vibrated again.

Theodore: I'm glad it's over. We don't need her.

Moses: Um. I know you're a kinky bastard and everything, but not even you can tame crazy. Get out while you can.

Mikel (admin): Try me.

Cian: RIP Tilda.

Moses: You will be remembered.

Moses: By someone.

Moses: Oh, who am I kidding, she doesn't even have a cat.

Gabriel: Try not to make a mess.

Niko: What the hell are you doing to her?

Mikel (admin): I'm not doing anything.

Elijah: I'm afraid to ask.

Niko: No, you aren't.

Elijah: Okay, I'm not.

Mikel (admin): Everything that is being done to her, she's doing herself. I'm just standing here on my phone. But the video should keep her on our side for a while.

He lifted his eyes from his phone again, realising Tilda had finished the bottle. Sloppily. There was wine running down the sides of her mouth.

"Put it inside you," he ordered coldly.

He wasn't even pretending anymore.

"Noo," she whined. "Come here and spank me instead. Choke me. Scratch me."

Predictable.

"What else?" he asked.

"Hurt me!" she demanded, clutching the bottle.

"You know what you have to do," he returned, tapping back into the group chat as he covered the microphone. "Get yourself off with that bottle and I'll make sure you're covered in my mark tomorrow."

For everyone to see.

For you to file a report.

He hated that he had been right.

He hated that there was no loyalty inside her.

He *hated* it so much that it was a shock to his system when he scraped a hand down his face in irritation and got a heady whiff of cherry. Isobel had been saturated in her own scent. Contented by Theodore and Kilian's efforts to comfort her ... but it was still a surprise that her scent remained so strong on his skin.

He swallowed as his anger and frustration melted into something else, his hand tightening around the phone. For the briefest, most disturbing second, his sight wavered, and he imagined another body on the counter, dripping in liquid and following his orders. A growl built up in the back of his throat and he dropped his phone down, cutting off the recording.

He walked out, slamming the door, his eyes closing for a brief second as he willed his half-hard cock to deflate.

He stalked into the elevator and texted the group a quick message.

Mikel (admin): We're set. There won't be any repercussions from Tilda.

To Tilda, he sent the recording.

Mikel: Nobody has seen it, and nobody has to. Don't ever try to trap me again, Tilda.

He briefly considered sending another, kinder message. Something like *I enjoyed our mutually beneficial arrangement*, or maybe to wish her the best for the future, but Tilda wasn't a sentimental person and she likely wouldn't appreciate the empty attempts at pleasantries.

It was better to just be honest, and he honestly wasn't thinking about their arrangement or her future at all by the time his feet hit the pathway leading back to Dorm A.

His focus had always been on the Alphas, and tonight was no different.

8

HOW ABOUT GO FUCK YOURSELF?

IT WAS DIFFICULT FOR ISOBEL TO DRAG HERSELF BACK FROM THE warm, fuzzy depths of sleep, and the closer she got to the surface of consciousness, the more she ached. It was a slow pain, a cinder sparking against a rough, cavernous wall, showing just how cold and empty she was inside.

It was confusing, because at the same time, she felt *amazing.*

She felt light as air, warm to her core, and blissed out on the most delicious aroma. Like a full-bloom meadow in spring, the bergamot-oleander blend was heady and drowsy, sweet and sunny. Light and fragrant, but utterly addictive. She cracked her eyes open, blurrily focussing on the ceiling of Theodore's room, her arms and legs flinging out as she unfurled in a heavy, lazy stretch.

The bed was empty, but still warm on either side of her.

She paused, her brow furrowing as she tried to remember what had happened the night before. Kilian. Theodore. The shower. And then ... *nothing?*

Panic sluiced through her, heavy and sharp, but there were no new scars on her arms. In fact, the scars she *did* have seemed to have faded slightly. They were smaller. Thinner. Less jagged.

The bed smelled only faintly of Theodore, and strongly of Kilian and Sato. They must have stayed with her.

She sucked in a lungful of air, trying to clear away the remnants of her panic as the door cracked open, Cian appearing with a cup of coffee and a plate of avocado toast.

"Morning, sunshine." He kicked the door closed behind him, eyeing her carefully. "Ready to go viral because the sexiest Alpha in Dorm A just brought you breakfast in be—" He froze, his eyes zeroing in on her chest.

She glanced down, freezing at the slight glow through her borrowed T-shirt. She yanked at the neckline, pulling it far enough to reveal the shining gemstone. The *new* gemstone. It was a few inches below the stone that had momentarily given her Kalen's powers. It was a cold, icy grey, like a cloudy diamond.

The panic tried to claw back into her, but Cian's panic was stronger, drowning hers out. He dropped the plate, shoving the mug onto the bedside table as he fell onto the bed, grabbing her head in his hands.

"Focus on me," he said quietly. "Take five deep breaths. Count them for me."

Panic, panic, panic.

It hammered into her, denting her barricade, knocking her off kilter.

"Y-You're the one freaking out," she gritted. "N-Not me."

He blew out a breath that was half laugh, half scoff, his emotion settling somewhat. "Right. Sorry. Tell me what you're feeling?"

He was still holding her face, his hands making her feel tiny, the roughness of his palms tempting her to turn her face to the side and brush her cheek against the texture, but she held herself back.

"I feel ... warm. Like nothing really. Are you trying to hold me in place by my head so I don't turn back time?"

He made that huffing sound again, his hands drifting, one of them slipping around the back of her neck, the other dropping to her shirt, weighing down the neckline as he stared at the gemstone ... and almost exposed her chest a little too much. "We don't know what this one does. It could be ..." He trailed off, giving her a guarded look.

"I know." She caught his forearm, brushing her touch along his skin, trying to soothe him the way he seemed to be able to do just by touching her.

His attention drifted, his teeth catching his lip as he pressed his knuckles forward against the chain embedded into her skin. His eyes flicked up to hers, watching her reaction, before he unfurled his fingers, pressing his entire palm to her chest. Her own hands fell back down to her lap, her heart stuttering beneath his grip.

He pressed, weighing her back, inch by inch until her head was sinking into the pillow, her hair fanning messily around her. He pulled in a steadying breath, licking his lips.

"How do you feel?" he repeated.

Well *now* she didn't want to tell him.

She folded her arms, inadvertently trapping his hand between her breasts. Something lit up in his bright gaze, the aquamarine colour glittering as his power swelled around her, dousing her in sun and saltwater. It pooled in the back of her throat, threatening to choke her. She was almost convinced that a cresting wave had sprayed her with sea mist as little beads of sweat tried to gather across her skin.

"I feel fine," she blurted, sounding completely scattered. "C-Can I have my ... um ... coffee? I don't think anything is going to happen."

He lifted off her immediately, grabbing the cup from the bedside table, drips of coffee stuck to the side from his haste in slamming it down. He pressed it into her hands and then just sat there, staring at the mug with a heavy, dark frown, before his eyes widened.

"Fucking *hell*," he groaned, examining her face. "Tell me to do something."

"Like what?" Some of her nervousness dropped away at the shocked look on his face.

She gulped at the coffee, but he reached out, grabbing the mug again.

"Anything." He stole the coffee off her, slapping it back onto the bedside table, clearly wanting her to focus.

"How about go fuck yourself?" she grumbled, quickly reaching for the coffee again. She might be a Sigma, but anything getting between her and caffeine first thing in the morning turned her into a prissy, bossy Beta.

Cian was tugging at the tie in his sweatpants.

"W-What are you—" she started, but her question was cut off as his hand tunnelled beneath the waistband, dragging it just low enough to show her the hint of another tattoo swirling up from where the waistband of his underwear should have been. If he had been wearing any.

"You might want to tell me to stop before we get the *Ironside Show* banned from the family-friendly time slot, sweetheart."

He sounded like he was joking. There weren't even any cameras in the room, but his expression was entirely serious. His hand shifted and it looked like he had wrapped it around his length, his jaw clenching. "Isobel …"

"Stop! Jesus Christ, stop!"

He breathed out a short sigh of relief, pulling his hand out of his pants and holding them both up in an innocent gesture. "You've got Elijah's power, love. Hypnosis."

"What?" she rasped, staring at his hand.

His scent had changed. It didn't remind her of the ocean anymore, but of steam-choked gasps and sweat-dusted skin. He was sun-soaked sex, and it was the *single* most drugging scent she had ever experienced.

She grabbed his hand, driven entirely by instinct, but stopped just short of pressing it against her face, leaving them both to stare at their clasped hands, held between them for no reason.

She quickly dropped him, and he leaned back, levelling her with a calm look that didn't give away any of his thoughts, but he was half hard, making his sweatpants look a little obscene as the material clung to the outline of his cock, the edge of his tattoo still peeking out. It looked like a branch of some kind, with flowers on it.

"That didn't feel very hypnotic," she said, trying to mimic his relaxed posture, ignoring her thundering heartbeat and forcing her voice to sound normal.

And her gaze to stay on his face.

"You aren't practised with it like Elijah is." His lips crooked into an amused half-grin. "And thank all the levels of hell for that."

"It sounds super illegal." She pulled her legs up to her chest, wrapping her arms around her knees. "That makes five of you: Theo, Moses, Easton, Sato, and Reed."

"Sato, hm?" His head tipped to the side, golden tendrils of hair escaping the way he had knotted them at the back of his head, curving down around his face. "That's new."

"He told me." She reached out to him with her foot, nudging his thigh with her toes, drawing a small smirk onto his face to chase away the look of arrogant inquisition that had taken over his features.

"Just like that?" Cian asked. "Didn't ask for anything in return?"

He was regarding her like he *knew*.

Maybe Kilian and Theodore had already told him, and he was just pretending to hear it for the first time.

"Why don't you check your group texts?" she suggested, pushing him with her toes again. "I bet they told you all about it."

This time, he grabbed her foot, trapping it against the bed. "The content of the group texts got a little explicit last night. I don't think you want to see that."

"Explicit?" She blinked at him, her mind racing. "How? What do you mean?" She felt the urge before it really blossomed into her mind as an idea, and Cian stiffened as soon as he read the intention on her face.

"Isobel, don't—"

"Tell me," she said.

He groaned. "You're going to pay for that." He shook his head, closing his eyes as though he was fighting against something, but then he fixed her with a serious look. "Mikki ended things with his girlfriend. Recorded her fucking herself with a wine bottle as she begged him to hurt her ... just to keep her under his thumb. He didn't send us the recording, but he explained what happened after—oh for fuck's sake, Carter, don't make me say this—"

"Stop," she squeaked, blinking at him in astonishment. "Wow. Sorry. Wasn't expecting that."

He shook his head, but there was a tight smile tugging his mouth. "Impossible," he muttered. And then his head snapped up again, attention narrowing on her chest. "Why are you getting side effects? Especially after last night? Shouldn't you be more settled?"

She shrugged. "Isn't Easton's girlfriend an official? You don't *have* to tell me."

He chuckled, slipping off the bed. "Tilda is an official —our eyes and ears inside the control room. That means she's a human. She's a bit obsessed with Mikki. Practically stalked him before he was posted here as a professor, but she's ashamed of their relationship because he's Gifted."

"Why would she ask him to hurt her? Why would she ... ah, I mean, the thing with the wine bottle?"

Cian shook his head, his expression melting into amusement. "That's Mikki's business. How do you feel now?"

He was looking at her chest, where the glow from the gemstone was no longer peeking through her shirt.

"Honestly?" She frowned. "I don't feel any different. Shouldn't I be able to feel these powers? Do you know what it feels like when Elijah uses his hypnosis?"

"He doesn't use it." Cian stood up from the bed, leaning over to drag her up beside him. "Also not my story to tell. Kilian went to Dorm O to grab you some clothes. He should be back any minute. Want some more toast?"

It was Sunday, so she didn't have any classes, but that didn't mean she had a clear day ahead of her. She shook her head. "I'll grab breakfast after practice. I'm already late."

"All right then." He stood over her, glancing at the way Theodore's shirt threatened to fall off her shoulder. "Just a heads-up ... you aren't going back to Dorm O. Not today, not next week, not ever. Kilian is bringing back the essentials. You can keep them in his room until the end of term."

"I can't just—"

He ducked down, kissing an inch from the side of her mouth, shocking her into stillness and silence.

"This isn't a negotiation." He lowered his voice to a purr that rumbled through her, making her sway closer to him.

"It should be," she managed.

"You're right." He smiled. "It should be. But it isn't. Eve—and every single one of her pathetic, spineless little cronies—are dead idiots walking, but that doesn't mean we can take them out on live television. So until we can think of a way to get her permanently expelled, you can't be alone."

"You guys don't even *want* the bond," she snapped, completely aware that she was angry at *Eve*, not Cian ... but she couldn't stop the temper from flaring in her voice. "What does it matter—"

The asshole kissed her again. His lips pressed to the other side of her mouth, not actually touching her lips, drifting down until his teeth nipped at her jaw. "Aren't we friends?" he rumbled, his nose to her cheek, his sapphire eyes hidden from her view. "Do you enjoy seeing your friends almost murdered?"

"I wouldn't try to control their lives," she squeaked, her voice thin and wobbly. *Why did he keep doing that?*

Cian was always flirting, always teasing her, but he was acting ... almost sweet and sensual. Not like himself.

"If you die, we'll be hit with everything you're holding back," he said lowly. "Theo and Moses will feel the full force of being ripped from their mate and they'll probably lose their shit. Then we're all fucked. And whoever happens to be around them when it happens will be *dead*. And I don't even want to think about who Oscar will kill if someone breaks his to—" He cut himself off, inching back to stare at her as he tried to cover up what he had been about to say.

"Toy?" she deadpanned.

"I meant mate." *He* gave *her* a stern look. "And I ..." He chewed his perfect, sinuously curved lip, looking her steadily in the eyes. "You're a sweet girl, Illy. You're soft and kind, but stubborn and loyal, and I like having you around. I can't stand the thought of someone like you being hurt. *Again*. It doesn't have anything to do with the bond."

"Thank you?" She swallowed, wondering how to react. Should she compliment him? The first thing that flashed into her mind was how amazing his new ink looked against his beautiful, golden skin. Maybe that wasn't appropriate.

His eyes dipped to her mouth again, and he groaned. "You're welcome. Why the fuck do you smell so good this morning?"

"It's Sato and Kilian."

He laughed huskily. "No, it's not. I should go. I'm late for group session."

"You guys have group session on the weekend too?" she asked, surprised.

"Yeah. It's three times as long."

He collected the plate he had dropped on the way in and yanked open the door, leaving her to ponder his words as she touched her newest gemstone.

There was room for more.

There was room for *eight* more.

Eventually, she could get Theodore and Moses' ability. She needed to make sure she was ready for that. She needed to make sure she wasn't on *camera* for that.

GABRIEL FELL INTO STEP BESIDE HER AS SHE WAS LEAVING DORM A half an hour later. She was showered and dressed for the day in a pair of spandex shorts and one of Kilian's T-shirts that she was pretending she had picked up by accident after he unloaded most of her clothes into his closet.

"Puppy." Gabriel yawned, looking down over Alpha Hill as the sun climbed higher, turning the colourful desert flowers into vivid, beautiful hues of yellow, orange, and red. "Can I persuade you to reschedule your practise time and come to group session instead?"

Her shoulders hunched in a little, feeling the constrictions of her situation tightening around her, but she fought to keep her tone free from any of the strain. "Sure. Thanks for, you know—" She waved her hand awkwardly. "—the help."

He just stared back at her, his russet eyes murky, his features so perfect and symmetrical that they almost distracted her away from the fact that there was no emotion on his face whatsoever. "No problem. We've got the situation handled."

She pulled out her phone to reschedule her practice sessions, knowing that whoever was keeping an eye on her calendar would inform her father. He usually returned to the academy on Sunday evenings but didn't expect her to see him until Monday. He liked to question her on every single minute change to her routine, her classes, and her social media feed.

Reed caught up to them as they reached the bottom of the stairs, falling in on her other side without a word.

Halfway there, she stumbled, and both of them stopped, a hand on each of her biceps, staring down at her with narrowed eyes and sharp attention, watchful and alarmed.

They seemed even more worked up about Eve returning than *she* was.

"What is it?" Reed's attention swept down to her chest.

"Cian said this session is going to take a few hours." She swallowed as they released her. "Sorry, I was just wondering how you endure a few hours of ... that."

Reed rolled his eyes, and they both started walking again, Gabriel's hand low on her spine urging her to keep pace.

"It's a singing lesson," Reed—*Elijah* said. She might as well use his name, since he was now her sort-of roommate and she was his sort-of captive.

She might as well use all their names.

"It's hardly taxing," Reed added on. *Elijah, dammit.*

It was harder with him. He was so cold, so unfeeling, so analytical. She didn't feel like they were friends at all.

"Right." She focussed on the path ahead of her, the urge to ask Elijah about his illegal power and why he refused to use it popping back up into her throat no matter how many times she pushed it down.

When the urge grew unbearable, she pulled out her phone and sent a quick group message.

Isobel: I should know exactly what all your abilities are if they're going to suddenly appear inside me without warning.

Both Alphas pulled out their phones as Elijah pushed open the door to the fitness centre, leading them toward Easton's usual room. He groaned quietly. "Moses is going to jump on that."

They entered the room, finding it empty. It was the first time she had ever arrived before everyone else.

Elijah and Gabriel moved to dump their bags on the floor beside the door and Isobel dropped her own belongings, tying up her hair just in case Easton made her exercise with the others.

Theodore and Moses walked into the room, both of them adding their stuff to the now-growing pile.

"You really want to know?" Moses asked out of

nowhere, his dark eyes lit with some sort of challenge as he brushed past her, waving his phone in the air.

"Ah, yes?" she said to his back.

Theodore tucked his phone back into his bag before dropping his arm over her shoulders and steering her to the stretching mat.

"How you feeling, pretty?" His lips delivered the question into her hair a second before he pressed her down to the mat, and then scooted a few inches away to start stretching.

She arranged herself to copy his exercises, but before she could answer him, Moses was hovering by the edge of the mat.

"For the record, I don't think anyone will appear inside you without warning, so you don't have to worry about their level of ability."

"Shut the fuck *up*, you idiot." Theodore pounced forward, tackling Moses to the mat, the crash of their bodies narrowly missing her.

She scooted closer to the wall, continuing her stretches with an annoyed look on her face to hide the embarrassment that wanted to flush over her cheeks instead.

"You're an animal," she grumbled, as she bent over her outstretched legs and found herself face to face with Moses, Theodore holding his head tight against the mat.

He laughed darkly, throwing Theodore off him, and switching their positions.

"That's what you should be able to do by now," Niko stated dryly, standing at the edge of the mat, and pointing to Moses.

She glanced over his shoulder, noting that Kilian, Cian, and Sato—*Oscar*—had also arrived.

"Yeah, exactly." She bit her lip as she looked up at Niko. "So why can't I?"

They teased each other sometimes when they were wrestling, but he didn't usually react the way he was now: by falling silent, his nostrils flaring, his eyes tracing the way she stretched before darting off to the side.

"I guess you had a good sleep," he muttered, falling down beside her and pressing her back down again, forcing her deeper into the stretch. "No excuse to be lazy, though."

She huffed, trying to shrug him off. "This is Professor Easton's session, not yours."

He snorted. "This is *Professor Easton's* vocal session. He can keep your throat. I'm the one in charge of your body."

"*Ni-ko.*" Moses flopped off Theodore, his laughter sudden and deep. "You make it too easy."

Niko scowled. "I obviously didn't mean it like that."

Moses rolled to his side, that devilish eyebrow of his jumping up again as he leaned on his elbow, propping his chin into his hand. "Her spine is in the wrong position."

"It is not," Isobel snapped back.

"Actually, it is," Niko said. "Sit up."

He waited for her to obey before he shifted partially behind her, flattening his hand to her stomach, his other hand pressing just above her mid-back.

"Straighten up," he instructed, his breath brushing her neck. "You don't want that curve when you start to bend."

Niko *never* touched her like this.

She tried to correct the position of her spine, but Niko made a dissatisfied sound, both of his hands dropping to her hips, fingers digging in just above her hipbones and pulling back.

That strange, empty feeling that she had woken up with sparked back to life again, even more hollow and cavernous, an ice-cold itch creeping up through her organs.

"Better," Niko grunted. "Now keep that rotation in your hips, keep your spine straight, and ..." He pressed against her back, forcing her to bend over her legs again. He was right. Her spine had been in the wrong position.

She was too distracted to even stretch properly.

There was a spark of satisfaction in Moses' gaze that reminded her of Oscar for an uncomfortable moment. A glint of sadistic enjoyment, as though he had just engineered a moment of chaos. A private unravelling of something just for his own private viewing.

Theodore gripped her thigh and dragged her halfway

across the mat, refusing to look at the others as he went quietly back to his exercises. She returned to copying him, and Moses smirked like he had won.

"I know when people are lying." Niko was speaking to the mat, and several heads whipped up at his confession. "That's what my ability is." He directed his attention to the door, ignoring everyone else. "What's keeping Mikki?"

Isobel almost bit her tongue to hold back the barrage of questions. It wasn't polite to interrogate people about their abilities. But being able to tell when people were *lying*? That was powerful. It made her think about her own father, and his claims that he didn't have an ability. So far, all the Alphas she had met were in possession of very potent abilities. The ability to control time? To control the weather? To turn into murderous ... *somethings*? To read the future? To turn invisible? To create chaos? To *control* people? She still didn't know what Gabriel's ability was, but she was sure he had one, and she was sure it would be illegal.

Suddenly, it didn't seem so feasible that her father was born without an ability.

"He had a rough night," Cian answered, only a second before Easton stepped into the room, slamming the door behind him.

"You four—" He pointed to Moses, Theodore, Cian, and Elijah. "—and Carter. On the treadmills. Now." He grunted the words, barely even sparing them a glance. "Oscar, Gabriel, and Kilian. On the rowing machines. Fifteen minutes hard and fast and then switch." He clapped his hands together, making Isobel twitch an inch closer to Theodore. "Go!"

Theodore pulled her up with him, giving her a carefree grin, reassuring her that Easton's sharp mood was nothing to be concerned about. But she accidentally looked up at Easton as she passed by him, catching sight of a new scar on his cheek, deep and pink, and mottled bruising around his neck peeking up from the top of his collar.

She stumbled, her eyes stretching wide as his attention zeroed in on her, his eyelids lowering over mismatched pupils to make his gaze more severe as a hint of annoyance pinged against her chest from his direction.

"Something you want to say, Carter?" His tone wasn't quite as sharp as when he had been addressing the group, but there was a deeply unhappy undercurrent that made her want to tuck her chin and run away.

"N-No, Professor."

"Treadmill!" Theodore stepped between her and Easton, quickly pushing her toward one of the machines. "Hurry now." He waited until she was tapping the buttons to increase her speed, her neck prickling like Easton was still watching her before Theodore leaned over from the treadmill beside hers.

"Keep your head down this session," he whispered. "If you need to leave, just leave. One of us will go with you."

She reared her head back, blinking at him in confusion. "Because of Ea—" she began to ask, but he just put a finger to his lips and hiked up the speed on his machine, kicking it into a sprint. He even pulled out headphones, but he flashed her a short, apologetic smile in the mirror as he tuned out the rest of the room.

She found her attention drifting to the left, studying Easton in the mirror as he scrolled through his phone, snarling at the boys on the rowing machines for slacking off. He was definitely in a state, but she couldn't tell exactly what the state was, because every Alpha in the room seemed to be feeling something negative, and it was hitting her from all directions.

Wariness. Frustration. Exasperation. Dread. Distress.

They were all worked up, but they were hiding it remarkably well. On their faces, at least.

She fished her own headphones from the pocket of her shorts, choosing the latest playlist she had finalised for her practice sessions. With the aid of music, her body seemed to activate, suddenly willing and eager to move, the running belt moving too slow for the beat of the song she had chosen. She edged the speed past what she usually set it at, realising she might have a chance of running off the anxious edges of everyone in the room if she tried hard enough.

She lost herself in the music, in the process, slowly siphoning off hints of their jagged emotion until her heart skipped a beat and her legs almost failed her. A hand shot out, hitting the emergency stop button for her treadmill, and she jerked to the side, thrown off balance.

"You're done." Elijah's voice was cold, catching her easily, his arm wrapped around her waist as he set her on the ground, holding her up as she tried to gain her footing. Her headphones had fallen out, her music echoing back up to her from where they lay on the ground.

"Carter." *Easton. Shit.*

"Good luck." Elijah walked away, leaving her to raise her head and confront the scarred professor.

He looked like he had been pacing before the stretching mat, where the rest of the Alphas were lined up, half of them on their backs, the other half standing with medicine balls.

Gabriel was propped up, watching her closely as Elijah returned to him and snatched up the medicine ball, sending it down with so much force that it might have cracked Gabriel's ribs if he hadn't caught it so deftly, tossing it back up lightly. The whole time, he stared at her, until Elijah muttered something to him, and he returned his full attention to the task.

When she still hadn't moved, Easton frowned, his finger twitching. He was pointing at the ground before him, but he hadn't raised his hand at all ... it was almost like the movement was completely unconscious.

She swallowed, shuffling over to him, her system in shock. She hadn't noticed the others getting off the treadmills or beginning their other exercises. She didn't even know how long she had been running for, but she could feel the heavy weight of everything she had gradually stolen from them. It sat inside her chest, swirling painfully, a dark vortex hungry for more. Combined with that horrible, persisting emptiness in her gut that still plagued her, it was enough to make her limbs tremble as she stopped before Easton.

"Take over, Niko," Easton commanded, before striding to the far side of the gym, casting her a quick, loaded look like he expected her to follow.

She trailed him to a smaller stretching area where the mats backed onto a mirrored section of the wall. The air conditioner was right above her, making the hairs along her arm stand on end as her sweat dried under the frigid breeze. He pulled a yoga mat from the wall and flicked it out, settling it over the ground.

"I can do whatever the others are doing," she insisted quietly, just out of pure stubbornness. She *obviously* couldn't. There was strong, and then there was *Alpha* strong. If Elijah threw a medicine ball at her with that much force, it wouldn't just break her ribs, it would break *her*, and then probably go through the floor beneath her.

Easton smirked like he knew what she was thinking. "On the mat, Carter. Floor work for you. I'm sorry you had to be here, but I'm sure you can make use of the time?"

She shrugged, her attention snapping between him and the mat. "Of course."

"Professor."

She blinked. "Sorry, Professor." Usually, Easton let it slip when she didn't call him professor. Kalen was the one who pulled her up on it every time, a hint of iron lining the soft reprimand.

Easton stared at her for a second before sighing and sinking onto the seat of the nearest weights machine. "Carter." He paused, his mouth tightening. "Why are you looking at me like that?"

"Like what?" she squeaked.

His mismatched eyes narrowed. They were almost slits. "Cian sent a message—"

"Of course he did," she grumbled.

"Professor," he hissed.

She snapped her mouth shut, and he pulled in a deep breath, inching back until his shoulder rested against the machine behind him. He looked almost lazy, but his attention was far too heavy.

She waited for him to continue, and he waited for her to correct herself.

Swallowing, she muttered, "Professor."

For some reason, he laughed. The sound was short

and sharp, and his head fell into his hands as his broad shoulders shook, and then he was straightening again. "I know you borrowed Elijah's power," he said, shaking his head now. "You made Cian tell you what happened last night, didn't you?"

She quickly moved to the mat, seating herself so that she was facing the mirror instead of him, her legs crossed.

"Sorry, Professor. I don't know what you're talking about." She stretched out her right arm, notching it outside her left knee, and twisted her spine that way.

When she was finally, blessedly, turned fully away from him, her expression finally broke, her eyes growing wide and her lips twitching with the urge to mouth, "What the hell?" to someone. Except that the other Alphas were all busy beating each other up.

All of them except Kilian.

Since Niko had been his partner, he was mostly just moving between the other pairs, saying things she couldn't hear, his pale eyes regularly flicking back to monitor her and Easton.

"Help," she mouthed.

An amused smirk cracked over his face, but it was just as quickly wiped away, and he shook his head.

"Isobel."

Her head whipped to the side, connecting with Easton's stare before she could control her reaction. She switched her stretch to the other side, pretending it had all been part of the plan.

"Tell me what you know," he said plainly.

"I don't really think you want me repeating it, Professor." She tried to direct her attention to his chin so that she didn't break out into a nervous sweat, but she only found her attention snagging on the bruises rising out of his collar. "I don't know where you got those marks," she added.

"Would you like to know?" he asked, a little too casually.

An alarm immediately blared to life inside her head, telling her that she was being invited into a trap, but she couldn't seem to help herself. She nodded. A small motion, easily overlooked.

"It's called the Stone Dahlia." He dropped his voice until she had to lean forward to hear him. "The *clubhouse* your secret admirer is texting you about." He emphasised the word "clubhouse" as though it didn't even begin to describe it. "But we're pretty sure it isn't one of the students. We think it's someone from the Track Team."

"The ... track team? As in the—"

"No." He didn't even wait for her to properly voice the question. "I mean the group of stupidly powerful old men who run this whole show." He flicked his hand around, indicating the cameras stationed around the room. "The billionaires who decide which students get put on the Icon Track. They run the Stone Dahlia, and we're going to make sure you give them what they want."

"First ..." She quickly twisted to sit on her knees facing him, gaping at him as she held up a finger. "*Why?* And second—" She imitated his hand flick at the cameras. "—how do you know they aren't listening right now?"

He tugged his phone from his pocket and waved it at her. "Elijah and Gabriel have been developing a security app. If they try to turn the cameras on to spy on us during our private sessions, we'll all get a notification."

"Can I get that app?" She chewed on her lip, watching as his expression relaxed slightly.

Had he expected their conversation to go differently?

"Yes." He leaned forward, his forearms planted on his thighs, his hands hanging down between his knees. They seemed to have a fresh slew of healing scars scattered over them. "You did the right thing telling Theo and Kilian, Carter."

"Um ... you can call me Isobel, uh, if you want, Professor."

"You don't tell me what to call you. I decide that." He flinched back, like he was reacting to his own sharp tone, his palms running over his thighs. "Sorry." He grimaced. "It's been a night."

"I heard."

"About what?"

"About the girlfriend."

"Hm." The sound was a rumble in his chest. "I don't have one of those."

"Well, you forgot about *her* pretty quick."

Easton chuckled. "Don't be a brat, Isobel. You can tease the other Alphas all you like, but it won't get you anywhere with me. Nowhere you want to be, anyway."

She bit her tongue.

"I've gone easy on you because you hadn't been accepted into Dorm A yet, but you're as good as moved in now, which makes you my responsibility. I'm more than a dorm supervisor or a mentor to these boys. I'm here for everything they need but most of the time, I'm also the one who decides what they need. Are you ready for that?"

"I'm not very good at being told what I need." She quickly dropped her eyes to her knees, confused about when she had turned to face him so readily, like an eager fan straining to hear his every word. She relaxed her posture, stretching her legs out in front of her to ease the ache in her muscles. It wasn't from her run, but from the heaviness she had sipped out of each of them, and that hollow sting persisting beneath her skin.

Easton watched her. "I've noticed."

"I already have someone dictating what I need."

"That's your first free pass," he informed her calmly. "Compare me to Braun Carter again and I'll show you how a real man disciplines."

She frowned, wriggling her toes. "You're very threatening for a professor."

"You're remarkably unafraid for a girl who was almost murdered a month ago."

She felt her lips tugging up at the sides. Was she enjoying *talking* to Easton? It felt like she was. "I've had worse."

"No, you haven't," he said softly. "But you're one of mine, now. Nothing like that will happen to you again."

A shudder travelled up her spine, making her vision hazy at that word.

Mine.

Her toes stopped wiggling, curling in shock, before she curbed the reaction.

"You ... I ..." she stumbled. "Thank you, Professor?"

His lips lifted at the corners. "You're welcome, Isobel."

She stared at him, struck dumb. "I feel weird," she blurted. "I feel like you just took away all my problems and made them all sound so simple, but they're *not*. Like, why would the Track Team be threatening me into trying to figure out a way to contact them? Why wouldn't they just *talk* to me? And if the officials know about your ... ability—which they do, if they have the blackmail video —how are you still here?"

"Not all of the officials," Easton said. "The Track Team is only a percentage of them, and they *want* to know damaging things about people. It's how they enslave them. If they can't find anything damaging on you and they want you on their side, they'll force you into doing something incriminating, just to make sure you're properly under their heel before they take you on board."

"And you want them to recruit me?" she asked, a frown furrowing into her brow.

"They need to know that what they have on you is enough." His eyes grew dark, his emotion suddenly pressing heavily up against her, roiling and bitter. "If you resist, they'll try harder. If this is them—and we think it is—then they're going easy on you, which means they're desperate for you."

"For me to ... what? What do they do?"

"What don't they do?" He sucked in a breath through his teeth. "The Stone Dahlia is almost the same size as the academy, tunnelling so far down below us that they could host an entire concert down there and we would never suspect a thing up here."

"Down ... down *where?*" she spluttered.

"Beneath the main lake. The entrance is through the boathouse—well, the Gifted entrance, anyway. The human entrance is from the other side of the hill leading up to the academy. They hire out rooms. Hire out Gifted. They put us on display. Make us entertain crowds of humans who have paid obscene amounts for an invitation. The Track Team has information on *everyone*. Not just us, but their human guests, and each other."

He was giving her so much information—so much *insane* information—but for some reason, she could only think of one thing in that moment. The back of Gabriel's door, and the message that had been spelled out with individual sticky notes, arranged so heartrendingly obsessively.

I am not for sale.

She swallowed, tears springing up before she could stop them. Horrified, she looked back down to her lap. "Did my ... does my father know about this?"

"Undoubtedly." Easton's voice deepened. "It seems like a game of popularity, but it's the Track Team who *actually* decides the winner every year. And they continue to control their Icons long after they leave the walls of Ironside."

She tapped a freckle on her thigh. "I don't want to get involved with them."

"You have no reason to trust me, but I've protected every one of my Alphas since the day they arrived here, and I'll protect you too. I'm asking you to trust me. Trust Kalen. Trust Elijah. Trust your friends." He cleared his throat. "Don't trust Oscar."

She picked her head up, surprised. "You, Kalen and ... Elijah?"

"There are a lot of contingencies to plan in the situation we find ourselves in." His grin almost twitched into being again. "Elijah is our planner. If he tells you to do something, you should do it. He usually has a good reason."

She chewed her lip. "And Oscar?"

"Is damaged." Easton's expression closed down. "And reactionary. Attuned to his instinct instead of his conscience. Before he had a mate, he was manageable. But you've just added a whole new level of primality to his brain that might make things a little difficult with you living in the dorm. You'll need to learn to manage him."

"Why can't he learn to manage me, instead?" she grumbled.

Easton smiled—his first full, real smile since they had begun talking, and even though it twisted all his scars and made the shadows beneath his eyes even darker, she felt something in her chest flip, the hollow ache inside her turning just that little bit more painful.

"I'm afraid Oscar has a habit of breaking his toys," Easton warned.

Isobel groaned. *This again.* "I'm not a toy."

Easton's smile dropped away, and he leaned forward again. "You're a born and bred *puppet*, Carter. I'm not saying that to be cruel. I'm saying it because it's the truth. You're a toy to anyone who wants to play with you. Whether you *let* them or not—well, that's the part that's up to you. I'll protect you from the other Gifted, from the psychotic bitch who hurt you, from your asshole of a father, and from the officials at Ironside ... but you're going to need to protect yourself against the other Alphas. Decide your boundaries. Make them clear. Learn how to manage the volatile personalities and find your space with the peaceful ones. Nobody else is going to do that for you. We have too much respect for each other to dictate how you interact with each of us. Those are *our* boundaries. Am I clear?"

"Crystal." She chewed her lip, and his eyes flashed with amusement, as though he knew she had more to say. Eventually, she just blurted, "Everyone calls you Mikki."

"You'll have to earn that," he said, standing, his eyes passing over her. "Floor exercises only for the rest of the session. I don't want to see you back on that treadmill and if I catch you siphoning off anyone's shitty mood, you're in trouble. I think you've taken enough for today."

She swallowed, waiting for him to walk away, but he didn't. He waited. She ducked her chin, and he knelt before her.

"Nod if you're going to obey," he said gently, sensing that she was completely overwhelmed.

She nodded, her gaze still stuck to her legs.

"Good girl," he said, low and soft, the words a caress that fluttered through her on a gentle breeze, lifting her chin as he stood and walked away so that she could watch him.

She had no idea what kind of man Easton—*ah, fuck it.* His name was *Mikel.* She had no idea what kind of man he was, but her chest ached with the need to trust him, to see what might happen if she became one of "his Alphas." Though she would never be one of *them*, she still wondered what it would be like to be one of *his*.

Her entire life, people had claimed that they were protecting her. Doing things for her own good. But none of them ever looked like Mikel when they claimed it.

None of them ever made her feel like it was true.

9
Adorable Sex on a Stick

Elijah and Gabriel both came to her practice session that afternoon, using the other half of the room to quietly do their own thing as she picked her song and did a few stretches, sneaking glances at them from beneath her eyelashes.

They had said they wouldn't intrude on her session, but she was still uncomfortable enough to surreptitiously spy on them for a few minutes.

They had paired both of their headphones with Gabriel's phone and seemed to be working out the choreography for a song she couldn't hear. It seemed complicated—too complicated for her to follow, until she realised it wasn't just a dance for one or two people. It was group choreography.

She forced herself to tune them out, grabbing her phone and watching through the last recording she had made of her end-of-year piece for Dance Acrobatics. After identifying her problem areas, she restarted her music and cycled through the routine. Once, and then twice, and then three times.

With each repetition, she only grew more frustrated. The moves were good, but they weren't *great*, and Professor Lye had announced that he would be grading their final performances over the last two days of class. He was restricting his third-year class to the top ten performers, which made it incredibly competitive, especially when most of the other students were pairing up to better their chances. She wasn't sure if it was her slow recovery from the Vermont attack or not, but something was off with her dancing.

"Need a hand?" Gabriel's quiet tone made her head whip up.

She focussed on the bench where he and Elijah had relocated to at some point without her noticing.

She spun on her heel, approaching them, and hitting Pause on her music. "Is it that bad?"

"It's a little forced." Elijah leaned up against the wall, his posture relaxed. "But you're still healing."

Gabriel shrugged, apparently agreeing with the other Alpha.

"Forced how?" she demanded, a little too quickly, before focussing on Elijah. "And what are you doing for your final performance?"

“For Lye?” he asked, cocking his head. “I choreographed a dance, but I’ve run into casting issues.”

“Casting issues?” she asked, as Gabriel snorted.

“He doesn’t want to dance with anyone,” Gabriel supplied. “But since Lye’s third-year class is a partner class, he still prepared partner choreography.”

“Oh.” She glanced between them, waiting for Elijah to get upset that Gabriel was teasing him, but Elijah remained relaxed, a small smile hooking at the edges of his mouth. “I didn’t realise. You barely come to class. I don’t know how you get away with it.”

“I send Lye weekly recordings of my progress.” Elijah leaned forward an inch, a spark lighting up his gaze. “He seems ... content. Are you scoping me out, Sigma?”

“You are my competition.” She sniffed, crossing her arms. “I want to get into Lye’s class next year too.”

“Why?” Gabriel cocked a brow. “It’s an Acro Duo class. *Duo* being the key word.”

She widened her eyes at him in mock horror. “Are you saying I don’t have any friends?”

He smirked, but it wasn’t cruel. It was ... weirdly intimate. And it was *Gabriel*, so that added a whole other layer of weird to the intimacy.

“He’s saying you’re very selective about who gets close to you.” Elijah sounded almost bored.

“Yep,” Gabriel’s lips popped on the word. “And Acro Duo work is a whole lot of getting close.”

“Are you on the wait list?” she asked, because it really

sounded like he was, which was surprising. She couldn't picture Gabriel dripping in sweat, with chalk-dusted hands, tangled up with a dance partner.

Gabriel crooked his finger at her instead of answering. She glanced at Elijah, but he only dropped his head to the side, his eyes sweeping over her, a challenging glint entering his expression. She stepped toward Gabriel, stopping between his knees.

"Come here," he muttered, tilting his chin up.

She ducked down, assuming he didn't want his words overheard, her eyes flickering nervously between his.

He was showing her that spark of personality again, that little hint of interest that he usually buried behind a wall of cool, calm, and collected.

"Closer, Puppy."

She made a face at him. It probably looked scared.

Elijah chuckled, and the sound urged her to quickly duck her face beside Gabriel's, his dark blond hair brushing her nose. His scent was soothing and gentle, so subtle it made her want to press her nose to his skin and inhale. He was clean and crisp like fresh linen hung out to dry in the sun. It was so comforting it almost made her toes curl as she imagined slipping into a bed with fresh cotton sheets drifting against her skin.

"We're going to need to know all the classes you want to waitlist for next year."

"Why?" She drew back just enough to look at him in

the eye again, but he nudged his head to the side, silently demanding she move closer again.

When she tucked her head back beside his, this time, she felt his fingers on the back of her knee. The touch seemed experimental, just a light brush of his fingertips testing out the surface of her skin. She immediately got goosebumps, the hollow ache inside her growing just that little bit sharper.

"Because we need to make sure there's at least one of us in each of your classes," he whispered.

She started to draw back again, to demand *why* again, but this time both his hands wrapped around the backs of her thighs, jerking her forward until her chest slapped against his, her thighs pressing between his. She could even feel the hard brush of muscle against her stomach through their clothes. His scent was something she could have easily gulped up just for the rush of comfort it gave her, but his touch had the opposite effect, making her so nervous she almost felt sick.

"*Because*," he muttered, answering the "why" she hadn't had a chance to ask, "bad things happen when we leave you alone."

"Welcome to the world," she whispered back, feeling Elijah's silent attention on the side of her face. "Bad things happen. You can't stop them."

"Dance with Elijah."

"No," she said reflexively.

"Why not?" he sounded amused.

"B-Because." She drew back again, and this time he let her. She flicked a look to Elijah, but his expression was blank and relaxed—*still*. It was actually mildly infuriating at this point. She wanted to see him ruffled.

"Because?" Gabriel prompted.

"I don't know." She disentangled herself and quickly restarted her playlist, running through her routine a few more times before finally giving up. It was getting worse. She wasn't as fluid as she had been before the settlement tour, and her stamina wasn't the same.

AFTER WORKING IN THE LIBRARY FOR THE REST OF THE DAY WITH Gabriel and Elijah, she trailed them to the dining hall for dinner, still preoccupied with the task of choosing her classes for the next year. Her father had already emailed her to advise on which classes she *should* take, and to inform her that they would be deciding her class list on Monday night after he returned to Ironside.

It was an improvement on him deciding everything and her finding out what she was in store for without even a conversation, but she wasn't sure she liked the fact that there was progress. He was trying to loop her in because he thought she was playing the game and was *proud* of the cunning he thought he had perceived in her.

But she was only trying to survive, just like she had every day in that penthouse apartment with her mother.

The only difference was that her father wasn't the only monster under her bed anymore.

"That's our booth." Elijah pointed to the alcove she usually saw the Alphas in. "Meet us there after you have your food."

She watched them walk off with a bemused expression. They *knew* booths weren't reserved, right? They had to. But still ... now that she thought about it, nobody else dared to approach that particular table.

Must be nice to be untouchable.

She grabbed a tray and stopped before the food bar. It was Japanese-themed, with an extensive noodle and ramen section, a colourful sushi section, and a section for meats and tempura, which she passed by without a glance. She picked up a bowl of rice, a smaller bowl of vegetables, and some noodles in a miso broth, the steam curling up from the food making her stomach clench.

She hadn't had much of an appetite lately, so it took her a few moments to realise she was *hungry*. She also hadn't had to pause any of her activity to have a sneezing or coughing fit, and her head was clear of the fuzzy, disorientated feeling that had been plaguing her for weeks.

With a frown, she pulled out her phone and quickly navigated to the group chat, not really looking where she was going.

Isobel: What did you guys do to me last night?

"You're running out of time."

She pulled up short, her attention snapping up past her tray as someone grabbed the other side of it.

Crowe was glowering down at her, looking like he wanted to flip her tray up into her face. After a moment, he forcibly released it, spilling miso soup across the surface.

"What?" she managed, catching sight of Eve hovering a few tables away, pretending to talk to her friends, her gaze fixed sharply on Isobel and Crowe.

"You're running out of time." He enunciated each of the words like she was hard of hearing. "It's almost summer break."

Her mind went blank, her lips parting in shock. "It was you."

He didn't answer.

"The messages?" she pressed, an unfamiliar spark of fury igniting somewhere inside her. "You took that video."

He still didn't answer, but his complete lack of shock or confusion seemed to speak volumes.

"Did you hear me, slut?" He leaned over the tray, smelling like sweat and fear. "You're out of fucking time. Do you have an answer or not?"

No ... he didn't smell like fear. He *felt* like fear. It was so strong it reached out to her even though he wasn't an Alpha and her walls were still solidly raised.

He was *swimming* in it.

"I do," she said, simply.

The look of hatred in his eyes burned hotter. "What's it called, then?"

"The Stone Dahlia."

"And how do you get in, Sigma?"

"You enter through the old boathouse by the lake."

"Then why haven't you?" He turned his head, spitting on the ground. "They'll be making their offer to you tomorrow morning. It's just a formality. You can't actually refuse."

He stalked off, and she glanced over at Eve, but the other girl was now pretending not to have noticed the interaction at all, laughing easily with her hand on the arm of an Omega girl. Isobel narrowed her eyes, noticing again that Eve seemed to have lost weight, her usual clothes hanging off her frame. The dark circles beneath her eyes unceasing.

Not Isobel's problem.

She hurried over to the Alpha booth, slipping onto the edge of the bench seat without looking to see who else was there, except Gabriel, who sat opposite her and had been half-raised from his seat like he was about to come after her. He eased back down when she did, and she felt his attention on her. Not just him. She smelled saltwater and sunshine, and heady whiskey nearby. Cian and Niko.

Still, she didn't tear her attention from Crowe, zeroing in on his table. He sat alone, staring down at an untouched tray, a vacant look on his face. Bellamy sat separately, surrounded by his usual group of loyal supporters. Crowe's hair had grown longer and now hung shaggy and choppy, the unwashed length dangling over his eyes. He had put on weight, and his skin was sunken and sallow. Whenever someone passed by too close to where he sat, his eyes darted about in a panicked sort of way before resolutely fixing back to his tray.

He looked *terrible*. Defeated. Afraid. Traumatised.

"It was him?" Elijah's soft whisper broke into her thoughts. "The behemoth?"

She nodded, barely, aware they couldn't discuss anything openly.

"What did you guys ..." She cleared her throat, glancing up to do a quick inventory of who was sitting in the booth: Elijah, Gabriel, Cian, and Niko. "I mean ... did any of you do something to him?"

"That's not us, doll." Cian nodded toward Crowe. "That's someone else's doing." He dipped close, his breath brushing her ear as he whispered, "Several someones."

"Are you sure?" she pressed, biting on the inside of her cheek to keep from blurting out accusations. Mostly directed toward Theodore or Oscar.

Cian slapped a napkin onto her tray to soak up the spilled liquid. "Mostly sure. I think you got a message."

She pulled out her phone with a frown.

Theodore: You've forgotten?

Kilian: What do you remember?

Oscar: Bad things.

Moses: Filthy things.

Theodore: Moses, what the actual fuck.

She shook her head, typing out a reply.

Isobel: I know you weren't there, Moses. You smell like stomped-on flowers. It's hard to miss.

Moses: YOU CAN SCENT US?

"Little wolf." Niko laughed out loud, reading his phone like it was a novel he was particularly invested in while he shovelled food into his mouth with the other hand.

Kilian: What do you remember, baby?

Cian groaned next to her, muttering, "This fucking guy."

Isobel: I remember taking a shower?

"Suitably vague," Elijah mumbled.

They were all on their phones, preferring to have this conversation away from the prying ears of Ironside.

"Yeah, we might need specifics, Carter." Niko seemed to be enjoying himself.

She scowled, quickly tapping out another message.

Isobel: I remember taking a shower with Kilian and Theo.

Kilian: You fell asleep.

Isobel: In the shower?

Theodore: On me.

Isobel: ... In the shower?

Cian snorted.

Theodore: A few steps out of the shower.

"Don't apologise." Theodore's shadow fell across her, his eyes glancing at the screen of her phone, where she had begun to do exactly that.

She quickly scooted over on the bench, accidentally bumping into Cian. He slid all the way to the back of the booth, pulling her with him, and then he dragged their trays over. The rest of the Alphas filtered in, some of them bringing extra food for Niko, who must have been texting them his orders.

Kilian slid a plate of sushi down the table to Niko and then sat, announcing, "We asked the officials to put a couch in my room big enough for me to sleep on." He let his voice carry naturally, probably wanting the cameras to pick up on this particular conversation. "They should be done by the time we finish dinner."

"You didn't run into any issues?" Elijah asked.

Kilian shook his head, gulping down half a glass of water before he pulled his tray closer. "Some of us are acting as Isobel's surrogates. That means keeping her safe. They must have expected us to do something when they brought Ev—"

"Don't say her name," Oscar snarled. He had been sitting quietly with Moses on the other side of the booth, acting disinterested in the lively conversation between Theodore, Cian, and Niko, but now his head was lifted from his food, his dark eyes furious.

"When they brought the Omega back," Kilian smoothly corrected, instead of acting like Oscar was being ridiculous. "Anyway, you can sleep in my bed, and I'll sleep on the couch." Kilian glanced up at her, his expression crafted into a polite, friendly arrangement of his angelic features. "You already have enough popularity points for a spot in Dorm A, right?"

Isobel nodded. "My father said the Mate Finder campaign took care of that." Her father had actually said the *Vermont attack* had taken care of it, but if she repeated those exact words, she might actually vomit before she reached the end of the sentence.

"Good." Kilian lifted a shoulder in a shrug, his muscles shifting beneath his shirt. A shirt that looked pretty good, actually. She might have to hunt it out of his closet later. "Then we're agreed, right? You'll stay with me until they give you your own room? You've more than earned it."

Her phone vibrated before she could answer, and she checked her messages.

Unknown: Hey.

Unknown: It's Sophia.

She blinked at her screen in surprise. Cian and Theodore both drifted closer, peering down into her lap, giving her no privacy.

"The girl from the hospital?" Theodore muttered lowly, sounding confused.

Unknown: I got your number from Mama's records.

She saved the number and was about to reply when Cian caught her hand, stopping her.

"Let's see what she has to say," he murmured against the top of her head.

"Who?" Gabriel asked from across the table.

"Tell you later," Theodore said, watching as the typing dots popped up on her screen again.

Sophia: I need your help.

Sophia: It's urgent.

Sophia: I feel like such a dick but ... nobody else will listen to me. I need you.

Sophia: Full disclosure, when I say you, I mean your Alphas.

Isobel's grip tightened, a chill creeping up her spine.

Beside her, Cian let out a low whistle. "That was fucking ballsy."

Sophia: Please.

"Finish your food." Theodore closed his hand around her phone, forcing it face down on her lap.

She had completely lost her appetite, her stomach clenching sickeningly as she stared at her tray. She forced her jaw to unclench, her fingers to snap around her chopsticks, but she was shaking too much, her breath sounding too loud in her ears. She wasn't even sure why she was overreacting so much.

"I'm going." She dropped her chopsticks, waiting for Theodore to make room for her.

He didn't, but he sighed, staring at his tray. "Of course you are. And I'll go with you, but you need to eat something first. If you lose any more weight, I'm going to drag you onto my lap during mealtimes and hand-feed you myself. Is that really something you want?"

Objectively, it wasn't ... her *mind* knew that she wouldn't want the entire academy to see that, let alone everyone else in the world. But her body thought it sounded like a wonderful idea. Theodore's firm thighs beneath hers, his muscular arm wrapped around her, grip tight, while he teased the seam of her lips with salty snacks and sugary treats.

Her stomach swooped low, that hollow ache turning sharp with enough pain to make her wince. Theodore turned to her slowly, his nostrils flaring.

"Oh." His eyes dipped over her face. "You would."

"Don't be ridiculous," she growled out.

"It's natural." Elijah surveyed her from across the table, caressing the edge of his bowl of rice with his chopsticks. "Soul infractions remind the body and mind that it should have perished in the Death Phase. You're reaching out for your mate to remind you that there are reasons to remain in this world. Pleasures, comforts. Like food. Unfortunately, your mate isn't here, so you're looking to us instead. I implore you to make use of your surrogates. Kilian, Cian, and Oscar are all well aware of what they volunteered for."

He seemed to leave out Theodore and Gabriel on purpose. Probably because of their "girlfriends."

She made a sound of frustration at him, wanting to kick him for vocalising all of that before the cameras, but then she realised it was probably a ploy of some kind to clear up the rumours circulating online that all of the Alphas were surrogating for her.

"Cian," she huffed, refusing to look at the tall Alpha beside her, his skin warm as his arm brushed against hers. "Are you busy later?"

"How much later?" he returned, his voice carrying that husky quality that he usually reserved for flirting with everyone on camera.

He didn't seem to give a single shit about his reputation.

"Five minutes." She shoved some of her food into her mouth, eating as quickly as she could.

"For what?" Cian was leaning on the table now, bending down to peer at her, his eyes crinkling in amusement as her cheeks grew puffy with the amount of food she was trying to push through her lips.

She swallowed. "I want to go to the chapel."

He nodded sagely. "You should definitely atone before you use me to ease your bond."

"I'm not going to do anything to you." She rolled her eyes, quickly filling her mouth again in the hopes that he dropped it.

He didn't. "Should I use you, then?"

There was a hard thump under the table, and Cian let out a low, deep chuckle. "Fine, fine. Let's go confess, Carter."

"Thanks." She managed around the rim of her soup

bowl, having lifted it to hide the blush spreading across her cheeks.

She tried to set her chopsticks down several times, but each time Theodore only shook his head, nodding to the unfinished food on her tray. After the third time, he ducked his head down beside hers, whispering in her ear.

"I'll let you go if you agree to watch a movie with me before you go to sleep tonight."

She glanced at him, sucking in a short breath at how close his face was before quickly turning away again.

"Why?" she muttered.

"Dessert," he answered.

"Fuck's sake." Oscar stood up suddenly, jostling his tray. "Let me out."

He paused when he was out of the booth, glancing back to her and Theodore. "Group movie night," he said stiffly. "In the common room."

"Offer still stands," Theodore whispered.

She dipped her head in a slight nod and he stood up, tugging her out of the booth. "Ready?" he asked Cian.

The other Alpha nodded, following them out of the hall and around the lake. Isobel was about to branch off and head to the residence on the other side of the chapel when Cian caught her arm, encouraging her into the chapel instead.

"There's another exit through here," he said, leading the way to a door mostly hidden along the back wall, behind the altar. He tried the handle, showing that it was unlocked, and opened it wide to reveal the outside wall of the Guardian's residence.

"How'd you know that was there?" she asked.

"I come to the chapel sometimes." For some reason, his eyes dipped to her chest. *To the chain hidden beneath her shirt ...?*

"You follow the Gifted religion?" she guessed.

He only shrugged, nodding at the open doorway. She skipped past, Theodore following wordlessly, and the three of them skirted the wall, finding themselves at the propped-open gate.

She approached the front door, knocking softly, but it was also ajar, and it squeaked, falling open further as her knuckles connected with it.

A soft, strangled sob carried out to where they stood, and she almost darted forward, but Cian caught her shoulder, holding her back. Theodore pushed the door open the rest of the way, striding into the small kitchen.

"What happened?" He sounded alarmed. "Is anyone else here? Is he okay?"

"It's just us." Sophia sounded strained.

Isobel shrugged out of Cian's hold and pushed into the room, finding Sophia and Luis on the floor, leaning against the kitchen cabinets. Luis was curled into a ball, his arms wrapped around his legs, his sobs small and terrified.

"Carter." Sophia looked up at her, tension and relief fighting across her expression. "You came."

"What happened?" Isobel tried to step forward, but Cian caught her again, his hands at her hips this time.

She glanced over her shoulder, catching his apologetic look before he tugged her back, pressing her hard against his body.

With a short sigh, she realised neither of the Alphas were going to let her near any strangers anytime soon.

"He has dreams," Sophia explained, as Theodore knelt on Luis' other side.

"You okay, little buddy?" He set a hand against Luis' shoulder, completely dwarfing the small boy.

"What kind of dreams?" Cian and Isobel asked at the same time, the same note of wariness in both their voices.

Luis lifted his head, looking at Theodore, and then Cian, his eyes wide. When he glanced at Isobel, he paused, his glasses slipping off the edge of his nose, hanging precariously by his left ear, his face soaked in tears.

"We're g-going to d-die," he whimpered.

Cian cursed, releasing Isobel. They both fell to their knees before Luis, who kept staring at Isobel like he thought she could somehow save him.

"T-The gods like y-you," he stuttered out, pointing to where her chain was hidden. "Y-You can ask them for help."

Sophia pressed her hands over Luis' ears, her attention passing between Isobel and the Alphas. "He said he heard sirens, screaming, alarms going off. And he said he saw me and mama dead in the chapel."

She released Luis, popping up to fill a glass with water before returning and pressing it into his hands.

"Hi." Cian held out his hand after Luis pushed the glass away. "I'm Ashford."

"I know." Luis quickly tried to right his glasses, his hand trembling violently as it disappeared in Cian's grip. "I'm L-Luis."

"How often do you have dreams that come true, Luis?" Cian reached over and straightened his glasses.

Luis made a squeaking sound, like he suddenly couldn't talk.

"Maybe once or twice a year," Sophia answered for him. "They're never good ... but they always come true."

"That's his first mistake." Cian painted on a reassuring smile. "The divination ability is never certain. Unpractised users will make their own predictions come true simply by believing they will."

Luis' watery, mahogany stare was growing wider by the second.

"How far apart are the dreams from the incidents that occur?" Cian asked Sophia.

"Sometimes a month, sometimes the next day." She slipped her hands beneath Luis' arms. "Come on, grasshopper. Let's go lie down, okay?"

They all stood, watching as his eyes grew unfocussed, his stance wobbly as Sophia pulled him to his feet.

"He's about to crash hard," Sophia explained. "If you have any other questions for him, you have a few minutes until he passes out."

"I'll take him." Cian bent down, banding an arm around Luis' legs and pulling him up to his wide chest. The little boy's head immediately lolled onto Cian's shoulder, his eyes fluttering shut.

"Bedroom?" Cian asked.

Sophia gave him directions before motioning the kitchen table. "Please, sit. I'll make tea."

Her accent deepened with a wobble, her eyes filling with tears now that Luis was out of sight. Isobel caught her shoulder and steered her to one of the chairs.

"You sit," she instructed the other girl gently. "I'll make the tea."

Isobel glanced to Theodore as she filled the kettle, hoping he would understand that she wanted him to distract Sophia so she could siphon away some of the worry. His expression darkened, and he glanced once at the Delta girl who was too busy staring at the table and trying not to cry to notice the minute shake of his head. Isobel pushed out her lower lip, silently begging him.

His gaze narrowed, his arms crossing tightly over his chest before he let out a short, sharp breath, turning back to Sophia. "If this is *any* sort of trick or—"

"It's not," Isobel muttered, interrupting the threat before he could voice it. She had cracked open her walls, and was slowly, subtly sipping on Sophia's emotion. It was a chilling cocktail of terror and disbelief, made frigid with shock.

"I'm not here to play the stupid game," Sophia snapped, immediately furious with Theodore. "I'm here to *help* people. I don't give two shits about tricks and traps unless they might cause harm to *my family*."

"Where's your mother?" Theodore asked, without even missing a beat, his tone unapologetic.

Isobel bit back a wave of nausea, cutting herself off from Sophia's emotions as she pulled four mugs down from the cupboard, able to see where they were through the mottled glass cabinet doors.

"She's at the hospital for the next hour," Sophia answered. "She'll be mad if she finds out I told any of you this. She doesn't trust any of these Ironside narcissists. No offence."

Isobel poured the hot water and carried the cups over to the table before claiming a seat.

"You're here." Theodore said. "You're an Ironside person as well."

"I'm here to *serve* the Ironside people, so not really." Sophia shrugged, curling her hands around the mug like she needed the heat to warm her. "Look, I'm sorry ... I don't know why I thought you could help." She shook her head. "Luis was having a massive panic attack and I just ... for a second I thought it was going to happen like *now*. I wasn't thinking straight."

"Were you trying to get to me?" Cian asked, entering the room again. He picked up Isobel's chair, nudging it up against Theodore's before dragging another chair to her other side and dropping into it, boxing her in.

Isobel shifted nervously, uncomfortably aware of the tension lining both of the Alphas, of the hardness in their guarded eyes and the way they were treating Sophia like some sort of double agent trying to lure Isobel into a secret lair full of Ironside spies, just salivating at the mouth for the opportunity to tear back into her skin.

She leaned forward a little, drawing Sophia's focus. "Ignore them," she suggested. "Cian was there in Vermont and Theodore had to spend all that time in the hospital with me. They're just being careful. But ... I am a little confused. Isn't this something you should be taking to the officials? To your mom? If your lives are in danger, you need to tell someone."

"Oh, I will." She laughed dryly, all humour wiped from the sound. "Watch them double security for themselves and their precious Alphas. No offence." She flicked a quick glance to either side of Isobel. "Again." This time she looked a little guilty for the harsh words.

Theodore and Cian stayed quiet, Theodore's hand falling to the top of Isobel's spine, his fingers brushing against the base of her neck.

"You said in your message that you needed the Alphas," she prompted Sophia.

Sophia nodded, staring down into her mug. "Ashford, specifically." She glanced up to Cian, her expression wary. "Have you seen anything?"

He responded, "I need to already be aware about something before I can use divination to find out more about it."

"So?" Sophia swallowed, her face wincing. "Could you? Find out more?"

"About someone running around the academy murdering people?" Cian asked dryly. "Yeah, I think I could spare the time. Thanks for bringing it to my attention."

"First step is to take it to the officials," Theodore said firmly, his grip drifting up so that his fingertips could reach more of Isobel's skin above the collar of her shirt. "Make it official, make a big deal about it, and do it tonight. Then follow it up again in the morning. Ask them outright what they're doing about it. You're right—they will tighten security for themselves, but singling out us over the rest of the student body is far more difficult and impracticable than simply tightening security around the entry and exit points to the academy. That should handle the situation if the attacker is from outside."

"And if they're already in here?" Isobel asked, masking a shudder.

She had seen enough of death and almost death.

"That's what I need to figure out," Cian announced, standing. "We should get going. We'll be in touch. You need to convince Luis that *believing* things will happen does half the work."

Sophia arched a dark brow at Cian, some of her fear making way for curiosity. "You follow the religion, don't you?"

"What's it to you?" he shot back, glancing at Isobel like he was contemplating bodily tossing her over his shoulder so he could leave.

She stood, moving with him to the door.

"Just wondering what your thoughts are on Carter's long-distance bond," Sophia said, using her sleeve to wipe away the dampness that still marked her cheeks. "If you follow the religion, then you know it's never happened before."

"Look at her." Cian suddenly spun Isobel around, his hands tight on her shoulders, his tension leaking into his grip. "Adorable sex on a stick right here, and it's even sweeter because she would never dirty herself with someone like me, even if I am an Alpha. I've got a bit of a reputation around here, haven't I? The only thing I *think* is that I'm a bastard who's going to be cursed by each of the gods for every day I take advantage of this situation."

Sophia's brows both popped up. "O-kay."

Isobel just stood there, her face heating.

"I think that's enough prying for one day." Theodore opened the door, ushering them through.

"Carter!" Sophia called out when they were halfway to the gate. "Thanks."

Isobel nodded at her, waiting until they were back in the chapel before she cut her attention to Cian. "That was a bit much."

He smirked, rubbing tattooed hands against his mouth, flashing her a tongue piercing that had her pulling up short.

When did you get that? It was on the tip of her tongue, but she bit back the question because it was none of her business.

"Which part?" he asked, brimming with fake innocence.

"Cut it out." Theodore punched his shoulder. "Let's go. We've got shit to figure out."

10
PROBLEMATIC

Isobel leaned against the tiled wall of Theodore's shower, completely exhausted. The Alphas had called a group meeting to go over every detail of the "Ironside Employee" with the divination ability, who had foreseen "a terrorist attack" on Ironside. The details had been twisted as much as possible to make sure the story couldn't be skimmed over.

Cian and Theodore had made it sound like they had been in the chapel with her, the three of them "praying for the officials to find her mate in good health" when two Ironside employees stumbled in, and the situation escalated from there.

The level of performance needed for the entire conversation had drained her.

She washed her hair and scrubbed her skin, wishing for the first time in years that her father hadn't organised for her body hair to be lasered off. He had been getting annoyed at how much her morning shower routine was cutting into her rigid schedule, but now she wished she had something else to do, something to take up more of her time before she had to drag herself out again to deal with *yet another* attack that may or may not even happen.

It wasn't that she wasn't taking it seriously, but there was some sort of block in her mind, her thoughts recoiling whenever she tried to acknowledge the possibility of what Luis had seen.

There was a horrible, dark place inside her that whispered, *You won't survive a third time.*

GABRIEL CLOSED THE DOOR TO HIS ROOM WITH A SILENT *SNICK*, pulling off his shirt and dropping it into the laundry hamper as he walked into his bathroom. They were all having showers before reconvening for "movie night." He was pretty sure they all just wanted to sleep, but it was hard to go their separate ways. Isobel had been slipping them little hints of her own pain all day, and she didn't even realise she was doing it. She should have been completely settled after last night, but something was off, and he couldn't figure out what it was.

He had watched her most of the day. Whenever she touched her stomach, that confused dip weighing down her brow, that was when he felt it. The little twinge of pain. Elijah had felt it, too, and he knew from the shift in everyone's scents over dinner that they had also felt something.

Whatever it was, he knew they all wanted to keep an eye on her.

Maybe it was that infernal chain hooked into her skin, or maybe it was a brand-new layer of hell in the form of a new side effect they had yet to encounter. Whatever it was, she was one of them now, and they would deal with it together.

Well ... that and nobody wanted to leave her alone with Theodore.

He turned on the water and stripped off the rest of his clothes, setting his phone beside the sink. After folding a fresh set of clothes onto the bathroom bench, he stepped beneath the spray. He had just ducked his head beneath the warm water when the world around him tipped off its axis. He stumbled into the wall, shooting out a hand to steady himself as his vision blurred.

Suddenly, he wasn't staring down at *his* shower.

He was staring at a similar shower floor, the small blue tiles glittering with the shower spray as small, pale feet paced back and forth.

He could feel everything.

Her frustration, her fear, and the giant block of trauma that hovered over her head, threatening to crush her if her mind twisted down the wrong path. She walked from one side of the shower to the other, muttering low to herself.

"You can handle this. You can do this. You've dealt with worse. *Nothing has even happened yet.* Get a hold of yourself."

She felt alone.

Didn't she realise nobody would ever hurt her again?

They couldn't control every variable in the known world, but the girl had *ten* half-bonded mates. It was as close as she could get to complete and utter protection.

Except they had already failed once, hadn't they?

She sank onto the tiled ledge, her head tipping back to stare at the water pouring down from the giant rainfall shower head.

"Think of literally anything else," she instructed herself strictly.

Gabriel contained a smirk, leaning heavily against the wall—since the sensation of being inside two bodies was so disorientating. He hadn't pegged her for a person who talked to herself, but maybe it was the stress getting to her.

She suddenly looked down, and he froze, getting an eyeful of nipples the exact same shade as her soft lips, and long, pale legs stretching out to catch the spray of water.

Shit. He managed to push away from the wall, feeling his way out of the shower and cringing at the water that sluiced all over the floor as he felt for his phone.

He made it back to the bench, probably drenching his

phone as he tried to focus on the screen. Isobel's tired sigh travelled through him, and he fought off a pounding headache as he focussed just long enough to navigate into a secure message screen.

He snapped straight back into her head as soon as he stopped fighting it, watching as she rested her hands against her thighs, rubbing up and down in an attempt to calm herself. It took several rounds of deep breathing to fight off the sick feeling that threatened to make him black out from his brief rebellion against the side effect.

The bond did *not* fuck around, apparently. He would have to make note of that later.

Gabriel raised his phone to his mouth, knowing intuitively where the text-to-speech button was.

"I'm in your head."

She looked up when she heard her phone, leaning out of the shower to snatch it off the counter.

Hidden member: Preview unavailable.

She tapped on the message.

Unknown: I'm in your head.

She swore softly, clicking on the "unknown" contact. It gave her the standard error when secured messaging was turned on.

This feature is currently hidden.

Her fingers flew over the screen. *Isobel: Who is this?*

"You have ten guesses." He spoke the message, hearing her slight chuckle as it popped up on her screen.

She started typing again, before stopping, fixing her

gaze to the wall. "Why am I typing?" She shook her head, another tired sigh slipping out. "Will you text me when you're out of my head, please?"

"Yes." He kept his finger on the button, pausing. "Are you okay?"

"I just want to think about something *other* than death or disaster for a second," she huffed out. "Is this a professor?"

"No."

"Are you telling the truth?"

"Yes."

She waited, before whispering, "Then why? Is it—"

"Isobel." He sent the message, cutting her off as she glanced at her screen.

He swallowed. She didn't realise she had dropped the hand holding her phone, and he got another goddamn eyeful as she glanced down at her screen.

He couldn't close his eyes, couldn't block her out.

"Call Isobel," he grumbled, raising his phone to his ear.

"Gabe-Gabriel?" She saw his name flash across her screen before she answered.

"Yeah."

"Are you okay?" she asked, fixing her eyes back to the wall after she clicked the speakerphone button and set the phone onto a small shelf behind her head—probably so that she wouldn't keep accidentally looking down at her lap. "I'm ... sorry—"

Why was her pussy completely shaved? Must have been a rich girl thing, because he highly doubted it was to keep herself tidy for a sexual partner. He had never even *met* a more obvious virgin.

"For something you can't control? I'm fine. Are you okay?"

"Of course." She lowered her voice as though it might prevent him from detecting her lie.

He was starting to feel the pressure of needing everything to go right, but he pushed back his own agitation, working hard to gentle his tone.

"Something has been happening to you all day. Do you want to tell me what it is?"

"Just this weird feeling." She was holding her stomach again. He couldn't see it, but he could feel it. Soft skin wrapping subtle muscle, smooth as silk beneath her touch, water dripping from her fingertips. She had a beautiful body. It was like it had been created specifically to dance. It didn't seem to matter what she wore or what she was doing, clothes fit her figure like they were made just for her, even when they were five sizes too big.

"Describe it?" he prompted.

"Just ... hollow pain. Sharp. I don't know. There's just this emptiness inside my stomach."

"Like hunger?"

"I guess, but different."

"Longing?"

She paused, but her soft stroking across the gentle muscles of her stomach continued. She must not have realised that he could feel what she was doing.

"Maybe," she whispered. "Something like that."

"Close your eyes," Gabriel ordered, forgetting to make his voice soft.

She flinched in shock, but his vision suddenly filled with darkness, and he let out a relieved breath.

"Good." He kept his voice no more than a gentle exhale. "I want you to press your hand to the ache and think about what you want, what you need."

She obeyed him again, like she always did. It made him itch with the need to give her another order, but it also made him inexplicably furious.

Was this how the Omega bitch managed to get her hooks in so easily?

Isobel was a people-pleaser. She was too fucking easy to take advantage of.

He focussed on her body, on the hollow pain that she was sharing with him. It was awful. Sharp and cavernous. Not so much longing as keen desperation.

"I don't know." Her words were shaky. "I think ..." She pulled her hand away, breathing a broken sigh. The ache eased, somewhat. "Touching myself makes it worse."

Ah, fuck.

Of all the side effects, she had to get *this* one.

"I think I know what it is." He swore softly, shifting on the bench. "But there's nothing we can do to fix it."

"What are you talking about?" She was touching her stomach again like she couldn't help herself.

"It's one of the more ... brutal side effects. A sort of frenzy that only eases when you have sex with your mate."

She laughed, sudden and hollow. "How many of them?"

"I wasn't advising it." A growl tried to ride Gabriel's tone, but he bit it forcefully back. He cared more than he thought he would—not that the Sigma might fuck one of the other Alphas, but that she wasn't ready, and he knew it.

And maybe he also cared if she fucked one of the other Alphas.

That would be very inconvenient, if true. Because it was inevitable, at least with Theodore.

The two of them were like magnets, orbiting around the edge of a force that snapped them together the second they were close enough. It was like they belonged to each other.

And maybe Gabriel cared a little bit about that.

Maybe he cared a lot about that.

Maybe that made him extremely uncomfortable.

"I know," she said. "How long does it last? It's bearable at the moment."

He felt a muted little pang of something in his own

body, but he was too tuned into her to recognise what it was, not that he was very good at recognising feelings in the first instance anyway.

"I can actually feel what you can feel right now," he decided to tell her.

"And?" She sounded combative. Stubborn. "It really isn't that bad."

"It might get worse." He grunted when her fingers drifted up, over the chain embedded into her skin. "But if I remember correctly, it won't last more than a day."

She glanced down, and all the breath left his body. He had seen her naked earlier in the year when she pulled herself from the lake and onto the dock. He remembered thinking back then that she looked like a painting, and the errant observation popped up again.

The alabaster tone of her skin seemed to sparkle, a mist of water scattered across her chest, each little droplet shifting and dribbling with each gentle swell of her breath. Her hair twisted across her skin in wet spirals, looking like an artist had painted them there with adoring brush strokes.

"Shit," she hissed, diverting her attention from the chain and back to the wall. "Are you still ... um, with me?"

"Yeah." His tone was husky, and he hated it.

"Sorry," she muttered. "I'll try and get dressed without looking." She stood, reaching for the taps.

"Sit down," Gabriel said, his tone soft but laced with

iron. She did, and he drew in a steadying breath. "Now look down. Show me the chain."

She dropped her chin, one hand delicately covering the junction between her tightly crossed legs, her other arm banded across her chest.

A laugh tried to bubble up in his chest. "I've seen it all, Illy."

"Illy?" she echoed, a note of confusion in her tone.

"Just this once, just while we're alone."

"I don't understand you," she muttered, before dropping her arm. She kept her other hand on her lap.

"Does it feel like anything?" he asked.

She passed her fingers over the delicate links, pausing on the two gemstones that had appeared. "Only when it changes."

"I would have torn it out by now," he admitted quietly. "I never understood people like Cian, people who can inject ink and metal into their skin. It's disgusting."

She scoffed quietly, seeming to enjoy the feel of the links dragging against the pads of her fingers. "I think it's ... beautiful, actually."

Well on *her* it was. Every-fucking-thing was beautiful on the painting herself.

"Are you asexual?" she asked, conversationally.

It was easier to talk this way. She apparently agreed.

"No," he said. "Or sometimes, maybe. I'm sure there's a classification for it, but I've never been fond of classifying myself. It takes a special someone for me to go past a certain point."

"I don't think I'm asexual," she said. "I think I'm very, very, very not asexual."

His stomach tightened. "Weird way to announce that you're horny."

She dropped her fingers from the chain, her hand falling to her thigh. She didn't bother averting her gaze as she stretched her legs out to catch the water again.

"I wish I wasn't a virgin," she grumbled. "I wish it wasn't such a big deal. I wish I could just go get a normal boyfriend who isn't a mate and just get *rid* of all these feelings ..." She trailed off, and he realised there was a low rumbling emanating from his chest. It was rough and furious, and he could feel the spark of fear that jolted through her.

Dammit. Gabriel wrangled back the flash of furious possessiveness, not wanting to lose their moment. "Sorry," he rumbled. "I like ... talking to you like this. Being inside you makes me feel like I'm completely in control. I can see everything and you ... can't. I feel like I could tell you anything. I don't think I've ever felt like this before."

"What about Elijah?" she asked, keeping her voice free of the alarm that he could feel flash through her anyway.

She thought he was fucked up.

She would be correct.

"Other than Elijah," he said.

"You said you have two best friends. You said they both sacrificed for you. Who is the other one?"

"Niko."

She was silent for too long, and when she spoke again, her vision had blurred like there were tears gathering in her eyes. "Gabe?" she whispered.

"Hmm." He couldn't trust his voice.

"Do you think we can do this?" The tears spilled over, briefly clearing her vision before filling it again. "Like ... forever? I don't want to be in pain forever. I don't want to be dancing this dance forever."

"You won't." *What the fuck are you saying, asshole?*

"How do you know?" She sniffled.

"Because I'm promising you." *Fuck, fuck, fuck, don't do that.*

"Say it properly." She trembled on the edge of openly sobbing. Her breath hitched as she waited for him to pull her back, and *god-fucking-dammit,* he didn't want to see her fall.

"I promise, Isobel."

Her sigh was shaky, her body falling limp against the wall.

"Where's your hand?" He needed to distract himself. Or her. Or both of them.

She held her hand up before her face, and Gabriel could feel her face twisting in confusion. "Right he—"

"Not that one." His purr was supposed to be

deliberate. Instead, it slipped out before he could *force* it out. "The other one."

"B-Between my legs," she stammered. "I didn't want to accidentally flash you."

"You're already covered in water and tears. You might as well be wet everywhere. Rub your clit until you are."

"W-Why?" Her breath stuttered out. Poor girl thought she needed a reason to come.

"Because as soon as you're wet enough, you're going to stick a finger into your honey and then suck on it so I know what you taste like. I've never been a huge fan of fruit, but ever since I met you, I've been craving cherries."

She choked on a tiny whine, a jolt of surprised pleasure sizzling through her body. It echoed into his, and he felt his dick filling with blood as her fingers drifted down over the flat plane of her belly.

It *broke* him the way she always obeyed.

She skipped right past her little button, finding a warm, wet channel already waiting for her, as though his order had instantly sent a rush of nectar where she needed it. It dewed her thighs as she pushed a finger inside herself.

"Jesus Christ, that's a good girl." Gabriel didn't even realise he was feeling for the heavy length of his own desire laying against his thigh. It was thickening with every little pant she caught in her throat.

"A-Are you ..." She seemed to get shy, before pushing her fingers into her mouth.

Sweet, sticky cherry burst over his tongue.

"Fuck. Shit." He gripped himself tightly, pumping once, the movement rough. "Am I what, Isobel?"

"Sure you might be asexual?" she burst out, her fingers falling out of her mouth.

He laughed, a weird spark of joy lighting inside him, the feeling so bright he couldn't figure out if it had originated from him, or from her. "Fingers back in your pussy, brat."

"I don't usually do this," she admitted breathlessly, her touches lazy, almost shy. "I mean I *have* done this, I just ..."

"You've been too busy trying to survive," he grumbled. "You forgot to live. Lucky for you, I prefer to take control. Touch your nipples, beautiful girl."

"You never talk to me like this," she gasped, her hips jerking at the reverence in his voice.

"Just this once, just while we're alone," he repeated his earlier sentiment.

She pinched one of those pretty little nipples. "I think you would be better at this than me."

"I *am* doing this." Gabriel's dick was wet before, but now he could feel his own excitement leaking from the tip, making the glide of his hand even smoother as he thought about her annoying teleporting side effect and how very convenient it would be if it activated at that moment. It was best this way, though. He wasn't sure he would be able to keep his hands to himself with her cherry essence on his tongue and the knowledge of how smooth and soft her skin was in his mind.

"Are you sure you want to live without pain, Illy?"

"W-What?"

"Two fingers," he grunted. "Now. Good. *Good girl.* Now three."

Rein it in, asshole.

He could only have sex when he was in complete control of everything that happened, and sometimes he needed to push his partner, just to make doubly sure that he was *still* in control, that they would still obey his every command. But he wasn't having sex with Isobel.

He was ... *shit*, it was so much worse than sex.

He just wanted her to feel good for once.

"Tell me what feels nice." He tried to temper the dominance wanting to rise up in his throat, to bark commands at her, to push and push and push until she cried again, because there was something not right in him, and he thought she sounded pretty when she was sniffling and calling him *Gabe.*

"I like your voice," she whispered back. "It feels good."

She was going to kill him.

Gabriel eased his hand from his throbbing length, stretching out his fingers as the need to drive into her until he had somewhere wet and warm to release into seized up in his spine.

He preferred to wear condoms, usually, and to tear

them off at the last second so that he could come on his partner, instead of having it sticking to his own flesh.

This fantasy was a new one, and he wasn't sure he liked it.

He needed to end this.

"Time to come," he demanded, the harsh edge creeping back into his voice.

But she liked it. Of course she did. She liked when he took the pressure off her shoulders and demanded she make herself feel good. Her fingers slipped from her channel, rubbing over her clit, and she flinched as she pinched her nipple too hard, almost making him explode on himself.

"I told you to do something," Gabriel said calmly. "So do it now, Illy."

She let out a small whimper, her release flooding through her body in a strong wave that had him biting his lip hard enough to draw blood. The intense feeling must have somehow jerked him back to his own body, but he barely noticed.

He had intended to deny himself, but his hand was a magnet, drawn to the flesh that was already twitching, already exploding along with her. He couldn't have held it back if he tried, and he thought he might have tried, but that was almost a distant memory, pushed aside as his thoughts filled with her taste, her breath, her scent, and the waves of her orgasm that pulsed through them both, leaving him with the violent aftershocks.

She swore quietly, the sound carrying through his phone speaker as he settled back into his body. Her next whimper was a nervous one. He stroked himself slowly, feeling his own release against his still-hard cock, too distracted to be grossed out by it.

"I think your chain is beautiful," he said on an exhale.

I think you're beautiful, he wanted to add, because she deserved pretty words and platitudes, but she deserved clear boundaries even more. There wasn't going to be a romantic relationship between them.

There couldn't be.

The Alphas were his family, and he had bet his entire life on what they were doing at Ironside.

One wrong step with Isobel was all they needed to collapse the whole foundation.

Isobel grew still, pain lacing away the gentle aftershocks that shivered through her body. She clutched her stomach, the empty cavernous feeling turning into a cyclone of horrible, sharp agony. When Theodore had touched her, it had helped ... *a lot*.

Maybe Gabriel was right about this particular side effect ... but if he had thought that sexual pleasure would help her, he was *so* wrong.

"You aren't in my head anymore, are you?" she gritted.

"No." His tone turned sharp with shock. "What happened? You sound like you're in pain."

"It's worse," she groaned.

He swore viciously. "I'm going to hang up so I can get some things together. Do you need help getting out of the shower?"

"No." She stood up to prove it, but her knees immediately buckled as pain travelled like an electric shock through her limbs.

"That's a yes, isn't it?"

"Kilian," she whispered, curling into a ball, and hugging her arms around her knees.

He was silent for a moment, but when he spoke again, it was on a soft exhale. "Okay. I'll send in Kilian." He hung up, and she focussed on trying to draw in one breath after another until the door flew open.

"Hey, baby." Kilian turned off the shower, kneeling in front of her, his hands gently lifting her face. "You okay? What happened?"

He was stroking her cheeks, his pale eyes wide with concern, his beautiful mouth cinched into a tight line.

"Pain," she moaned. "In my stomach."

"Okay. Shit. All right." He yanked a towel off the rack, squeezing out the water from her hair and doing his best to dry her off without disturbing her position. "You feel warm." His hand pressed against her forehead, a frown digging down the sides of his mouth. He switched out the towel for a fresh one, using it to bundle her up and lift her onto the bathroom counter. He caught her legs as she hugged the towel around herself, helping to lower them slowly.

She winced. “Sorry you have to take care of me all the time.”

“I like taking care of you,” he rumbled, narrowing his eyes on her face. “Take that away from me and you’ll find out what a stage-ten clinger looks like in an Alpha’s body. It isn’t pretty. You feel like being squashed into a pancake?”

She laughed, but it cut off immediately on a pained groan. Kilian extracted panties from the bundle of clothes she had brought into the bathroom with her, his fingers tucked into each side as he hooked her feet into them, his palms gliding up the sides of her shins, her thighs ...

The pain doubled.

She fell forward, her forehead catching against his shoulder, a whimper tumbling out of her throat. He stepped between her legs, quickly lifting her with one arm as he tugged the underwear around her hips.

“Almost done,” he soothed, cupping the sides of her face, and kissing each of her temples. “You’re doing so well.”

He tugged the oversized shirt over her head, pretending not to notice that it was his, which just made her want to cry and hug him at the same time. He lifted up the silk shorts she had brought in, a brow arching.

"You can't even see them under the shirt," she defended.

"I'll get something more comfortable." He ducked out of the bathroom, and she caught a glimpse of Theodore and Gabriel on the other side before the door fell closed again.

When Kilian returned, it was with a pair of loose sweatpants that swallowed her legs and needed to be rolled five times at the hips to stay on.

"Let's get you settled." He gathered her up, striding halfway across Theodore's bedroom, obviously intending to go into the hallway. She opened her mouth to protest him carrying her, and he cut her a sharp look.

"You don't feel right." Theodore appeared beside Kilian, his voice deep and uneven, his hand rubbing at his chest as he reached out to open the door for them. "Usually I can't feel you at all."

She glanced at Gabriel, but he was wearing his blank expression, only the slightest furrow between his brows. Guilt clawed at her, but it wasn't her own. It was his. It scratched and tore its way into her chest, leaving her gasping as Kilian turned into the hallway, stalked to the common room, and carefully sat her on the couch.

Niko, Cian, Oscar, and Moses were already there, leaving plenty of space around the couch that someone had obviously prepared for her. They watched on quietly, Cian pausing whatever they had been watching. Elijah walked in with Mikel and Kalen, and she twisted her fingers together, completely at a loss for what to do or say with all of their eyes on her, their concern and confusion buffering against her already-tight chest.

As soon as Kilian set her down, Gabriel pushed him away. It wasn't rough, but Kilian still arched both brows at him, his watchful gaze travelling over Gabriel's tight expression before he backed off, muttering something low to Theodore, who was also watching Gabriel with a frown.

Gabriel placed a warm, fluffy thing in her lap, and she blinked down at it in surprise.

"Hot water bottle," he grunted.

"It's pink." Her voice cracked with pain.

"And hideous." He watched as she hugged it. "It was the only cover left, and I didn't want to wait for more to come in stock in case you needed it."

It really was hideous. The cover seemed to be made of thick sheepskin, frothy and fluffy and delectable to sink her fingers into, but it was quite a sight. Also ... *when had Gabriel ordered her a hot water bottle?*

He extracted one of her arms from the pink fluff, wedging a cool glass of water into her grip, and then he was shaking pills out of a bottle, holding them before her mouth.

"Open," he demanded.

She popped her lips open, and he dropped the pills onto her tongue, the fierce look still digging into his features. She washed the medication down and he took the glass from her again, tapping a thermometer against her lips.

"Under your tongue," he demanded.

She let him take her temperature, which he seemed to note on his phone, before he pulled up a bag from the floor.

"I didn't know what you might like, so ..." He set the bag onto the couch beside her, and she peered into it, seeing a dozen different types of chocolate and candy.

"I ..." He glanced to the side, not really looking at anyone—though everyone was definitely looking at *him* with varying degrees of curiosity and confusion. "If it's what I think it is, sugar is supposed to help. There's ice cream in the freezer. Do you want ice cream? I'll get it." He spun on his heel, stalking out of the room.

Elijah gave her an unreadable look before turning and following him.

"The fuck is up with him?" Oscar grunted.

Kilian picked her up and claimed her seat, bundling her into his lap. Theodore moved the bag of snacks and fell down next to them, dragging a throw from the back of the couch and passing it to Kilian.

"Thanks." Kilian lifted her a little so that he could wrap the blanket all the way around her, tugging the edges closed over her disastrous hot water bottle.

Mikel and Kalen shared a look, Kalen arching a dark brow at the other Alpha before striding off. Mikel focussed back on her. “Let me know immediately if you need to go to the hospital.”

She nodded, and he also left.

She supposed it would look weird for the cameras if they hovered around her like concerned mother hens.

Cian grabbed the remote, pressed Play on their movie and turned the sound up until it filled the room, vibrating along the walls.

They were trying to minimise the whole incident, likely wary of saying the wrong thing or acting the wrong way. Whatever the reason, Isobel was immensely grateful. The last thing she needed, on top of the pain, was for everyone to discuss how the bond was trying to force her to have sex with one of them.

“Any news about Luis’ dream?” she asked Kilian softly, the sudden noise of the movie allowing her to speak freely.

“Cian is getting similar warnings about death, more or less,” he whispered back, as Theodore pulled her legs into his lap. “But we have no idea what it is or when it’s going to happen, which usually means it isn’t going to happen today.”

“What are we going to do?” she whispered.

“We’re sticking close together until the end of term. One of us always needs to be with at least one other Alpha, and we have to answer Mikel’s check-in messages in the group chat as soon as he sends them. So make sure you can always see or hear your phone, even while you're dancing."

What about everyone else? She wanted to ask the question. It was on the tip of her tongue, but she swallowed it back. She couldn't even protect herself, and she suddenly had more than herself to worry about.

A Tether couldn't survive without an Anchor.

If something happened to one of the Alphas, what would happen to her?

Theodore had been brushing his thumb along the arch of her foot, but he suddenly dug his nail into the sensitive skin of her ankle, drawing her attention to him with a snap, her lips parting in shock. He widened his eyes, giving her that innocent look he used to be able to pull off so well.

Not so much anymore.

"He's pretty sure nothing is going to happen tonight." Theodore wrapped his hand around her ankle, squeezing it in reassurance. "Try to relax. There's nothing more we can do about *that* problem tonight, so let's focus on this problem instead."

She schooled her face into a blank expression. "What problem?"

"Yeah," Moses drawled, his hands tucked behind his head, his dark grey gaze fixed to the screen. "What problem?"

"There's a problem?" Niko managed to sound confused and genuinely concerned.

"Wow," Oscar drawled, also refusing to shift his eyes from the screen. "You just called your little girlfriend a problem. Real smooth, Theo."

"Wallis is a problem?" Gabriel asked distractedly, walking back into the room with a tub of ice cream, a bowl, and a handful of spoons.

"Wallis is actually quite tall," Elijah added, directing the statement to Oscar.

"This conversation got problematic real fast," Kilian mumbled against her temple.

Gabriel shot him a look, holding the tub of ice cream out to Isobel. He jiggled it when she didn't immediately reach for it. As soon as it was in her hands, he quickly scooped some out into the bowl, then dropped a spoon into the tub for her, handing the rest out to the others. The bowl was for him, of course. There was no way he was going to double-dip that spoon of his.

Theodore leaned over her legs, digging his spoon into the frosty, creamy concoction.

"You all suck," he said, after licking choc chip and mint cream from the cold metal.

11
KINKY SOUR

CUDDLED UP IN THE COCOON OF KILIAN'S ARMS, ISOBEL FELT something settling inside her that had felt uneasy for months. She was swamped by his calming scent, with Theodore gently tracing his fingers over her calves and the rest of the Alphas spread out around them. For a precious half an hour—with random, muscled arms reaching over her lap to steal chocolate or candy—she felt like she belonged somewhere.

It didn't really have anything to do with *her*, though.

It was the way the Alphas were with each other. The easy, warm camaraderie they possessed. The inside jokes that sprang to their lips effortlessly, causing familiar groans and chuckles in response. It was the tension that had dissolved completely from Moses' face, the easy smile that crept over Niko's, and the way Oscar closed his eyes and kicked his legs up onto Gabriel's lap—who immediately shoved them off with a retaliatory kick.

They seemed to be so comfortable with each other that they had almost forgotten she was there at all. Just another warm body on the couch, another sweet scent mixing with Theodore and Kilian's aroma to create a light, harmonious fragrance that balanced itself out perfectly. They acted more like brothers than friends or roommates, their bond so obvious that it warmed her even though she wasn't a part of it.

Cian, Niko, and Moses had moved to the floor right in front of her, resting back on cushions they had dragged from the couches and armchairs, their long, toned limbs spreading out in every direction. Moses had a hand tucked behind his head, one of his legs bent, swinging side to side to collide with Niko's leg in a casual touch that didn't even seem to be intentional. Niko's foot was jiggling as though he would rather be doing something more active, but he laughed in a relaxed way whenever Moses muttered something sarcastic beneath his breath.

Cian's shirt had ridden up and he was absently stroking his own skin, his thumb passing back and forth across the hint of a black tattoo curling up from the waistband of his pants. When Niko hit his chest, he sat up quickly, sucking in a breath, and Elijah looked down at them in disapproval.

"Careful, it'll get infected," Gabriel grumbled.

Cian cupped a hand over where one of his nipples

would have been, pouting at Niko. "I *just* got that one done, asshole."

"Is there anywhere left you *haven't* just gotten done?" Niko tossed back casually. "You're really milking this special permission thing. Weren't you only supposed to get one tattoo finished?"

"Surrogating is hard." Cian's pout deepened, but it only made him look delightfully sultry, instead of truly pathetic. "No offence," he added, tipping his head back to glance at Isobel.

"You have my sympathies," she returned dryly.

"Appreciate it, doll. And"—he swung his head back to Niko—"for the record, I definitely have a few places left." He waggled his eyebrows.

Niko rolled his eyes, turning back to the screen. Isobel pulled out her phone, peeking over at Theodore beneath her lashes as she considered the message she wanted to send.

It was his birthday today—his and Moses'—but had they celebrated it the night before? It didn't really seem like they celebrated anything. They just performed for the cameras and then went to sleep.

She pulled up a message to Theodore, but then found herself stuck, realising that if she sent a private message to Theodore, she would have to send a private message to Moses. She switched to the group chat.

What should she say?

Kilian's chin brushed her head as he looked down at

what she was doing, and she completely lost her nerve. There were a dozen things she wanted to say to Theodore, but not too many sentiments for his brother.

She dropped her phone with a small huff, glancing over to Elijah, who was jotting things down on his tablet with an electronic pen, flicking his attention back to the movie every now and then. He was sitting closest to her on the perpendicular couch, his elbow notched on the armrest, close enough for her to reach out and tap hesitantly.

"Would you mind if I borrowed that when you're finished?" she asked, leaning toward him as much as she could without testing whether too much movement would hurt her stomach or not.

"This?" He held up the tablet, a blond brow quirking in surprise.

She promised, "Just for a little bit."

His attention switched between his screen and her face a few times, and then he tapped on it and handed it over.

"Thanks, Elijah."

His other brow jumped up at the sound of his first name. "So casual, all of a sudden."

"Do you mind?" She set the tablet on the arm of the couch, gently trying to shift her position to lean over it slightly, accepting the pen he handed over.

"I might." He didn't sound like he did. "But what will I call you? We're running out of petting zoo animals."

Gabriel scoffed, his eyes still fixed to the screen.

Oscar flicked dark eyes to Elijah, but it was impossible to tell if he was frowning because of what Elijah had said, or if that was just his relaxed face.

"Petting zoo animals?" Theodore asked distractedly, paying more attention to the movie than to their conversation.

"Rabbit and puppy," Kilian supplied.

Elijah was watching her too carefully for him to be teasing her. It was like she had taken away his main source of entertainment, so he had turned his intellect on her instead. He was poking at her like she was a trick puzzle he had only three minutes to solve, and he was happy to break her apart if he could still get to her secret centre.

For a moment, she was buffeted by the weirdness of her own thoughts, but then she realised his agitation was itching at her chest, his fingers twitching for his phone like he needed something else to do now that she had taken his tablet.

"I'm just going to draw something," she said, cocking her head at him, her hair falling over his screen.

His brow smoothed out, moving on from their brief exchange as though they had just had one of those silent conversations he and Gabriel had all the time.

Oh my god. Maybe they *had*.

He reached over, gathering her hair in his hand. She thought he was just moving it off the screen of his tablet, but he held onto it loosely as he leaned closer, pushing up his reading glasses with his other hand before tapping on his tablet, bringing up a sketching app for her.

He released her without a word when Oscar turned in the opposite direction, his head by Gabriel's thigh as he kicked his feet up into Elijah's lap, his eyes switching between Elijah and her. Elijah shoved his legs off with a disgusted murmur; Oscar immediately pulled them back up again, and then they were smiling and kicking each other with a little too much force, until Gabriel joined in, shoving Oscar off the couch.

Isobel bit back her smirk because she wasn't confident she wouldn't face retaliation if Oscar caught sight of it. She turned her attention to her task and began sketching a rough outline.

Drawing had never been one of her strengths, but there wasn't a single artistic pursuit that her father hadn't provided tutoring for, so she at least had the basics down. She detailed a bouquet of flowers, slowly losing herself in the task. Theodore was bold and charming, wily and roguish, only sometimes allowing her to glimpse the wide-eyed boy from her first year at Ironside.

She drew savage desert flowers and dark thorns, stems tangling in twine, fraying in places where the thorns cut like talons. But she added softness, too: sprays of delicate buds, wild like weeds, and puffs of pale, frothy colour.

It wasn't a typically beautiful bouquet, but it was compelling. Hard to look away from. Just like Theodore.

"Beautiful," Kilian whispered, his arm stretching out onto the table as he leaned down beside her.

She smiled to herself, saving the image, and starting on the second one. She thought it would be difficult, but it wasn't. Moses wasn't all *that* bad. He was tough and prickly, but he was also playful and flippant, fiercely loyal to his brother and his friends. She paused to pull up her phone, googling which flowers were associated with loyalty.

Iris.

She outlined a bunch of irises, using them as the base of her arrangement and colouring them a deep, midnight blue. She added wildflowers of every colour, bright and dramatic, untamed and threatening to burst from the confines of the twine she drew around them. Dark thorns popped up in between vivid flashes of colour, completing the image.

"Who are these for?" Kilian whispered, reminding her that he was still curled around, her, still leaning with her, like he didn't want her out of the cocoon of his embrace.

"What are you two whispering about?" Theodore grumbled.

Kilian's body jolted, Theodore jostling him from the other side.

"Nothing," she said, sending both images to her phone before turning off the tablet and sliding it across the table, back to Elijah. "For their birthdays," she added lowly to Kilian, as she gently pulled herself back up, careful not to move the hot water bottle too much.

Kilian pulled up with her, and she realised the credits on the movie were rolling. Cian, Moses, and Niko jumped up, slipping back into a bickering match over all the "special privileges" Cian was managing to wrangle out of the officials. Oscar rolled off the couch, stretching out his whole body before leaning over Isobel and snatching the Twizzler she had been idly sucking on while she had sketched right out of her mouth.

"Night, rabbit." He bopped her on the nose with it before sticking the still-damp end between his teeth and stalking out of the room.

She immediately swiped at her nose, wrinkling it like ... like a ... *like a rabbit.*

Theodore, who had been watching her, choked on a sudden laugh, and tried to cover it up by taking a massive swig from his water bottle. He stood, obviously thinking heavily about something as he looked down at her.

"How you feeling, pretty girl?"

Like ass. "Awesome."

His brows grew heavier, his eyes narrowing.

"Kalen and Mikki are going to want to have a quick word with you before you go to bed," Elijah warned, standing to help Gabriel, who had started collecting all the stray cushions with a frown on his face.

"Oh ... okay." She set the hot water bottle aside and opened the blanket, testing out how easy it was to stand.

Gabriel stopped what he was doing, the rest of them watching her as she shot out a hand, Kilian easily catching her as he stood behind her. Her head swam dizzily for a moment, but there was no debilitating clench of pain. It had dulled to a faint throb at some point, probably because of the medication Gabriel had given her.

"Are they ... um ..." She glanced toward the hallway. She had no idea where they even slept. "In one of the offices?"

"Try Kalen's office," Gabriel suggested, his russet eyes travelling over her slowly, an oddly calculating look pinching his features. "It's the first door after you enter the dorm. Their residences are above their offices, but they're probably still downstairs."

She nodded, giving Kilian a grateful smile before she moved to the hallway.

"You can take the bed when you're ready," Kilian called after her. "I'll sleep on the couch in my room."

She scrunched up her nose again, wondering if he had practically shouted that on purpose. Theodore and Niko needed to give him acting lessons. And that was coming from *her*. She knocked on the door to Kalen's office.

"Come in," his deep voice commanded, travelling faintly through the thick wood.

She eased the door open, glancing quickly at Kalen and Mikel before she slipped through and closed it behind her. As comfortable as she had been a few minutes ago surrounded by all the other Alphas, she was now equally as uncomfortable standing before the professors. They were quiet, both of them in chairs by the window, a book in one hand and a drink in the other. Mikel also seemed to have his laptop pushed to the side, and Kalen had another small stack of books by his elbow as though he regularly changed his mind about what he felt like reading.

She raised her head again, her face flushing as she shifted from foot to foot.

"Isobel," Kalen greeted. "Pull up a seat."

She caught the flick of his hand gesturing to a stool not far from them, and she moved to nudge it the rest of the way to their table, before perching on the edge of it. Her heart was pounding, her breath stuck in her chest, and she wasn't sure why.

Mikel held his glass out to her. "Been a day, hm?"

It took her a moment to realise he was offering it to her. She accepted it, staring down at the yellow liquid, garnished with a bright cherry and a twisted orange slice. He must have just made it because it seemed like he hadn't even taken a sip yet, but he didn't get up to make himself another. The glass was cold, little diamond patterns wrapping around the sides poking into her palm.

"Whiskey sour," Mikel explained, watching her calmly.

She sipped it and then licked her lips to savour the taste. It was rich and mellow with a zesty tang, a hint of sweetness and an undercurrent of bitterness to balance it out. She liked the drink ... but she had spent quite a lot of time training with Niko over the past month, growing familiar with the scent of whiskey in her nose and the taste of it filling her throat.

Mikel slipped a leather bookmark into his book, closed his laptop, and set the book on top of it, his gaze speculative as he watched her savour his drink.

"The Track Team approached you through a Beta," Kalen cut straight to the point, shifting in his chair to give her his full attention. He added his book to the stack by his elbow without marking his page.

Her stomach immediately churned, and she focussed her attention on the bright orange slice in her drink as she nodded. "Crowe said they would make their offer tomorrow, but that I wouldn't be able to refuse."

Kalen affirmed, "That's how it works."

He wasn't wearing his contact.

She hadn't noticed when she walked in, but she glanced up as he spoke, and now she was suddenly staring at him, her lips parted in surprise, unable to tear her attention away from his honey-brown iris. Familiar gold specks watched her in return, still circled by his gold Alpha ring.

"They irritate my fucking eyes," he explained, taking a swig from his glass.

"S-Sorry." She fiddled with Mikel's glass, not sure what else to say.

"Not your fault." He shared a quick look with Mikel. "And the Beta was right—you can't refuse the Track Team. You've seen how they recruit people. Playing hard to get only increases the amount of collateral they gather to control you. You need to come across as easy to control."

She nodded, sipping more of the sweet and tangy liquid to calm her rioting nerves. "What happens when they recruit me?"

"You'll have to wait until someone offers to become your sponsor. Usually, they parade new recruits through the Stone Dahlia for one night, and then they aren't allowed back in until a sponsorship offer is put before the Track Team by someone who is already a member. Or you could find your own sponsor and avoid all that. Since we're so close to the end of term, you could probably push it out until the start of next year. The club doesn't operate over the summer break."

"A sponsor?" She grew still, glancing between him and Mikel, waiting for further explanation. Kalen closed his eyes, rubbing the bridge of his nose and then he set his drink down, leaning forward, his face canted toward hers, his elbows notched over his strong thighs.

"You have to be sponsored by a fully-fledged member to get full membership to the Stone Dahlia," he explained. "You're the sponsor's responsibility for a year before you get your own access card. It's their way of making sure you're properly taught the rules, and also that you stay quiet."

"Okay." She sensed there was more, and for some reason, both of the professors were finding it difficult to have the conversation. There was no small amount of unease emanating from them, arcing into her and dancing around inside her chest.

"Either one of us could sponsor you." Mikel was leaning back where Kalen was leaning forward. "But that would mean you can't step into the club without us."

"That doesn't sound so bad?" Her confusion deepened. If she had to stick to *anyone* inside the club, she would prefer it to be one of them.

They were strong, stern, and ... dominant. But they were still Gifted. They weren't secondary citizens because they weren't even citizens, and if humans ran the Stone Dahlia, then there would be people down there far more powerful than Kalen and Mikel.

"The club is large." Kalen reclined again, snatching up his drink like he was annoyed at the spark of hopefulness that had briefly shot through her—and might have shown on her face. "It encompasses varied ... activities. Most of them illegal. That's where the money is made."

"Do you do illegal things?" she asked.

His lips twitched, and Mikel let out a low laugh.

"No, I don't." It was Kalen who answered, Mikel remaining quiet. "But that doesn't mean other people don't." He let her absorb that before continuing. "What Mikel and Oscar do is too dangerous. You don't *have* to end up in the same part of the club as your sponsor. You could transfer out to a different section after your sponsorship period, but more often than not, people stay with their sponsors after the year is up. So we don't think it's a good idea for you to shadow either of them."

"Elijah and Gabriel are options," Mikel added, before Isobel could utter a single, surprised word. "But they both entertain in the same section as Kalen—he sponsored both of them. I sponsored Oscar."

"So it doesn't matter if you're with me or them, you'll still be in the same section," Kalen summarised.

"And the others?" she rasped quietly. "Has everyone been recruited?"

"Not yet." Kalen's frown was deep. "They usually don't start recruiting in the first two years. Oscar, Elijah, and Gabriel were special cases. And now you. I suspect they didn't want to sit on you. You're too ... unpredictable."

"I'm *very* predictable," she countered.

"That so?" Kalen's firm lips quirked.

His easy attitude made her suddenly self-conscious, her attention snapping to Mikel again. Kalen had asked her to speak to him informally when they were alone, but Mikel hadn't.

"Am I ..." She swallowed past the crack in her voice. "Should I be calling you Professor?"

"While I'm enabling underage drinking?" Mikel winced. "I don't fucking think so. When you're outside this room? Yes."

She rolled her tongue against the roof of her mouth, trying to keep the surprise off her face. "So what do you mean by 'entertain?' What do the Gifted actually do down there?"

"Some of them just fill the space," Mikel answered. "Flitting from section to section and socialising until someone important decides to spend a small fortune to get all their attention for a night—"

"You mean like—" She immediately interrupted, horrified, but Mikel was already shaking his head.

"They just have dinner and drinks or watch the other entertainment in private booths. The humans quite literally pay *just* for their company. We're talking about the most popular, the most famous Gifted at Ironside. The biggest celebrities in the world, other than the Icons themselves. People pay through the roof just to be part of the scene, and we're the ones who create the scene."

"What do you both do?" She lifted a finger from her

glass, gesturing between the two of them nervously. They were dancing around the point too much and it was making her antsy.

"What I do isn't exactly legal," Mikel admitted. "There's an unregulated ring down there. We fight, and the humans bet on us. It's one of the most popular sections of the club."

"Do they *make* you do that?" she asked quietly, unable to read his face. "And Oscar?"

"No." His eyes flashed in amusement. "I was originally with Kalen, but when I realised they were trying to recruit Oscar, I switched over. I thought it would be a good outlet for him."

"You get beat up for Oscar?" she blurted, before sinking her teeth into her lower lip, her face flooding with colour.

Mikel only regarded her with cool amusement. "No, Carter. That would imply I *lose*. I never lose."

"Not even against Niko?"

His amusement deepened. "You think Niko was born like that? Someone had to teach him."

"Right." She shuffled back on the stool. "Of course." She was starting to sweat. She crossed her legs distractedly and then uncrossed them again, the giant sweatpants making her movements ungainly.

"W-What about you?" She barely managed to flick her eyes up to Kalen long enough to let him know she was speaking to him before she hid away behind the sweep of her eyelashes again.

"I also hurt people," he admitted, trying to make his voice soft. Instead, it just came out as a low, growly rumble. "But they ask me to. The club has fetish rooms."

"Like ... whips and leather?" Her eyes widened, twitching up to his—except they didn't make it past his angular chin.

"I'm sure there's someone dressed in leather in one of the rooms, and yes, I've used whips before. Members of the club can assign themselves to a fetish room and the humans will either pay to play or pay to watch. Some of the rooms are so popular they have waitlists months long. All of us in Dorm A send our Ironside stipends home and those of us who work in the Stone Dahlia make our earnings available to the others."

So *that's* how the boys were affording expensive gifts from Ironside Row.

She finally managed to hold Kalen's stare, her attention flitting over the stern mask of his features. He was watching her carefully, warily, flashing the tiniest spark of amusement that disappeared from his eyes when he blinked it away.

"You said Elijah and Gabriel work with you?"

"Not *with* me, exactly," Kalen specified. "They run a room together."

"What's the um ... what do they ... you know ...?"

"Ask me properly anyway," Kalen suggested. He seemed to be trying to speak lightly and casually, likely for her sake, but his voice was too deep and textured, his stare far too heavy and focussed.

Mikel arched a sharp brow at her, somehow able to prompt her without a word, like he was giving her a shove in the middle of her back.

"What's their fetish?" she quickly asked, hiding her blush behind Mikel's glass as she hurriedly swallowed the rest of his drink. The cherry slipped into her mouth, and she caught the stem, sucking off the whiskey flavour coating its skin.

For a single, insane moment, she wondered if that was what it would taste like if she kissed Niko. Tart and smoky.

And then she realised she was thinking *ridiculous* thoughts, and she quickly shoved them out of her brain.

And then Mikel decided to drop a bomb on her.

"Degradation," he said plainly. "Humiliation. Sexual and physical torture."

Her mouth fell open and the cherry tumbled onto her lap. Both of the professors watched quietly as it rolled along her thigh and tipped onto the floor, bouncing twice.

She had so many questions, they all tripped over themselves on the tip of her tongue, giving her the precious few seconds she needed to realise that she shouldn't voice any of them. She had no right to judge what people chose to do of their own free will.

If a human wanted Elijah and Gabriel to *humiliate* and *torture* them, then ... fine? Right?

And if Elijah and Gabriel wanted to ...

She swallowed, carefully setting her glass on the table beside Kalen's. She fiddled with her fingers in her lap as she waited for them to continue. They were trying to baby-step her into this conversation, and she had already made it uncomfortable enough.

Kalen's eyes traced her face, reading something there that sparked satisfaction in his expression.

He licked his lips, saying, "My speciality is Shibari. It's a form of rope bondage. It's not all about sex. It's an art form, a kind of meditation for some people."

Rope bondage and torture.

Artistic expression and humiliation.

Degradation and meditation.

She bobbed her head, trying to visualise what Kalen was talking about before realising they were laying out her options before her, waiting for her to decide.

She could shadow Gabriel or Elijah and watch them torture people, or she could shadow Kalen and watch him tie people up. It didn't sound like Mikel and Oscar were on the table as options, and she was coming to the uncomfortable realisation that Mikel might have been as scarred as he was from those fights, and she wasn't sure she had the stomach to watch it happen night after night.

"How often?" she asked quietly.

"Generally once a week." Mikel tipped out of his chair, leaning over her to snatch the cherry from the floor. His stormy scent flooded over her as he popped it into his empty glass and resettled in his armchair. "Kalen could always transfer somewhere else, but his fetish room might present a more ... private and controlled environment for you—if slightly confronting. He has a firm hand over his audience. He can't control everyone else in the wider club if he decides to become a floater for you. We don't know exactly why they wanted to recruit you so early, so playing it safe might be a good idea."

"Mhmm." She chewed on her lip as she nervously turned to properly face Kalen. She wasn't sure if there was any kind of formality required, but she didn't want to do it wrong. "Will you be my sponsor?"

His lips firmed into an unyielding line, approval rushing over his expression fast enough that she was sure she had misread it when it disappeared. He wasn't saying anything, and she wondered if she had to say more to appease their concerns.

Whatever they were feeling, it wasn't negative, because there was only her own nervousness churning in her stomach. Either they were feeling nothing at all, or they were expelling an impressive amount of effort to keep their feelings under lock so that she wouldn't be influenced during what was clearly an important conversation for them. That fact alone stopped her from lowering her wall and reaching out to feel their emotions against their will.

Kalen let out a short breath. "If you were one of our Alphas, this conversation wouldn't even be happening. We would decide what was best for you based on your individual capabilities and needs, and we would assign you to whoever suits you best. That's how we work here. It's the *only* way any of this works."

"We're at a bit of a loss," Mikel added, his tone low. "We don't know enough about you. If we assign you to Kalen and then later find out that you can't handle—"

"I can handle anything," she interrupted, straightening her spine. "Put me in the ring with Oscar, I don't care."

Mikel's grin twitched into being, his eyes sparkling. "Maybe another time. Please understand what we're saying here, Isobel. We're talking about throwing a virgin into a kink club and asking her to swim."

She opened her mouth and then closed it again, an embarrassed sound catching in the back of her throat. "I'm not a child," she muttered. "And I have some experience. What makes you think I'm a virgin? Because nobody would want to date a Sigma?"

The last part was tacked on with a wince, and she wished she could have taken it back as soon as she said it.

"Because you're the colour of the rug," Kalen remarked calmly, pointing to the Persian carpet beneath them, where scarlet thread twisted in bright patterns. "And Moses was your first kiss, wasn't he?"

"Maybe." She firmed her lips. "You Alphas really like to gossip."

Kalen scoffed. "It's our job to monitor them. And now it's our job to monitor you. If Moses was your first kiss, who would you have had time to fuck between then and now?" He frowned, eyes flicking over her face. "Not to mention you just flinched when I said 'fuck.'"

She tossed her hands up. "Test me, then! Give me a ... a kink ... exam."

Mikel's smirk turned into a full-blown smile, his scars twisting around his face, his mismatched eyes crinkling at the sides. She had seen a picture of his full smile once. The comments had been brutal. Saying he was *unnaturally* ugly. Saying that Alphas were supposed to have perfect skin. None of the comments explained *why* they thought all Alphas should have perfect skin, so it wasn't likely that they all knew about the Alpha healing abilities. Perhaps their healing abilities made all the other Alphas who had starred on the *Ironside Show* over the years appear somewhat perfect.

Mikel's smile was a short, aching flash of nostalgia. A brief window into a version of him that had once smiled and laughed often, and easily. A version of him that was now dead. His smile was a memorial, and it was too sad to be beautiful, but her heart ached as much as it did for one of Theodore's picture-perfect, superstar smiles.

Kalen laughed, but it died too quickly, the deep, husky sound fading away and leaving her feeling like she had been dropped from a cliff with the way her stomach swooped. "There's one more problem," he said. "Mates are possessive by nature. I'm sure you would know that —your parents being who they are. When Theodore finds out what you're doing in the club—and he will— how do you think he's going to react?"

She frowned. "Well, wouldn't I just be standing in a corner or something? Or will I be like ... your assistant?"

"You'll do whatever I tell you to do."

The silence that stretched between them was heavy, making her clothes feel too hot and cumbersome.

"W-What will you tell me to do?" She tried to peer past the mask of his calm composure. She was finally beginning to feel little trickles of their emotion. Drips of discomfort and feelings of being *trapped*. They were being forced into this by the Track Team, and they didn't like it.

"To not touch anyone, talk to anyone, or look at anyone except me." Kalen's voice had lowered to a growl, the words delivered to her with some sort of weighted, grave subtext.

"Isobel." Mikel drew her attention immediately, and she turned her head his way. "Do you think you can do that?"

She lifted a shoulder. "I don't really have any friends here anyway, except Theodore and Kilian. And Cian. And

Gabriel, I guess. And maybe Teak and Charlie, but they aren't even students."

Both of them seemed mildly amused at her listing out everyone she might consider a friend.

"You won't be permitted to play." Mikel emphasised the words carefully. "Or to experiment."

A sudden image of Kalen wrapping her wrists with rope dropped like a cement block into her mind, crushing all rational thought. Her skin grew sensitive and hot, and the dull ache in her stomach briefly turned into a sharper pinch.

"How is that fair?" she managed to get out, her voice strangled. "Do the others get to do whatever they want?"

"Elijah, Gabriel, and I do not have sex in the rooms," Kalen rumbled.

"But you do other things." She hated that she didn't know the specifics of what those *things* were. It made her sound so inexperienced. "What if I want to h-humiliate someone?"

"Try it out." Kalen leaned back, folding thick, muscled arms over his chest, his posture relaxed as he settled a hard stare on her. "Insult me."

"You're bossy," she said immediately.

"You can do better than that," Mikel goaded. "What else?"

"He's ..." She trailed off, chewing on her lip.

Wonderful. Kalen is wonderful. He saved her life.

"Say it *to* me, Carter." Kalen's voice was deepening, her surname slipping out like a whip.

"You're not very good at modulating your tone."

Wow. Way to go, Isobel. That'll teach him.

Kalen drew all the way forward, his arms uncrossing, his hand cupping her chin, his scent digging into her pores. "Degradation isn't your thing, princess." Despite the pitiful insult she had slung at him, his voice had turned into a *very* pleasant rumble, the pet name making her brain short-circuit as she tried to remember why it sounded familiar and where she had heard it before.

The first time he taught her to climb.

His touch was soft, barely brushing her skin as his thumb skirted along her jaw. "You prefer to be praised, isn't that right?"

She found herself nodding, not entirely sure she understood what she was agreeing to.

Praise sounded good. Better than humiliation, anyway.

The purr of his voice combined with the intensity in his eyes was making her dizzy, his smoky vanilla scent flooding her senses. His thumb reached the edge of her jaw, right beneath her ear, and then he drew away, his hand falling back to his thigh.

She blinked rapidly, jerking to her feet. "Fine." The word tumbled out of her. "It's not like I was going to have my first time in a secret society dungeon beneath the lake anyway." She laughed awkwardly, the sound weak. Kalen and Mikel watched her with tensed bodies and hard eyes. "It just seems like a double standard, that's all. Gabriel, Elijah, and Oscar are clearly allowed to look at people and touch them and speak to them. Why can't I?"

"Because if anyone gets close to you, they're dead," Mikel said flatly.

It didn't sound like a threat. Just a simple fact.

"It's only a matter of time before the other Alphas are recruited into the Stone Dahlia. We can't have Theodore going feral or Oscar deciding to ... assert his dominance in public. The mate-bond is repelled by outsiders touching what it assumes to be theirs."

"I watch Wallis touch Theodore all the time," she returned.

"You're practised at managing your own emotions." Mikel was shaking his head. "Anyone else in your position would have had a complete mental breakdown at this point, but you've barely got a wobble in your step. The others aren't Sigmas. They don't have the same ability."

Sounds like an excuse, she wanted to say.

Years of seeing her father lose control and having her mother blame it on his Alpha instincts was niggling at her, but maybe Mikel had a point. Not about them, but about *her*.

She frowned, her feet brushing across the rug as she began to pace. "I can control my emotions because I *had* to." The words spilled out of her without her permission, tumbling unfiltered and flopping onto the carpet before her agitated footsteps. "There wasn't any space for me and what *I* feel. It isn't because I'm a Sigma; it's because I was only allowed to be *this* small." Her voice had risen, her fingers hovering an inch apart before her face as she whipped to face them. "And if I could make myself matter so little so that everyone else could matter so much, then anyone can, and if anyone can, then maybe *all of you* can make room for me."

Kalen pulled in a deep breath, his scent like burnt sugar as it filled her lungs, curling around the room like smoke, an acrid bite to it that tasted like sulphur, which she attributed to Mikel.

"The boys are killing themselves every day to work out as much Alpha aggression as they can," Kalen said calmly. He didn't *sound* angry at her, but his anger was there all the same, pounding into her skin with enough force to make her stumble. "And you're one of us now. That means nobody touches you, nobody hurts you, nobody makes you feel *small* ... and that includes Braun fucking Carter."

"You're never going to be alone with your father again," Mikel added, a rough promise that raised the hairs on the back of her neck.

She ducked her head down, shame dribbling through her. "What happens if they don't train so hard?"

"They surge." There was a note of warning in the way

Mikel spoke. "There's a part of the Alpha brain that just seems to ... flick off. Like a humanity switch. Suddenly, we're nothing but animals with entirely animal instincts."

"For most Alphas, it isn't a problem," Kalen explained calmly, shaking out his cuffs. It was hard to imagine him losing control in any way. "But when large groups of us cohabitate for too long, it seems to make it happen more often. It *was* comfortably manageable thanks to Elijah's plan and Mikel's guidance, but adding a *shared* mate into the mix has basically electrocuted all those instincts we were trying to keep dormant. Nobody will hurt you, but they might hurt other people if they see someone as a threat to you, or if the bond is being defiled in any way. They won't be able to help themselves. And that includes women touching them, not just men touching you. Our instincts go both ways. Both scenarios are dangerous, you just haven't witnessed the discussions we've had with them that resemble the discussion we're having with you right now."

She frowned, gripping the back of her neck as her pacing slowed to a stop. "If the bond can't stand being defiled by other people, then how can I handle Theo, Gabriel, and Elijah with their fake girlfriends? And why are they still carrying on with their fake girlfriends if it causes them so much distress?"

Kalen stood up, straightening out his shirt, his thumbs smoothing over the material to tuck any loose fabric back beneath his belt, drawing her attention to the large stature of his body and the muscles that were briefly defined when the material pulled tight, even though it was a typical business shirt, an ironed fabric with enough structure that it definitely shouldn't have just given her an outline of abdominal muscles.

He cleared his throat. "It's clear that you've been mistreated, Isobel. That's not what we were referring to earlier. Your Sigma ability is still an ability, even if you've had to use it for unfortunate purposes. Sigmas are incredibly strong-willed. Their mental fortitude is unparalleled. I'm not saying that you *should* be mistreated because you can handle it. I'm saying you've handled it better than an Alpha would have, because they don't have the same mental fortitude. And it's essential that we show the world just how well you can handle seeing the boys with their fake girlfriends, because we're playing a very delicate game here, trying to cover up the fact that you're actually half-bonded to every Alpha here."

"Any one of our boys would have snapped and snapped someone's jaw if they had to endure even a small fraction of what you have," Mikel added. "But that doesn't mean we aren't all training every day to maintain control over our impulses. None of us are using it as an excuse not to manage our aggression."

"You told me today that I have to learn how to manage Oscar," she accused quietly.

"And I've told him the same thing." Mikel's mouth hardened, tension lining his face. "You'll each need to figure out how to do that in your own ways. Assuming neither of you are about to change?"

He stared at her expectantly, waiting for a confirmation that she could be just as stubborn as Oscar, but she ... stubbornly didn't want to admit it.

"I'll be your sponsor," Kalen announced, stepping around her and heading to the door. "But I'm also giving you a day to change your mind if you need to. Make sure you think this through. This isn't an option I would be giving any of the others, so take advantage of it." Before he opened the door, he glanced back at her, waiting to see if she had any other questions.

She nodded, saying a quiet goodnight before heading toward Kilian's room. The lounge was empty, looking like a cleaning crew had slipped through while she had been in Kalen's office.

One probably had. Or Gabriel had beaten them to it.

She raised her fist to knock on Kilian's door, but then figured he was probably already asleep since there was no light spilling out from beneath the door. She cracked it open, trying to keep quiet, and breathed a short sigh of relief when there was enough moonlight spilling through the wide bay windows to illuminate her steps as she crept toward his bed. It was neatly made, her hot water bottle on top of the covers waiting for her. Kilian's form was stretched out on a brand-new couch, a blanket tugged up over his hips, his chest bare, his pale skin flawless in the soft shadows, every muscle sharp with definition, his hand resting on his stomach.

Kilian was an angel. Dropped into the mortal world to make everyone else feel the sharp sting of inferiority and the sharper burn of *want*.

She quickly looked away, climbing into his bed, and hugging the hot water bottle against her stomach, as she texted the pictures of her flower bunches to Theodore and Moses with a simple "*Happy birthday*" message for each of them. Theodore texted back almost immediately.

Theodore: Wow.

Theodore: I would say that nobody has ever given me flowers before, but Kilian beat you to it.

Isobel: Kilian gave you flower, singular. I gave you flowers, plural. I am still the top gentleman around these parts.

Theodore: You're smiling right now, aren't you?

Isobel: A little.

Theodore: Come in here so I can see it.

Isobel: No. Cameras.

Theodore: Bring your gentleman apprentice and make yourselves invisible.

Isobel: To do what?

Theodore: With Kilian around, nothing. But we could make him leave.

Isobel: And then what?

Theodore: Fuck.

Theodore: Fucking fuck.

Theodore: Nothing at all.

Isobel: You okay?

Theodore: Peachy. You okay, Illy-stone?

Isobel: I feel like I'm hanging off the edge of a cliff and someone is up there picking off my fingers one by one.

Theodore: I know it's scary, but you'll always have me to catch you. I'll never let you fall.

She typed out *Why?* but then immediately deleted it. It didn't matter. Maybe he still thought he owed her his life after what happened during their first year in the library, or maybe it was because she was his mate, but the truth was, she *knew* the feeling. If Theodore ever fell, she would catch him in an instant, and not because of her Sigma nature. She would catch him even if it crushed her.

Isobel: Thank you, Theo.

In response, he sent a screenshot of the home screen of his phone. He had saved her flowers as the background picture. She felt her stomach flip, and a stupid, wobbly smile overtook her entire face, remaining until she finally put her phone aside, resigned to the fact that Moses wasn't going to respond at all.

12

THE TWO SIDES OF TORTURE

Kilian couldn't sleep.

He tossed the covers from his lap and sat up on the couch, stretching out the kinks in his neck. He glanced toward the bed where Isobel was curled onto her side, her limp arm reaching across the mattress in his direction. She had tossed and turned for a while before finally succumbing to sleep, her subtle scent clawing across the room and begging him to crawl into bed beside her.

She smelled distressed, but also dizzyingly, delicately happy, and he wasn't sure which note in her perfume drew him in the hardest.

No, it was the delicate, airy sweetness. That was his favourite.

He pulled out his phone, staring at the dull reflection

of moonlight across his screen before he finally tapped it and brought up the secure messaging app.

Kilian: Anyone awake?

He could have called a group meeting, but it wasn't a good idea to mess with the cameras too much when Isobel was in the dorm. They would be watching too closely. It was safer to talk over text.

Mikel's response came first, which was hardly surprising. He slept with his phone on a table right beside his head, the volume turned up as loud as possible, always worried that one of them would get into trouble.

In all fairness ... they often got into trouble.

Mikel (admin): Are you okay?

Kilian: I'm fine.

He fiddled with the worn buttons along the side of his phone, waiting for someone to have something to say.

Mikel (admin): Isobel okay?

Kilian: She's asleep. She was exhausted.

Theodore: I'm awake.

Moses: Awake now.

Cian: What's on your mind, Kili?

Oscar: Awake.

Niko: mup

Niko: mop

Niko: up

Theodore: Niko is up.

Niko: Ye

Niko: p

Kalen (admin): Is this about Eve again?

Oscar is typing ...

Oscar has been muted.

Kilian: ... yeah.

Moses: Pretty sure I just heard Oscar's door open. He's already worked up after Carter came out of the shower smelling like ... well, you know.

Elijah: Gabriel, lock your door.

Gabriel: What?

Gabriel: I always lock my door.

Gabriel: Who the fuck is banging on my door?

Gabriel: Wait ... reading the other messages.

Moses: What does this have to do with Gabriel?

Theodore: Why am I always the last person to know everything?

Kilian: Guys.

Kalen (admin): Mikel?

Mikel (admin): On it.

Niko: Jesus Christ. Honestly. What happened now?

Elijah: I thought we all knew.

Niko: That Carter was touching herself in the shower? Yeah. We might be dumber than you, but we have these things called NOSES.

Elijah: That Gabriel was responsible.

Niko: Say what now?

Moses: I just heard Theo's door.

Kilian: Guys.

Kilian: You're going to wake her up.

Kilian: Please.

Mikel (admin): I think everyone should be nicer to Oscar. He's a good guy, really.

Moses: Hey Oscar.

Mikel (admin): Hey dude.

Moses: Where is Mikki?

Kilian's vision of the screen began to blur, his heart pounding for no reason at all. He quickly blinked through the haze, tipping his head back against the couch and counting slowly to ten as the phone kept vibrating in his palm.

On the bed, Isobel's forehead scrunched up in a tight wince, like the giant ball of anxiety he had almost choked on was trying to climb into her while she slept. He closed his eyes and counted again, ignoring his phone until the ball loosened, and Isobel's face smoothed out again.

Mikel (admin): I'm back.

Oscar has been unmuted.

Theodore: Kili?

Theodore: You okay?

Cian: All good, Kil?

Niko: Let me know you're okay or I'm coming in.

He scoffed at the tremble in his fingers, the remnants of the panic that had tried to drag him under.

Kilian: I'm good.

Kilian: We need to decide what to do about Eve. She knows everything.

Kalen (admin): Our contacts in the OGGB are saying that no new intel has come from Eve or Aron.

Kilian: Are we still waiting to see if Aron will talk?

Even typing his ex's name made him want to stumble to the bathroom and throw up, his brain pinching with an immediate headache. Aron hadn't been the love of his life or anything, but he had been Kilian's closest friend at Green Mountain before Kilian applied for Ironside. Aron had always been selfish and indulgent. Even manipulative, sometimes. And sometimes that manipulation had looked like cruelty ... but this was beyond anything Kilian could have suspected.

Kalen (admin): No. Aron has stuck with the same story. Eve sought him out when she went home for the break, told him you were secretly mated to Isobel, and told him she had a plan to break the bond. Apparently, he didn't know Eve was going to cut her. He thought Isobel's light would manifest on the outside and Eve could snatch it up. But he did nothing to stop her.

Mikel (admin): He's repeated that same story over and over, and then he "demonstrated" Eve's power. They forced him to sign a confession absolving Eve of all responsibility, and now he can't talk anymore.

Kilian blew out a sharp breath, his body jolting with

the memory of what had happened when the officials pulled him from Ironside.

Kilian: I have to tell you all something.

None of them replied, and he gnawed on his lip as he tried to find the right words.

Kilian: They didn't really put me up in the official's building while they questioned Aron.

Still, they didn't reply, and an awful, sinking sensation shot through Kilian.

They *knew*.

As soon as he was called to the front of the academy and ushered into a car with two silent, suited officials, he knew he was in for a rough interrogation. They had blindfolded him before the car even left the curb, driving around for the better part of the night. It was all for the sake of intimidation because as soon as they pulled him from the car, he knew he was beneath the academy. His footsteps echoed, the air temperature had dropped, and they pulled off his blindfold in the hallway outside his interrogation chamber, showcasing a brief flash of the opulence that he knew rested inside the Stone Dahlia, even though he had never stepped foot inside it before.

The floor was a shining mosaic of rare, polished stones with glittering pearl and gold accents twisted from wall to wall like luminescent veins. There wasn't a single scuff mark or footprint in the highly reflective surface, only a glittering spatter of soft, warm light from the tiered chandeliers above. The air was lightly perfumed with the faintest hint of an exotic scent that probably intrinsically made people want to spend money, and there was soft music spilling from hidden speakers, crooning at him to *relax*, even as the officials pushed him into the room and locked the door with stern, unflinching faces.

He wasn't sure how long he was kept there, but their process had been ... intense.

At first, they simply questioned him.

It was clear they didn't think he was Isobel's mate, and he supposed it made sense, since Theodore had spent almost a week refusing to leave Isobel's hospital bed, clutching her lifeless body against his as though he could somehow assimilate her into his skin ... and Kilian *hadn't* torn his best friend apart.

But the officials questioned him all the same, and they acted like they were unhappy with the answers they were getting out of him. That was when they brought the shock device in. They slapped electrodes to his skin and tapped a button whenever they decided he was being less than forthcoming.

Just a little jolt, they assured him, while he ground his teeth against the pain. *Research shows it helps to prompt the memory centre of your brain. You're an Alpha, so you'll recover in no time.*

They asked him if he had *organised* the attack. They

asked if he was in love with Theodore and wanted Isobel dead.

They asked how long he had been stringing along Eve *and* Aron *and* Isobel, and if he had gotten what he wanted.

They asked how he had formulated the plan, and how he had communicated it to Aron.

And then, suddenly, they changed tack again, asking if he knew who Isobel's mate was.

They swapped out their interrogators and continued until he was blacking out between electrocutions, and then it just ... stopped. They transferred him to the hospital for a "wellness check," and he didn't see any of them again.

He stared at his phone screen as it went black due to inactivity, realisation settling into his gut with a sickening lurch. He tapped on his screen to bring it back to life.

Kilian: I thought it was the Track Team.

Kilian: I thought it was them interfering in the interrogation to recruit me.

Kilian: I thought that's why it stopped.

Finally, one of them responded.

Elijah: No. It was Kalen.

Kilian: What the fuck, Kalen?

Kalen (admin): Don't start with me. You shouldn't have kept quiet about this for so long.

Kilian: I thought we had enough to deal with. I just wanted to wait a little bit.

Kilian: What did you give them in exchange?

Kalen (admin): I agreed to one private session.

Kilian swore roughly, before hiding his phone screen and darting a look to the bed to make sure he hadn't woken up Isobel. The Track Team had been trying to convince Kalen to take on private clients since he started at the Stone Dahlia, even going as far as to offer him a larger cut of his room fee. It was the difference between one thousand dollars and ten thousand dollars, but Kalen continued to refuse.

It was somewhat of an unspoken expectation that he would have to do whatever the client wanted if he allowed private sessions.

Kilian: Did everyone else agree to this?

The responses came immediately.

Mikel (admin): No.

Oscar: Fuck no.

Gabriel: None of us agreed.

Elijah: Kalen didn't call for a group vote. He told us what he had done after he did it.

Kilian: You should have fucking left me there.

Kalen (admin): This was my decision, and it's final. I can handle one private session.

Kilian: How do you plan on doing that?

Kalen (admin): I'll figure something out. Stop worrying about me, Kilian. You've got enough on your

plate, and it's my job to worry about you, not the other way around.

Elijah: I've already figured it out.

Kalen (admin): Do not bring that up again.

Elijah: It's a perfect solution.

Cian: First I'm hearing of a perfect solution?

Niko: Elijah's plans always work. What's the problem?

Elijah: There's no problem. Kalen just thinks he can refuse until I come up with a different plan that doesn't threaten his delicate sensibilities.

Kalen (admin): Watch your mouth.

Elijah: Save your bossy voice for Isobel. You're going to need it.

Theodore: What? What does this have to do with Isobel?

Gabriel: Ah. Yes, that makes sense.

Moses: We'll be the judges of what makes sense.

Moses: After you explain everything to us.

Gabriel: The club is trying to recruit Isobel. If she asks Kalen to be her sponsor, she can shadow him to all his engagements, even the private ones. If some rich cougar was hoping to get her claws into Kalen by spending a small fortune on a few hours in a private room with him, Isobel's presence will prove disruptive.

Cian: So? What's so bad about that plan?

Kalen (admin): That wasn't the plan.

Elijah: The plan was a little more comprehensive.

Gabriel: Okay, never mind. I'm with Kalen on this one.

Theodore: No need to get comprehensive.

Moses: Can we go back to a few minutes ago when Gabriel was actually wrong about something?

Gabriel: No.

Elijah: If Kalen changed his act, we could mitigate all risk. I think the comprehensive plan is better.

Oscar: Isobel Fucking Carter is a virgin Sigma who still can't meet our eyes while she's talking to us half the time. She isn't in the same league as a Shibari bunny.

Moses: Bunny, huh?

Gabriel: Awkward.

Elijah: Freudian slip, Oscar?

Oscar: I'll Freudian slip my fist through your teeth.

Oscar: As soon as I'm done with Gabriel.

Kilian: Where are you right now?

Oscar: In Gabriel's room.

Niko: What the fuck, Gabe. You let him in?

Gabriel: He was being loud. And I never touched Isobel. He has nothing to break.

Kilian: Then what is he doing?

Gabriel: He's currently standing in the corner, glaring at me, and trying to figure out how I could possibly have anything to do with Isobel touching herself in the shower when I wasn't even there.

Mikel (admin): For crying out loud, Oscar. Don't make me come down there again.

Oscar: I haven't hurt him yet. Everyone keep your panties on.

Moses: Speaking of panties. Want to search Gabe's hiding places while you're in there?

Theodore: Isobel isn't ready, Kalen.

Kalen (admin): I know.

Elijah: You could get her ready.

Kalen (admin): I know.

Niko: But you won't, right?

Kalen (admin): I need to get a better gauge of where she stands with all of this. She already asked me to be her sponsor.

Kilian: Don't push her.

Kilian navigated out of the chat and flopped back onto the couch, staring at the shadowed patterns on the roof. Isobel was in good hands with Kalen, and they all knew it, but there were parts of the club that even Kalen couldn't protect her from.

Things were getting more complicated ... but a weight had just been lifted off his chest.

He didn't usually keep secrets from them for so long, but he had thought it would be better if all their focus was on protecting Isobel.

He should have realised they already knew.

Isobel woke up an hour before her alarm was set to go off, her mind buzzing. She checked her phone just to make sure nothing terrible had happened while she slept, and then she snuck into Kilian's bathroom to get ready for the day. She was halfway out of the dorm before she paused, remembering that Mikel had ordered them to go everywhere in pairs or groups.

Thankfully, Elijah also seemed to be an early riser. He padded out of his room in rumpled sweats and mussed hair, heading toward the stairs leading up to the kitchen before he turned, pinning her with a look, his nose twitching.

He assessed her quickly, before mumbling, "Give me a minute," and disappearing back into his room.

He re-emerged dressed for dance practice, his bag slung over his arm, and met her at the door. "Where to this early? You don't have practise for an hour."

"I thought I'd check on Sophia and Luis."

"All right." He pushed the door open, holding it and nodding for her to go first.

"How'd you sleep?" he asked as they reached the stairs.

She felt awkward trying to make small talk with him, but he didn't seem to suffer from the same problem. He peppered her with polite, surface questions until they reached the chapel, where they both stopped short inside the doorway. The Guardian, Maya, was vacuuming around the dais, an old set of headphones strapped to her head, her foot tapping absently. She stopped when she saw them, shifting the headphones to her neck and turning off the vacuum.

"Carter," she said, her tone surprised. Her steady, gold-ringed, mahogany gaze moved to Elijah. "Reed, is it? I apologise, my son is a big fan, but I don't keep up with the show much."

Elijah only reclined his head a little in acknowledgement.

"Maya Rosales." She wound up the vacuum cord and strode over, sticking her hand out to Elijah.

"A pleasure," he said, pretending not to notice her hand. "I've heard ... things."

"A sceptic, huh?" She chuckled, amused by his cool reception, before turning her attention back to Isobel. "What brings you here this morning? Have any other artefacts appeared?" Her eyes darted right to Isobel's chest, even though the chain was hidden by her over-large shirt.

"Nothing since Sophia and Luis last updated you," Isobel answered blandly.

"I *am* a Guardian, Carter." Maya's lips thinned. "My children might have a knack for Gifted occult, but they don't have my years of experience. Of course they consulted me."

"And what do you have to say?" Isobel asked, crossing her arms.

The woman had only been polite to her, but it made Isobel *extremely* uncomfortable that Maya and her children were walking around with the knowledge that both of Isobel's eyes had changed.

After Eve ...

She stiffened, forcing the thoughts out of her mind to concentrate on Maya, who was pushing out little currents of anxiety to tease into Isobel's chest. It felt different to when Isobel's father bulldozed over her with his emotions, or when the Dorm A Alphas sent their emotions colliding against her body. This was softer, subtler, as though Maya was as practised as Isobel at keeping her emotions under lock and key.

Maybe she was.

Her entire occupation was maintaining a dead religion and a group of gods that most Gifted had long forgotten. She likely had to suffer just as much ridicule as Isobel did for being a Sigma.

"I think that the gods don't bother with curses," Maya answered. "But there is one god who must maintain the balance when the other gods go overboard with their gifts."

Isobel nodded, trying to recall the name of the god Sophia and Luis had shown her.

"Stygian," Maya supplied.

"Right." Isobel glanced around the chapel, but it wasn't like any of the shadows were about to shift away from the wall and turn into robed, celestial beings. It was just a chapel. Not even a very elaborate one, considering it belonged to Ironside. "The mysterious god."

"The Duskfall Warden," Maya corrected. "The Gifted don't have a 'god of mystery,' just as we don't have a 'goddess of love,' or a 'god of the seas.' Our gods aren't so simple as that, with only one segment of the world they are relegated to. The Duskfall Warden is named for the fact that he guards the space between light and dark. Sometimes, even the space between life and death. Without him, we have no balance."

Isobel wanted to bite her tongue, but the words spilled out anyway. "You call this world balanced?"

"The gods don't exist to serve *us*, Carter. We exist to serve them. They give us our abilities, our gifted blood, and in return, we are supposed to keep their temples and follow their edicts."

"I'm curious," Elijah spoke up suddenly, his voice calm and soft—definitely not as riled up as Isobel felt. "The chain you took from Isobel—has it shown any signs of sentience?"

"None at all," Maya answered immediately. "It was not intended for me."

"Have you studied it further?" Elijah pressed.

"Of course." Maya looked him over a little more thoroughly, arching a thin, elegant brow. "It's identical to Aphelina's chain. I've cross-referenced it across every picture I could find, and all the written accounts of bonded people receiving Aphelina's chain in the past."

"It can be gifted to more than one person at the same time?" Elijah's expression was almost bored, but he spoke quickly, his tone bordering on sharp.

"It would seem so." Maya brushed some cleaning

dust from her faded, button-down shirt. "The chain always disappears after some time, but it has *never* fused itself to a person's body. Not in any record I can find."

"Did you find any records of the chain being cut or deformed?" Elijah barely paused to digest Maya's words.

"No—" Maya admitted, but Elijah was already speaking again.

"What was so distinctive about the chain that you're so sure it's the same as those mentioned in your records?"

"It's not a metal of this world." Maya looked amused now.

"And how did you test that?" Elijah's disappointment reached out to Isobel, like he had already concluded that Maya couldn't possibly verify what she was saying.

Maya responded with her small smile curving out even further, her amusement over Elijah's rapid questioning obvious now, with just a small spark of something that might have been approval or respect glinting in her expression. "The officials are as interested in Carter's unique situation as I am. They allowed me to make contact with a certain professor at UCLA, who invited me into his lab for the day. He showed me how to test the metal, and I managed to convince him that the test itself was confidential."

"What kind of test?" Isobel asked, as Elijah's suspicion dropped out of her chest. His face was now painted in curiosity.

Maya shifted around them, closing the doors to the chapel firmly before she started up the vacuum again, but she didn't resume her work. She beckoned them closer, explaining lowly, "You never know with this place." She indicated the loudly humming vacuum. "The test I did was for thermal diffusivity. I flattened and smoothed out a section of the chain and set it up between a laser and an infrared detector. No matter how much I pulsed the gold with the laser, the infrared detector didn't pick up on an ounce of heat. No matter what I did, I simply could not heat the metal."

"It heats up all the time," Isobel argued, her fingers drifting up to her chest. "Whenever it changes."

"It's still changing?" Maya asked sharply.

Elijah's arm landed over Isobel's shoulders, pulling her back an inch and huddling her against his side. He turned slightly, putting himself between her and Maya.

"Have you said anything about Isobel's eyes?" he asked quietly, his tone now smooth as silk—yet that somehow made it more frightening. "Have your children said anything?"

"No." Maya frowned, rearing back slightly. "I already gave my word. And I kept the conclusions of my experiments to myself as well. They think the Gifted religion is a bunch of nonsense, so they weren't surprised when I told them there were no remarkable results."

"Why would you do that?" Elijah narrowed his eyes

on her. "That's anti-loyalist behaviour. What's in it for you?"

"What's in *this* for *you*?" Maya returned, gesturing the way Elijah was cuddling Isobel close enough that even her cheek was pressed tight to his shirt. "You aren't on Carter's medical records as a surrogate."

"And you aren't on her records at all," Elijah returned.

"Guess who *is* on my records?" Isobel grumbled. "Yeah, it's me. You can both stop talking about me like I'm not even here."

Elijah's grip didn't loosen. "What's in it for you, Guardian?" he insisted flatly, a hint of Alpha voice creeping into his words.

"You just answered your own question," she returned, just as flatly. The two of them were actually ... weirdly similar. "I'm a Guardian. I *exist* to protect and preserve the Gifted religion, and soul-bonded pairs are one of the fundamental pillars of that religion. All Gifted are supposed to have a bonded mate, divined by fate, but with all our people segregated into camps—and watched so closely—it's impossible for mates to find each other, or to be near each other when they enter into the Death Phase. Those who do find their mate are to be protected at all costs."

"Mama?" Sophia raised her voice over the sound of the vacuum, closing the back door to the chapel as she stepped inside. Luis was almost stuck to her back, his face pale, his hand tangled in her shirt. "Oh." Sophia's attention caught on Isobel and Elijah. "Hey—" Her expression suddenly crumpled. "Did Ashford have a vision? Does he know something?"

"Nothing new," Elijah said, as Maya turned off the vacuum.

Isobel lowered her walls a little, tasting the overwhelming, sickening terror that rolled off Luis in large waves. She walked over to them, kneeling before Luis and examining his pale, sweaty face.

"You had another dream?" she guessed.

Luis nodded, his lower lip trembling, and then he hid his face in Sophia's shirt and started crying. Isobel stood, her chest hurting, but it was nothing on the heartbroken anguish she felt from Sophia. She sipped some of it into herself, realising that she had gotten better at siphoning off people's emotions without them noticing, and then she raised her wall again, breathing a little easier and feeling guilty for it.

She shared a brief look with Sophia, who had schooled her expression until it only revealed the slightest pinch of pain.

"The same dream," Sophia explained. "No new details. This is the third time."

Isobel glanced down at the boy again, making a decision that she already knew she was going to pay for.

"Don't—" Elijah was stepping toward her, but it was too late.

She yanked down her walls and gulped at Luis' fear, dragging it into her own body in heaping amounts, barely able to catch her breath before another mountain of terror landed inside her. It was stacking into her body like great big lead blocks, forming a precarious, menacing tower.

Elijah caught her arms, spinning her to face him, his cold eyes flicking between hers, his handsome, aristocratic features a little blurry. "Stop it," he whispered harshly. "You can't afford to be sick right now, Carter. This attack could happen at any moment."

She grappled with her walls, pushing out of Elijah's hold so that he wouldn't feel how badly she was shaking. She didn't want him to know how much she had just shoved into herself.

She glanced back down at Luis, but he wasn't clinging to Sophia anymore. He flung himself at Isobel, launching at her so heavily that she actually thought she was being attacked at first. His thin arms wrapped around her hips, his head pressing into her stomach, and she waited for him to squeeze too tight, to assault her with a hidden weapon, to try and force her to the ground where his mother and sister would be able to pin her ...

But he was just hugging her.

His breaths were short and choppy, his tears wetting her shirt, his arms shaking as much as hers were. She slipped to her knees, and his arms unlatched only to fling up around her neck, his trembling body crashing against hers again.

"It-it's okay," he hiccupped. "Y-You'll be o-okay."

Why was he comforting her?

Why were her cheeks wet?

She hugged Luis back, trying to hide her tears as his shaking hand patted over her hair in clumsy, soothing motions. Heat suddenly surrounded her spine, the scent of spiced cloves and unfurling woodsmoke wrapping her up and whispering to her limbs that *true* comfort was only a breath away. She released Luis, and Elijah caught her instantly, lifting her back to her feet, and then higher, until she could wrap her legs around his waist, her arms hooking around his neck, her nose buried in his throat.

"She took everything the boy was feeling," he explained, his arms wrapped tightly around her.

"Is she okay?" Sophia whispered.

"She will be," Elijah grunted. "Can we have a minute?"

"Of course," Maya responded softly. "Luis, come here, darling. We'll give you five minutes, but you shouldn't stay in here too long. They'll send a crew to check on you."

"I'm aware." Elijah's voice was short, but he seemed to wrangle it into something more polite. "It was ... interesting to meet you, Guardian."

"Take care of her." *Alpha voice.* Maya's voice.

"Can I say bye?" Luis whispered.

"Another time, grasshopper," Maya soothed him. "We need to give them a moment. Come on."

As soon as the door closed, Elijah moved to a bench, yanking it away from the wall so that she wouldn't have to unwind her legs from around his waist. He sat, his hands catching her face and lifting it from its hiding spot against the warm security of his neck, where her sorrow unfurled in thoughts of woodsmoke.

"Are you going to pass out?" he asked. His face was blurry, but she was pretty sure a heavy frown weighed down his lips.

"No." She grimaced. "I just took it really *fast*, and it was ... he's so ..."

"He's a child dreaming of his entire family being murdered," Elijah supplied dryly. "I'm sure he's thoroughly traumatised. You taking away the emotion won't even touch that trauma."

"Stop it." She swatted weakly at his chest. "S'my power," she slurred. "I do what I want with it."

His lips seemed to quirk, his thumbs rubbing at the drying tears on her cheeks. "I've only seen you cry once. The day you died."

"Which time?" She tried to bury her face in his neck again, to draw that powerful scent back into her lungs, but he held her face firmly.

"You're so strong," he said quietly, those cold eyes boring into hers. "But you're not unbreakable. Stop pushing your luck."

"I heard about what you do," she blurted, feeling embarrassed by his scrutiny as her vision began to clear, Luis' emotion finally finding space inside her to settle properly. "I heard you like to humiliate people."

Elijah's grip loosened, falling to her waist. The edge of his mouth twitched even further until it was half a smile. "Really?"

"I thought you hated bullies."

"I do."

"Then why?"

His regarded her flatly. "Why what, Carter?"

"Why do you like to degrade people?"

"Did you 'hear' that I like to degrade people, or did you 'hear' that it was something I did? Because there's a difference between doing something and liking it."

"Why do it if you don't like it?"

"Now that's a better question ... but I never said I didn't like it."

Isobel groaned, swatting his chest again. "You're—"

He caught her wrist, and then her other, twisting both of her arms behind her back, and then he straightened his posture, using his grip on her arms to press her chest against his. She had to tip her head right back to still meet his eyes.

"I like to be in control," he explained in a whisper. "But the fetish room isn't about what I like. It's about what people want to see. What they would pay to see.

And they love to see other people *begging* to be reduced to vessels for whatever we want to do with them."

"What do you do with them?"

"You're very curious today. Why?"

She shrugged—as much as she could with her arms twisted the way they were. "Just wondering."

"Well ..." He transferred both of her wrists to one of his hands, using the other to grip her hip and draw her closer. "I wouldn't worry, sweet girl. You're going to love what Kalen does. And when he does it to you, it'll be a nice experience."

When, not *if*.

"How do you know that?"

His cold gaze was crawling over her face, categorising the drying tears on her skin. She could still feel the wetness clumping her eyelashes together.

"Because of what happened last night with Gabriel," he finally admitted. "You aren't that close with him, but you still let him tell you how to touch yourself, didn't you?" He continued before she even had a chance to respond. "And not because of the bond." He tugged her even closer, ducking his head to whisper the words against her cheek. "It was because he offered to take it all away for a moment. The stress, the decisions, the danger. He was completely in control, and you trusted him enough to know that he would keep you safe if you gave it all up. He would take care of you and make you feel good, and you didn't need to give anything in return except your sweet submission."

She suddenly felt restless, her breath coming in short gasps, her entire existence narrowing to the way her legs were still locked around his waist, her arms twisted behind her back, one of his hands tight on the curve of her waist. She was straining toward him, her wrists stuck together obediently even though she might have been able to get them free if she surprised him with the effort. She was happy for him to position her however he wanted ... because she *felt* safe with him.

But he was wrong that it had nothing to do with the bond.

It was his *scent* convincing her to trust him, and she could only smell him because of the bond ... though she supposed that didn't mean his scent was a lie. Alphas could scent everyone around them, and that didn't make them trust everyone around them. Heck, they didn't trust *anyone.*

Did she trust Elijah?

She wasn't sure.

"Interesting," he muttered. He had pulled back, examining her face as she remained silent. "You think I'm manipulating you." It wasn't a question.

"Aren't you?"

"Maybe." He released her wrists, his hands lightly squeezing her arms as he lifted her, standing and setting her back on her feet. "Don't take it personally. I find it easier to deal with people this way."

"Why don't you just say what you really mean?"

He smirked, covering his mouth with the back of his hand as a short chuckle fell out of him. "Okay, Carter. I think your innocence is liberating ... in a way I didn't quite expect. I think your asshole of a father didn't prepare you for the more ... well let's just say *social* aspects of Ironside, because he doesn't really see you as a person, does he? And your mother—"

"Careful," she hissed, stepping into his personal space, her eyes narrowing into slits as she stared up at him.

For some reason, that smirk broke out over his face again. "Your mother," he continued, ignoring her warning, "was likely traumatised by her own *social* experiences, and preparing you for something she would never have wished for you wasn't high on her list of priorities, I'm guessing."

"When you say social—"

"I'm talking about sex and romantic relationships, yes."

"Right."

"You've grown up with a very twisted notion of romance playing out right in front of you, with Ironside influencing your ideals every other night, and Hollywood adding in a sprinkle of uncertainty on the side. Which version do you believe? The environment that created your father? The relationship he has with your mother before your own eyes, or the movies he acts in? You're remarkably good at holding all those twisted influences inside you while you let go and just *feel,* and I believe that makes you incredibly dangerous to us. It's beautiful, and there's no room in our world for sweet, beautiful things."

She glanced down, staring at the puckered scars running down her forearms. She didn't even bother to cover them up, but there was no doubt that she no longer felt *beautiful* the way she once did.

Dance used to make her feel beautiful, but something had changed.

She didn't dance to soar, anymore. She danced because she was a scratched record on a turntable, stuck repeating herself over and over because there was nothing more to her than the things her father had raised her to be. She was just wobbling along, singing the same song, dancing the same dance, waiting for someone to lift the needle and shatter her for good.

"I like ... what you see," she managed. "I ... wish it was true."

"Hmm." His finger suddenly appeared beneath her chin, lifting her face delicately until she was forced to meet his eyes again. "When is your next appointment with the bond specialist?"

"This afternoon. It's usually on Thursdays, but—"

"The Day of Consolidation is tomorrow," he finished for her. "And then we break for the summer. Is she going to come up with a plan for how to keep the bond stable over the summer break?"

Isobel nodded, forcing his finger to drop, but his eyes stayed fixed on hers, his stare narrowed and unblinking, his attention making the hairs along her arms stand on end.

"Good," he grunted, straightening away from her. "You should ask to continue your sessions with her over the break. Phone or video meetings."

She blinked at him, but he was already striding for the door.

13
BABY

"It still isn't working," Gabriel muttered, watching as her arms fell limp to her sides, the song over the speakers fading into silence before restarting. "Dance with Elijah."

Elijah was sitting there quietly, considering her with that same hard stare that hadn't shifted from his face since they had left the chapel an hour ago.

"Not this again." She sighed, switching her attention back to Gabriel. "Professor Lye didn't say it *had* to be a partner dance for the final assessment."

"And yet the point of the assessment is to apply for his third-year class, which is a class specialising in partner work," Gabriel returned. "Why don't you give it a try? What's the harm?"

She glanced between them, realising they *both* had that sharp, assessing stare. This was another special "Reed and Spade" test, but she didn't feel like being assessed anymore. If they thought they saw something they didn't like, then that ugliness was bound to grow in gruesome power the deeper they looked.

The truth wasn't pretty.

The truth was so unsettling that she didn't even want to admit it to herself.

She walked over to the door and flicked off the light, and then strode to the windows, drawing the heavy curtains until the room was doused in darkness. It had turned into a miserable day, so there wasn't much light to sneak in around the fabric.

She felt better like this.

Like she was in one of Kalen's climbing sessions. Terrified, but sure that she would never fall, because each time she had climbed with that blindfold stealing her vision over the past few weeks, he had guided her safely back to the ground. She had never stumbled.

And this way ... the difference between her and Elijah wouldn't be as glaring. There would be no witnesses to just how broken and scarred she looked beside someone like him. She walked back to the Alphas, finding them with ease since the blinking lights from the audio panels were right above them.

"Pick a song," she muttered, snatching up her phone and thrusting it out to where Elijah and Gabriel still sat, unflinching, barely even showing a hint of curiosity over her strange actions.

Elijah leaned forward, scrolling through her phone

for a moment, the light from her screen illuminating his perfect, impeccable features.

He tapped on something, and she tossed it back to the shelf, only catching a glimpse of a song called "Baby" before it started booming over the speakers. Elijah held out a hand to her, barely visible in the darkness, and she hesitated for a moment.

She couldn't do this.

She couldn't dance with Elijah.

Maybe she should just ...

He caught her hand, pulling her into his body with a tight yank, just as the first heavy thump of the song vibrated along the floor.

"Just let go," he murmured, so softly she almost missed it. "Forget about how you look, how you feel. Just follow my lead for three minutes. You can do anything for three minutes."

He moved her slowly, gripping her shoulders and twisting her torso, bending her back and then stroking up along her spine, drawing her up and into his body. He flicked up her arm and she turned to watch the shadowed limb drop back to her side, her instincts kicking in just in time to make sure the fall was graceful and weightless.

Even in the dark, she could see the hesitation in her movements.

He shifted his leg between hers, his foot brushing the inside of hers, making her step where he wanted her to step. At first, his movements were slow and deliberate, the pressure of his hands firm, but as she loosened up and followed the suggestion of his touches, he used less pressure, until even the slightest shift in his posture managed to move her one way or another. He guided her with his hands, his legs, his feet, his weight and size, bending her and twisting her until she felt like she was made of rippling silk. Her only purpose to decorate his body as he created slow, beautiful choreography seemingly on the spot.

She might have floated away if he wasn't bending her over his thigh, his fingers trailing over the front of her shirt, skirting the bumps of the chain embedded into her skin.

For the briefest second, her doubts came crashing back.

Perfect, impeccable Elijah. And her. A Sigma with scars like ladders up her arms and a foreign chain hooked into her skin that could turn her into a monster at any second.

But then he was pulling her up and his knuckles brushed beneath her palms, her arms obeying the unspoken command to move into a new position, and she lost herself to the dance again, her focus narrowing on his cues, her attention straining in the dark to follow his lead.

It only took a quick flick of his wrist to send her into another dip, and this time she let her whole body unfurl, her arms stretching up above her head as he pressed her into the arc. The second the pressure of his fingers against her stomach eased, she pulled up, searching for his hands again, closing her eyes as he transitioned her into a series of crisscrossing, intertwining steps that had a huge smile breaking over her face as her heartbeat thudded, marvelling at how perfectly he managed to move them both.

He spun her, but it wasn't a big flourish, only a chance for her to twirl back into his body like a magnet, his hands already raised to catch hers ... except he didn't catch her. He didn't grab her. He didn't grip her. He held out his hands and her fingers brushed lightly against his palms as he guided her.

He was *conducting* her.

She was the one who pressed closer, looking for his next leading touch, his next guiding step, moulding her body to his to try and anticipate him better until she could even feel the uneven breaths that rattled his chest.

His movements became more complicated, but her body only obeyed with more ease, allowing him to lift her, to toss her just enough that his grip was able to switch rapidly from her waist to her thighs. She tightened all her muscles to keep her balance as he spun her around, before he tossed her again, spinning her this time, catching her just as perfectly, his hands cinching her waist as her back landed against his chest.

He raised her, bending her back over his shoulder, his

hand running along the outside of her thigh. She stretched out her leg, still following the flow of his subtle touches, even though he was now tossing her around. He suddenly gripped the inside of her thigh, turning her again as she bent her other knee, keeping her elongated leg strong as she caught her free foot and bent completely over his shoulder.

She released the pose as soon as his hands shifted, keeping herself pliant and willowy as his palms wrapped her hips, twirling her again as he lowered her, his feet already nudging hers across the floor in turn after turn after turn, until her breath dropped out of her chest completely and she was too dizzy to do anything but cling to him when he drew her back in.

"Sweet girl," he said, holding her close, his voice rough, his hands dragging her suddenly up his body, his hips grinding into hers.

The movement was so sudden, so forceful after his drugging, guiding movements that a sound actually hiccupped from her chest, her legs hooking up to cling to his hips on instinct.

He was ... *hard.*

And pushing right between her thighs, the solid length of him pressing tightly to her suddenly throbbing centre like her tights were only a momentary barrier that could be torn away with one of those magical flicks of his wrist.

"I think that's enough for today." He suddenly set her

down, and she realised his song had already finished, and a new one was playing.

"Sorry," she choked out, unsure what else to say.

He ducked to whisper against her cheek, "It's enough for today because reducing us to shadows won't hide a thing if I put you on your hands and knees and see how prettily you'll bend with your hair wrapped around my fist and all that sweet-smelling, desperate heat wrapped around my d—"

"Your delightful self-control?" Gabriel was suddenly behind her, spinning her around, but his eyes seemed fixed over her head.

She swayed between them, her thoughts scattered.

What?

What the ... hell?

Had Elijah just *lost his composure?*

"Focus," Gabriel snapped.

"I stopped, didn't I?" Elijah returned, a growl still riding his tone. "You try having her damp fucking tights rubbing all over the head of your d—"

"*My* delightful manners remain intact." Gabriel pulled her away. "But I'm sure one of the other cavemen can empathise with you—"

"*Stop.*" Alpha voice. "*Bring her back.*"

"Ah, shit." Gabriel froze, and a shudder travelled through Isobel.

"Ignore," Elijah gritted, the word a breathy snarl.

"That." He made a sound that was halfway between a growl and a groan. "Take … her … away."

Gabriel marched her over to the bench, snatching up all their stuff in the dark before guiding her back to the door, his steps quickening as the room grew suddenly, ominously silent now that her phone had stopped playing music.

"Fucking hell." He pushed her out of the door and slammed it behind him, before grabbing her hand and tugging her into a run. "First class?" He shot out over his shoulder, before answering his own question. "It's not time for your first class yet—"

"Shouldn't I—" She tried to twist away from Gabriel, worried that Elijah was surging and that running away would only make it worse, but Gabriel interrupted, tugging her harder.

"You shouldn't."

"Why not?"

"Because *that* particular issue has absolutely nothing to do with your safety."

She frowned, keeping her head down as he dragged her toward the dining hall. She could hardly demand answers with students spilling over the pathways on their way to grab breakfast and cameras leering down at them.

"There's Theo," Gabriel said, pointing out the tousled dark head of hair ducking into the dining hall, taller than most of the students around him. "Go straight to him. No detours. I can't leave Elijah alone and you aren't allowed to be alone either. Mikki's rules."

He spun on his heel, jogging away from her, and she followed the slow slog of students into the dining hall. Theodore had already grabbed a tray and was filling it to overflowing. It seemed that the food theme that morning was just "pancakes," because that's all she could see.

They were all different shapes and sizes, stacked onto labelled warming plates and surrounded by tumbling displays of fruit, selections of yogurt, flavoured creams, an assortment of syrups, and an entire section of miscellaneous toppings. There were thick and fluffy buttermilk pancakes, spotted blueberry and choc chip, orange pumpkin and pecan, buckwheat, wholewheat, ricotta, lemon, oatmeal, and cornmeal ... and then there seemed to be an international section. Thin stacks from Sweden; puffy, jiggly towers from Japan; savoury samples from Korea and Japan; tiny little Dutch puffs; and flat, sugary Hungarian crepes.

She scanned the other labels with distracted eyes. Chinese, Finnish, Mexican, Persian, Bhutanese, Hungarian, and Indian ... it was one of the most elaborate breakfast displays Ironside had done since she had arrived. She was used to it on special occasions, but she couldn't remember anything special about that particular day. It was the day *before* Consolidation Day.

Theodore was mixing so many different types of pancakes it actually made her stomach start to turn, but then she realised he was checking his phone as he piled things on. Kilian, Cian, Moses, Niko, and Oscar were already tucked away in their booth, and only some of them seemed to have food.

"Need a hand?" she asked.

"Just the Illy I was waiting for." He immediately doused her in a smile that made her stomach flip before he transferred the tray to her hands, pulling out a fresh one. He paused, his smile disappearing as he glanced around her. "Elijah and Gabriel are supposed to be with you."

"They ... got held up."

"Hmm." He examined her expression quietly, but he didn't press her, turning back to his task until the second tray was also full. He added on what she wanted to eat, and then they carried all the food back to the table, setting the trays down as the other Alphas descended, grabbing for plates and muttering their thanks.

"Hey." Moses caught the hem of her shirt, pulling her firmly down beside him. "Thanks for the flowers."

She peeked over at him, but he had already released her shirt and was entirely focussed on his food, and then a sudden, booming voice distracted her, making her jump in shock.

"Attention students!" The voice reverberated through the room, projected by a microphone.

They peered out of their booth, watching as a group

of officials strode into the hall, wheeling what looked like a projector on a small stand.

"If you could all give us your attention for a few moments, we have a special announcement that concerns all of you."

It was a woman speaking: a brunette in a navy suit, her fringe sweeping over her face in a harsh fashion. "An incident has been brought to our attention," the woman continued, stepping into the centre of the room as the other officials set up the projector, casting a light over the back wall of the dining hall.

Moses caught Isobel around the waist, lifting her out of the booth and setting her on her feet again as the other Alphas slid out, gathering around her.

She pulled her phone out as all the other booths emptied, everyone spilling out to watch the back wall. Navigating to Sophia's contact, she sent off a quick message, asking if everything was okay on their end.

Sophia: Nothing out of the ordinary yet.

She began to reply, but the back wall suddenly filled with an image, distracting her.

Because it *was* her.

Her face was blurred, but the dress Kilian had gifted her wasn't.

"The fuck is this?" Theodore growled out lowly, apparently also able to tell that it was her.

"This video was taken last term by a student who was hesitant to turn it in," the woman announced, as the video remained paused, stuck on the image of Isobel ... *stepping out of Dorm A?*

"We have very strict rules when it comes to bullying and sexual assault," the woman barked into her microphone.

"Bullshit," Moses mumbled beneath his breath.

"Let this video be a warning to you all," the woman said ominously. "We're always watching, and inappropriate behaviour will be met with severe and swift action."

The video started, then.

Crowe lumbered onto the screen, and Isobel sank backward, closer to the booth, wishing she could hide from all the cameras in the room. Crowe's face was blurred, but the fuzzy circle was much smaller than the one protecting Isobel's identity, still revealing the limp, dark strands of hair that fell around his face—not to mention he was easily one of the largest boys on campus, and his only slightly muffled voice rang through the room the second he spoke.

"Let's try this again, shall we?" He was dragging her away from the entrance, and the projection blurred as whoever had been secretly videoing him shifted quickly to follow, refocusing and zooming in as Crowe held her upright against the back of the dorm.

"I knew you'd give in eventually," Crowe crooned, his voice more distant now as her body pitched and wobbled to the side, her limbs falling limp and unresponsive.

The video cut off abruptly, and the official paused with the microphone raised to her lips, a small, cruel smile concealed as a storm of whispering broke out through the hall.

The officials wanted to publicly shame Crowe ... but *why*? He was a Beta, and it definitely wasn't to protect anyone from bullies or predators. The officials had known about—and were *gossiping* about—all the attacks made against her, but not one of them had tried to speak to her about them.

There was a commotion toward the back of the room, students scrambling away from a person standing near the entrance to the hall.

Crowe.

He glanced over at her, his eyes empty, his mouth forming a word. "*Welcome.*"

Welcome ... *what*?

Someone shoved him several steps backward, almost knocking him off balance despite his massive size. Bellamy was standing before the bigger boy, fuming, his eyes spitting furious fire. His mouth was moving in a furious gush of words, but Isobel couldn't hear a thing he was saying from the other side of the hall.

He shoved Crowe again, but Crowe didn't even bother to fight back. He spat out what looked like a curse before spinning on his heel and stalking out of the hall.

What the hell was going on?

"It saddens us that it took so long for this footage to

find its way into our hands." The official spoke again without warning, everyone jolting their attention back to her. "We want all of our students to know that they can *come to us*." She emphasised it as though she had already spoken it a dozen times and was frustrated that nobody was listening. "If you have something to report ..." The woman motioned to the wall behind her, reminding everyone of what they had watched. "Then you know where to find us. We would like to assure you that confidentiality is *absolutely* key."

"That's one way of delivering an invitation," Moses grumbled from behind her. He was standing surprisingly close. She could feel the heat from his body, his words stirring against the back of her head. She wasn't sure when he had last stood so close to her. *On purpose.*

The others were also shifting closer—not just to her, but to each other, forming a tight circle with her and Kilian in the centre, Theodore to the right, Cian slightly in front of everyone, and Niko to the left. Their bodies were tense. Theodore and Niko's expressions tight and wary. Oscar was somewhere behind her—she could smell his strong oleander scent rolling over the fragrances of the other Alphas like a cloud of smoke, muddying them all up. The sensation was unsettling. It smelled like a forest set on fire, with tinges of Niko's whiskey turning into gasoline and Cian's sunshine smouldering far too hotly.

"Invitation?" Isobel whispered, barely daring to

move her lips as she turned her head, too focussed on the woman to look all the way back at Moses.

The official was staring out over the sea of gathered students, her brows raised in expectation. When she found Isobel tucked behind Cian, she paused, repeating, "You know where to find us," before clicking her fingers at the other officials to follow her as she stalked from the room.

"Wait ... that's it?" Isobel stared after the woman. "She ... she didn't even say where to find them."

Theodore, who had been leaning up against the side of the booth to her right—his shoes touching hers, his arms crossed—curled closer, his lips by her ear. He even raised his hand to block the cameras from reading his lips. "The Track Team told you to find out where the club was. You found out. This is them summoning you. *You know where to find them*, and *confidentiality is absolutely key*."

She snapped her mouth shut, unable to properly reply in the busy dining hall. The other students had broken out into a confused mass of whispers, one of them calling after the official.

"What about Crowe?" The shout was a little too loud, and Isobel craned her neck to peer around Oscar to see who had spoken.

A second-year Beta. One of Crowe's friends ... or was she? It seemed like Bellamy's fan club of Betas were trying to distance themselves from Crowe.

The official paused in the doorway to the hall, turning to look back at the Beta. "Alaric Crowe—along with others—have been questioned in relation to this incident. All students must be cautious not to start baseless rumours, as this is a form of harassment in itself. The person in the video will be found and dealt with by the academy board."

Theodore scoffed quietly, and it seemed like not even the Beta girl could find the words to respond, her fists clenched by her sides as the officials left the hall in a swift clicking of heels and tapping of business shoes.

Isobel didn't move, and neither did the Alphas. They waited, watching and listening, for something else to happen. Finally, Theodore slid back into the booth, pulling Isobel in beside him. The rest of them filed back in and all the plates were rearranged as they settled into new positions.

"Should we do an end-of-year party?" Theodore asked casually, acting like nothing at all had happened as he violently shoved a buckwheat and muesli pancake off his plate to get to the fluffy Japanese pancake beneath it, which was beginning to cave in from the dolloped cream and sliced strawberries he had piled into the centre of it. Apparently, he was having a treat day.

"Obviously," Niko said, at the same time as Moses said, "No."

"It should be Consolidation Day themed like last year," Cian added, though he didn't look particularly excited by the prospect. "We can hang the Gifted-American flag all over the place, and have a red, white, and blue cake."

"Or we could just chill," Moses muttered, stabbing up the buckwheat pancake Theodore had abandoned.

"I think Elijah said the officials already offered to sponsor another Dorm A party."

"Must be nice." Isobel froze, staring down at her plate. *Did she just say that out loud?* She glanced up. They were all staring at her. "To have coffee," she finished lamely. "I forgot to get one."

"Here." Theodore shifted his mug her way.

"That's okay." Her face was starting to burn. Theodore hated people stealing his food or sharing his utensils. He was almost as bad as Gabriel.

"What dorm are you trying to get into again?" Oscar asked blandly, leaning forward to fix narrowed dark eyes on her. "Correct me if I'm mistaken, but you'll be prancing through Dorm A in your rich-girl pyjamas next year right alongside the rest of us *spoiled* Alphas."

If Oscar had said that to her a year ago, she would have tried to crawl beneath the table and die. She still wanted to slump down and disappear a little bit, but she also knew that the spark of annoyance in his eye was something he only showed to his *friends.* If he truly thought so little of her, he would have been ignoring her completely.

"I can't tell if your issue is with me thinking you're

spoiled or if it's just my pyjamas." She popped a mouthful of chocolate chip pancake into her mouth.

"It's definitely the pyjamas," Cian supplied, leaning back in his seat to chug half a cup of coffee. "He's as obsessed as Gabriel is with your underwear."

Moses glanced up from his breakfast, scanning the faces around the table before he blew out a disappointed breath. "Such a waste. Gabriel isn't here."

"Where are those two?" Niko didn't even look up from his food.

"They got held up," Isobel muttered.

Everyone glanced at her. Even Niko, who stopped eating for half a second to do so.

"Elijah, um ..." She glanced nervously around the table, trying to find the right words in front of the camera. "He overdid it in dance practice. Surged his movements too much."

Theodore's brows knit together. "Surged his movements?"

"Uh, yeah, I mean he overextended himself."

They were silent, several of them checking their phones.

"Can't wait to question him about *that* later." Oscar finally spoke, his tone full of dark humour.

Cian sighed, shaking his head. "Any idea why he might have ... overextended himself?" he asked Isobel.

"No idea," she said quickly.

"Oh?" Niko—who had gone back to his food—suddenly looked up again, his eyes narrowing.

She felt her face, neck, and chest all start to heat up, and she quickly pulled up her palms to cup her cheeks, turning even redder as the warmth flooded into her hands.

"You really don't know?" Niko asked, his gaze pulling her in.

"I might know," she blurted, before quickly shaking her head. "I've gotta get to my first class." She shot to her feet, realising she had somehow been sandwiched into the back of the booth with three Alphas either side of her.

She turned her pleading look to Theodore, and he met it with a small, amused smile.

"I want to say that won't work on me, but nothing's ever worked better," he declared, pushing Cian out of the booth and reaching over to drag out an annoyed Moses, who tried to take his plate with him.

Cian grabbed his bag and slung it over his shoulder. "Let's go, doll." He snatched up her bag before she could, and then he hoisted up a third, sending it flying into Moses' chest. "You're with us. Sorry to break your absent streak."

"Was hoping to finish the year without going to a single one of those ridiculous classes," Moses grumbled beneath his breath, abandoning his breakfast to follow Isobel and Cian out of the hall.

14
THE HEALING POWER OF CRYSTALS. OR NOT

ISOBEL HAD BEEN IN SUCH A RUSH TO ESCAPE BREAKFAST THAT she didn't even realise how early they were until they spilled into the still-dark, empty classroom. Cian flicked on the lights and took hold of Isobel's wrist, pulling her to the back of the room. He nudged open the swinging door to the supply closet where Professor Vega kept her psychic paraphernalia. He twisted his body at the last second, pulling her ahead of him and into the cramped space. He stepped in after her, his face carefully blank, and Moses moved in beside him, dropping his bag by the door and reaching over for Isobel's bag as Cian pulled the door closed behind them.

It wasn't too dark to see their faces, but the shadows now settling into their features made the flat set of their mouths look more like scowls. She felt along the shelf behind her, knocking over a stack of tarot card boxes.

"What are we doing in here?" She stepped onto a pile of divination textbooks, just so that they wouldn't be towering over her, and Moses flicked his attention down to her feet with a small shake of his head.

"You're hiding something." Cian stepped into her personal space, reaching out to the shelf beside her head. His scent washed over her, saltwater and gentle heat seeping into her pores and making her lick her lips as she tracked him warily with her eyes.

He only grabbed a long, smooth crystal from the shelf, turning it over in his palm with a thoughtful expression.

"Hiding what?" she croaked, glancing between them.

"Elijah and Gabriel." Moses stepped over a box of meditation cushions, nudging them back toward the door to make room for him and Cian to crowd her up against the shelf. She had no idea if they were trying to intimidate her or simply trying to keep their voices low. "What really happened? Why couldn't you say it in front of the cameras?"

"Because Elijah surged." She stared down at her feet. "Gabriel said we had to leave him—"

"He actually surged?" Moses interrupted, like he still couldn't believe it.

"Surged how?" Cian cocked his head to the side, looking more curious than surprised, a lock of dark gold hair slipping over his forehead, tattooed fingers brushing it absently back.

"What do you mean how?" She switched her attention from her shoes to the roof.

"Isobel." Cian's voice lowered to a purr. "Look at me."

Her attention darted back to his face, her jaw set stubbornly, teeth grinding together.

He cupped her jaw, his thumb slipping up above her chin, brushing beneath the swell of her lip, his eyes darkening to a velvet sapphire, his Alpha ring glittering almost menacingly. He tipped forward, whispering close to her face, "Did he want to fuck you, doll?"

She blinked at him, her stomach swooping. "W-We were just dancing."

"Hm." Cian's attention switched to her mouth. "Do you know what it looks like when someone wants to fuck you? Do you know what it feels like?"

She lifted her chin. "Yes."

He licked his lips like he was tasting her deception, and his grip on her chin tightened, his eyes darkening further, his Alpha ring beginning to swell.

"Get it out of her now, or I do it my way," Moses snapped, his acidic and sweet scent growing sour. "This class is going to fill up in a matter of minutes."

The door to the classroom opened as if on cue, and a small group of students entered, chattering animatedly about what had happened in the dining hall. The storage cupboard had slats in it, just big enough to let in a small amount of light, and angled to show them a hint of the classroom beyond.

Isobel tried to pull her chin out of Cian's grip, but he only shook his head, making a quiet sound of reprimand before his hand fell to her neck, pushing her tightly to the shelves. She darted a look to the slats, but there was no way they could see inside the dark closet without angling the slats in the other direction. Her eyes snapped to Moses, finding only annoyance.

"Why are you so stubborn?" he asked, mouthing the words more than anything.

"Why are you?" she returned, but Cian tightened his grip, and she immediately returned her attention to him.

He had switched the smooth crystal to his other hand to grab her, but now he reached up to set it back onto the shelf.

"What happened?" he asked softly.

His grip had been incrementally tightening, so subtly that she didn't even realise when she stopped breathing. She reached up to grab his wrist, and the second her fingers hit his skin, he loosened his hold, his expression unchanging, chillingly blank.

"You're freaking me out," she grumbled, as the students began loudly replaying a recording of the dining hall incident on someone's phone.

"Please." Moses rolled his eyes, shrugging back his shoulders until he found a comfortable spot to lean against the shelves, tucking one of his feet behind the other and crossing his muscled arms. "Nobody's nose is as good as mine. You're not freaked out."

"Then what am I?" she flung out in a distressed whisper.

"Turned on, honey." Cian breathed the words against her ear, his grip tightening again. "Tell us what happened with Elijah."

She wanted to snap back at him, but her knees had gone weak, and he had pushed one of his thighs between hers like he knew he would need to hold her up, his spare hand dropping to her hip.

"Be a good girl and I'll give you what Elijah couldn't," he purred into her ear.

She felt her eyes fluttering shut, but then immediately pulled them open, wide with embarrassment as she stared over Cian's shoulder at Moses.

"H-Have you guys spoken to Kalen?" she asked, her voice trembling.

Moses watched her carefully, his dark eyes impassive as they captured every tick and twitch in her expression. "No ..." His gaze brushed down her body, taking in the way Cian was pressing her into the shelves. "But we don't need to. It's written all over you. You're built for praise."

"And I'm remarkably good at finding people's weak spots," Cian added, a smirk in his voice. "So how hard should I try, Carter? How much should I push you?" His tongue flicked out against the edge of her jaw. "This hard?" He gripped her hair suddenly, pulling her head back and licking along her jaw until he got to her chin, which he nipped at sharply. "Or harder?"

Her mind went completely blank. "Yes."

Cian groaned, pulling back slightly. She was staring at his lips, wondering if they tasted like salt water, and if kissing him would feel like drowning. He turned his head, narrowing his eyes on Moses. "Someone needs to keep her quiet while I'm persuading her to talk."

Moses arched a dark, winged brow, his expression challenging despite the quiet tone of his words. "I'm not laying a finger on her." His attention drifted to Isobel. "No offense, Carter."

"None taken," she muttered, Moses' even tone helping to clear the hazy fog Cian had managed to scatter her thoughts with.

The classroom was starting to fill up, louder than usual as they rode the wave of drama from earlier. Moses pushed off the shelves, but instead of stalking out of the closet, he only reached over Cian, gripping her shoulder and pulling her forward, her front smacking into Cian's hard chest. Cian caught her hips, pulling her off the stack of books she had been standing on and turning their bodies until she could feel Moses at her back, the three of them stacked sideways into the cupboard. She finally had a full view of the door, and she swallowed nervously at the light slanting in across the floor, missing Cian's shoe by an inch.

Moses nudged her stack of books back beneath her dangling feet and Cian set her down again.

"Now let me be very clear," Cian whispered, ducking back to her ear. "This isn't a punishment. It's a lesson. You're going to be one of us soon, and you need to understand who you're dealing with. Consider this my initiation task. If you beg out, you lose."

"Pity you won't be able to use your mouth," Moses mumbled, his body pressing up against her back, his hand suddenly wrapping around the lower half of her face, his grip tight enough to alarm her.

"Do you know how to tap out, doll?" Cian's hand settled on her neck again, his fingers flexing in a loose grip.

Her eyes widened, her nostrils flaring with desperate breath. Last time, he had eased his grip as soon as she touched his hand. Hesitantly, she reached up and tapped Cian's wrist, and his hand immediately eased away, caressing along her collarbone. As soon as he moved, so did Moses, dropping his grip to her shoulder and steadying her as she gulped in a harrowed breath.

Her body was starting to shake, but she couldn't figure out the emotions tripping through her. She was so wet, she *knew* she would have been saturating the closet in her scent, but her stomach was flipping nervously. She had a feeling she had upset Cian, but he had made a point of saying that she wasn't being punished, and Moses? He wasn't a person she would ever think to put her trust in. Not to mention she still didn't know *what* was happening, but she recognised the way Cian's Alpha ring was swelling and the intent look in his eyes. It was the way Theodore had looked after he kissed her. It was the way Oscar had looked before he kissed her.

Cian wanted to kiss her.

"That's exactly right," Cian purred softly, nuzzling her cheek. "Don't forget your gesture. You might need it." He hooked his fingers in her tights as Moses wrapped his hand around her mouth again. With a rough tug, her tights were torn down her legs, a surprised shriek dashed against Moses' calloused skin as he lifted her enough for Cian to rip off her shoes and yank her tights over her feet, flinging them to the shelf behind him.

She jerked, gripping Moses' wrist, and both Alphas paused.

"Is that your gesture, Carter?" Moses asked huskily, his voice deep and low.

She shook her head.

"Show me you remember it," Cian demanded quietly.

She reached shaking fingers up to the back of Moses' hand, tapping it, and he dropped it just as Cian leaned forward.

"Such a good girl," Cian praised, his lips barely brushing against hers, not really a kiss but more of an acknowledgement. "That's the last time I remind you, do you understand?"

She whimpered breathily, and Moses' hand silenced her again.

"Just nod," Moses rumbled against the back of her head.

She nodded, and Cian reached for a box on the shelf beside him, flicking up the lid as Isobel stared at the picture on the side. Whatever it was, it was a rounded tower shape, and that had confusion and slight panic sparking to life in the pit of her stomach, but when Cian drew the object out of the packaging, it was just a crystal, like the dozen other sizes and shapes of crystals and gemstones lined up along the shelf and stacked away in boxes along the back wall, except this one was apparently big and special enough to warrant its own box.

Cian ran his fingers over the smooth, veined pink stone like he was testing it for cracks or imperfections before he tapped the end of it against Moses' hand. Moses peeled his fingers back, setting them on her hips as Cian tapped the cool, rounded crystal against her lips next.

"Open your mouth."

She parted her lips, and he pushed in without warning, flattening her tongue as he filled her mouth, the end of the stone hitting the back of her throat. The sudden invasion had surprised tears filling her eyes, but the way Cian was watching her also had liquid heat pooling low in her stomach, making her press and rub her thighs together in an attempt to ease the ache.

"Make sure it's nice and wet," Moses warned lowly, "or this is going to hurt."

That spark of alarm burned hotter, and it must have also spiked in her scent because Moses let out a short grunt of approval against the back of her head, enjoying the fear he had encouraged her to feel.

Cian pulled the stone out of her mouth, and then several things happened at once. The chain on her chest began burning, Cian ripped her panties off with his free hand, and the stone was pushed immediately between her thighs, forcing her to quickly clamp it there by half crossing her legs so that it wouldn't fall to the ground and alert all the students to what they were doing.

Cian must have seen the chain glowing, because he tugged down the neckline of her shirt, staring at the new gemstone that had appeared.

They all waited, panting quietly, suddenly painfully aware of the students on the other side of the door.

"Looks reddish." Cian was peering at the gem. "Feel anything?"

She was feeling *a lot* of things. And Moses was still silencing her.

She narrowed her eyes on Cian, like she didn't appreciate the question, and he smirked.

For the love of every useless fucking god don't let it be me.

The words popped into her head, growled out in Moses' voice, full of trepidation.

"Isobel?" Cian prompted.

It could be fun if she goes feral.

Cian's voice this time.

Inside her *head.*

She slowly shook her head, and Cian's brows lowered dangerously. He twisted the stone she didn't realise he was still holding, and it slipped against her clit, causing another sound to escape her throat and disappear into Moses' palm.

"Eyes normal?" Moses grunted. *I'll fucking pray if I have to.*

"Eyes are normal," Cian confirmed. "My girl is soaked." *I've never been so hard.*

"Call her that again and I'm done cooperating," Moses growled, somehow sounding threatening while also barely audible.

Cian only chuckled, twisting the stone again and making Isobel slacken back against Moses, who had to tighten his hold of her hip to keep her upright.

"She'll be begging for me so much you might as well have the words tattooed into your palm before I'm done here." Cian angled the stone to push against her entrance, his eyes tunnelling into hers. "You want to tell us what happened with Elijah, baby?"

She nodded, her body trying to twist away from the intrusion. The top book on the pile she had been standing on toppled off, smacking into the ground, and they all froze again, waiting for someone to come and investigate. The class was still loudly discussing the incident in the dining hall, replaying all the videos that had popped up on social media as they gathered at the front of the room. Vega was sitting at her desk by the window, peering out of the glass with a frown on her lips, either uninterested in the class without Cian there, or else simply acknowledging that she had no chance of wrangling the students into focussing.

After a few horribly tense breaths, Moses tutted out a disapproving sound, looping his arm around her middle as he lifted her a few inches, the stone slipping back between her thighs as he carefully toed away the stack of books and began lowering her to the floor again.

Except Cian refused to lower his hand.

She gripped Moses' arm tight in warning, her nails digging in as he lowered her slowly, the stone pushing between her soaked lips again, trying to nestle further into her entrance. Her words of protest were muffled against Moses' palm. She kicked at Cian, but he only flashed her a dark, heated smile.

Need inside. It was both of their voices layering over each other, along with other thoughts and disjointed statements that were suddenly too loud for her to sort through.

This is bad. That had been Moses. *Shouldn't do this to Theodore. Going to kill me.*

One of the Alphas could hear people's innermost thoughts.

That didn't bode well for her.

Especially since they hadn't thought it necessary to *tell* her.

Moses lowered her down another inch, despite his thoughts, and their words inside her head quickly became a jumble again.

So soft.

Smells so good.

Could bathe in this.

Want to taste.

So pretty.

Hate this.

Could watch her face like this for hours.

Want to kiss her.

Want to lick her.

Want to fucking punch something.

Moses' breath rattled, the fingers digging into her hip flexing as he pushed her down further. She tried to bow her body away from the invading object, but Cian's hand flashed to her other hip until they were both pushing her down. Her nails razed Moses' arm, and she caught a brief whiff of copper, his quiet grunt in her ear telling her that she had drawn blood.

"You want to tell us now?" Cian asked, his gaze on fire as he licked his lips.

She nodded desperately, but Moses still refused to remove his hand.

"You want to tap out?" Cian's whisper was almost lost as they pushed her down further, the stone stretching her, filling her in a way she had never felt before. She was standing on the very tips of her toes, unable to get any higher, her body straining upwards, but there was a niggling little thought in the back of her mind as they both surged closer at the sound of her tortured, muffled groan.

She could suddenly feel how hard they both were, Cian's dick pressing into her hip, Moses' curved into the small of her back, and she wondered what it would feel like if it was one of them pushing inside her instead of the smooth crystal.

Somewhere in the classroom, Vega was now attempting to waffle on about moon cycles, and the fear of being caught or found out should have hindered her lust, but the growled thoughts hammering into her brain sent her inhibitions swirling away.

"Fuck, Isobel." Cian groaned quietly. "What are you thinking about? You just got so wet it's coating my fingers."

She immediately reached for his hand, twisting her thighs together to keep the stone in place as she pulled his grip away.

She felt wild.

Unhinged.

He must have seen it in her eyes because he allowed her to shift his grip, watching her with a mix of curiosity and heat. She scrambled for the drawstring on his pants before pushing both of their hands past the waistband. She circled his fingers around his own length right at the top of his cock as it pushed up into their searching grip, spreading her nectar over his length as she pushed their hands down to the base. Cian's eyes flared, his nostrils flared, even his Alpha ring seemed to pulse bigger, a deep rattle emanating from his chest.

"Fuck, Illy." He tugged down Moses' hand and kissed her fully, his tongue spearing into her mouth, the cold metal of his piercing a shock as his hand gripped her throat, squeezing lightly like he was trying to send her a message. His steely length throbbed in their hands before he pulled her fingers out of his pants, groaning at the way she tried to twist her fingers against his skin to leave behind as much of her stickiness as she could. He snapped her hand to his wrist, and she realised he was letting her know that her gesture was still there, that she could still tap the back of one of their hands.

And then he squeezed her throat again, his other hand twisting into her hair.

"Want to tell us now?" he growled out breathlessly, pulling back an inch to let her breathe.

She tried to say yes, but he surged forward again, filling her mouth with his tongue before she could muster up a single word.

“You can stand on those pretty toes all day, can’t you, Carter?” Moses whispered silkily.

She waited for his thoughts to let her know what he had meant by that, but belatedly realised that the stone on her chest had grown cold again. She felt his rough fingers drifting across her thigh and realised he was about to take control of the stone. She tried to beg for him not to touch it, but Cian flexed his fingers against her neck threateningly, biting down hard on her lip.

“Aw, baby,” he crooned softly. “Is there something you wanted to say?” He flicked his eyes over her shoulder, connecting with Moses for a brief moment. “Stepladder behind you. Lift her legs.”

Moses reacted far too quickly, swooping down, and picking her up by the backs of her knees, knocking her off balance and back into him as he lowered himself to the thin stepladder shoved into the corner of the cupboard, one of his boots planted on the lower rung, the other steady against the ground to keep them balanced.

Cian had caught the crystal as it slipped out of her, and he held it now, staring down at her as Moses peeled her legs apart, his head falling into the crook of her neck. Moses seemed to inhale her deeply, his chest vibrating with a rough, almost inaudible sound. He thrust his hips up, his erection grinding into her ass as his hand brushed up her torso, between her breasts, stopping at her neck. She expected him to cover her mouth again, but instead, he wrapped her neck in his grip, squeezing with a deeper groan falling against her ear. His other hand drifted between her legs as he hooked his knees beneath hers and spread her out wider, wide enough that she could feel the air from the door slats against her heated, swollen skin.

Cian watched with hooded eyes, gripping her chin and absently stroking her lower lip as his eyes fell between her legs. When he raised his gaze again, he sucked in a sharp breath.

"Stay just like that, doll." He pinched her chin higher, lifting her gaze fully to his as he stepped forward, towering over both her and Moses on the short stepladder. "Don't take your eyes off me and I'll let you leave your scent all over me, okay? Take your eyes off me and I'll wipe it all away."

She nodded, a whimper catching in the back of her throat. Cian must have handed Moses the stone without her noticing, because she could suddenly feel it slipping between her folds again, the head notching at her entrance as it came to rest there.

She wanted to flutter her eyelids closed at the sensation, but held them open instead as Cian pushed down the waistband of his pants, pulling out his cock. It was long and tanned, the golden tone of his skin flushed with a ruby glow, the veins pulsing as he gripped it and squeezed. She briefly glanced the full tattoo curling from his inner thigh and around his groin. Twisted branches and delicate, scattered tufts of flowers. It looked like a gust of wind had torn through the knotted tree, sending petals fluttering around the stem of his cock and to the other side of his groin. The petals were coloured in a delicate pink, the rest of the tattoo black.

"You want to cover me with saliva, baby?" His scent swelled, filling her lungs to bursting point.

She nodded, and Moses' hand gave her a quick warning squeeze before he shoved the stone into her several inches at once. She jolted back and almost shrieked, but Cian took advantage of her mouth popping open in shock and suddenly thrust into it, pushing all the way to the back of her throat in one brutal movement.

She choked on him instantly, the gagging sound cut off because he was filling her mouth completely, her jaw straining to accommodate him, her tongue flattened. She clenched around the stone, and she knew she was dripping her excitement over Moses' hand because he bit down against the back of her neck almost in retaliation, punishing her for enjoying herself.

He forced the stone all the way into her, thrusting as suddenly as Cian had, his teeth still latched onto her skin, and she let out a keening wail that never escaped her throat and only seemed to cause her mouth to vibrate around Cian's pulsing length.

Cian growled and Moses cursed, pulling the smooth crystal out and forcing it back in, all the way to the base, the movement strong and smooth, powerful enough to jolt her and have her desperately grappling at both of their arms in an attempt to suck air back into her lungs. They both eased off a bit, Cian pulling halfway out of her mouth, staring down at her with pinched brows, combing his fingers softly through her hair, gentling her as Moses tapped his fingers against her neck in a distracted, agitated pattern, like he was counting down the seconds until he could squeeze the breath out of her.

"*Please*," she tried to whisper around Cian's hot length, blinking blurry tears out of her vision as she stared up at him, but he only gripped the back of her head and slid inside as far as he could push again.

Cian's thumbs stroked beneath her eye, swiping at the strained tears that gathered there before popping his thumb between his lips to lick away the salty drop from his skin. She felt momentarily hypnotised, but then Moses distracted her by thrusting the stone in and out of her again, his movements jerky like he was trying to stop himself. He licked over the spot on the back of her neck where he had bitten her, but then his teeth scraped her again, in a different spot, and then again, and again.

He fucked her with the stone, faster and harder, and she licked her tongue along the swollen flesh before her face, wanting to taste the tang of saltwater and the burn of sunlight as badly as she wanted to cover Cian in her own scent. She licked and licked and tried to keep her whimpers to the back of her throat as their scents thickened into the headiest mix of salt and sap, so thick she could almost feel it dribbling over her skin.

"Baby ...," Cian rasped out. "That's enough. I'm going to lose control."

He was going to take it away? There were parts she had only licked once. She gripped the base of him, quickly closing her mouth around the head and trying to push all of him back into her mouth.

"Illy, fuck. *Fuckk.* You need to stop, baby girl. Or I'll come all over you—"

"Get a single fucking drop on her and I will literally break your fucking dick, Cian Ashford. I'm not fucking around," Moses ground out, his quiet Alpha voice radiating through his body and into Isobel's.

She squirmed back against him and pulled back to lick the salty liquid drops that were gathering on the tip of Cian's cock.

"Isobel," Cian whispered, his voice barely more than a rasp, his eyes unfocussed. "You need to stop, honey."

Something swooped low in her stomach, some kind of rejection she didn't understand at all. It was like the bond had taken over, forcing her to *need* certain things she couldn't even make sense of. She *needed* Cian to *let* her lick him, mark him, claim him, and he didn't want her to. Her vision flooded with tears—different tears this time—her stomach twisting painfully, and Cian blew out a long breath before pushing the head of his cock against her trembling lips.

"This isn't part of your initiation," he said huskily. "This is just what happens when you pout at me." He pushed back into her mouth, twisted his hands into her hair, and started to fuck her mouth roughly, pushing in as deep as her throat would allow before rocking a few times and forcing himself even deeper, and then pulling out and shoving back in, repeating the brutal movements until he stilled, pulsing and spilling hot liquid deep into her throat.

Moses kept his grip on her light so that she wouldn't choke, but she still struggled to swallow it down, her body so on edge that she was squirming uncontrollably in Moses' lap, causing him to push his hips up, seeking relief by rubbing his erection against her.

Cian was still growling lowly in the back of his throat when he pulled from her mouth, tugging his pants up over his glistening dick immediately like he was already fighting off the urge to ease it back into her.

He crouched down in front of her, gently laying his hand over her mouth.

"Do you want to tell us now, sweetheart?"

She nodded frantically, her hips now moving in synchronisation with the drag of the stone in and out of her gripping channel. She had never felt so desperate before in her life.

She just wanted *relief*.

"Then tell us, and we'll let you come." Cian peeled his hand away, bending close so she could whisper to him. "Why did Elijah surge, Illy?"

"H-He liked dancing with m-me."

"Was he hard, baby?" Cian crooned, an oddly calculating look flashing into his eyes.

She nodded.

"Did he want to get inside you as desperately as Moses wants to get inside you right now?"

She whimpered, clenching around the stone. "I d-don't know. Moses d-doesn't ... it's not like that—"

"Shut the fuck up," Moses whispered gutturally, allowing the stone to slip out of her, holding it up in front of her. "Clean it. With your hands."

She wrapped her hands around the slippery crystal, coating her palms in her own juices before he pulled it away, handing it off to Cian. He lifted her, spinning her around and tugging her legs around his hips as he resettled her in his lap.

"On me," he demanded, tugging at the waistband of his pants until his erection broke free, angry and purplish, thicker than Cian's, but not as long.

She quickly wrapped her hands around him, appreciating that he didn't even question her insane need, and had even anticipated it. He groaned as she twisted her hands over his length, trying to cover every inch, fascinated with the way he twitched and throbbed against her fingers.

As soon as she pulled her hands away, confident that she had spread her essence everywhere, he snatched her hips and pulled her over his damp stiffness.

"More," he grunted quietly, his voice rough and

gritty. He ground her pussy over him, making her gush all over him and squirm with the now dire need to come. "Goddamn it, Carter."

"Moses ..." There was a low, quiet warning in Cian's rumble. "You can't fuck her."

Moses razed his teeth along her collarbone before tugging down her shirt and sports bra, bunching both beneath her breast in his fist while he sucked her nipple into his mouth. He had lifted her off his lap and she only had the head of his dick to grind against, so she tried to push her hips down onto that, making him hiss out a breath and bite her nipple.

She exploded, and he shifted his hips so that she couldn't press down on him the same way, dropping her back to his lap and letting her ride out the waves of her orgasm against his thigh before he stood, a torrent of curses slipping out of his mouth one after the other, his eyes a dark inferno as he set her trembling body on the stepladder and pressed his weeping cock to her lips.

"I can't come on you," he whispered brokenly. "It'll cause a riot." He seemed to be asking for permission, and for a moment, she was just as confused as he was. She didn't have that kind of relationship with Moses.

He didn't even *like* her.

But her lips were parting anyway, and he slid against her tongue with a husky groan. She could see Cian over his shoulder, watching her face with a guarded, calculating look, assessing her even though there was still a spark of heat in his expression as she took his friend's cock all the way to the back of her throat.

Moses started thrusting unevenly, fucking into her throat as he gripped her cheeks, puffing her lips out as he looked down at her with angry dark eyes.

"Wish you weren't sucking it all off," he muttered in a distracted way before his hips jerked and he exploded against the back of her tongue. "Fuck ... *fuck* ... Jesus Christ ... why do you have to look like you were made for me? Swallow it all. Every drop, Carter."

He stroked a line up her throat, and then pulled out of her mouth, tucking himself back into his pants before tugging her up, into his arms.

He held her against his chest, saying something quietly to Cian, who seemed to be shifting around behind him. The sounds of the classroom on the other side of the cupboard seemed piercingly loud all of a sudden, and she felt dizzy, and overwhelmed. There were tears spilling down her cheeks, and she didn't know how to stop them.

She had just done *what*?

And with *Moses?*

Cian seemed to be tugging her tights back on while Moses held her, and as he settled them against her hips, he saw her face.

"To me," Cian demanded, grabbing her off Moses and sitting on the stepladder so that he could bundle her into his lap. "Shh, you're okay, doll. You're safe."

He brushed her hair from her face so gently she could have been made of glass. "You did so well. You're so beautiful, so perfect."

She liked Cian ... Cian was safe ...

But right at that moment, Cian felt more than dangerous.

Without Cian, none of that would have happened.

She screwed her eyes closed, willing her body to teleport away, but of course, it didn't work like that, so instead, she slumped into the overheated body holding her, her cheek falling to his shoulder, and she started counting inside her head.

He whispered to her that she was stunning, she was perfect, she was *such a good girl*, and she pushed all those words away before they could weave her back under his spell.

She wasn't very experienced, but she also wasn't an idiot.

What she had just done was *irresponsible*.

She almost lost her virginity in a *CLOSET*.

WITH MOSES.

"Pathetic," her father would say. "What a desperate, pathetic little Sigma."

15
Red Light, Green Light

Despite her best efforts to ignore him, Cian still managed to calm her somewhat. At least he managed to stop her crying and fix up all her clothes so that she looked presentable again, but the effort to tell herself that his heat *wasn't* comforting and his whispered voice *didn't* sound like heaven had completely sapped all her energy reserves, and when the classroom finally emptied, her legs were too wobbly to move.

She scooted away from both of them when they tried to help her, shoving the long pink crystal into her bag because there was no way she was leaving it in there for the students to play with. She burst out of the closet, keeping her head down as she stalked toward the fitness centre. Her next class was Mikel's small group session, but there was no way she could face the other Alphas.

Unfortunately, luck wasn't on her side, because she

was on track to run right into Kilian, Niko, and Theodore outside the fitness centre. They were walking toward her from the other direction. One of them called out, but she tucked her chin down tighter, quickening her steps to a jog as she yanked open the entrance door and hurried toward the climbing rooms, her heart beating all the way into her throat.

She was on autopilot, her brain tripping over itself, her chest growing tight and painful, dark spots flashing before her eyes. She briefly considered stopping and looking for Niko. He would know what to do. He would hold her hands and tell her to squeeze him until the heavy weight of dread stopped crushing her.

But no ... she just wanted to get to her session with Kalen.

The sign wasn't up on the door yet, but she shoved her way inside anyway, staring around at the empty room.

No ... this wasn't right. It was time for *Mikel's* session, not Kalen's. She started pacing, moving to the rack of harnesses out of habit as she pulled out her phone. Her vision blurred over with tears, and she froze, forcing her eyes to go dry with an iron will that did nothing to ease the crushing panic threatening to pull her under. She flicked open a group message because she couldn't remember if she had Kalen's number or not.

But what could she say?

He was probably busy.

She would just practise until it was time for their session. She started strapping herself in, and the door opened. She glanced up, her nose flaring. She usually couldn't smell any of the Alphas from so far away, but Cian and Moses were wearing her like a cloud of perfume. The others had joined them: Theodore, Kilian, Niko—and Oscar, who must have caught up to the others at some point.

"Illy." Theodore stepped ahead of the others, a careful, cautious mask over his features. "Are you hurt?"

"Hurt?" She snapped out the word in a confused way, unable to look at him for long. "No, no. I'm just climbing." She turned away, wishing she could draw a full breath, but her chest was too tight.

"Isobel." It was Cian this time, his voice low and regretful. It threatened to break her heart, and that made her *furious.* Since when did she care about Cian so much? *Sure*, they went through a lot together on the settlement tour—

"Yes, we did."

She froze, her head snapping up to the climbing wall, the back of her neck prickling. "Did I just say that out loud?"

"Just that we went through a lot together. Do you think you could step away from the wall and talk to us for a little bit?"

She winced, the panic flaring bigger and brighter, her breath a rasp. "N-No, I can't, sorry. I'm training."

"What's going on?" Gabriel's voice carried through the room. "We could literally follow her scent all the way here."

Gabriel.

Gabriel could read minds.

She knew the abilities of everyone else. He was the only unknown.

"Why don't you tell me?" she shot back, spinning on her foot and glaring at him.

He didn't look guilty. Only considering.

Elijah, who had followed him into the room, narrowed an icy gaze on Isobel's face. "You know that thing I don't use anymore, Isobel?"

His power?

She nodded once, short and sharp, sensing a reprimand incoming.

"Gabriel is the same."

Great. Now she had nobody except herself to be angry at again. Unless ...

She sought out Moses, wishing she could *do* something with the furious energy bubbling in her veins.

"Oh, we're getting into it, are we?" He stayed where he was, but it looked like he had shifted his stance. It was eerily similar to something Niko did just before he pounced. She didn't like that she could see the confusion and alarm bleeding out of the darkness of Moses' glare. She didn't like that she could *feel* it cracking against her body like a whip, opening up wounds so that it could bleed into her, infecting her with her own forced empathy.

She tore her eyes away from him before she could crack open her walls and suck his turmoil into herself. "No," she relented. "Sorry."

Anger. Moses didn't like that she wasn't rising to the occasion and fighting with him.

Too bad.

She turned to the wall again and reached for the first handhold, hoisting herself up.

"All right, that's enough." Niko appeared beside her, plucking her away from the wall as though she was just a bug. He set her back onto her feet and caught her face in his hands. "What's wrong?"

Out of the corner of her eye, she saw Oscar moving to her backpack and pulling it open. He picked up something from inside, raising it to his nose, the object still hidden.

The crystal.

Fucking hell.

She tore out of Niko's hold and tried to grab onto the wall again, but he plucked her off as easily as he had the first time, setting her back onto her feet.

"Isobel." Oscar's Alpha voice lashed through the room, whipping against her mind. "Come with me."

She didn't have an ounce of strength to resist him, but at least he was leaving the room and walking away from the others. She stripped off her harness and tossed it aside as she trailed after him.

"Just her and Cian," he barked over his shoulder as he flung open the door again.

She followed a good few strides behind the two Alphas, her eyes on the backs of Oscar's shoes as they passed out of the fitness centre. Cian was texting as he walked while Oscar glared everyone out of their path. Her first thought when they reached the family centre was that they were dragging her to her father for punishment, and she let out a low whimper as she started dragging her feet. They both stopped and turned around, taking several steps toward her. She scattered backwards, holding out her hands.

Cian ... golden, beautiful Cian ... had suddenly become as dangerous to her as Oscar.

Cian's jaw was flexing, his eyes burning, but Oscar only nodded, spinning on his heel and continuing into the family centre. She huddled into one corner of the elevator as they leaned against the opposite side, and then before she knew it, they were standing outside the room she usually met Teak and Charlie in.

Cian knocked, but there was no answer.

"Sorry!" a harried voice called out as the elevator dinged again. Teak and Charlie were rushing toward them. "Got a bit held up. Hi, sweetheart." Teak gave her a brief smile before unlocking the door and motioning her inside.

Cian moved to follow her, but Teak shook her head, her smile suddenly disappearing. "You two can wait downstairs."

Isobel sank into her usual chair, her body on autopilot. The panic hadn't disappeared, but it had lessened as Oscar commanded her body, simmering away somewhere in the back of her mind. Now she was just going through the motions.

"You okay?" Charlie squeezed her hand, kneeling by Isobel's chair. "Want some water?"

Isobel raised her head, glancing between Charlie and Teak—who had moved to the other side of her chair, picking up her free hand and just ... waiting. Waiting for her to talk.

"I think I messed up," she whispered.

"You know what I do whenever I think I messed up?" Charlie asked, a small, understanding smile curving along her mouth. "I imagine someone I love and respect doing that same thing. Does it still look like such a big mistake, or are you just being way too hard on yourself?"

Isobel lifted her head, settling miserable eyes on both women. "I almost had sex with Moses Kane."

"*Moses* Kane?" Teak echoed, eyebrows shooting up.

Charlie swallowed a laugh, trying to look sympathetic. "Okay. Unexpected."

Both women fell back to their usual chairs, sharing a look with each other. "Well ..." Teak cleared her throat, shifting nervously. "This is ... a little outside my purview as a bond specialist, but who you sleep with is a personal choice, even if you have a mate. It certainly isn't recommended, but that's from a health perspective. Only you can decide what's right and wrong for your own body on a moral scale. I might have to intervene if you were fully bonded, though. That could be dangerous."

"Yeah," Isobel said blankly.

"That's not actually what you're upset about, is it?" Charlie prodded.

Isobel clenched her jaw and shook her head. "I might have feelings for Cian. And ... a few of my other surrogates."

"So you're worried about upsetting your surrogates by becoming romantically involved with Moses?"

Isobel scoffed. "It wasn't romantic. It was in the closet at the back of a classroom. *During* class."

Charlie smirked. "Gotta say, I'm enjoying this open communication."

Teak swatted her partner's knee before refocussing on Isobel, her expression stern. "You don't owe anything to any of those Alphas, Isobel. They volunteered to surrogate for you, knowing that you already have a mate."

"I ..." Isobel played with her fingers in her lap. "It wasn't really them I was thinking of. It's ... me. I don't *want* to feel anything for anyone. Not them. Not my mate. Ever."

Teak leaned back, crossing her legs, her heel jiggling

as she bounced her foot, her toned arms flexing like her body had suddenly grown tight with tension. "Not every Sigma is the same," she said, gentling her expression. "And not every Alpha is your father. Have they done anything to hurt you? To make you feel unsafe?"

"Uhh." Isobel swallowed, flicking her attention between the women. She was pretty sure Cian and Moses choking her and fucking her with one of Professor Vega's crystals wasn't exactly what they meant. "Not really."

"Not really?" Teak asked sharply.

"I could have stopped them at any point. I didn't want to."

"Them?" Charlie's brows jumped up, her mouth falling open.

"Um. Him?" Isobel flinched.

"It wasn't just Mos—*oh.*" Teak flicked a look to the door. "Ashford was there too?"

Isobel nodded miserably.

Charlie looked like she wanted to high-five her, but resisted. "Colour me impressed."

Teak's foot stopped wiggling as she stared at Isobel. "Who else have you been involved with?"

Isobel shrugged, feeling herself grow a little smaller. "I guess Theodore, Oscar, and Gabriel. And Kilian, a little bit. And there was a weird moment with Elijah and Niko. And—" She cut herself off, about to say something about Kalen.

"And?" Charlie choked out, as Teak fell against the back of her chair, eyes wide with shock.

"And nothing." Isobel hugged herself. "It sounds bad when I say it out loud."

"Not bad," Teak immediately cut in. "Just different. Do they all know about each other?"

"Well, they like to gossip and they tell each other *everything*, so ... probably."

Teak chuckled. "Sounds like you know them well. So why did Sato and Ashford drag you here and why did Ashford bring your appointment forward?"

"How did he even do that?" Isobel returned, frowning.

"He asked for my contact details in case of an emergency," Teak explained. "Why did they think you needed to speak to us?"

"Because I wouldn't speak to them."

"Why?"

"Because ... I guess ... I don't know how to."

Teak cocked her head to the side, a strand of chocolate brown hair unwinding from around her ear. "You know, as Sigmas, we're taught that we're not really allowed to have emotions of our own. We're expected to exist to serve others—at least in the eyes of the people who still believe we have any power at all. If a Sigma has a breakdown, then they're basically nonfunctioning, because how can they level other people's emotions if they can't even control their own?

We're held to an impossible, inhumane standard. Even for the Gifted."

"You're allowed to feel whatever you're feeling," Charlie added. "If you want to be mad, *be* mad. If you want to cry, then *cry*."

Never let them see you cry.

"I can't." Isobel straightened her shoulders, pulling her chin up a little higher. "I just ... can't."

"You can't *yet*," Teak corrected. "We're all just works in progress, try to remember that. It's okay to do things differently."

"You also can't stop them from reacting how they're going to." Charlie shared a guarded look with Teak. "There needs to be space for you to have feelings *and* for them to have feelings. You can't control theirs and ... you also can't control yours, I'm afraid."

Isobel smiled a little, suddenly feeling tired enough to sink into the armchair and fall asleep. "I'm discovering that."

"What's the worst that could happen if you accepted the bond you're hiding from?" Teak suddenly questioned, turning the conversation in a direction Isobel hadn't been expecting.

"I could lead an empty life locked away in an apartment in the sky with nothing to fill my time until the day I disappear without a trace."

Teak nodded, sharing another quick look with

Charlie, who nodded glumly, before she shifted to the edge of her chair, reaching for Isobel's hands.

"Your mother didn't disappear without a trace. She died of cardiac arrest."

Cardiac arrest.

Her heart stopped.

Suddenly, Isobel couldn't breathe again. It was everything she had feared. Her mother had taken on all of her father's darkness without Isobel there to share the load ... and it had proved too much.

"And what's the worst that could happen if you stopped fighting your feelings for ... well ... your feelings?" Teak prodded, squeezing Isobel's fingers, and ducking her head to catch Isobel's attention.

"I could lose the person I've found here that finally feels like *me*," she rushed out, realising that she was shaking so much, she was causing Teak's sleeves to tremble slightly. "I could lose this awful spark of happiness that scares the hell out of me. It's not that I felt invisible before and now suddenly I'm famous. I still feel just as invisible, but now there are people who seem to understand me. It's like they know me better than I do, and I don't want to lose how that makes me feel. I'm discovering myself through *them*, and I wish I wasn't. I wish I was doing it all on my own."

"We don't go through life all on our own," Teak said soothingly. "Changing your environment is how you change yourself. Your environment has changed in a big way, and it looks like the Alphas in Dorm A are a big part of your environment here. If you like the way they're influencing you, then maybe don't fight it so much. If something happens to pull you away from them, you'll still have everything they taught you. You won't lose any of it."

"And it makes total sense that they're having such a profound impact on you." Charlie moved to sit on the arm of Isobel's chair, draping her arm over Isobel's shoulder and giving her a gentle squeeze. "Their lives have been the opposite of yours in every single aspect. They're respected where you're looked down on. They're powerless where you have all the wealth and influence of an Icon's daughter. They're celebrated and you're disregarded. They have impossible standards to live up to, and you're underestimated every single day, in every way possible. They have so much to teach you and you have so much to teach them. It's not surprising that you're drawn to each other ... I mean *some* things are surprising—"

Teak swatted at her again. "Stop it."

"Do I *sound* like I'm judging?" Charlie laughed.

"No," Teak grumbled. "You sound impressed."

"She counted out *eight* of them," Charlie stage-whispered. "And then she said *and*."

"I was just trying to count Cian twice because he's so ... hot," Isobel protested weakly.

The two women retreated, Teak checking her phone while Charlie just sat back in her chair, still smirking.

"I asked your father for an update on what his plans were to help you through the summer break." Teak frowned as she scrolled across her screen. "It looks like he still hasn't replied. Has he spoken to you?"

"Not since last week." Isobel shrugged. "He's really preoccupied with getting this new superhero movie. He's up against Bellamy's dad and things are getting a bit tense. I've met with his assistant and Cooper more than I've met with him the past few weeks."

"Cooper's the guy with the goatee, right?" Teak asked, tapping her chin. "I saw him in some of the coverage of your settlement tour. Is he *your* official manager, or your father's?"

"Mine, now. Dad made me sign a contract to keep him on after I got out of the hospital. But he's more of a messenger than anything."

"I'll try to get into contact with him instead." Teak sighed, slipping her phone away. "I'm worried your father won't prioritise the need for surrogates over the break. He should have submitted an application for one of them already, and there's been nothing. At this point, it's going to have to be an emergency application."

Isobel's blood ran cold. "Maybe he forgot. He's been really busy."

"All right, well we can leave it there for now. I think we should continue our sessions over the break. At least once a week. We can video chat and I can intervene if I see that your health is at risk."

Isobel stood, chewing on her lip. "I didn't last very long on the settlement tour without a surrogate."

"I'll video call you three days into the break," Teak assured. "You're not just your father's responsibility anymore. Now you're ... Ironside's."

"You were about to say yours, weren't you?" Charlie teased, sending Isobel a wink.

"Also mine." Teak sniffed, looking Isobel over. "Give me your phone. You'll need my details for our online sessions."

After they exchanged information, the panic dropped back into Isobel's gut, and she found herself with nerves dancing all the way to her fingertips.

"You've got this," Charlie muttered, patting her on the shoulder before opening the door and striding out.

The hallway was blissfully bare, and she slipped into the elevator with Teak and Charlie, wishing she could just follow them all the way to wherever they lived and never have to face the Alphas again, but there was no such luck.

It wasn't just Cian and Oscar waiting for her.

The rest of the Alphas were gathered in the family centre, spread out around three of the tables with Kalen and Mikel leaning against the wall between two of the windows looking out toward the front of the academy.

"Well, well, this is surprising." Teak stopped as soon

as she exited the elevator, her gaze drifting over the gathered men, taking in their carefully guarded expressions. "Professor West, Professor Easton." She turned her attention to the tall bodies at the back of the room. "Can I help you?"

"No," Mikel replied, "we're good." His tone wasn't harsh, but it wasn't sugary sweet either. He examined Isobel closely before settling his attention back on Teak. "Is there anything I need to be aware of?"

"What could you possibly need to be aware of?" Teak feigned ignorance, putting on a calm, confused demeanour.

It made Isobel like her that much more.

It wasn't every day she saw a Sigma stand up to ten guarded Alphas, all radiating tense, overwhelming energy.

Actually, it wasn't *any* day.

"Carter is one of my Alphas." Mikel nodded toward Isobel. "Her welfare is my concern. Is there anything I need to be aware of?"

"Um, Carter is a Sigma," Charlie inserted, raising her hand.

"You should prepare emergency paperwork for some of your Alphas to travel if the need for a surrogate arises," Teak said, surprising everyone. "Have them ready to be filed. It would appear that Isobel's father hasn't arranged a care plan for the summer break."

"She's going home alone?" Cian growled, jumping up

from the edge of the table he had been sitting on, his tattooed hands curling into fists, which he quickly shoved into his pockets.

Pockets that pulled the material of his pants tight around his crotch.

Which reminded her that his *dick* had been in her *mouth* an hour ago.

Shit shit shit.

She sucked in a deep, shaky breath, looking away from Cian. "I'm going to be late for my next—"

"You're with me right now," Mikel interrupted, a hint of iron to his tone.

Kalen pushed off the wall, stalking closer. "Thank you." He aimed that at Charlie and Teak before stopping short of Isobel and returning his heavy stare to them over her head. "We'll make sure the paperwork is ready."

"Right. Well ... okay. I'll be speaking to you soon, Isobel." Teak squeezed her shoulder quickly before striding for the entrance, her heels clacking hastily.

"Later, kiddo." Charlie waved at her, flashing an unbothered smile before following Teak out of the family centre.

MOSES WAS HAVING A HARD TIME WRANGLING HIS EMOTIONS under control, and as soon as the other Sigma walked away, he lost his grip on the barrier he had been hoarding it all behind—something they had all been practising lately.

He felt the crack in his efforts, felt the pressure in his chest ease as some of it slipped out. Isobel didn't even flinch, even though he was sure several of the others had probably just done the exact same thing.

To stand there and get battered by anger, worry, and confusion from ten different angles wasn't an easy thing to do, but the girl was a professional sponge. She rubbed her nose with the heel of her palm, eyes diverted to the windows as they all fell into silence.

"Luckily, the film crews are tied up at the moment following around their picks for the Icon winner this year," Kalen groused out in a terse voice, though his scent didn't match the burning, smoking sugar he emitted when he was angry. He stroked his chin, considering Carter. "I think we could probably keep you here without them interrupting. Until you finally tell us what's happening, that is."

Isobel squared off her shoulders, setting her jaw as she tried to muster the energy to face them all. Usually, Moses liked the fight in her. The stubbornness that matched his. The steely backbone he liked to bend just a little too much for his own comfort. But not right now.

He didn't want her to have to fight when she was scared.

He would rather do that for her. He would do it for everyone, if they let him.

"Look ..." She started to pace across the tiled stone floor, her steps hurried and nervous. "This is getting a little complicated. I ... I thought ... with the surrogacy thing—" She cut herself off, shaking her head like she was already disagreeing with the train of thought she had just gone down.

Was that *what was bothering her?*

She hadn't freaked out getting close to Theodore, Oscar, or Gabriel. Maybe the problem was *him*. Maybe she needed really clear boundaries.

"I applied to be a surrogate," he announced, lying through his fucking teeth.

Everyone's head whipped around to him. Elijah and Gabriel looked expectant—Elijah even a little impatient, likely annoyed that it had taken Moses too long to get on with whatever action he had predicted Moses should take. Theodore's eyes flashed dark with anger.

Kilian shifted, discomfort lining his shoulders.

Nico nodded slightly.

"W-What?" Isobel stuttered, spinning to face him.

Why was his face hot?

Why was his face burning with the slightest tinge of colour *now?* He had just fucked her with a goddamn crystal and exploded in her mouth but *now* he was blushing? *Awesome. Great. Perfect.*

"Yeah." He cleared his throat, focussing on Oscar for a moment. The other Alpha had an angry challenge simmering behind a hard stare. That was going to be a fight later. Moses looked forward to it. "I'm sorry, I forgot to ask you. Is that okay?"

"Uh." She seemed shocked silent, her throat working as she tried to dredge up an answer. "Yes? I mean sure. Yes. Thank you?" She smiled, the motion trembling across her lips, relief flashing in her eyes. "So all of that was—"

"Just doing my part." He waved her off.

Her shoulders inched down, relief visibly flooding through her body.

Jesus Christ what the fuck?

Most people would be weeping with rejection by this point.

Kilian, Theodore, and Cian also relaxed, but the confusion on their faces deepened. Moses wanted to punch something to ease his frustration. The level of intellect required to keep up with this *one* girl was off the charts. She never did what he expected.

Especially not in the closet.

"Things got a little out of hand," Cian said, as though his thoughts had naturally gravitated to the same place. "It definitely wasn't supposed to go that far. Do you understand, Illy?"

Theodore stiffened, flashing a glare from Cian to Isobel. Moses knew his brother better than anyone, and while Theodore had an impressive amount of self-control, he also tended to lose it in a spectacular way. They had pushed him pretty far today.

"I ... yeah, I didn't mean for that either." Isobel copied Moses' dismissive hand wave, her eyes darting to the floor.

"Maybe some ground rules would help," Niko spoke up.

Kalen and Mikel seemed to have taken a backseat in the discussion for now. They preferred for the rest of them to sort out their own messes, but they seemed tense enough that they would probably step in this time if things got too heated. Luckily, they had Niko. If anyone could make this whole situation sound all nice and neat and reasonable, it was Niko.

"Do you have any in mind?" Niko prodded Isobel gently. "Anything that's absolutely off limits to you?"

Isobel nodded. And then shook her head.

They waited, but she didn't say anything.

"Okay." Niko looked like he wanted to smile. "Anyone else?"

"She needs a proper safe word," Cian announced.

"What the *fuck* would she need one of those for?" Oscar growled, jumping out of his chair and prowling toward Cian.

Moses quickly inserted himself between them, trying to catch Oscar's eyes, and everyone was too distracted to notice Theodore slipping past them and slamming Cian against the wall.

"WHAT DID YOU DO TO HER?"

"Enough," barked Kalen, his Alpha voice like a wave through the room. "Everyone sit down. Now."

"Oh my god." Isobel was staring at Cian in horror as they all moved to obey Kalen, Oscar choosing to stand just to prove he could.

Cian had three deep gouges cutting across his neck and into his chest. He was holding both hands over the wounds, but blood was trying to spill through his fingers.

Theodore slumped into a chair, gripping the table in front of him with a black-clawed hand, the talons elongated and painted crimson at the tips.

"Someone do something!" Isobel shifted around restlessly in her chair.

"It's fine," Cian rasped. "Barely a scratch."

"Barely a scratch?" she repeated, her voice sounding numb with shock as she turned to stare at Theodore. "Do I rip open Wallis' neck every time you touch her?"

Theodore gave her a strained smile. "I barely touched him."

Theodore's scent was growing more and more acidic by the second, his eyes flashing with a warning precursor of darkness. Moses was seconds away from snapping at Kalen that he needed to go to his brother, but Isobel seemed to soften at the last second.

"I'm worried about you too, Theo," she whispered.

He just stared back at her like he was going to demand

she prove it, but then he seemed to shrug off the compulsion, shaking out his arms until his talons retreated into blood-stained nails. Despite the situation, Moses felt a pang of pride. The sheer amount of *effort* it took to pull back from the brink like that was unbelievable, but there wasn't a single line of strain on Theodore's face.

"A safe word is necessary for playing with half-bonded or fully bonded Alphas." Kalen drew the attention of the room easily as he surveyed them. "Regardless of personal tastes and proclivities, we tend to be aggressive when our emotions are heightened, and where bonds are concerned, mated Alphas are known to be dangerously territorial and possessive. If I had foreseen ..." He paused for a moment, his discerning gaze landing on Cian. "Things progressing so suddenly, I would have arranged to speak with Isobel privately so that she could be better prepared."

"It really wasn't that shocking," Isobel murmured weakly, her cheeks stained bright red.

She had found a seat close to the window, as far as she could get from all of them. Niko and Kilian were closest to her, both of them angled toward the other Alphas as though they might need to jump up and protect her.

"You quite literally went into shock afterwards," Moses snapped, immediately regretting his sharp tone ... but she didn't glare at him or tense her posture. She just tossed him a quiet, thoughtful look. Which was so much worse. It made him feel like she was peering right through him, tasting his emotions, and silently categorising his thoughts. He did a quick mental check to see what he was putting out there, but he wasn't feeling anything too serious or embarrassing.

Maybe he was in shock as well.

"A safe word is non-negotiable," Mikel rumbled. "I suggest the traffic light system. Green for when you're good, yellow for when you're nearing your limit, and red to stop everything immediately, without repercussions. How does that sound?"

"G-Good. Green?"

Mikel and Kalen both smiled, Mikel flexing his hands like he suddenly wanted to grab her and squeeze her cheeks and say that she was disgustingly adorable, using her safe word in normal conversation. Or maybe Moses was projecting.

Ugh, he made himself want to vomit.

"I have a rule of my own," Kalen announced, causing Isobel's brows to jump up in surprise. He continued, "I know Cian and Moses, and even while Moses might not be the friendliest Alpha, neither of them would treat you badly after a sexual encounter, which means you robbed them of the ability to give you the proper aftercare you needed." His voice grew softer, more like a gravelled purr. "You ran to the climbing room because I take care of you in there, isn't that right, princess?"

Isobel nodded, looking both entranced and confused.

“Cian and Moses would have taken care of you in the same way, isn’t that right?” His amber eyes were suddenly boring into Moses and Cian.

“Obviously.” Cian spoke lowly, the blood finally ceasing its attempts to escape his fingers. He was the only one, other than Kilian and Oscar, who didn’t seem to have calmed down at least a little bit.

Oscar was frightfully quiet, like a predator stalking along the edges of a battlefield, waiting for them all to wear each other down before he pounced and feasted. Kilian just seemed generally unhappy with everything that was happening.

They were all watching him, Moses realised. Waiting for his answer. “I think Cian cared more than I did about that,” he admitted. “I would have taken care of her, but I think he needed to.”

“Aftercare is important for both parties,” Mikel agreed quietly.

“Let’s make things perfectly clear.” Kalen sighed, like he hated what he was about to say. “If you’re going to play hard,” he was directing his words to Isobel, who swallowed, “then you’re going to crash hard. Nobody is allowed to touch you until you can assure us that you won’t be running away from aftercare and won’t bury your own needs. It’s not safe. If you’re willing to ignore your needs afterwards, then you might also ignore your needs during and refrain from using your safe word, which is unacceptable.”

He watched her like he was waiting for her to verbally agree, but she seemed too overwhelmed.

"Nod if you understand," Mikel spoke up, and she quickly jerked her head up and down a few times.

"Good." Mikel stopped by her chair, his hand landing on top of her head. He bent closer to her, whispering something that sounded like *brave girl*. She closed her eyes, a slight tremor travelling through her body that made Moses want to toss her over the nearest table and aggressively interrogate her until he knew *every single word* that made her tremble like that.

His feelings were getting out of hand. Was this what Theodore felt like? It was impossible to tell with his brother. Oscar definitely felt it. It was written into every crease around his frowning mouth as dark eyes tracked anyone who even blinked in Isobel's direction. And the others?

He swallowed back a frustrated groan, scrubbing a hand down his face. This was impossible. He needed to get a handle on it. They couldn't *all* have her—and if she was going to choose any of them, it wasn't going to be him. It was going to be his brother. Even though Moses kissed her first.

And an inch of his cock was inside her first.

Yeah, nice one, dickhead. Because that counts.

He had no chance. She didn't want him to be her first kiss and the fact that he almost lost *both* their virginities in a closet in the back of a full classroom was exactly why she was going to pick Theodore.

Or *anyone* else.

Hell, she would probably pick Mikel before she picked Moses.

16
THE GUILTY FINGER POINTS FIRST

ISOBEL SLIPPED OUT FROM BENEATH MIKEL'S STEADYING TOUCH, approaching Cian. He watched with a heavy, guarded stare that made her want to turn tail and run again, but she forced herself to step between his legs as he shifted upright, his eyes flicking over her face in question.

The wounds on his neck were now just red lines, but blood was soaking his shirt, so she kept her chest away from his as she wrapped her arms around his neck, eyes fluttering closed as his scent washed over her, still mixed with her own heady syrup.

"Sorry," she mumbled.

He gripped her hips, and Isobel stiffened, swallowing back a whimper as her body chose that moment to recall the feeling of him and Moses forcing her down over the crystal by her hips. A gravelled sound vibrated out of Cian's chest, and she quickly skipped away, hurrying over to Moses. She fell clumsily into him more than anything, but he caught her easily, standing as she reached his chair.

He had said that Cian was the one who needed to take care of her, but he pulled her tight against his body, bowing her back slightly as he inhaled deeply against her neck, his hands tight on her waist.

"Forgiven," he rumbled. "But just this once."

She pulled back, giving him a searching look, which he turned away from. She didn't understand him at *all*.

"Well ..." Mikel cleared his throat. "It looks like my session is over. Does anyone have a change of shirt for Cian? He can't leave looking like that."

"On it." Niko pulled a shirt and a water bottle out of his bag, tossing both to Cian, who tugged the bloodied shirt over his head and poured water onto a clean section of it, using that to wipe away the blood from his neck. He didn't look at Theodore, and Theodore didn't apologise.

Isobel blinked at the second nipple piercing Cian had acquired at some point, realising his ink had spread further again. It practically *covered* his chest and his sides. She tore her attention away when she felt eyes burning into the side of her face.

Gabriel.

He had his head tilted, his russet gaze open and curious—not his usual cold detachment. After her encounter with him, hadn't she also avoided him?

Swallowing, she inched his way, watching the hint of amusement that sparked to life in his expression.

"Me too?" he guessed, though there was a slightly ironic or sarcastic note to his voice.

She hovered by his knees, wondering how to proceed. He would probably prefer she *didn't* try to hug him. He opened one of his hands and parted his legs, so she stepped closer, her arms twining around his neck as his hands pushed beneath her loose top, settling against the bare skin of her lower back.

"I thought you didn't like touching," she whispered into his skin.

"You smell like other people," he rumbled back. "It's infuriating."

"We smell fucking amazing and don't even pretend we don't," Cian said, examining his fingernails. He was starting to sound a little more like himself. "Anything else you need to share with the group, doll?"

Isobel pulled back from Gabriel, shaking her head. "No."

She met Theodore's stormy stare, and he smiled slightly, like he had won some kind of competition. Maybe he had. She had been sexual with him, but she *hadn't* run away from him.

"I have to go see my father," she announced, suddenly full of tension again. "I don't think I can wait until tonight. I feel too ... overloaded. I just want to get one thing off my plate."

"Then let's go." Mikel strode for the elevator, barking over his shoulder. "Everyone, get your shit together before next period. The next person to start a fight will have me to deal with. And clean all the blood off the floor before you leave."

Isobel stared at his back, her brows twitching up as he called the elevator. She moved to his side, smoothing her shirt down nervously.

"You don't smell like anything," he reassured her, his attention shrewd as they stepped into the elevator. He leaned against the side wall, crossing his arms, his eyes dipping from the top of her shirt to her hips and back up again. "*They* smell like you marked them as much as possible."

"Is that a thing?"

"That is, most definitely, a thing. Leaving behind your scent and essence on your mate is a type of claiming."

She felt her forehead scrunching up and quickly turned her eyes to the floor.

"No," Mikel said calmly. "Tell me."

The elevator dinged open, and they both stepped into the hallway, but he gave a minute shake of his head when she moved to step toward her father's apartment.

She cringed. "It's not appropriate."

"We're past appropriate. Tell me what you were thinking."

"Just that they didn't do the same. They actually made a point not to."

"As they should." Mikel nodded. "You have eight other mates—and even aside from that fact, if one of them had tried to claim you in any sort of way in front of the other, we might be looking at a far messier situation right now. Likely a bloody mess. And blood can be hard to hide in a place with a camera around every corner. Are you upset that they didn't?"

"Upset?" She shook her head. "I would have been upset if they didn't let me do what I did ... but they encouraged it."

"They tried to take care of you, pet." He raised a hand, his fingers brushing beneath her chin, barely even a touch before he dropped his hand. "Let's get this over and done with." He nodded down the hallway.

"You can just wait outside if you want," she said, moving to the door of her father's apartment. She could already hear his voice booming from within, and it sent a tremor of apprehension down her spine.

But she had to do this.

For her mother.

"Not a chance," Mikel muttered, reaching past her to knock briskly on the door. "You're never going to be alone with him again."

His body was close behind hers, but as soon as the door handle turned, he melted a few steps away, standing slightly off to the side.

"Isobel?" Braun Carter filled the doorway, a look of annoyance in his face as he became momentarily distracted by his phone.

"You've got it, Stan!" he thundered enthusiastically. "I'll have Bellamy email you right now and we'll get this little mess all cleared up, eh? Great." He hung up the phone, the annoyance in his face creasing deeper. "What are you doing here?" He only seemed to notice Mikel, then, and most of the annoyance filtered out of his expression. "Professor Easton. What a pleasure." He flung the door open, motioning them inside. "What brings you both here? Shouldn't you be in class right now, Isobel?"

"This is more important," she managed to get out, the giant ball of anxiety in her throat making it difficult to speak. "There's something I need to ask you."

"By all means." He rocked back on his heels, folding his meaty arms and setting his jaw in a warning flex. "I'm at your disposal."

He wasn't even trying to hide his sarcasm in front of Mikel ... but then again, he probably expected Mikel to share his disdain.

"I need to know what happened to Mom."

Her father's thick brows drew down, heavy over his eyes. "That's a conversation for private family time, Isobel. Come back at the time we have scheduled. No guests—no offence, Professor Easton, but it's just so rare that I get alone time with my daughter, her being so famous now." His attention flicked up to Mikel for a moment, seeming a little confused over the other man's continued silence.

"No." Isobel forced her eyes up to her father's, flinching at the wave of his rage as it swept over her, threatening to send her to her knees. "I'm free now. We can meet now."

He stared at her for a moment. Calculating. And then he fell back another step, motioning for them both to take a seat on one of the couches facing the floor-to-ceiling windows that looked over the front of the academy. His assistant walked in from the other room, holding a tablet in one hand and a phone in the other. She paused when she spotted Mikel, her eyes going wide before she quickly turned and left the room again, closing the door quietly behind her.

"Your mother had a heart attack," Braun announced, rounding the couches to stand by the window and look down on Isobel. Mikel had stayed behind the couch, right behind Isobel, and Braun glanced to the other Alpha, his stare growing hard, with a hint of curiosity peeking through. "Is there something I can help you with, Professor?"

"Yes, actually." Mikel spoke formally, his tone detached. "But my issue can wait. Please continue." The hint of Alpha command in his voice had Isobel almost turning around in surprise, but she managed to keep her focus on her father.

"What was she doing?" Isobel pressed. "Where was she? Were you with her?"

"I was there," Braun confirmed, easing down into an armchair, the same grief Isobel had felt the day he had told her about her mother edging past the rage he was pushing out at her. She resisted the urge to pull down her walls and take it all from him, the way she had been taught.

"I deserve to know what happened." She tried to sound unyielding and unafraid, but she was pretty sure it had come out sounding more like a question.

"I know you think it's my fault." Braun turned away from her, looking out the window, his jaw tensing again. "You were always so much weaker than Caran. She could handle me. She didn't die because she was levelling me out. She died because she weakened herself. She stopped taking her medication."

"What medication?" Isobel frowned, unsure how to react to her father actually talking to her instead of dismissing her completely.

He stood and walked to where his soft leather briefcase was sitting on the hall table. He pulled a small white bottle from inside and brought it over to his chair, sinking down again as he smacked the bottle onto the coffee table before him.

"The surrogate pills," he said. "They were keeping her alive. Along with me."

"S-Surrogate?" Isobel stuttered.

"God, you really can be stupid, Isobel." He pinched his nose, annoyance now overtaking his tendrils of grief.

Behind her, Mikel let out a low sound of warning, but Braun didn't seem to hear it. It was almost as though he had forgotten the presence of the other Alpha altogether.

"Mom wasn't your mate?" Isobel asked, something like fear choking up the back of her throat.

"Her mate was my brother. He was her Anchor." Braun levelled Isobel with a tired look. "He died, and I offered to help. I'd heard about the pills, but they weren't available in the settlements—hell, the people in the settlements *still* don't know about them. I pretended she was my mate, otherwise, they never would have issued the pills to me. It was simple enough, since we have a similar eye colour. They issued the pills on the basis that I would be travelling most of the year for work and she would be home alone. Between me and the pills, she survived."

Isobel's mind was spinning, her eyes fixed to the little white bottle. "What are they?"

"Surrogate pills. Do you listen, girl?" He snapped his fingers in front of her face. "They stop the bond side effects and sustain people when their bonds aren't available."

The anger rose within her so swiftly she spluttered for a moment before the words burst out of her. "Why didn't you give them to *me*?"

"I've been carrying them around in case you need

them." He rolled his eyes like she was being overly dramatic. "Your need for a surrogate has brought you more attention and screen time than any plan I could have possibly come up with. I would have stepped in if the situation had become dire or if none of your little boyfriends offered to help."

"That's fucked up." She stared at him, shocked into disbelief. "Is that what you did to Mom? You stopped giving her pills?"

"Accuse me of killing Caran Carter one more time, I dare you," he growled, suddenly turning his full attention on her, his fury clawing over her skin. "She stopped taking them on her own. Stashing every second one away. She was trying to build up a stash so that she could run away. It was stupid. Reckless. How was I supposed to know she had grown so weak? I barely gave her an *inch* of what was supposed to be *our* burden to carry before she collapsed."

Isobel jumped up. "I'm done here." She was trembling, vibrating anger and grief—half of it hers, half of it his.

"Not so fast." Braun snatched up the pill bottle, stuffing it into his pocket. Even now, he wasn't going to offer it to her. "We have to discuss what's happening over the break."

She paused, her back still turned, waiting for whatever he wanted to say.

"I've arranged a surrogate for you. He'll be coming to stay with us."

She met Mikel's eyes, and he shook his head slightly. *It wasn't one of the Alphas.*

"Who?" she croaked.

"Adam Bellamy."

She spun around, her mouth falling open. "I already have several surrogates. I'm not even friends with Bellamy."

"I don't care who you're friends with, Isobel. I made a deal with Adam's father. It's a Hollywood thing—you wouldn't understand. He's going to step down from the movie role I'm interested in, and in return, you're going to give Adam the bump in popularity he needs before the start of year three. This is how the business works."

"No." The word fell out of her mouth before she could even think it through.

Braun's honey-gold eyes narrowed into slits. "This isn't a discussion. It's happening whether you like it or not." He took a threatening step toward her but paused, seeking out Mikel again. "I think you've intruded enough, don't you, Professor? This should have been a private discussion between me and my daughter."

"The matter of *my* student's safety is a discussion for us all," Mikel countered calmly. "And that plan isn't going to work."

"Did I miss the episode where they made you her new daddy?" Braun gritted out, making a grab for Isobel.

She slipped out from beneath his hand. For a moment, he seemed too shocked to move, and then he barrelled forward again, but Mikel was there in an instant, gripping his wrist and twisting it behind his back until the larger man was bent forward and twitching with pain, a grunt vibrating out of his throat. Mikel's movements were so fast that the whole thing happened in a blur. He released Braun just as quickly, and Isobel found herself blinking at his back as he planted himself before her.

"Think you're gonna hook your cart to her cash wagon, eh?" Her father laughed cruelly. "Too bad, Professor. She already has a manager. Signed a contract with him and everything. And she's under my control until she graduates."

"The academy retains the right to intervene where they see fit." Mikel's voice was chillingly calm.

"Aren't you getting a bit greedy?" Braun asked. Isobel peered around Mikel to see the smug look overtaking her father's face. "Don't you already have eight perfectly fit Alpha horses in this race? Why don't you leave the silly little Sigma foal to me? Adding her to your roster won't do shit to overcompensate for that god-awful face."

"Why don't you shut the hell up for once?" Isobel stepped out from behind Mikel. "I'm done with your abusive crap. Why don't you *watch what you say* for once? Why don't you try to talk like an *adult* for once?"

Her father didn't look at her like he was surprised

that she was finally learning to stand up for herself. He looked at her like she had plotted out the most annoying thing she could do to stand against him, and had gone ahead and done it just to spite him.

She wasn't being strong in his eyes. She was being small.

She wasn't making him hear her, she was just making noise, and it was pathetic.

"Oh, you're a big girl now." He raked his eyes over her, his mocking smile growing a vicious edge. "Don't forget who *made* you, Isobel. And you." He turned his stare on Mikel, seeming to grow bigger, his shoulders wider, his expression tight. "I don't know what the little twit promised you, but she has a contract with Cesar Cooper. She already has a manager, a publicist, *and* an Alpha to make all her decisions for her, so you and your boys can get back in line and wait to be called on."

"I don't think so," Mikel said mildly. "But thanks for the ... enlightening chat. I think we'll be on our way, now."

"I'm not done with her," Braun spat.

Isobel's head was pounding. Her father had been pushing his emotions onto her as he usually did whenever she was in his presence, but with every passing minute, the spitting mass of his fury was increasing in size, growing heavy against her chest like a huge boulder weighing against her bones and threatening to cave them in.

"I still have to pick her classes for next year—"

"I'll pick my own—" she tried to interrupt, but he continued speaking like she wasn't even there.

"And go through her timetable for the summer break."

Mikel pulled out his phone, glancing at the screen. "You likely have until the end of the day to submit your *proposed* timetable and bond care plan to her bond specialist. I will be submitting several alternative solutions within the hour, and just in case you've forgotten: the officials don't like to sit on welfare decisions for very long. They're a waste of time. My plan will be comprehensive." He moved for the door and Isobel turned to follow him, but her father's words stopped her in her tracks.

"You always were a selfish, manipulative little bitch."

She flinched, and the weight of fury against her chest swelled until it was too much. She caught a whimper at the back of her throat, focusing on the door Mikel was holding open, resisting the tears that wanted to break free and funnelling all her energy into taking just a few more steps. She just needed to get out of that room ...

But her father wasn't that kind.

"Just like your mother."

Mikel caught her eye, perhaps seeing the battle in her expression because he closed his eyes for a second before gritting out a quick warning.

"I can't get away with murder today, Carter. Best to ignore him."

"You get away with murder *weekly,*" her father snarled.

Mikel only raised a brow in polite question. "Oh?"

Isobel turned her head slightly, just enough to take in how her father's face was growing purplish red. He needed to calm down or else she was going to collapse under the pure weight of his outburst.

"You think I don't know why she brought you here?" Braun laughed. "You think I don't know the Track Team approached her? You think I haven't seen you down there, week after week, putting their own enemies into comas?" He snorted. "Icons aren't just pretty faces, Easton. We're predators with survival instincts and if I can beat out hundreds of vicious Icons-in-training without so much as a scratch, then I sure as fuck can outsmart a washed-up Alpha who wasn't even selected."

Mikel smiled then, the gesture pushing and tugging at the scars marring his face. "Are you trying to goad me into a fight, Braun?"

Isobel felt her own lips tugging up on one side, a tiny spark of pleasure shooting through her. It was stupid that it mattered to her at all, but at Ironside, she had become *Carter*, referred to by her last name just like everyone else, but when she was with her father, he was the one given the respect of formality, and she just became Isobel. Usually, it was normal to give the oldest person in the room the respect of formality, which was why the show referred to Theodore as Kane—even though he was only older by a few minutes—while Moses was always Moses. Mikel's subtle rearrangement of respect was doing weird things to her insides.

The feeling was quickly drowned out as her father took another step toward her. Mikel immediately moved away from the door, and Isobel forced her legs to work again before a fight could break out. Mikel caught her elbow, steering her toward the door and depositing her through it.

Before closing it in her face.

"Uh." She stared at the closed door and then jerked back a surprised step when what sounded like a massive body was thrown up against it.

Mikel's Alpha voice growled clearly through the wood, making her shrink a step back. "If you want to fight me so bad, then submit an application and pay me what I'm due, just like everyone else."

"Get the fuck off me. The hell is wrong with you, psycho?" her father barked back, also in Alpha voice.

Isobel was trembling, even though none of the orders were for her.

"I don't think I will." Mikel sounded like he was smiling again. "Well now, isn't that something? Mr Big Bad Icon can't even influence a washed-up Alpha. Boohoo. You had no chance, boy. Better behave yourself from now on."

A form materialised beside her, so suddenly that she jumped back another step. It was a man who seemed vaguely familiar, but it wasn't until he sucked the air in through his teeth in an aggravated gesture that she realised who he was, because that *sound* pierced a memory deep within her. She tried to grip it, but it filtered away, leaving behind a name.

"G-Grandpa?" she whispered.

"Not anymore," he grunted, dismissing her as he tried to open the door. His hand passed straight through it, and his face began turning red. "The heck is going on here? I can hear that useless good-for-nothing son of mine. He hiding from me, is he?"

Buddy Carter whirled on her and then looked around like there might be a tool he could use instead of attempting to try the handle again. "Annoying piece of shit," he muttered.

Isobel had only met him twice that she could remember, but he seemed ... *achingly* familiar. Her first memory was of his broad, plum-coloured, rage-filled face as they spilled from his house and into the car, leaving in a rush. She had no idea how old she was. She only remembered her mother crying in the front seat, her father's rigid tension, and the feeling of *wrongness* that pervaded everything. The second memory, he had been sickly sweet. Laughing jovially and tossing a present into her lap. Braun had given him some money. She remembered now.

He was happy when Braun gave him money, and the calls stopped when the money did.

The weight was tossed off the door, and it swung open, giving Isobel a clear view of her father crashing over the sofa and into the coffee table, which thankfully wasn't glass. Still, the splintering of wood gave her pause, but Mikel snapped the door closed before she could hesitate.

"Let's go," he said, far too casually for someone who had just called her father *boy* and tossed him across the room. "I think it's going to storm, and you need to get to your session with Kalen."

"Storm because of yo—"

He quickly spoke over her. "Yes."

"Why?" She nervously watched as her grandfather looked between them and the closed door, before deciding to follow her. "He can't see me, can he?" Buddy eyed Mikel curiously. "So you can see ghosts, eh, girl?"

She didn't even know he had died.

Mikel punched the button to open the elevator doors and waved her in before him. "Sometimes it slips out and I can't help it," he explained.

"Are you okay?" she asked, trying to ignore the apparition as Mikel leaned against one wall of the elevator and she propped herself against the other, her arms wrapped loosely around her torso. He didn't *feel* okay, but she was too sick from her father's influence to properly sort through how much of the anger she felt was leftover from him and how much was Mikel's.

His eyes dipped from her face to where she was holding herself, his nostrils flaring slightly. "Forget about me. What did he do to you?"

"Gave her a bit of discipline, I reckon," the apparition of her grandfather grunted. "Always told that boy taking the Sigma under his wing was a bad idea. Bitches like that are bad news. I only have so many sons for her to run through."

She sucked in a deep breath, closing her eyes and willing the apparition to disappear. "Nothing, really." She popped her eyes open and gave Mikel a weak shrug. "Some emotions are just heavier than others. Darker. And with him ... I just can't seem to shut him out like I can the rest of you. Mom said all Alphas are stronger than our barriers, but he's something else."

Buddy harrumphed with pride.

"He's not stronger. He's just conditioned you to be weaker around him." Mikel narrowed his gaze. "Do you believe what he said about your mother? About their bond?"

She dropped her attention to her shoes and kept it there as they walked out of the family centre, Buddy following along like he simply had nowhere better to be. "You know ..." She hesitated, her own uncomfortable emotions mixing with the toxic cloud of fury her father had left her with. "I'm embarrassed to say this, but I don't think I've met his eyes enough to be able to tell the minute differences between them and my mother's. I know she definitely had two slightly different shades of brown, but—"

"Are you fucking dumb, girl?" Buddy laughed at her, a few steps behind them. "You didn't know?"

She broke off, swallowing back a sudden wave of grief. "I've always thought I have my father's eyes. But if they were truly mated ... why have I never thought that I have *their* eyes? How would I know which colour was his and which was hers?"

"You must have noticed on some level," Mikel agreed quietly. "It's hard to tell from afar, especially if she had eyes like mine. I know people always wonder if I'm bonded when they first see my eyes, even if they don't ask outright. Maybe she had just enough of a variation."

"Can't believe I'm still picking up the tab for that useless bitch even after all these years. Can't even be dead in peace," Buddy grumbled, forcing Isobel to halt.

Mikel also stopped, his eyes finding hers.

"What the hell are you talking about?" she asked, flicking her attention to the apparition just long enough to let him know she was talking to him before she refocussed on Mikel, whose brows had pitched together.

Somehow, he was smart enough to keep his mouth shut, also flicking his eyes to the spot she had glanced to.

"Oh, *now* you want to talk to me," Buddy groused

sarcastically. “So honoured the Sigma girl has time for the likes of me.”

“You’re an Omega,” she shot back. “Don’t get so far ahead of yourself. What were you talking about just before?”

Mikel let out a low, short whistle. “How long have you been carrying on two conversations?”

“Not long,” she said quickly. “But thanks for confirming my theory that the men in Dorm A gossip more than every Omega girl in Dorm O combined.”

“Oh, great,” Buddy muttered sarcastically. “We’re at Ironside. Better call security, girlie. I can’t even afford a fucking glass of water here. Not even if I drink it from my hands.”

“Naturally” was all Mikel said.

Isobel sighed, glimpsing students along the path ahead of them. She needed to wrap this up.

“What did you mean you’re still picking up the tab for ... for her. Are you talking about my mother?”

“Caran Hoity-Toity Baker?” Buddy was trying to lean into her sight, his thick brows jumping as he deliberately used her mother’s maiden name instead of the name she shared with him.

“Carter,” Isobel inserted. “Caran Isobella Carter. You already know her name, so use it.”

“My mistake,” her grandfather stated blandly. “Must have forgotten. It’s hard being dead.”

"So you are dead? And what, now you're a ghost? A figment of my imagination?"

Buddy *tsked*, wagging his finger in her face. "Those are the questions that got you banned from your mama, girl." He pulled back, suddenly pensive. "Actually ... go ahead and ask them. Then I'll be banned too."

"Um." She was struggling to stay focussed on Mikel. "W-What are you?"

"A remnant," he answered, looking a little confused himself.

"Are you real?"

"As real as remnants can be."

"Where do you go when you aren't here?"

"Elsewhere, nowhere." He waved a hand like she was asking stupid questions. "I rest. I sleep. I've earned it. This is the first time my rest has been broken."

"Have you seen my mom?" she whispered hurriedly, hearing the group of students drawing closer.

"Nah." Buddy looked up to the sky, like checking what time of day it was. "Don't know how I know I took her place today. I just know it. This really isn't working—oh, never mind. Yes, I can feel him calling me back no—"

Isobel turned her head as he disappeared, searching along the path for any sign of him.

"Gone?" Mikel guessed, after the students had passed by them, shooting Mikel wary glances. They were probably skipping classes.

Isobel nodded, and he started walking again, his pace

deliberately slow. Above them, the sky was growing dark, clouds gathering fat and heavy, the wind picking up speed. She was grateful for his pace because her steps were growing shorter and stiffer, a sharp pain shooting up through her ribs. Her face pinching with confusion at his continued silence. "You're not acting at all weirded out by the fact that I'm seeing dead people."

"I'd be more surprised if there was nothing more to our abilities than what the officials tell us," he responded lowly. "There was some quiet chatter back in the San Bernadino Settlement around five years ago about a Sigma. Apparently, she was seeing visions of her dead husband, but then the visions changed into other people, and she never saw him again, so she finally killed herself to be with him, thinking he was alive somewhere in some sort of afterworld."

"Do the Gifted believe in an afterworld?"

"Not from what I recall."

"Oh." She tried not to sound disappointed. That would have been convenient.

"They believe in fragments." Mikel shot her a guarded look. "Like memories. Kept alive by the people who knew them and kept safe by one of their gods. They believe that lighting a candle can bring back one of the fragments on loan from the god who protects it. You can speak to the dead that way. They just don't speak back."

"What do you believe?" she dared to ask, shooting him a quick, timid look.

As much as standing up to her father had given her a wobbly boost of confidence, having Mikel belittle him and toss him around like a rag doll made the stoic professor far more terrifying than he had ever been before.

"I believe it's going to rain," he responded shortly. "And this is where I leave you."

They were standing by the doors to the fitness centre. "Go straight to Kalen. No detours."

"Okay."

"Okay?" One dark brow twitched up.

"Professor." She swallowed.

A flash of lightning and the sudden crack of thunder had her flinching violently, but Mikel didn't look furious. He didn't even feel furious. She had gained enough distance from her father to be able to tell where all the rage was coming from, and none of it was originating from Mikel.

It was almost like he was directing it all into the sky instead.

She reached out like she was going to catch him when he turned away, but he smoothly slid his hands into his pockets, looking at her hand. She pulled it up, tucking a flyaway strand of hair behind her ear just to give it something to do. He didn't say anything, but he was clearly waiting for her to explain why she had almost stopped him.

"Is it happening so that I don't have to feel it?" she asked quietly.

His gaze flickered upward for just a moment, and the rain started to lightly pitter-patter around them. A short melodious few notes rang out over hidden speakers all over the academy, signalling the end of the third period.

"Yes," Mikel admitted, sighing slightly. "But don't feel bad. The lake could use a top-up." Then he turned again and stalked off without waiting for her response.

"Thank you," she whispered anyway, wishing he had stuck around to accept it.

17

GOOD LUCK WITH OSCAR

ISOBEL STEPPED INTO THE CLIMBING ROOM, SURPRISED TO FIND Kalen already waiting there since the fourth period had yet to begin.

"Cameras are already off," he told her, stepping around her to hang the Session in Progress sign on the door, before closing it. He flicked the lock and then eased back so that he wasn't crowding her as he quickly surveyed her, his broad face clear of any particular emotion. "It didn't go well?"

She laughed awkwardly. "It was fin—"

"The truth, Isobel." There was a sharpness to his words, a subtle command, but there was no anger brushing up against her from his emotions.

"It was awful." She rolled her shoulders back, trying to loosen some of the tension that held her muscles in such a tight grip. "My parents weren't even bonded.

There's a special medication that can sustain a Tether indefinitely—unless you skip every other day, which my mom did. It seems like she was probably trying to save up enough pills to run away from him. Anyway, that's how she died. She weakened herself so that when he went to dump his usual load of emotional filth onto her, her heart just stopped. Apparently, I'm selfish, manipulative, and stupid. And I can't even argue with that because who doesn't even notice that the two people she spends *every day* with don't even have matching eyes?"

"A person who doesn't make a lot of eye contact." Kalen's gravelled voice lowered to a gentle hum. He drifted closer and touched her chin, easing her gaze up to his. "A person who has been taught to stay out of the way. That doesn't make you selfish or stupid, and only manipulative people call other people shit like that. You're perfect the way you are."

She scoffed, searching his face for anything resembling humour, but he looked completely serious. "You don't even know me that well," she managed. "You can't say that."

"I'm an excellent judge of character." He rolled his eyes, releasing her chin and motioning to the harness hanging on the wall.

She immediately put herself through the motions of preparing for their climbing session. It was almost a guilty pleasure, and sometimes she worried that he *knew* how much she looked forward to him tying that blindfold behind her head.

It was strangely exhilarating to hand over complete responsibility for her well-being to someone she trusted instead of having it forcibly taken away from her by people she didn't trust. It was slowly cleansing her, session by session. Instilling a fragile hope inside her that one day she would be able to blindly trust someone outside the climbing room, and they would never let her down—just like Kalen had never let her slip or fall.

He reached out to tighten her harness, and then he spun her around, pulling the blindfold down over her eyes.

"You're perfect because you're angry," he said. "Deep down, that's what you have at your core. A quiet, persistent fury, kicking to get out. But what are you *choosing* to give people? Measured words, thoughtful gestures, and relief from their ugly emotions. I don't think you have a single bad intention in your body, and I think perfection is all about intention, because if it depended on action, none of us would ever achieve it."

He was right, of course, but it was harder to apply his words to *her*, specifically. She wished she felt anything like how he saw her, but it didn't seem real. Maybe he was just used to his volatile Alphas, and a quiet Sigma was a novelty to him.

She waited for his hands to land on her shoulders, to direct her to the wall as his heat crept over her spine, his rich vanilla scent digging into her muscles and forcing them to loosen.

"But what if I did?" she finally responded. "Have bad intentions? What if I changed?"

He leaned closer to her, his hands finally settling over her shoulders, warm and big, his breath tickling the back of her ear. "Even the most perfect girls can be bad sometimes."

She shivered and then jumped up and down just to try and mask the tremor in her limbs as her body prepared for the climb.

Either Kalen didn't notice, or he pretended not to. He just held onto her as she bounced around for a few seconds, and then he stepped her forward and lifted her hands to the first holds.

An hour later, she was sweating and shaking, and her mind was blissfully blank. There was no room for her to agonise over what her father had said or his plans for her summer break, because if she missed a single word Kalen said, she could hurt herself. When her feet hit the ground again and she pulled off the blindfold, the sound of the storm outside seemed louder than ever, crashing up against the windows.

"Is Mikel ... I mean, is this okay?" She gestured to the rain lashing the glass on the opposite wall.

"He'll be fine," Kalen assured her. "It'll ease up before the end of the day. What class do you have next?"

"Film Aesthetics."

"You're skipping it," he said. "They don't have any final assessments, do they?"

"No ..."

"Good. Give me a minute, then we can walk to my office. We need to sort out your classes for next year."

KALEN CAST ANOTHER QUICK GLANCE TO THE WINDOW BEFORE he pulled out his phone. The group chat without Isobel had half a dozen messages from the other Alphas asking if Mikel was okay and what had happened with Isobel's father. Mikel had written back only a few minutes ago, saying:

I'm not going to lie ... we have a slight problem. Braun Carter made a deal with Matthias Bellamy to get a movie role. In exchange, he said Adam Bellamy could stay with Isobel as her surrogate for the summer. He hasn't submitted it as a proposal through any of the official channels yet. I've already submitted five separate proposals. One for Isobel to stay with the Kanes in the Hudson settlement—since two of her surrogates would be available there—and another for her to stay in the Piney Woods settlement with Elijah and Gabriel, for the same reason, even though Elijah isn't one of her surrogates, he still lives with Gabriel. The other options are for her to stay with Kilian or Oscar, and finally ... the last option is really fucking shit. I'm holding onto it until it seems like they're going to reject all the other proposals. But I've suggested that Theodore, Moses, and Oscar should all accompany her to Vermont to stay with Kilian. They went to all the trouble of bringing Eve back to Ironside, so they're clearly hoping for an altercation of some kind and so far, Isobel has been denying them that.

Mikel: I'm sorry, Oscar. I know home time is crucial for you right now.

Kalen shook his head, checking on Isobel. She had hung up her harness and was picking through her bag for what turned out to be painkillers. She popped two of them and then sat down against the wall, tilting her head back and closing her eyes. He flicked through the replies that had come after Mikel's messages.

Moses: I haven't actually submitted an application to be her surrogate.

Mikel (admin): I did it for you.

Oscar: The last plan is worse than shit. Why Theo, Moses, and me?

Gabriel: For the drama. Theo's secretly in love with her, you're a complete asshole who nobody can figure out the motivations of, and Moses just volunteered to surrogate for the girl his brother is secretly in love with.

Theodore: I'm ignoring that.

Theodore: Why are you letting it storm, Mikki? What else happened?

Mikel (admin): Isobel was overloaded. I had to make sure I was directing all my shit elsewhere.

Kalen (admin): What shit?

Mikel (admin): Her father is an abusive waste of

oxygen. There are pills that can sustain a Tether without their mate, and they've been around for a long time. The officials have been hiding their existence, probably because they're expensive to produce and the Gifted aren't worth the investment. Braun and Caran Carter weren't even mates. Her Anchor died back in the settlement she came from, and she's been using Braun and the pills to survive ever since.

Elijah: That ... is a lot.

Kilian: Is Isobel okay?

Kalen (admin): She's on autopilot right now, but she's going to crash tonight. Theodore and Oscar, can you hold off killing each other for a night?

Oscar: No promises.

Kalen (admin): Let me rephrase. The only person you touch tonight is Isobel. Comfort the bond only. She needs time to process, not another sexual encounter to freak out about and I haven't even spoken to her about birth control yet.

Niko: Let me. She's too intimidated by you. She might just agree to whatever you say.

Cian: Maybe Teak should do it.

Niko: No. I'll do it. Nobody has a better chance of gauging where she truly stands with all of this than me, and I'm sick of entrusting her to everyone else and watching everything go to shit.

Kilian: Okay seriously, what the hell? When did you catch feelings for Carter? Like what the actual fuck is going on here?

Niko: I didn't. She's just an innocent girl caught up in all our Alpha bullshit and she needs someone looking out for her who ISN'T trying to fuck her.

Moses: If anything, she tried to fuck me.

Kalen (admin): Moses.

Moses: Yeah, yeah. I know I fucked up.

Kilian: I want to be there too.

Kalen (admin): Kilian and Niko—talk to her together and do it soon. Everyone else ...

Kalen (admin): We need to have a meeting.

Elijah: I'll sort out a loop for the cameras tonight. The cleaning crew is usually there an hour before midnight and usually finishes just before midnight, so let's say 12:30?

Gabriel: Works for me.

Theodore: With Isobel?

Kalen (admin): Yes. It's time we looped her into the bigger plan. Her mistrusting us and us mistrusting her has only caused problems. We do this as a team from now on, or we don't do it at all.

Niko: Shouldn't we vote, first? About whether we bring her on?

Theodore: Are you saying no?

Niko: My vote is yes, actually. It's not me I'm worried about.

Kilian: My vote is obviously yes.

Elijah: It's the only option.

Gabriel: I agree.

Cian: It was going to happen anyway. There's no point fighting it.

Theodore: It's a yes from me.

Kalen (admin): Mikki and I have already spoken. He's on board. Oscar? Moses?

Moses: I can hardly say no after today, can I?

Oscar: I can still say no.

Moses: But you won't.

Oscar: Why's that, dead-man-walking?

Moses: Because you recorded her singing in Mikki's session the other day.

Theodore: You know she's good. You know she could be incredible. And you want to win.

Gabriel: Initially, I couldn't see how adding another person to the plan could be anything less than a burden, but I agree. She could be the piece we didn't even know we were missing.

Oscar: Or she could be the final straw, and we could lose everything. I can't afford to lose everything. I'm Lily's guardian. If I get out of the settlements, so does she.

Kalen (admin): You knew this was coming, Oscar. We've been biding our time, but we can't actually win separate from Isobel. Now more than ever, we have to do this together. She might not survive without us, and she's as much a victim of this situation as we are.

Oscar: I know.

Oscar: But if we're finally acknowledging everything—what the hell does that even mean? Theodore said the bond specialist confirmed that sex outside the bond could cause another soul infraction. So none of us can be with her and none of us can be with anyone else? We're all just going to fight over her and pretend we aren't fighting over her for the rest of our lives while she tries to take all of our shitty aggressiveness into herself?

Elijah: No. We'll figure something else out.

Moses: Not even you can make that math work, Elijah.

Cian: You don't know that.

Kilian: What possibilities have you seen, Cian?

Cian: I've seen her in my future. I've seen you all in my future. Nothing more concrete than that.

Moses: You've seen us miserable and trying to kill each other?

Cian: No. They were happy dreams. But they were just dreams.

Kalen glanced over to Isobel with a sigh. Her head was starting to loll to the side like she had accidentally fallen asleep waiting for him. His phone kept vibrating, but he slipped it into his pocket, crouching before her and gently clasping her shoulder.

Oscar would come around.

They really didn't have any other choice, and it was best to get it all out in the open before summer break, so everyone would have the space to think and process before coming back for their third year. He was going to need them all to come back strong and ready.

Isobel jolted awake, her fists raised in defence, her

eyes wide and panicked as she sucked in a heaving breath.

"P-Professor." She quickly lowered her fists. "Sorry, I fell asleep."

"Sorry to keep you waiting." His fingers twitched with the need to sweep the fretful strands of hair falling into her face back behind her ears, but he only turned it, offering her his palm instead.

She hesitantly placed her smaller hand into his grip, and he helped her up.

Isobel trailed Kalen back to Dorm A, feeling guilty every step of the way. He was holding an umbrella over her head like he was her bodyguard or something—while he got absolutely drenched. But she was also too terrified to scoot closer to him, and he seemed to prefer maintaining a suitable distance between their bodies.

She had tried to take the handle of the umbrella off him a few times, but he only grunted out a sound to make her hand drop. He didn't speak until they were both inside his office, and even then, it was just to curse out Mikel under his breath as he slicked back his wet hair.

"Come on up." He opened a door, revealing a set of stairs, and nodded toward them.

She slipped past him and hurried up the stairs, finding herself in a room much like the other bedrooms on the first level, complete with an en suite and a bay window, though this one obviously couldn't be climbed out of.

He snatched a change of clothes from his walk-in and disappeared into his en suite, emerging clean and dry—this time in one of the suits he wore when he wasn't training her to climb, though he left the jacket and tie off.

"Take a seat," he suggested, motioning to the bay window. "Do you have a shortlist of classes you're interested in?"

"Uh—yes. I want to do Professor Lye's Acro Duo class."

"Duo?" He questioned, gripping the back of his desk chair, and spinning it around to face her before sitting, his ankle planted over his knee as he shifted his hips to get comfortable, his big arms crossing over his chest. His vanilla scent was mild and sweet, his influence a low hum of comfort. She wasn't sure how he was doing it, but it seemed deliberate, somehow.

"Yeah." She frowned. "Why do you say it like that?"

"Because you won't dance with Elijah. They've given you several opportunities to."

"Okay, firstly." She reared back in surprise. "Was that some sort of ploy? His whole 'running into casting problems' thing? Why do you even know about it? And secondly, I did agree to dance with Elijah. And we did ... um, dance."

Kalen ran his tongue over his firm lower lip, eyeing

her quietly. "It wasn't a ploy. They noticed your name on the sign-up sheet for Lye's audition list and also signed up in case you wanted to audition with a partner, but then ... well, I suppose when they realised you were too scared to dance with Elijah, then they wanted to figure out why. Sometimes it isn't good to pique Elijah's curiosity."

"That goes for both of them," she muttered.

Kalen's lips twitched. "Perhaps. So, any other classes?"

"Urban Dance, Interpretive Choreography, Hip-Hop Fusion, and Lyrical Dance."

"That leaves one free slot."

"Will I be continuing with the small group sessions next year?"

"Yes, and your tutoring sessions with me and Elijah. Since Elijah and I will take up two sessions a week, I'll work out a way to spread those over your classes with the lowest priority. But ... I would suggest you drop Urban Dance from the list. Interpretive Choreography is basically the same thing, except the professor for that class is organising a guest choreographer each week and you'll gain far more experience. And you should add in Icon Matters, the introduction class. It's a whole lot of bullshit, but they teach you how to manage your social media and all the associated skills you're going to need to play the game going forward."

She nodded quietly, dropping her attention to her lap as she played with the hem of her shirt.

"Talk to me," he suggested. "What are you thinking?"

"Just that I need to start taking this seriously." She raised her chin, swallowing as she met his eyes. "You guys will all be fine if something happens to me or if we're all separated, but I won't. And the only way I get those surrogate pills is if I stay out of the settlements. The only way to secure my future is to win this game."

He nodded, regarding her seriously. "Welcome to the club."

"I'm not asking you to help me or anything." She went back to fiddling with her shirt, her cheeks heating. "I'm just asking you not to sabotage me."

"What if there was a way for all of us to win?" he asked quietly, his deep rumble tunnelling shock through her.

"What?" her head jerked up. "No. They only choose one winner."

Kalen sucked in a deep breath, shaking his head. "It's a conversation for later. With everyone. We need to do this as a group. From now on, we need to do *everything* as a group, understood?"

"I think so."

"You understand, princess. So let me rephrase. Do you agree?" He leaned forward, notching his forearms on his knees, drawing his face close to hers, his fierce amber eyes digging into hers with a glint of something she couldn't quite read.

"Can I think about it?" she dodged.

For some reason, that amused him. "You really think you can do this alone, Carter?"

"No." She chewed on the inside of her cheek. "Yes. Maybe."

"Do you want to?" He caught her hand in his, ducking his head to catch her eye. It wasn't like when Teak or Charlie grabbed her hand. His was so warm, his palm so rough, and he was so much bigger than her—her own hand practically disappeared. "Because *we* want to do this together. I know the Alphas fight amongst themselves, but we've known each other far longer than the years we've been here. They're supported by myself and Mikel, and by each other. We trust in the group and we protect the group. We don't keep secrets—though some of us try, for a little while. I'm not saying it's simple or perfect, but you need the group and none of us want to see you suffer on your own."

"Why not? I haven't known any of you longer than a couple of years. I'm not like your family. I'm just a really annoying thing that happened to all of you."

"Technically—" Kalen smirked. "—every one of them were an event that 'happened' to me at some point in time. I collected each of them and added them to the group to protect them because all of them need to win this game. Now I'm doing the same with you. You're *exactly* like them, not some annoying outlier."

"What do you mean? Why did you have to protect them?"

"Let's talk about it tonight. Are you in, Isobel?" He squeezed her hand, that comforting brush of his power settling over her shoulders like a hug.

"Okay how are you *doing* that?" she finally blurted, widening her eyes at him. "How are you pushing out good emotions on me? I usually only feel negative stuff."

"Just something I thought I'd try." His lips twitched into a half smile. "I'm glad it's working."

"But *how*?"

"Elijah found some interesting information about people influencing emotions through a bond. We're not fully bonded, but I guess it still works to some extent. I just think about what I want you to feel and push it at you. Why don't you try it?"

"Me?" She reared back, blinking at him. He looked serious. "You want me to push my emotions on you?"

You want me to treat you like a Sigma?

"I wouldn't have asked if I didn't." He caught her other hand, tugging both until he could hold them against his knees as he shifted forward. "Close your eyes, if you need to focus."

It was an immediate relief to close her eyes, to pretend that Kalen wasn't holding her hands and asking her to trust him and use him like a Sigma sponge.

She pulled in a deep breath. “Okay, now what?”

“Pick a feeling.”

That would require her to actually sort through her feelings. She twitched, a second from pulling her hands away, but he seemed to anticipate her reaction, tightening his grip on her before she could actually move.

She huffed out an annoyed sound, turning inwardly to sort through what she was feeling. Scared—terrified, really. Betrayed. Angry. Sad. Surprised.

But there was a tiny, *miniscule* little spark of hope in there too. Clinging on to the promise Kalen dangled over her.

She might not have to be on the outside, anymore. She could make a choice and it really seemed like they were *giving* her this choice instead of demanding she become one of them.

She clung to the sliver of hope, pushing everything else away, but paused as the sad feeling persisted, floating back into the forefront of her mind.

Her grandfather had died at some point, and nobody had told her.

She *still* didn’t know how or when it had happened.

With another sigh, she shoved that aside and gripped onto the faintest thread of hope. “Now what?”

“Push it. Literally, just give it a mental shove toward me.”

She frowned, unsure how to do what he was asking.

"Imagine it's an object of some kind," he suggested.

It was already like a thread in her mind, so she turned it into a needle instead, and then imagined stabbing Kalen through the chest with it.

He grunted, dropping her hands. Her eyes flew open, staring at the hand he held over his chest.

"Crap. Did that hurt?" she blurted.

He laughed. "Did you just *stab* me with ... *hope?"*

"You said to turn it into an object!"

"And you chose a *knife?"*

"A needle!"

"A needle that you ... stabbed me with?" He chuckled again, the yellowed amber of his eyes sparking to life.

"Well ... I mean ... I guess I thought about shoving it through your chest. I was just thinking that it needed to be inside you if you were going to feel it. I can't believe I just did that."

His phone started to ring, and he fished it out of his pocket, glancing at the screen before bringing it to his ear. Whoever was on the other line started speaking immediately. "Yes, she's with me. Wait, what? You felt that? Let me check." He hung up, and then tapped on his phone a few times before turning it to face her.

It was the group text that she was part of, and as each new message popped up, she found her brows shooting up in surprise.

Moses: The hell was that?

Cian: Was that you, Isobel?

Niko: Did we all feel that?

Gabriel: I'm guessing so.

Theodore: I just felt a cute little Illy-flavoured knife stab into my chest.

Kilian: And it felt kinda good?

Oscar: Stabbing usually does.

Gabriel: Felt hopeful.

"They all felt it," she said numbly.

"So, what do you think?" Kalen lowered his phone, his smile slipping as his regard turned heavy again. "Are we doing this together?"

"I don't even know what you guys are doing."

"I didn't mean that—that's another conversation. I mean are we dealing with the bond together from now on? As a group, no secrets, tackling everything together?"

"I guess that sounds nice." She bobbed her head slightly. "And what if there's a fight? What if someone changes their mind?"

"The bond happened to all of us," Kalen said gruffly. "Like a cyclone. You can't 'change your mind' about a cyclone. It's happening whether you like it or not. We're just deciding to board ourselves up in the same house, to try and survive it together."

"I understand. It just feels like a change of pace, suddenly." She struggled to vocalise how she was feeling, but Kalen seemed to understand.

"Bonds are just magic and mayhem to us." He frowned. "When our eyes changed, it didn't suddenly change our feelings or make our world tilt and crack open to include you. Our world was still the same as it was the day before. It was us against everyone else, and you were part of 'everyone else.' We had no idea *what* you were going to do or what kind of person you were going to turn into. We all have something serious on the line here, something we can't just throw away because you appeared out of nowhere and seemed nice enough."

She laughed awkwardly. "I never held it against you. It was pretty obvious you guys were all playing a larger game. But I hated being alone with this secret while you all had each other."

"And you put your trust in the wrong person and look how it turned out." His fingers drifted up over the scars on her arm, making her shiver. "So you understand the risks we were facing while trying to decide whether we should trust you or not. Our game here at the academy aside, if you had told anybody about Theo and Moses' abilities, they would be *dead*, and the rest of us wouldn't be much better off. I promised to protect those boys, and that's exactly what I did, even if it was against you. Now, I'm promising to protect you too. And I'm so fucking sorry this had to be so hard for you."

"I guess it's okay." She let her eyes fall, watching as his hands settled against her forearms, that comforting feeling tingling all over her again. "But I have a ... request. Can I have a request?"

"Sure." He sounded like he was smiling again. "Why not."

"I don't care if Alphas are more aggressive and territorial. Whatever they're allowed to do in the Stone Dahlia, so am I. If they're allowed to do it with whoever they like, then so am I. Just because I can emotionally handle it doesn't mean I should have to."

"You're right." He grimaced. "Elijah and Gabriel are already transitioning out of their rooms down there—"

"Since when?" she interrupted, confused.

"Elijah sent us a message this morning that they were going to become floaters instead. They're going to look around for something else to get into so that they're settled for when the Track Team tries to recruit the others."

"Oh." She wondered if that was after her conversation with Elijah that morning in the chapel. He hadn't really said that he *liked* what he did, only that other people liked it.

Maybe he didn't want to bring any of the other Alphas into something he wasn't even enjoying that much ... or more likely, there was a larger plan in motion, because it *was* Elijah.

"So I'm free to do what I like, then?" she asked, her eyes flicking up to Kalen's.

Immediately, his gaze narrowed. "No, princess. Not when you're in my room. And that has nothing to do with double standards. When you're with me, the rules I gave you last night still apply. When you're in my room, I *own* you." He eased back, clearing his throat. "Other than that, yes. But be as considerate of them as they are being of you."

"I thought they were just indifferent," she challenged.

He smirked. "Gabriel, maybe. Elijah is indifferent to no one. And Theo is definitely keeping Wallis at arm's length because of you. It would serve him better to be all over her for the cameras. At the moment, he's coming across as a shitty boyfriend and that doesn't help his reputation at all."

"Well." She shrugged, feigning indifference. "If I ever get a fake boyfriend, I'll be just as considerate."

Kalen's hands twitched on her arms, but his expression didn't shift. "Make sure he's not easily broken. Any other stipulations?"

"Don't the other guys need to agree to that one?"

"They'll do what I tell them to do."

"Even Oscar?"

"No. Good luck with Oscar."

She smiled despite herself, shaking her head a little. He sounded like he was joking, but he was probably serious.

"Okay." She gave him a succinct nod. "You have a deal."

18
GREEN IS GOLDEN

THE STORM HAD EASED UP A LITTLE, BUT NOT MUCH. ISOBEL spent the rest of her fifth period in Kalen's office, despite attempting to go back to class after their discussion. He had stopped her the second she picked up her bag, directing her to a seat opposite his desk downstairs instead, and then disappearing. He came back with a tray of coffee for them both, plus a few bowls of snacks, and she gave up her protests almost immediately.

She needed to prepare her audition for Lye's class, anyway.

She curled up in the chair, sipping her coffee and flipping through her playlist as she nibbled on a shortbread cookie. Her finger paused over the song she and Elijah had danced to, her brow crinkling.

Shoving the rest of the cookie into her mouth, she pulled up his number and sent him a private message.

Isobel: Do you still want to dance with me?

He didn't respond immediately, and she brought up one of her social media accounts, flicking through to see if any of the other second-years had posted pictures of their preparations for final assessments. When Elijah's name popped up along the top of her screen, she almost choked on the buttery cookie that threatened to lodge in the back of her throat. She quickly swallowed and clicked on the message.

Elijah: I organised with Lye to submit a video application.

Isobel: For us both?

Elijah: If you want.

Isobel: Why a video application?

Elijah: In case I surge again. Sorry about that, by the way.

Isobel: Um.

Isobel: That's okay?

Isobel: Can you explain why that happened and why Gabriel made me leave? I'm confused about when I'm supposed to stay and show that I'm safe, or leave to keep myself safe.

Elijah: You're always safe. Gabriel was the one who wasn't safe.

Isobel: Why?

Elijah: He was taking you away from me.

Elijah: And it happened because ... I wasn't expecting us to be so good together. I knew you were feeling self-conscious and that's why you didn't want to dance with me, but then you let go and the way you were responding to me was just ...

Elijah: It was lovely. You were lovely.

She had *felt* lovely dancing with Elijah. It was the best she had felt since waking up in the hospital, and she was almost deliriously happy that he was offering to dance with her again.

Isobel: Thank you.

Elijah: So you've taken on one of us. How about two of us?

Isobel: You mean Gabriel? But we didn't practise any three-way choreography?

Elijah: I have something prepared. I'm sure you can memorise it quickly enough. Gabriel wants to apply for Lye's third-year class as well.

Isobel: It sounds fun, actually.

Elijah: That's my girl.

She stared at the screen, re-reading his last message as he kept typing. He obviously wasn't trying to *claim* her as a mate or anything and she certainly wasn't hoping he would, but for some reason his choice of words had butterflies flaring up in the pit of her stomach anyway.

Elijah: Meet us in your usual training room for a few practice runs at the choreography before we go outside. Cian is going to film the performance. Wear something simple and easy to move in. We're going to make this count. I don't like coming in second place.

She began to type out the fact that it was raining but then backspaced over the words. Obviously, he *knew* it was raining. Instead, she told Kalen that she needed to get ready to shoot her submission video and padded into Kilian's room to sort through the dresses he had brought over from Dorm O.

She picked out a couple and laid them out over the bed, snapping a picture of them and sending it to the group chat, since Cian, Elijah, and Gabriel would all be involved in the video.

Isobel: Which one?

Gabriel: Send us photos of you in them, Puppy. Can't tell like this.

She dragged the options into the bathroom and stripped off her clothes, pulling on a high-waisted pair of black dance underwear. She considered a bra, but then decided to skip it, since she didn't want her sleeves to slip and show off any straps, and a few of the dresses were open backed.

She snapped pictures of the front and back of every dress she had brought in with her, and then sent them off all at once, leaning against the counter to wait and see which one they thought would fit their song choice best. She assumed they already had a song, since Elijah mentioned teaching her choreography.

Kilian's response was instant, even though he had nothing to do with the dance.

Kilian: The third one.

She checked back through the photos and clicked on the third one. It was a black mesh design made of thin, delicate silk. The sleeves were long and fitted, the neckline high, tight along her chest and flared out from there in silken ripples to her knees.

It created an interesting texture interplay over her skin and would probably look really nice in the rain ... the only problem was, the mesh was completely see-through. A bodysuit was supposed to be worn beneath it. She had arranged her arms casually over her chest when she took the photo, but she would need to swap out her underwear for a leotard if that dress was the choice.

She ducked back into the closet as her phone vibrated again.

Theodore: The third one. Hard to see the top of it, though.

Cian: #3. The others can burn for all I care.

Isobel: There's nothing wrong with the others.

Cian: But none of them are #3.

Kilian: Will the sleeves be too tight? Is that silk?

Oscar: Jesus Christ.

Isobel: Yeah, it's fine, just stretchy enough.

Isobel: Oscar?

Oscar: Did you just send us a topless photo?

Niko: She clearly has a dress on.

Oscar: She has a net on.

Isobel: Moving on.

Oscar: Oh no you don't.

Kalen (admin): The third option is the best.

Niko: I agree. It's pretty.

Isobel: Thanks, Niko.

Gabriel: We also like #3. But wear a leotard, Puppy.

Isobel: I was just trying it on!

She set her phone aside to extract a leotard from the drawer Kilian had cleared out for her underwear and was shocked when she felt a hand against her spine. She jolted upright, clutching the leotard to her chest as she spun around.

Oscar tilted his head as he watched her back into the set of drawers. "Fell into another trap, little rabbit?"

"I could have been naked!" She wasn't. She was wearing the last dress option. Still, she *could* have been. And why did Oscar have to move so quietly?

"You could have been." He shrugged.

She flicked him across the chest with her leotard. "Don't be rude. I'm allowed to be here. I'm allowed privacy."

"Not from me." He stepped forward and she tried to scramble back further, but there was nowhere to go. "Heard you had a thing for closets. Thought I'd see if it was true."

She tried to hit him with her leotard again, but he caught it this time, yanking it out of her hands and tossing it behind him, then his body was pressing up against hers and the little brass drawer handles were poking into her back.

"Are you jealous?" she asked, trying not to sound intimidated and thinking he would just laugh at her for the question.

Instead, he just quietly nodded, his hands tugging at her hips until she was pulled up to her toes, and then he ducked down, planting his lips by her ear.

"I thought I only had to worry about Theo, but everyone wants a little taste of cherry, hm?"

She sucked in a quick breath, feeling his teeth graze over her neck, her stomach clenching tightly. "They're my surrogates. They're h-helping me."

"Is that what they're doing?" Oscar chuckled darkly, easing off her a little, his dark eyes catching hers. "I have no interest in helping you. So how do you explain this?"

"You're trying to intimidate me." She frowned, pushing against his chest.

"Wrong." He pulled her up suddenly, catching her against his body. One arm wrapped around the back of her thighs while his other hand caught her face, drawing her lips to his. "I just want to get deep inside you because you're already deep inside me and I hate it."

He muttered the words against her lips before kissing her roughly, his tongue invading her mouth. She clutched at his shoulders, her body bowing into his, and as soon as he got the reaction he wanted, he dropped her, spinning her around to face the drawers.

"Stay like that," he muttered, his heat leaving her body for a moment before he was back, his hands teasing up the backs of her thighs. "Colour, rabbit?"

"G-Gr—yellow."

"Why yellow?" He sounded amused, his fingers

slipping beneath her dress to run lightly along the curve of her ass at the tops of her thighs. "Tell me."

"Because I don't want to be late."

"You won't be. I'm just making sure you're dressed properly." His touch drifted up higher, his thumbs hooking into the tops of her dancing underwear, and then he was pulling them down her legs, bending behind her to help her step out of them. He wrapped his hand around the inside of her calf, and as he rose, so did his hand.

She did a quick mental calculation, realising that Oscar was so much taller than her that there was no way his hand would stop short of her pussy if he straightened to his full height, and then he would know how wet she was just from his kiss. Hell, he would only need to hit her upper thigh to know that, because she could feel the stickiness there already.

Hit by a moment of panic, she immediately tried to clench her legs together, but he must have predicted her, because his boots were suddenly between her feet, kicking her legs out wider.

"This is the group's second debut," he murmured, his voice gravelly as he gripped her inner thigh, his other hand slowly wrapping her hair around his fist. "You should make everyone sick with jealousy. Violent with it. Nothing should look better than the three of you dancing together. Every single person watching should want to peel their own skin off just to *be* you."

He cupped her between the legs, one of his fingers lightly stroking against her clit. "But first ... you need to feel all of that for yourself."

She didn't know what to say or do. Her throat felt painfully dry, her limbs threatening to go weak and collapse her into a pile of bones on the ground.

"D-Does this feel so good because of the bond?" she squeaked out in surprise, her hands flying up to support herself against the drawers when he tugged her head back against his chest, bowing her body backwards.

"No." Oscar breathed deeply against the top of her head before drawing slow, gentle circles around her clit.

No?

She froze, and he quickly spun her around, leaning down to capture her mouth.

"I meant yes," he growled into the kiss. "So don't fucking worry." He knelt, pushed her dress up to her hips and buried his face between her legs, a second growl vibrating out of his body and into hers. He pulled one of her legs over his shoulder and began to lick her roughly, all gentleness dropping away from him. He sucked her clit and scraped his teeth over her, making her jolt in his hands before he thrust his tongue into her, pushing it deep into her channel before returning his attention to her clit, a groan building up in his chest. As soon as she neared orgasm, he pushed her dress higher and sank his teeth into her stomach, causing her to yelp out in pain.

"No orgasms. That's for later," he snapped, pulling

up and spinning her around again, kneeling behind her. "Step."

She glanced down, blinking in surprise at the leotard he held open, waiting for her to step into. She did, and he slid it up her legs and over her hips. He flicked her dress off, pressing behind her as he reached for her breasts.

"So perfect," Oscar mumbled, squeezing them gently at first, and then harder. "You're almost dressed, baby."

He released her, and she heard the rustling of his clothing before something hot and hard was pressing against her ass. He pulled open the back of her leotard, pushing his cock into the material, nestling it between her legs. He paused there—with her frozen in shock—and cupped her breasts again, his tongue running up along the back of her ear.

She shuddered, and he pulsed between her legs.

"Colour?" he whispered, his rough voice making her shudder.

"Yellow." Her voice was barely audible, but he must have heard her anyway.

"Because you don't want to be late or because you can feel my dick, Carter?"

"D-Don't want to be la—"

He started pushing against her, shocking her into silence. She could feel all of the honey dripping out of her, coating him as he sawed a few inches back and forth, and she almost came just from the knowledge that she was soaking him and he was allowing it. He pinched her nipples and she spasmed, her empty channel clenching desperately.

"Need more," she demanded quietly, wriggling to get some relief, but he was so careful to avoid her clit, to continue denying her the orgasm she had lost.

"Fuck." He pushed against her entrance and then backed off a little, suddenly gripping and jerking along his own length, the head of his dick bobbing at her slick entrance with every stroke.

"You're going to dance with me on you," he commanded. "In you. You're mine."

His other hand fell between her legs, finding her clit and pinching it roughly. "Ask me to come in you and I'll let you come with me. All you have to do is ask, baby."

She should have been thinking things like "Oscar is insane" and "will this cause the Alphas to surge" and "will this cause a public bloodbath," but instead, there was nothing in her mind past trembling heat and desperation.

She nodded and felt a sharp tug on her clit in response.

"I don't hear you asking," Oscar snarled, quickening his strokes in a threatening way, like he was going to go ahead and do it anyway.

"I w-want it." She tried to push back against him, and he grunted.

"Prove it, Illy." He increased the pressure against her clit until she felt her orgasm building back up again.

"I want to wear you while I'm dancing," she begged quietly, ashamed of her own words. "I want you all over me."

"Mhm." He pushed until he was firmly notched against her pussy lips, forcing himself in barely even half an inch. "Put your fingers in your mouth, baby. You're about to scream."

"W-What?"

"Do it," he grunted, swatting her right across the front of her pussy. "Now. Three of them. Suck on them."

She quickly slipped three fingers into her mouth.

"Good girl. Turn your head and show me."

She tilted her head, her cheek pressing to the drawers, and felt his cock twitch against her. "There's my pretty ... girl, fuck." He released his twitching length and briefly grasped her wrist, pushing her own fingers deeper into her mouth before he cupped her breast again, rubbing her clit harder as he teased her nipples. "Time to scream, Rabbit."

Her orgasm rushed up on her, but she still wasn't prepared to scream until he palmed his cock again and pressed another inch into her, stretching her opening so much that the burn sent an immediate wave of fright through her.

She hadn't even thought about the fact that he was so much bigger than the crystal, or that he might try to go any deeper, even though he was still only an inch or so inside her. He pinched her clit again right in the middle of her orgasm, and she screamed around her own fingers, a husky, desperate and shocked cry that had him groaning and pumping hot liquid into her channel. She tried to press further back against him, but he delivered a hard smack to her right ass cheek, pausing her movement.

"Pass me something from the drawer," he demanded quietly. "We don't want a messy leotard, do we, Carter?"

She slipped her fingers out of her mouth, wincing at the trail of drool that drooped between her hand and her mouth.

Oscar grunted, slapping her again, lighter this time. "Can't have a red ass either."

She pulled open the drawer with her own things inside, her body feeling warm and tingly as she extracted a cotton crop top, which was getting a little too small for her anyway, and handed it back to him.

"I can't show any stains on my leotard for the video," she said, completely in shock that she was even having to say that.

And to Oscar.

"I know, Rabbit." He sounded like he was smirking. He pulled out of her and spun her around to face him, holding the crop top between her legs. "You're addictive, you know that?"

She blinked at him, wondering at the unguarded look on his face. *So was he.* But she didn't want to say it.

"Do you think this is normal?" she asked instead. "This ... desperation. I feel like I could do that all day."

His eyes slitted, heat sparking in the dark depths. "Don't tempt me to go further. I'm trying to be good."

"That was you trying to be good?" she asked, a little breathless when his gaze fell to her still-exposed breasts.

"Yeah ..." The word was a rasp, and he quickly pulled her leotard the rest of the way up, hooking her arms through the straps and snapping them against her shoulders.

She had pressed her legs together to keep the cotton secure, but he tugged it out carelessly, fitting her leotard into place with a thoughtful expression.

"That was the least violent way for me to deal with my proprietary aggression. The real question is ..." He settled his big hands on her waist. "Why are you letting me? I'm a fucking monster and you're ... perfect."

She stared at him for a moment, too warm and tingly from her recent orgasm to feel anything except comfortable. "You've never hurt me."

"I lied to you. About being your mate."

"I would have done the same." She rolled her eyes. "I mean sure, I was angry you all hid it from me, but *I* wasn't ready to have a mate and I didn't know all of you either. I would have absolutely hidden it until I was sure I could trust all of you. I think you did the best you could."

"We try and separate you and Theo all the time," he

spat out, almost angrily. "Even though we all know how you two feel about each other."

She fell into silence again, wondering where the conversation was going. It was like he *needed* her to hate him.

"I hadn't noticed," she said mildly.

He scoffed. "You can't possibly be this beautiful, this pliant, this ... *soft* and *nice*"—he spat the words out like they were curses—"for all of us. Something has to give. Your feelings for Theo will grow and the rest of us will be forgotten. Or you'll figure out how much Kilian likes you and then not even Theo will measure up."

"Don't be ridiculous." She crossed her arms, keeping them there even when he picked her up by her biceps and carried her to the bed, setting her on the end of it as he cleaned up the closet.

She wished she had the perfect thing to say, but it had never occurred to her that the Alphas would be jealous of each other. Maybe Moses ... but he would be jealous of Theodore spending time with her because of *Theodore*, not because of her.

Now ... she was re-evaluating.

She had grown closer to Cian, especially over the settlement tour. And Niko, who she had spent more time with over the past few weeks than any of the others. And suddenly Moses was volunteering to be her surrogate.

And Gabriel was her friend.

And Elijah liked to dance with her.

Were they ... developing feelings?

Was *she?*

No. That was stupid. There were eight of them—or ten, if she included the professors. She wasn't exactly friends with Mikel or Kalen, but she was growing dependent on them both. It wasn't something they were trying to engineer, but both were so accustomed to taking care of the other Alphas that they had slotted her in as one of their charges, and she liked how safe it made her feel.

"I won't pick favourites," she whispered, so low she almost thought he didn't hear her, but he paused, her silk mesh dress clenched in his fist.

"Not even Theo?"

Beautiful, superstar Theodore. How could anyone ever match up to him?

Except Kilian did it all the time, with his lush smiles and sly gazes that made her giggle. And Cian could hypnotise her with the click of his tattooed fingers, wielding a power over her that nobody else seemed to hold. And Gabriel. Stoic and stern-faced, always seeming to quietly anticipate her needs. She would follow him anywhere because she *trusted* him. She trusted in his calm, cold confidence.

But nobody made her feel as safe as Kalen ...

She took a deep breath, meeting Oscar's eyes. "I meant what I said. I won't—I can't pick favourites. I like the person I've become since I met all of you, and I don't think I would be the same if even one of you had been missing from the start."

He dropped the dress beside her and started running his fingers through her hair, working out the tangles he had caused. "I feel the same way about them," he admitted. "That's why this is hard. All my choices have been taken away and I'm even more furious because you're ... you. If you were awful, I could be glad you belonged to them. I could forget about you."

"Kalen promised we're going to figure this out together." She knew she sounded afraid, and it was because Oscar and Moses were complete wildcards. Niko and Kilian didn't want mates, but they would do what was best for the group and neither of them wanted to see her suffer. Elijah also didn't want a mate, but if they were willing to include her in their plans, it was only because Elijah had already told them it would work.

But Oscar? He could throw it all back in their faces.

"You're a sweet girl." He sighed, catching her chin, lifting her face to his as he crouched over her. "We'll protect you, okay?"

She bounded up, throwing her arms around his waist. He grunted a surprised sound, but inserted his hands beneath her arms, hoisting her up so she could wrap her legs around him instead, his hands gripping her ass. His lips found hers, his kiss sharp, like he didn't know how to platonically hug someone. As soon as she began to squirm against him, he squeezed her and set her down, quickly dragging the dress over her head.

"Let's go," he said, his gaze sweeping over her. "You look fucking amazing."

THEY ARRIVED IN THE PRACTICE ROOM JUST AS THE SIXTH PERIOD started, giving her exactly an hour to learn all of the choreography and for them to film and submit it to Lye before the end of the period. Cian, Gabriel, and Elijah were already there, rehearsing camera angles, and the three of them froze when she and Oscar pushed into the room.

Cian ran a hand down his face, groaning deeply. "Jesus, Illy. Aren't you sore, honey?"

"N-No." She flushed bright red. "He didn't have a crystal, so—"

"Shit." Oscar suddenly froze, whipping out his phone. "Niko needs to talk to you about—about something."

"There were *rules*," Elijah snarled. "What the fuck, Oscar?"

Oscar just ignored him, moving to sit on the bench as he texted Niko. Gabriel turned on Isobel, his expression calm. "You okay?"

There wasn't much more she could say on camera, so she just nodded.

"Don't feel pressured to practise these dance routines just because everyone else wants to," Elijah said, still angrily eyeing Oscar. He was probably trying to cover up Cian's "are you sore" comment by making it seem like she and Oscar had been practising some choreography.

Isobel chewed on her lip and nodded. "Honestly, I wanted to dance. And I want to dance now, too, so ... let's just get on with it?"

The three of them turned to stare at her, and Oscar picked up his head from his phone, smirking darkly. "Wait until you get to practise the full routine, Carter."

Cian looked relieved. "Still haven't reached the end of the routine, then?"

"Not even close," Oscar answered for her, while Gabriel and Elijah shared a loaded look.

"How far into the routine, exactly?" Cian turned his attention to Oscar. "Since you're so fucking chatty today."

"Barely got through the basics." Oscar shrugged, throwing his hands across the back of the bench seat. "Don't you guys have some choreography to learn? I didn't bring you the star performer looking like *that* for nothing."

Elijah quickly took control of the session. Running through Isobel's part of the choreography while Gabriel stopped and started the music for them, and then they did a few rounds with Cian filming, watching it back each time to perfect their mistakes.

She had been given challenges to quickly learn choreography before, but she was extra nervous this time. Oscar had called it "the group's second debut," and she was starting to realise that what they were doing would of course be bigger than an application for Lye's class. It would be the first time Elijah and Gabriel had danced for the public, instead of hiding away in practice rooms and working on choreography with their headphones in.

It would also be the first time anyone would see her dancing with a partner. Even when Lye partnered people up for his class, she was always left on her own, and he ended up using her to demonstrate things for the rest of the students.

After their final run-through, Elijah picked up his phone to check the time. "We need to head out. The others should have finished setting up the floating platform by now."

"Floating platform?" she asked, jumping up and down to keep her muscles warm. It wasn't raining *that* much. What did they need a floating platform for?

"You'll see." Oscar dropped his arm over her shoulders, steering her from the room while Cian packed up the camera equipment.

Elijah fell into step on her other side, Gabriel waiting at the door for Cian.

"You two seem very friendly all of a sudden," Elijah

said, keeping his voice low as he glanced at Oscar. "What colour were you, Carter?"

"Fuck off," Oscar shot back. "You don't get to take notes on all her *dance rehearsals.*"

"Yellow," Isobel answered, ignoring Oscar. "Because I didn't want to be late."

Oscar scoffed quietly, and Elijah's lips twitched like he wanted to smile. "I see. So you did well, then."

"Don't you want to know how well Oscar did?" she asked.

Both Alphas chuckled.

"I think he probably did fine," Elijah answered. "But I'm glad he went easy on you."

"Hardly," she mumbled beneath her breath.

"Didn't know I was capable of going that easy," Oscar crooned into her ear, before straightening.

"Then you should be ready for me soon," Elijah stated, in such a matter-of-fact way that Isobel had to repeat the words in her mind a few times, positive that she had misheard him. When she tripped over her own feet, he caught her easily, that amused smirk still on his lips.

"I'm kidding, Carter."

Cian and Gabriel caught up to them as they left the fitness centre, the five of them ducking into the rain and jogging toward the lake, where it seemed like all the other Alphas had gathered. Theodore and Moses were in the water, Mikel and Kalen standing off to one side, Kilian and Niko off to the other.

There weren't many students lingering outside, but a few had begun to gather, huddling beneath the overhang of the old boathouse to observe what Theodore and Moses were doing.

"That should hold!" Theodore called out, climbing out of the water. "Need a hand onto the platform, Illy—" He froze, coming to a stop before her, his nostrils flaring.

Moses appeared behind him, dark grey eyes narrowing, his squared jaw clenching. Isobel refocussed on Theodore, apprehension eating away at her chest like a vicious parasite. His jealousy was a searing flash, like a hot knife stabbing into her skin, but as soon as she felt it, it was suddenly gone. He was schooling his handsome face, pushing wet tendrils of hair out of his eyes as he bent down to her eye level.

"We were supposed to share you tonight," he whispered. "But guess who just lost the privilege?"

"Worth it," Oscar grunted, striding away to stand with Kalen and Mikel—Moses following him. The two professors were both eyeing her like they could smell her from twenty feet away. Or maybe they could just smell her on Oscar. She dropped her eyes, trying to shove away her nerves.

As much as she had enjoyed Moses, Cian, and Oscar making her body feel so *good*, she was starting to get overwhelmed again, and she really needed a moment to settle herself.

"Don't get too excited, though." Theodore straightened away from her, flashing his superstar smile. "You're getting cuddles and treats and nothing else."

"Treats?" She winced, but somewhere inside her chest, there was a little spark of happiness flaring to life. "I'm not a dog."

"No." He reached out like he was going to touch her face, but then he clenched his fingers into a fist and dropped it back to his side. "You're a brave fucking girl who deserves some caramel chocolate, a massive hug, and a funny movie."

That spark burned brighter, her smile taking over her whole face. "Okay. Sounds good."

"Green?" he asked, smirking at her.

"So green." She could have hugged him in front of everyone, she was so relieved.

"There's my girl. Now go kick some ass. If this doesn't break the internet, then we aren't doing our jobs properly."

19

ISOBEL BLOODY CARTER

THEODORE HELPED HER ONTO THE FLOATING PLATFORM, WHICH didn't wobble and sway as she had expected. It felt secure, like walking on concrete with a few millimetres of water layered on top. She moved to the middle as Elijah and Gabriel set up speakers along the edge of the lake. Even during their run-throughs in the practice rooms, they had still used headphones.

Cian moved to the bank before the platform, setting up one camera to record them front-on and making sure it was protected from the rain before he lifted a second camera to record them while he moved around. They were taking it so seriously, and it made her want to do really well for them.

All the Alphas had come to support, just like they did with Theodore's debut ... except this time, they weren't just supporting Elijah and Gabriel. They were supporting her too.

Mikel and Kalen both nodded at her, silently encouraging her, and she took up position, one leg pointed behind her, her arms wrapped over her chest, her head lowered as the rain pattered down around her. Elijah and Gabriel moved to either side of her, and Cian raised his arm.

"Music starting in three, two ..."

Obsessed by Jake Daniels began playing, and she moved immediately to Gabriel, Elijah backing up to the edge of the platform. They came together easily, their movements light and fun, sharp and clean, timed impeccably to each beat of the song. The choreography was actually quite difficult and nuanced—especially on a floating platform in the rain—but the beauty of it was in making it look simple and playful.

She concentrated on making her body flow easily with Gabriel's, each roll and spin beautifully executed, every tiny movement precise and exacting. It helped that Gabriel was a *sensational* dancer, easily moving and influencing her body to keep them both in sync. Even the smallest movements of their hips and hands were aesthetically pleasing when they pulled them off at exactly the right moment, in perfect coordination. Gabriel's skill made them seem like they were sharing the same brain, their bodies reacting to a single command instead of two people moving independently.

As soon as the second verse was introduced, they separated, Elijah joining in on her other side as they started the three-person choreography. The style of dance was contemporary fusion, throwing in some difficult acrobatic work with a more casual lyrical and hip-hop style. It meant that she was using every inch of her body, from her posture to her acrobatic strength, her timing and precision, her full body extensions and even the arrangement of her hands and fingers.

It was harder when they weren't touching and couldn't see each other in the practice room mirror, and the effect of the dance wouldn't work unless they were in perfect synchronisation, so she tuned out everything to listen to the music, making sure she was always on time.

When the verse changed again, she spun toward Elijah, Gabriel stepping off to the side to watch as Elijah caught her, and they melted together as easily as she had softened into Gabriel.

Elijah tossed her up as the song slowed into the bridge, lifting his leg into a ninety-degree angle and angling his upper body to form a straight line from his ankle to his head. He caught her against the line of his body like he was a shelf, and she balanced there, crossing her ankles and folding her arms behind her head in feigned ease, gazing up at the sky despite the rain that spattered her face.

She heard cheers and whistles from the bank, and then Elijah rolled her down again. She found herself smiling like an idiot the longer they danced, and when they separated into three again, she chanced a quick glance to the Alphas on the bank, spotting Theodore's wide, bright smile and Kilian's beautiful, happily curved lips before she was forced to refocus.

Her smile faded a little as her concentration kicked in again. They were moving closer to the final stage of the choreography.

This was the only part they hadn't practised.

Elijah had said it was because they wanted to save it for the final video, but she suspected he was refusing to practise it on the hard floor in case she hurt herself. At least on the platform, one of them would be able to push her off course and into the lake if things went wrong.

Elijah picked her up and began to spin, his arm hooked around her hips as she bent forward, reaching out and turning herself limbless like a rag doll. He spun and spun and then released her, and her mind went blank.

This was the part where she needed to trust them. To not lock up her body and try to twist to safety, but it was over before she could even consider how many different ways Gabriel would be able to knock her into the lake if he wasn't going to catch her successfully, and the probability of her hitting the platform instead.

His arm slipped through the narrow space between her thighs and stomach, hooking her onto his arm and continuing the spin Elijah had abandoned, drawing out another round of cheers from the lake.

He spun her gently to the platform, a doll set aside to rest, and the song ended, just like that.

One of the best moments of her life, over in a flash.

"You guys!" Kilian bounded onto the platform, almost knocking over Cian. "That was *insane!* You did so well! Holy shit!" He picked up Isobel, and when he set her down again, she found Gabriel and Elijah both smiling at her.

Full, stunning smiles.

"Thanks," she managed, her throat tight. "For doing that with me."

"Won't be the last time." Gabriel rested his hand on her head. Maybe it was his version of a hug. "Get used to it. This is your life now."

She had never loved her life before, but she suddenly had the feeling that she did now. At least her heart felt like it was going to burst, and she couldn't stop smiling.

A brief flash of terror bubbled up, reminding her that Ironside wasn't *safe*, that people were still trying to hurt her, that the world she lived in was far from perfect and even the Alphas could leave her one day, but for now, she pushed the terror down and decided to savour the moment.

She never wanted to forget this.

"That was incredible." Theodore dragged her off the

platform, tucking her beneath his arm and leading her back to Kalen and Mikel, who seemed ...

Impressed?

By *her?*

"You only saw that choreography today?" Kalen asked as soon as she was within earshot.

More students had gathered, but they were keeping their distance from the two Alpha professors.

She nodded. "Elijah and Gabriel are really good teachers."

"They are," Mikel agreed. "But you're the one who just showed us choreography most professional dancers would need to spend weeks in back-to-back workshops to pull off as effortlessly as you just did."

"No, no." She quickly waved her hands before her. "That was really hard, not effortless at all."

Oscar stepped forward, gripping her cheeks with one hand and puffing out her lips. "Take the compliment. You were great."

"Aw coo hay doh beeh," she tried to speak, and he shook his wet head, giving her a severe look.

"You could have done better?" he guessed.

She nodded in agreement.

He released her. "I don't think so. You're pretty when you smile. Anyway." He glanced at the others. "I'm going to shower and change. Who did we decide is getting dinner?"

"We're getting it," Niko announced, approaching

with Cian and Kilian. He glared at Oscar for a moment, as though the other Alpha's uncharacteristically easy-going mood was grating on his nerves before he shifted his attention to her. "Anything you want, Isobel? We're picking it up from the dining hall so we can all relax tonight, since it's our last night."

She found herself shaking her head numbly, all of the happiness draining out of her. Tomorrow was Consolidation Day. Her father's threat to take her away from the Alphas and stick her with Bellamy refused to dislodge from her brain.

She scanned the faces of the other students who had gathered and spotted Rayne—one of the second-year Betas, who Bellamy usually hung out with—huddled beneath an umbrella with a few of her friends. Isobel started toward them, breathing out a sigh of relief when Bellamy stepped out from behind another Beta, tucked into a leather jacket with the hood pulled up to ward off the rain.

"Nice job, Carter." He eyed her as she approached. "I take it you've spoken to your dad."

"It's not happening," she said, stopping before him, her hands planted on her hips.

"Not what I heard." He shrugged, his light green eyes twitching over her shoulder to fix on whoever had stepped up behind her.

She turned her cheek a little, smelling something warm and resinous, with a tinge of smoking sweetness that curled around her like a warning. A very grumpy Theodore.

"Kane," Bellamy greeted. "I think Wallis was looking for you."

"A better question is what are *you* doing looking at *Carter*," Theodore shot back. "She has more than enough surrogates."

"And yet Daddy Carter still thinks she needs another one. Or maybe you guys just aren't very effective?" Bellamy shrugged. "Not my business, really."

A dark laugh reached their group, several of Bellamy's friends scattering away as another body stepped up behind her, oleander slowly descending over their group like a vaporous cloud.

"You have a death wish, Beta?" Oscar growled.

"He your boyfriend or something?" Bellamy asked Isobel. He couldn't quite seem to bring himself to look at Oscar. He shifted his weight, casually leaning in the other direction.

"No." Isobel crossed her arms over her chest. "I have a mate, remember?"

"Noo," he drawled sarcastically, his English accent thickening. "I totally forgot that *Isobel Bloody Carter* has a goddamn mate."

She found herself smiling because he ... well, he had a point. It was almost a guarantee that Ironside would use her half-bonded status as a source of drama at least once a week.

"If you refuse to be my surrogate, my father won't be able to do anything to force you," she said. "So just pull out. Please. Don't let them use us to negotiate with each other."

Bellamy closed his eyes, pinching his nose before dropping his hand and levelling her with a tired expression. "I'll try. But you haven't met my dad."

"I can relate."

"All right." Theodore tugged her back. "Enough bonding. Mission accomplished. Bye bye, Bellamy."

"Did you want me to tell Wallis to meet you at Dorm A or something?" Bellamy asked blandly. "I'm pretty sure she ran back to get an umbrella."

"Actually, we're having a dorm-only celebration tonight. Tell her I'm sorry and I'll call her later!" Theodore dragged Isobel off, and they stopped to collect all the camera equipment from Cian before they headed back to Dorm A as a group.

Kilian texted her to let her know that she could use his shower, so she went straight to his room and stood under the warm flow of water for several minutes, replaying the dance over and over in her head as though she could somehow tattoo it into her memory before she dressed in one of Kilian's shirts and a pair of shorts.

She made her way to the rooftop, following the noise and the smell of food, and paused at the top of the stairs, biting back a smile at the sight of all ten of them crowded into the kitchen, digging into the food Niko, Kilian, and

Cian had picked up. They still had one period left for the day and all their usual scheduled practice and training time, but for the first time since arriving at Ironside, Isobel felt okay with just letting it all go and enjoying herself. It wasn't just her, either. The others were relaxed and happy—even excited, though it was hard to tell since their positive emotions didn't have the same effect on her.

Kilian dragged her to a stool at the counter before disappearing to take a shower, and Theodore filled up a plate, sliding it over to her as Moses poured margaritas for everyone. It took her a moment to realise a new camera had been installed on the rooftop, covering the entire kitchen area, which had been a blind spot up until now.

"Should we be drinking on camera?" she muttered low to Niko, who snapped a glass down in front of her.

He shrugged. "We're celebrating, don't worry about it. Kalen won't let us drink much anyway. We're still on emergency standby."

She cut a look to Cian, who was sitting on the opposite counter, Oscar beside him. Oscar was halfway through an enchilada, a hint of amusement in his dark eyes as he watched Moses pretending not to understand what Theodore wanted on his taco and loading it up with pineapple instead. Cian's food was untouched and there was no drink in his hand. He held an easy smile on his face and was obviously keeping his emotions tightly in check, but it was clear that he was worried.

She checked her phone, but there were no new messages from Sophia. There was every chance that Ironside had increased security after Luis' and Cian's dreams, throwing off whatever plans had been in motion for an attack at Ironside. But that didn't mean it couldn't still happen in the future. She knew the health and safety of the Gifted wasn't exactly the government's highest priority, but *Ironside* was a billion-dollar industry for the country, and all of their Icon assets were within these walls, so even though they didn't put a lot of stock into the Gifted abilities, they were probably still taking the idea of a threat at least somewhat seriously.

She forced the thoughts from her mind to eat the vegetarian tacos Theodore had made for her, even though her appetite had dipped. She didn't really have a choice because Theodore was watching her, waiting to pounce the second she pushed her plate away. As soon as Cian spotted her covertly watching him, he also started eating, flashing her a carefree, cocky grin.

It was obviously fake, but the longer they held eye contact, the more it smouldered into something darker. She could *see* him remembering what they had done in the closet that morning. He even seemed to be staring at her lips, and it made her too nervous to eat, so she reached for her margarita instead, the cool, tangy liquid spilling across her tongue as she switched her attention from Cian to Niko, who was already on his third burrito.

He caught her watching and notched his chin up in question, his brows twitching up as he took another huge, tearing bite.

"Where do you put all that food?" she asked.

"He burns it off," Kilian answered, returning from his shower. "Most of his classes are sports."

"I'm three times your size," Niko defended, after swallowing the food in his mouth. He raised his arm and flexed it, and Isobel blinked at the immediate bulge of muscle.

He had grown. They all had.

They were all taller and more muscular than when she had first seen them in her first week at Ironside. Oscar's hair was growing out, his curls loosening the longer they got. He could almost pull half of it up into a ponytail now, and it looked like whoever had cut his hair last had given him a slight undercut.

Cian's maturing was a little more obvious than the others, with the tattoos and piercings now littering his body, whereas Niko, Theodore, and Moses had just grown stronger, the angles in their faces broadening and sharpening.

Kilian still had a more streamlined look with lithe muscles and a graceful posture, but there was less softness in his face. The angelic features were still there, but they were far more dangerous. He used to look like the perfect angel, but now he looked like he could probably tempt angels to rip off their wings and dive right out of the sky.

Elijah and Gabriel had grown taller and more intimidating with their matching deadpan expressions and standoffish personalities. Elijah always kept his hair at the same length, but something about his face had definitely changed. Unlike the others, it made him seem *decades* older instead of a couple of years. It wasn't that he looked tired or drawn, but there was just far too much intelligence in his eyes. It was like he understood more than he let on and was operating a few levels higher than everyone else. Gabriel's shoulders had widened to almost match Niko's, but his body was still far less bulky, both he and Elijah maintaining perfect dancer's physiques.

And she was more or less the same. She didn't have the crazy growth cycle the Alphas did. She was the same height, the same weight ... though her hair had grown a few inches.

Still, she had changed *inwardly*. When she looked back, she could barely recognise the girl she had been in her first week at Ironside.

As soon as her plate was empty, she washed it up and left the others on the rooftop, taking her margarita downstairs with her and slipping into Kilian's room. She climbed onto his window seat and propped up her phone to catch up on the last few Ironside episodes she had missed.

It wasn't that she really wanted to watch them—she already knew what happened because it was all anyone talked about—but she was searching for a moment of normalcy. She had been feeling a pervading sense of joy that refused to abate for long ever since she danced with Elijah and Gabriel, but the feeling was so foreign it was actually beginning to swirl into panic as it tried to make itself at home in her body.

She crossed her legs, sipped the dregs of her margarita, and let her mind go blank, dispersing the joy and worry and panic like none of it mattered, the way she used to do every night in her first year.

Not that there had been any joy, back then.

The Alphas must have sensed that she needed some time alone because even though she could hear them all coming downstairs an hour later, they didn't disturb her.

As the sun set across her outstretched legs, she jumped up to grab a blanket and drag it back to the window seat with her, where she curled into a ball, using her arms as a pillow as she stared at her phone. When the sky grew dark and her sight started to blur with fatigue, there was a soft knock on the door and Kilian poked his head inside.

"Can I come in?" he asked, flicking his attention from her curled-up form to her phone and back.

"Yes! It's your room!" She started to struggle upright, but he held out a hand.

"Don't." He stepped into the room and kicked the door closed behind him. "You look so comfortable."

"I was just catching up on Ironside."

"Do you want a hug?"

She blinked at him. "Actually, ye—"

He scooped her up before she could finish, claiming her seat and bundling her into his lap. She relaxed instantly, infuriating tears threatening to appear. It was just too much of a relief to have Kilian. Beautiful, perfect, *not-a-threat* Kilian. She could feel however she felt about him, and it would never mean anything.

"Today was a bit much, hm?" he rumbled into her hair, carefully stroking the strands out of her face as she rested it against his chest.

"I'm never going near a closet again."

He laughed, bundling her closer. "What about next time you want to come, baby?"

Hearing him rumble out those words in his soft velvet voice made her thighs immediately clench together. A reaction she attempted to ignore completely.

"I'll do it myself."

He exhaled a sharp puff of air. "When did you get so dangerous?"

"Huh?" She tilted her head to glance up at him and he quickly looked away.

"Nothing. You didn't have sex today, did you?"

"Um. I don't think so?" She dropped her head again, breathing in his bergamot scent.

He laughed again, the motion jolting her head slightly. "You'd fucking know, Illy. Especially with Oscar. Do you mind if I call Niko in here?"

"What for?"

"Just a little talk. Is that okay?"

She nodded, watching him curiously as he fished out his phone and sent a quick text, but his expression was soft and calm, preventing the anxiety from climbing back into her stomach.

When Niko came in, he walked straight over, picked up her phone and paused the Ironside episode before kicking off his shoes and sitting opposite them. He kicked up his legs along the edge of the window seat, lending her some of his heat without actually touching her.

"Big day?" he asked, his voice a pleasant rumble, free from any kind of inflection that could put her on edge.

"I ... guess so." She looked from him and up to Kilian, who only gave her a reassuring smile, his fingers running up and down her arms over the blanket she was still wrapped in.

"Are you okay with everything that happened today?" Niko asked, his beautiful mossy eyes showing nothing but kindness, no negative emotion emanating from him.

"Are you guys shielding your emotions from me?" she asked.

"We've been trying to." Niko tilted his head in curiosity. "Are you avoiding my question for a reason?"

She sighed, folding her arms across her chest, the blanket slipping down. "I wanted everything to happen. I'm just surprised at myself, that's all. I've never been very ... boy crazy, I guess. Or girl crazy," she quickly tacked on, for Kilian's benefit.

That seemed to amuse him because he chuckled.

"Do you think the bond is making you feel this way?" Niko asked, now watching her very carefully.

She shook her head. "I wanted to think that for a while. I thought—since I'm not supposed to be able to scent you—that your scents were like ... hypnotising me?" She looked down at her lap, embarrassed. "That sounds stupid."

"No, it doesn't." Kilian let out a low, short growl that he quickly cut off. "Nothing you say to us right now will sound stupid."

"And now?" Niko pressed, reaching out to lay his hand over her blanket, somehow knowing exactly where her foot was. He squeezed gently, forcing her eyes back up to his.

She shrugged, her embarrassment deepening. "Theo explained that people's natural scents smell better or worse depending on your level of attraction to them."

"So your feelings aren't from the bond?" Kilian asked.

She stiffened.

Who the hell said anything about feelings?

“The bond isn’t forcing you into sexual situations with the others?” Niko clarified, his eyes narrowing as they took in her expression.

“N-No.” She shook her head quickly. “I could have stopped it at any time. I knew I could. Oscar’s scary but he wouldn’t hurt me.”

“He might hurt you,” Niko said seriously.

He made her scream.

“Only when I want him to,” she answered quietly.

Kilian grunted. “What do you mean? We need you to be specific.”

“I don’t like when Oscar threatens to be violent to other people, or ... when I think he’s upset at me. I don’t like violence or anger in general. Cian made sure to tell me I wasn’t being punished for anything—if he hadn’t done that, I might have freaked out. But when they aren’t angry at me ...” She trailed off, at a complete loss for how to explain herself.

“When you want to be claimed by your mate,” Niko supplied for her. “You want it done forcefully.”

She peered at him curiously. “How did you know that?” The questions rushed out of her now that he had managed to vocalise what she couldn’t: “Is that weird? Is it like that for all mates? Is it because you’re Alphas? I’ve never heard of anything like this before.”

“It might not be normal for everyone, but that

doesn't make it weird," Niko answered calmly, his thumb now running along the bottom of her foot through the blanket.

It wasn't like him to offer her physical comfort, but he seemed to be doing it deliberately, making sure that she didn't feel like they were cornering her or lecturing her.

It was working.

She suddenly felt like she could tell Niko anything …

"Can you *force* people to tell you the truth?" she asked, a hint of an accusation in her tone.

He grinned the lovely lopsided smile he rarely gave her. "I can, but I'm not doing it right now."

"Doesn't stop everyone from telling him everything," grumbled Kilian. "He tricks you with his stupid 'friendly neighbourhood therapist' face."

Isobel snorted. "Okay, sorry."

"Don't be." His smile dimmed a little. "It's all speculation at this stage, but it might have something to do with Alpha natures—because your mates are Alphas, you may want to be claimed in a very 'Alpha' way, or maybe these are just your personal proclivities. You didn't have much experience before this year, so it's a little hard to speculate about that."

"Not that it really matters whether this is just how you prefer things," Kilian added. "Because preferences aren't set in stone. They can change whenever you want them to change. You don't need to be a certain way just to make yourself fit with other people."

She chewed on her lip, thinking it through before finally shaking her head. "I'm definitely not doing anything just to fit them."

"Good." He bent down, nuzzling her cheek, and she barely managed to contain the insane urge to lift her face and nuzzle him back.

"So you aren't being pressured—outside of what you like," Niko summarised. "And you aren't being controlled by the bond. And you're comfortable with the traffic light system?"

"I like it." She stared back at Niko, a creeping suspicion making its way into her mind. "Did they send you guys in here to have a sex talk with me?"

His smile was back, wider than ever. "I volunteered, but they all thought it was important. And we would really like to get you to a doctor so you can talk to her about contraception."

"I have the implant." She indicated her arm. "My father made my mom take me to get it a week before he dropped me off here."

"How long does that last?" Niko asked, quickly masking his surprise. "Three years?"

She nodded, and he released her foot, some of the tension she hadn't even noticed he was carrying seeping out of his broad shoulders.

"You can come and talk to me or Kilian if you're ever

uncomfortable with anything, okay? You can also go to Mikel and Kalen. It might be tempting to approach Gabriel or Elijah, since they always have an answer to everything, but I'm starting to think that might not be the best idea."

"Why?" She frowned, a tendril of concern working its way along her chest.

"Gabriel has been acting off when it comes to you," Niko answered honestly. "It's so rare for him to act out of character at all, so we're just keeping an eye on the situation for now. Elijah surging today is also a concern ... and ..." Niko cringed slightly as if he didn't really want to say what was about to come out of his mouth. "I saw the way they both looked at you today. And how you looked at them."

She froze again, everything in her mind rebelling against what Niko was trying to suggest.

"It's not every day I get to dance with people so naturally talented." Her tone was too sharp, so she worked to soften it. "That's why I enjoyed it so much. And the atmosphere was great. The song choice was great. The choreography was brilliant. It had nothing to do with us *looking* at each other a certain way."

"It's your choice." Niko tried to sound reassuring. "Just letting you know that Kilian, Mikki, Kalen, and I are always available. We want you to feel safe and comfortable here with us."

"Do you?" she asked, growing sombre. "I know we're

friends and everything, but I didn't think you'd accept me moving into Dorm A, and I really didn't think you'd be on board with us all dealing with this bond as a group. I thought you'd want to be as far away from anything to do with it as possible."

He seemed taken aback, his lips thinning, but then his expression smoothed out again. "I shouldn't be surprised that you think that." He tugged his hands through the dyed strands of his hair. "I still can't accept the bond—not when nine other people are involved. And even if they weren't, my parents would never accept an American girl. Which is so dumb, because they're hardcore followers of the Gifted religion. But none of that changes the reality that there *is* a bond and it's not just your problem to deal with. It's on all of us. We need to make it work together. We just needed a little bit of time to all get to a place where we trusted you enough to bring you into the fold."

"And now I'm in?" she asked. "Kalen said I need to talk to everyone together?"

"We'll wake you up tonight when Elijah schedules the cameras to start looping. We're going to have a family meeting. You'll be brought up to speed then. Until then ... you should know that we're all in agreement on this."

That persisting spark of joy inside her flared a little brighter, but so did the panic.

It was too good to be true.

"Thanks, Niko."

He nodded and slipped off the seat, stepping back into his shoes.

He stopped when he was right beside them, looking down at her.

"Do you ..." He scrubbed a hand over the back of his neck, looking unsure. "Mind if we touch a bit more? It's just making me feel like bugs are crawling under my skin to have you smelling like everyone else except me."

She quickly lifted onto her knees, opening her arms, the blanket falling around her legs. He stepped into her, pressing her all along the front of his body, both big arms banding around her back, squeezing some of the breath out of her as her heart stuttered in her chest.

"Thank you for checking in on me," she whispered.

"You make it easy to care about you," he rumbled back, his voice husky. He pulled away, flicking a look to Kilian. "Should I tell Theo to get ready? Isobel looks sleepy."

She had collapsed back into Kilian's lap the second Niko let her go, so she could hardly argue with that.

"Yeah, I'll come and get him now." Kilian picked her up and deposited her onto his bed, passing her phone back into her hands before leaving with Niko.

He switched the lights off before he closed the door, and Isobel squinted at her phone screen, realising she had gotten more than twelve angry emails from her father over the course of the day. She slapped her phone onto the bedside table without opening any of them, kicking her way beneath the blankets to get comfortable, sticking her face into the pillow and inhaling, because the freshly laundered material smelled like Gabriel.

She let out a small groan as the scent filled her lungs. What she would give to sleep directly on top of Gabriel ... but she doubted he would ever allow that.

She curled around a few pillows instead, deciding to rest her eyes until Kilian and Theodore got back. She didn't hear either of them re-enter the room, but she felt when Theodore slipped in behind her, and she immediately abandoned the pillows, turning to her warm, amber-scented Alpha and curling around him instead.

He hummed a sound deep in his throat, drawing one of her legs over his hip and dragging her as close as he could before he started stroking her hair back from her face, running his fingers gently over her scalp. He rumbled something to Kilian, who quietly answered, and then a few seconds later, the bed dipped on her other side.

Kilian shoved all the pillows out of his way, pressing in behind her, his lips skimming her shoulder and one of his feet hooking with hers before his body grew relaxed behind her.

She garbled out a sleepy "Goodnight" against Theodore's hot skin, but was asleep so quickly, she didn't even remember if they responded or not.

20
STRING OF FATE

Isobel didn't want to wake up. In fact, she refused to wake up. She felt Theodore's amused chuckle more than she heard it, and then she was being hoisted into his arms. She wrapped herself around him, dropped her head into his neck and wiggled to try and get comfortable again as he started moving around.

"You're going to want to be awake for this, Illy." He held her up easily with one arm, his other hand tickling along her side.

She grumbled an unhappy sound, lifting her head as he entered the living room. The other Alphas were all filtering in, claiming seats as Theodore continued to brush his fingers up her side.

She was slowly coming awake, and as soon as she stiffened with the realisation that the other Alphas were all just sitting there, staring at her and Theodore and waiting for her to wake up, Theodore lifted her away, claiming an armchair and setting her back onto his lap, facing the others.

"Anyone need a coffee?" Elijah asked.

They all shook their heads and so did she, her nerves working to make her alert.

"Then let's skip the small talk and get right into it," Mikel grunted. "Isobel ... what do you know about Silla Carpenter?"

She glanced at Kalen. "You mean—"

"My grandmother," Kalen supplied. "Yes."

She swallowed, confused. "She won the Ironside game and decided to stay in her settlement instead of living with the humans. For a while, she was allowed to earn money from all her endorsement deals, but then they cut her off and said that if she wanted to remain in the settlements, then she had to forfeit all her rights and prizes. She chose to stay, and the officials had to change the Icon contracts to stop anything like that from happening again. That's what my mom said about it, anyway."

Kalen nodded. "That's right. Silla's plan was to inject her earnings directly into the settlement, but that upset their entire controlled ecosystem. It had to be stopped. What people don't know is that it almost didn't work. She had a significant fanbase, with supporters all over the world, and she always used to say that if she had leaned on them, if she had decided to fight the officials ...

she might have won. So that was her plan with me. To create an Ironside winner so adored and skilled that the officials wouldn't be able to stop me from keeping my endorsement deals and bringing money back into the settlements."

"I guess that makes sense." Isobel surveyed the gathered Alphas, wondering where this was going. Kalen wasn't even in the running to be an Icon. "Without the fans, they don't have a show, right?"

"Right." Elijah folded his arms loosely over his chest, leaning back into the couch and crossing his long legs. "So this whole thing starts with Silla and Kalen, but it evolved into something else when Moses and Theo happened."

"Their mother contacted my grandmother," Kalen said. "Silla knew people, and she was famous for having ways to deal with the officials and for being a strong Gifted advocate. So Silla arranged for Juliette Kane to visit our settlement and she came with two babies, claiming that their eyes and veins had turned black when they were born. Silla promised to find a way to protect them. Initially, we decided that the safest option was to hide them in plain sight, to train them up the same way Silla had trained me up, and to make sure they each won the *Ironside Show*, one after the other."

"And then we happened," Elijah said, his smile tight, his expression guarded. "Gabriel and I are orphans. We grew up in Niko's settlement. The woman who ran the house for orphans liked to rent out rare Gifted to the officials—like Alphas or Sigmas."

Isobel swallowed, switching her attention to Gabriel. He sat there, still as a statue, his expression as blank as ever. It was like he wasn't even listening to Elijah.

"I wasn't in control of my ability back then." Elijah's attention drifted off to the side. "I just wanted it to stop. I willed it to stop. I accidentally killed an official and Niko's parents helped get us out of there."

Isobel blinked as her blood ran cold, tears spilling down her cheeks.

I am not for sale.

The message on the back of Gabriel's door had haunted her ever since she had seen it, and now its true meaning finally landed like a heavy iron in the pit of her stomach, making her queasy.

"Elijah could protect himself with his ability most of the time," Niko said, cold fury written all over his expression. "But Gabriel could only hear the thoughts of everyone he was rented out to. The night Elijah killed that official, Gabriel was hurt so badly, he was brought into the clinic my dad ran. Elijah came with him, and my dad got the full story out of them both. I was listening at the door, so I knew exactly where to find the piece of shit Elijah killed. I burned down the house and the body inside it. My dad had heard about Silla Carpenter, so he contacted her, asking for her help with all three of us, since we were all involved at that point. She organised to have Elijah and Gabriel transferred to a different settlement."

"And then the plan changed," Kalen announced. "We decided to push the limits of Ironside a little further and create a group that could win the game. We told Juliette Kane to move settlements and pretend the boys were the same age—"

"What do you mean?" Isobel interrupted, blinking in confusion.

"I'm a year older," Theodore admitted, sounding a little guilty, "than you and Moses."

"Oh." She turned in his lap to look up at him.

"Sorry," he cringed. "Pretending to all be the same age was a crucial part of the plan."

She turned slowly, looking at the others.

"We gave Elijah and Gabriel new ages, and we started actively recruiting Alphas," Kalen said. "Elijah and Gabriel are two years older than you, and Niko is three years older."

"Right." She swallowed, wondering what else they had been hiding. "And then?"

"We decided that I wouldn't apply for Ironside because the plan would be more effective if we deprived the show of Alphas for a while and then hit them with a group of them at once. This way, I could enter when they did, as a professor. I could keep an eye on them and continue training them. We waited to see how much pressure the officials would apply since Alphas are so rare. They weren't happy, but we managed to strike a deal that made everyone happy. I would work in the Stone Dahlia, which would give us enough money to bribe the officials when we needed to transfer people from one settlement to another, and it would give the officials another Alpha to control and put on display."

"I struck the same deal," Mikel added. "Silla hunted me down, and I thought it was more important to help in the settlements than try my hand at being an Icon, so I was happy to work in the club. We figured with four Alphas we had a chance of stirring things up but with *more* Alphas, we could really shock the world into seriously paying attention. So we convinced Niko to join as well—"

"More like I didn't give you a choice," Niko grumbled.

A small smile stretched over Gabriel's lips. "He said he needed to protect us."

Kalen also looked over at Niko with a thin smile. "After Niko joined, we found Oscar. He had lost both of his parents and needed medicine for his sister badly. He joined us in an instant, even though he despised the idea of training to be an Icon and learning how to sing and dance like the others."

"How old are you?" Isobel asked, frowning at Oscar.

"Twenty-two," he answered.

He was four years older than her.

She chewed on her tongue, considering him for a moment, before breathing out a sigh. "I get why nobody has told me anything before now, but it's still annoying. It makes me feel like an idiot."

"If you're an idiot, then so is every other person out there," Elijah answered immediately. "Everyone has bought our story and it's because decades have gone into crafting, refining, and gatekeeping how to push an Icon —or two, or five, or eight—along the track to victory. I'm sorry we couldn't tell you before now."

"I get it." She ran her hands through her hair, hoping to detangle the sleep-tousled mess while she gathered her thoughts. "So, who was next?"

"Me." Cian smiled at her, but it didn't reach his eyes. "I was already training to be an Icon. My mother always used to take pictures of me when I was a kid and tell me that I should be a model or an actor, then she died, and I found out she had been selling those pictures. Honestly, I think that's why she killed herself. Alphas and Sigmas are rare commodities in the settlements, and child exploitation is a significant problem. My dad took over my training after that and reached out to Silla because he was worried about how many times I had been approached by people in the settlements asking if I was interested in doing some modelling for the officials. Silla confirmed his fears that those people were running child prostitution operations and then Kalen and Mikel applied for a visit. They convinced me on the spot to join their group, and I switched to vocal and dance training. I'm twenty-one, by the way."

She just stared at him, working her throat nervously.

Cian would have been a beautiful baby with those aquamarine eyes and tousled golden locks. The idea of anyone trying to harm him made her physically sick, and she curled her hands around her stomach, hoping the story didn't get any worse.

"I was the final addition," Kilian said, his pale eyes watching her carefully. "I'm also twenty-one. My adoptive parents knew Silla. They heard she was open to training up possible Icons, and they sent her my picture."

"Kilian didn't need protecting from anybody," Mikel explained. "But like Elijah, he had a staggering amount of natural talent. We decided he was going to be our secret weapon."

"So you're all going to try and win the game? As a group?" she summarised. "What kind of group? Like a band or something?"

"More than that." Kalen looked amused. "A performance group. A mix of genres and styles, but they can all sing and dance at an elite level, and by the time they graduate, they'll be the most popular group in the world. Everything we've done up until now has just been to create mystery and stir up interest. As of next year, every single performance piece is going to be as a group or for the group, and everyone is going to be expected to pull their weight cultivating the group's fan base. It's going to be tireless and constant, far beyond what people normally do to win this game. Their careers are starting inside Ironside, not *after* Ironside."

She could imagine Theodore and Kilian singing as they performed complicated choreography, because Theodore was good at everything and Kilian was graceful, with a beautiful voice. She could easily see Elijah and Gabriel pulling it off, as well. Even Cian, if she was honest. But Oscar? Singing and dancing? And Moses? And Niko?

"We want you in the group, Isobel." It was Elijah who spoke, his arms still loosely folded, his cold eyes expectant. "You're a fantastic dancer and you have a killer voice. With a bit of Mikel's fine-tuning, you could be a complete ace, like Theodore."

"Why are you an ace?" she asked, tipping her head back to the smirking Alpha.

"He's just a natural at everything," Kilian answered, rolling his eyes. "Picks up choreography like that"—he snapped his fingers—"and he has a stable voice with a natural range that barely needs any work, unlike the rest of us. We had to train for years to match what he was born with. You're a lot like him."

"Please." Theodore rolled his eyes. "Elijah has perfect pitch and an eidetic memory. I'm not the ace."

Elijah just shrugged.

"What about you two?" she asked, looking at Mikel and Kalen. "You put all this work into the group and then you get sent back to the settlements when they win? How does that keep us all together?"

"Actually." Mikel grinned, his scars twisting along his cheeks. "The group has signed a contract with me and Kalen as co-managers. It has a ten-year term, and it was signed three years ago. Starting next year, we'll be making no secret of the fact that we're managing you and the boys, and the fans will begin to think of us as just as much a part of the group as anyone else."

"You really think the officials are going to let this happen?" she asked, trying to keep the doubt from her tone.

"I look forward to watching them try to stop it," Kalen said, far too casually. "What do you say, Carter? Do you want to play this game on your own, or do you want to play it with us?"

If she chose to go her own way, she would win. The officials would make sure of it, even if it was purely to stop the Alpha group from winning. She could get her hands on the surrogate pills and live her own life exactly the way she wanted to, without any mates to answer to.

That reality hit her suddenly, and heavily.

She could *win* the game.

They had to have reached the same conclusion, but they were still giving her the option. They were giving her everything. Even the power to destroy them. It would have been wiser to secretly get rid of her. To find a way to get her expelled.

To forget about her.

The longer she sat with her thoughts, the less control they seemed to have over their emotions, and little flashes of anxiety, fear, and uncertainty began to bat away at her chest. Theodore had gone a little too still, his breath no longer stirring against the top of her head.

"What about Cesar?" The thought popped into her head unbidden. "My dad made me sign a contract assigning him as my manager already."

"We'll find a way to deal with him," Oscar promised darkly, making her head snap in his direction. He looked too serious.

"Mikel and I will deal with him," Kalen corrected with a frown.

"What's the name of your group?" she asked.

Moses barked out a laugh. "We don't have one. Been trying to figure that out for years. Maybe you should name it, since you'd be the final member."

She felt suddenly put on the spot, her mind racing for an idea that wasn't terrible. "What about Eleven?"

"There are nine of us, doll." Cian was smirking at her.

"There's eleven." She pointed to Kalen and Mikel. "You want the fans to include them, right?"

"That's actually not bad." Elijah sat up straighter. "That wasn't on our list of options at all."

"The list is long," Gabriel added.

"Infuriatingly long," Niko chimed in. "Sometimes,

when I can't sleep, I read it just to pass out from boredom."

"Does that mean you're joining?" Theodore asked, his deep voice uncertain. "We're really doing this together?"

That little spark of joy was back again, threatening to turn into a bonfire if she wasn't careful.

"I ... guess I'm joining," she said, squealing when Theodore suddenly squeezed her and stood, spinning her around.

The others all stood as well, gathering together in the middle of the living room. Kilian snatched her as soon as Theodore set her down, pulling her back against his chest.

"Is that everything?" she asked, a little breathless from the rush of adrenaline. "No more secrets now?"

For some reason, several of them glanced over her head at Kilian, who stiffened.

"Maybe one more secret," he admitted gently. "Please don't hate me, Illy."

"What?" She spun around, getting whiplash from her own emotions.

"I'm not gay," he said plainly.

She just stared at him.

"All right, let's leave them to it," Kalen snapped. "Everyone back to bed. You two—go to your room for this discussion before the cameras reset."

Kilian brushed past her as the rest of the Alphas left

the room, and she was left standing there alone with her mouth unhinged for a few minutes before she stormed into the room after him, slamming the door.

"What?" she whisper-yelled. "The *fuck*, Kilian?"

His pale cheeks flooded with colour, and he sat on his window seat, his head falling into his hands. "I'm sorry I didn't tell you."

"So ... you're bi?" she choked out. "Or is the ex-boyfriend also fake?"

"No, he's real. And I'm sexually fluid. Sometimes I feel gay, sometimes I feel bi, and whenever you're in the room I feel straighter than Niko dancing to a 90s playlist."

"I don't understand." She choked on an unwilling laugh, and then quickly cleared her throat to pretend it didn't happen at all. "Why would you have to keep that secret?"

"I didn't have to. At first, you just assumed and usually I just let people assume whatever they want, but then ... I guess I felt like I was your only safe option and that you needed me to stay that way. And since everyone else here also made the assumption that I'm gay, I figured it would be good for you to have at least one public surrogate that people didn't gossip about."

She winced. "Obviously I'd prefer you didn't hide who you are to make me comfortable."

He groaned. "I know, Illy. I've just been really worried about you."

"I've been really worried about you!" she shot back, planting her hands on her hips.

"I know, baby." He was actually pouting.

Colour flooded high into her cheeks. "You can't call me that anymore."

"Why not?" His pout grew more pronounced.

"Because ..." She started pacing, pausing every now and then to glare at him. "Oh my god, I can't believe this."

"I can still be a safe option for you." He stood up, interrupting her pacing path by planting himself in her way. "Nothing has to change."

"You kissed me," she said numbly, staring up at him. "To ..."

"Because I wanted to," he inserted. "Aron was my first boyfriend and I've never had a girlfriend. I guess I was a late bloomer. I don't know. I just really needed to kiss you."

"And?" she asked, afraid of what else he might say.

"I want to do it again," he rumbled, before his eyes widened and he quickly straightened, almost like he didn't realise he had been looming over her. "Just to be honest. But I can control myself. You don't have to worry about me."

"H-How long have you felt like that?" She gaped at him, her stomach flipping over, nervous tingles running all through her limbs.

"Since I snuck into your room while you were

sleeping, saw your note to Theodore and found out it was your birthday."

"What?" she croaked, her mind going blank. "I … the next day there was a cupcake—"

"That was me." He surveyed her warily. "And I took a photo of your note and showed it to Theodore. That's how he got your number. That's why he texted you."

"You … asshole," she finished lamely. "I'm so mad at you."

"You don't sound mad." He stepped forward, tilting his head in curiosity.

She wasn't at all.

She was relieved.

Because she really, really liked Kilian. And not as a friend.

And not just him.

She released a nervous laugh, shaking her head. "You're right. I'm more embarrassed that I never actually asked if you were gay or not. I just assumed. You must get that all the time. I'm sorry."

"So you forgive me?" He caught her cheeks, drifting another step closer, their bodies almost touching. "I'll still be your gay bestie in public so that you have a safe option in front of the cameras. But … do you want me to keep pretending in private?"

She bit her lip, a sound catching in the back of her throat. She wasn't sure what it was, exactly, but the sudden awareness that sparked in Kilian's pale eyes implied that he did.

"I don't know," she answered honestly. "I just want you to be yourself, but it was nice to have someone I could always touch without it having to mean anything."

"I can manage that," he said softly, still cupping her face, his thumbs brushing along the tops of her cheekbones. "I'll be whatever you want me to be, Isobel. Just don't change anything between us."

She swallowed, blinking back tears, and nodded silently. He kissed both of her cheeks, tasting the errant tear that slipped out, and then he bundled her up, lifting her into his arms as he turned off the light and carried her back to his bed. She refused to release the fistfuls of his shirt that she had grabbed, so he slipped into the bed beside her, pulling the blanket up around them both.

"I'm so much happier now than I was when I first got to Ironside," she whispered. "But I cry more now. How does that work?"

"You were disassociated when you first got to Ironside," he returned. "You walked around like a pretty little zombie, never letting anything affect you because you were never safe to just stop and feel anything."

She felt his inhale, like he was going to say something else, but then the door opened. It was hard to see in the dark, but it looked like Theodore. He approached the other side of the bed, falling into it before turning to face her, his head propped up on his hand.

"Kissed and made up?" he teased.

Not Theodore.

Moses.

Kilian reached over her and shoved at his chest. "What do you want?" he grumbled.

"Came to remind Miss Carter that she's neglecting her obligations," Moses replied flippantly. "She was supposed to destroy Wallis. She didn't even try."

"I thought about it a lot," Isobel defended, sounding just as grumpy as Kilian.

Moses leaned in closer, his powdery, crushed petal scent teasing into her nostrils like a whiff of perfume. "You thought I'd go easy on you just because of what happened in the closet?"

She deadpanned. "Which closet?"

He smirked, pinching her chin. "Oscar went too easy on you. You're getting cocky."

"I think you should go easy on me too." She gripped his wrist, only because he was holding her chin, but as soon as her fingers wrapped around his skin, they both paused. He stared at her fingers for a second, and the smirk dropped right off his face when his eyes returned to hers.

"Why is that, Sigma?" His tone was low and rough.

She pouted. Just like Kilian. And just like it worked

for Kilian, it seemed to work for her. Moses narrowed his eyes on her lips.

"You almost had sex with me," she said, inserting a slight whine to her voice as she trailed her fingers down his arm. "You aren't even nice to me, and you almost fucked me in a closet."

"Why are you pouting about it?" His voice was almost a groan, his gaze confused and frustrated, like he knew exactly what she was doing but still couldn't control his reaction.

"Can't you help me out?" she pleaded. "Just this once?"

He closed his eyes, trying to block her out.

She inched closer, placing her head on the pillow right beside his, their noses touching.

"Please, Moses?"

His grip dropped from her chin, skimming her neck. He paused there, his fingers stretching out before he quickly formed a fist. "Stop it, Carter."

"Stop what?" She brushed his nose with her own, her knee inching forward until it touched his thigh.

Behind her, she was pretty sure she could hear Kilian trying to smother a laugh.

"Stop trying to flirt your way out of this," Moses growled, reaching beneath the blanket, gripping her knee, and pulling it up over his hip, bringing her flush against his erection. He wasn't half hard either. He was throbbing. He pushed it against her stomach, and she swallowed a squeak of surprise.

"Why?" Her voice was suddenly shaking. "Is it working?"

He laughed, the sound full of darkness, and then his eyes popped open. "I don't know. Maybe you should try harder."

"Or maybe we should cool down," Kilian suggested, his arm hooking around her waist and drawing her back an inch.

"I'm not surging." Moses rolled his eyes, even though Kilian couldn't see him. "Just letting the little Sigma think she can seduce me."

"It feels like I can," Isobel said.

His hands drifted from her knee to her thigh, his fingertips slipping beneath the edges of her shorts. "Let's make a deal," he suggested. "Go and sleep with Theo for the rest of the night and I'll help you destroy Wallis."

"Okay. Why? You hate when I'm with Theo."

"It's our last night, Carter. He's barely gotten a minute with you, and I know he needs you. I don't want to deal with all the shit he's bottling up and have him going feral if your asshole dad decides to separate us for the summer."

"Done. Now help me."

"So demanding." He squeezed her thigh, and then released her, pulling out his phone. He tapped his screen for a few minutes and then turned it around, pointing to a button that said Process Transaction.

"Just click here," he said.

"Wh—"

"And don't ask what it does. I'll tell you after."

She surveyed Moses over the top of the phone, but his expression gave nothing away.

She clicked the button, and he tucked his phone back into his pocket.

"Done," he said. "Her bank account is empty. All her savings and Ironside stipends from the last two years completely stripped."

"What?" Isobel croaked.

"You just donated it all to The Huts. It's a section of the Hudson settlement where all the elderly people who no longer have family or a means to support themselves are shoved into closet-sized homes to die."

She almost choked. "How can you even do that?"

"Oscar hacked her and got into all her accounts when you stole her phone. Now ... it's time to go." He suddenly tore her out of Kilian's arms and set her on her feet, before taking her hand and dragging her from the room.

"Cameras are still down," he noted, checking his phone. "We've got a few minutes. Kili will have to come and get you in the morning. Say goodnight to your not-gay best friend."

"Goodn—" she started, but Moses was already pulling her through the door. He closed it and tugged her to Theodore's door instead, but he didn't open it. He took her by the shoulders and backed her into it.

"I'm not very good at doing things out of the goodness of my heart," he admitted lowly, planting his hands either side of her head on the door. He dipped forward, leaning his forearms on the door, bending until his lips hovered over hers. "Aren't you curious? Don't you want to know if our second kiss will feel like our first?"

She licked her lips, too nervous to speak, before shaking her head.

"Did you just lie to me?" he breathed out, his stormy eyes darkening.

Slowly, she nodded.

"Come to me," he demanded in a whisper, refusing to press his lips against hers.

"No," she whispered back.

He smiled, his breath misting her lips. "What colour if I make you, Carter?"

She didn't want to admit it.

His lips skimmed her cheek, brushing against her ear. "Just nod," he murmured.

She jerked her head down, heat flooding her cheeks, and he rumbled with a groan, his body pressing into hers.

"Come to me," he repeated, this time in Alpha voice.

It was such a relief to press up on her toes and fit her lips to his. Moses made her feel alive. He filled her with fiery emotion and demanded she rise to meet him with every interaction, but he also made her dizzyingly nervous. She didn't want to come between him and Theodore, but the ten-foot wall they had propped between them had crumbled, leaving her to face the fact that there was a burning attraction between them demanding to be acknowledged.

He cupped her face, one of his hands falling to her neck as his tongue slipped into her mouth. The kiss was slow, heady, exploratory. It cut her open and left her bleeding and confused, reeling with so many conflicting thoughts that she quickly tore her mouth away.

"R-Red," she gasped.

He didn't even look shocked.

That made it worse.

His thumb stroked across her jaw, his expression unreadable. "Night, Isobel."

She turned away, fumbled for the door, and disappeared into Theodore's room. He was sitting up in bed, staring at the door, his brow deeply furrowed.

"He likes you" was the first thing he said, and Isobel stopped short, her breath sawing in and out of her chest. Theodore's gaze travelled over her, coming to a rest on her face, his jaw tight and flexed. "He likes you and I can't even blame him."

"I think I messed up," she whispered. "I ..."

"No," he interrupted. "You've just been your sweet, wonderful self. You haven't done anything wrong." He patted the bed beside him, and she dragged her feet all the way there, flopping down beside him.

"I've been thinking," he murmured, shifting down to lay beside her. He opened his arm and she curled into his side immediately. "If you weren't showing any interest in them, we might have ended up with a far bigger problem. I think your openness is the glue keeping us all in check right now. Oscar was so smug today, he might as well have been skipping along and singing with the fucking birds. I've never seen him so ... relaxed. He needed to know that you would accept his claim, and then he immediately backed off."

She stared at the ceiling, quietly listening to him vocalising his thoughts. "Are you upset? Everyone expects you to overreact and I think it's making me think the same way."

"I want to rip off their hands every time they touch you," he admitted calmly. "But I think it would be worse if you were unhappy."

"You make me happy."

"I know." He rolled his head to the side, looking at her. "As amazing as you smell when you're turned on, you also smell a lot like my brother, and it's really off-putting right now."

"Oh." She shook herself around on his sheets, making him crack a smile. "Better?"

"No," he grunted, tugging her on top of his hips. He sat up, pulling his shirt over his head, and then he tugged off her shirt, tossing it away from his bed before pulling his over her head, never once letting his eyes stray from her face. She thought he would be happy with that, but then he stood, picking her up in the same motion as he dragged her shorts down her legs. He tossed those, and dropped back to the bed, sitting her back on his hips, the hem of his over-large shirt pooling in her lap.

"Better." He squeezed her waist. "You can borrow my shirts too, you know."

"Really?" She felt her smile pushing into her cheeks.

"Yeah." He ran his hands down her thighs, and then up again, slipping beneath the shirt to lightly circle her hips. "Fuck. You look good." He quickly shifted her off, dropping her back to the mattress. "I'm glad you're here, Illy." He turned her around, tugging the blanket around him as he pressed close behind her, his arm wrapping around her front.

Maybe there was something wrong with her, because all she could think about was how amazing he smelled and how much she desperately wanted him to touch her the same way he did the night she was released from the hospital.

"I'm glad I'm here too." She hugged his arm, feeling a persistent nudge of fear against her chest. She wasn't even sure if it was his or hers, but she was suddenly terrified that she might have to leave him the next day.

She wasn't sure if she could.

“Don’t worry.” He nuzzled into her neck, his warmth spreading through her body. “I’ll apply to visit whatever settlement you’re in if you’re not with me. I won’t leave you.”

She sucked in a shaky breath, and then turned around, his arm lifting to allow the movement before resettling over her.

“What if I have feelings?” she whispered, already wanting to take the words back. Or cry. Or throw up.

His eyes flicked between hers, his jaw flexing. “What kind of feelings?”

She pulled his hand to her chest, pressing it over her pounding heart. “Would that be okay?”

“Yeah, pretty. I think that would be fucking fine.” His voice was a growl, his Alpha ring growing bigger, making his eyes appear darker. “Ah, fuck the rules.” He grabbed the back of her neck and pulled her mouth to his, his tongue staking an immediate claim.

After the turmoil of everything that had happened that day, kissing Theodore was like coming home, and a sob built up in the back of her throat, quickly swallowed by him as he eased her backward, rolling on top of her, his knee kicking one of her legs wide before he settled his hips to hers, rocking his erection against her.

His kiss grew more demanding, his hands tearing his shirt off her body before she even realised what was happening. He paused, his forehead notched against hers, his body vibrating as he pulled in a few deep breaths.

"You okay?" she whispered, touching his jaw.

"Better." He kissed her again and then trailed kisses down her neck. "Just pent up. Don't want to lose control. Not going to fuck you tonight."

"Why not?" she asked, her mind full of his scent and the feel of his hands dragging down her sides.

He grunted, ripping her panties, and pulling them from her body in one ruined length of fabric.

"Shit, sorry." He stared at his hand, and then at her, his eyes travelling slowly over her chest, following the chain embedded in her skin down to her belly button and then dipping between her legs as he slowly pressed her knees apart.

The breath left his chest in a heavy groan. "Right now, I can't think of a single reason why, but I know I don't want to rush you."

He lowered over her again, his mouth drawn to hers like a magnet, his tongue thrusting deep as his fingers clenched against her hips, his cock rocking between her legs again. Though this time, only his boxers separated them.

"You want me to make you feel good again?" he rasped against her mouth. It was more of a demand than a question, but she nodded anyway.

She felt something tickle against her hand but ignored it as Theodore suddenly slid down the bed, forcing her knees wide apart, pressing them back against the bed, his tongue laving at the wetness he was creating between her thighs.

Her body bowed, a whimper catching in the back of her throat as her hands flew to his head. He moved to her clit, showering it with attention until she was losing her mind. It was fast and hard—ruthless, almost. He brought her to orgasm so quickly her breathy moans were interrupted by a hiccup of surprise, and then he climbed up her body again, propping himself up with one arm as he freed his cock, his knees trapping her legs together as he forced his hard length between her thighs, dipping it into the sticky, warm heat he had created. He thrust it in and out of the space between her thighs a few times, spreading her own honey over her skin before he pulled it out and started stroking himself, his eyes dark, his teeth sinking into his lower lip, all of his glorious muscles tensed.

"Was just going to focus on you," he gritted. "But I need you covered. Need it all over you. You're fucking mine. Fuck." He squeezed himself, and the first ribbon of white streaked across her chest, then her ribs, then her stomach. He kicked her knees wide, stroking himself a few more times as the final drips landed right on her pussy. She never would have thought she would be fantasising about anyone covering her in their semen, but some primal part of her brain was glowing and preening at the stark claiming. Her fingers were twitching to push the drops on her pussy lips inside herself, but that might be going a little too far.

He sat back, still hard, his length still twitching as he stared at her body before his eyes crawled up to hers, shadowed with desire.

"I wish I could keep you like this forever."

She swallowed, her voice husky as she said, "This is a family-friendly show."

He cracked a grin, leaning over her to kiss her softly. "I'll get a towel."

Despite the statement, he didn't move. He remained exactly where he was, eyes trailing leisurely over her, his dick still hard, his breath sucked sharply between his teeth.

"Okay, going," he rasped.

He pulled his boxers back into place and disappeared into his bathroom, returning with a damp washcloth. He gently cleaned her up, but when he returned from the bathroom again and caught her reaching for his discarded shirt, a gravelled sound of warning burst from his throat.

He looked like he surprised himself, and he shook his head. "Sorry, baby. Cover up if you want to."

She held up her hands in surrender, a laugh building up in the back of her throat, and he rolled his eyes, pouncing onto the bed and rolling her into his body, tugging the blanket up around her before wrapping her into his arms and pressing his nose to the back of her head, inhaling her deeply.

Her hand pricked again, and she glanced down, freezing at the hint of red on her skin, but it wasn't blood, it was only ... string. She raised her palm, and Theodore shifted behind her, his head lifting to also stare.

The string was tied around her pinkie finger, the other end disappearing into the blanket, she rolled onto her back and blinked at Theodore, who was holding up his hand. The other end was tied to his pinkie.

There was the softest, most subtle glow to the thread, and it felt like it hummed. It began drawing their hands together, and Isobel laughed as their palms met, the thread only relaxing when Theodore forced her fingers to part, threading his between them.

He didn't say a word, but he twisted behind her again, resting their clasped hands in front of her, where he could see them. He didn't feel tense, but she could tell that he stayed awake, just watching the thread, and she eventually drifted off to sleep before he did, her body filled with warmth and happiness.

21

CONSOLIDATION DAY

SHE BLINKED HER EYES OPEN BLEARILY, TRYING TO CLEAR THE fogginess from her mind as the world spun around her dizzily, the bed falling away from her as she dropped onto something much harder than a mattress. The something grunted, and a male voice swore roughly.

"Niko? What was that?" a woman's voice demanded. "Is there someone in your *bed*?"

"*Okaasan*. Mama. No."

Suddenly, a blanket was being tugged up over her head, Niko's hand gripping her shoulder underneath it, keeping her still. "See? It's just me. I just kicked my foot on the end of the bed. Why did you call so early?"

The blanket was flipped back from her head, revealing Niko half sitting up in bed, his broad, muscled chest bare, his hand landing on her shoulder again and squeezing. He didn't look at her, though, keeping his attention on his phone screen. His mother was chattering on about a dream she'd had, and something called *omikuji* and how it all meant something especially bad.

"Everything's fine, Okaasan." Niko sighed, his fingers still tightly holding Isobel in place.

"Are you getting sick?" she demanded.

"No, I'm just tired. You woke me up."

"Okay, Niko-kun, get some more sleep. Be careful today, okay? I'll text you later."

"Love you, Okaasan." He hung up the call and tossed his phone aside, peeling his hand off Isobel one finger at a time as he stared down at her in shock. "Are you naked, Carter?"

She was huddled between his legs, her hands still braced on his hard thighs, her mind completely still with shock.

"Would it be less awkward if I lied?" she asked timidly.

"No." He slitted his gaze. "You smell ..." He breathed deeply, his pupils dilating. "What were you doing?"

"Sleeping," she grumbled. "It was very confusing to wake up like this."

She started to lift up, but his eyes suddenly widened, and he yanked her back to his body, upsetting her balance and sprawling her across his chest.

"Shit," he swore, releasing her again. "Sorry, I thought you were going to drop the blanket."

"You never seen a girl naked before?" she asked, folding her arms over his chest, and propping her chin up, since it didn't look like she was going anywhere anytime soon.

"Of course I have," he groaned. "But none of them were my mate."

"Does your mom know about them?"

He glared at her. "I'm starting to see why you need a safe word."

She gasped, a laugh building in the back of her throat, and Niko's lips twitched like he was thinking of laughing as well.

"I don't think it's very common to discuss your sexual experiences with your parents," he said. "So ... that would be a no."

"What difference does me being your mate make?" she asked, cocking her head to the side.

His hand flashed up, brushing away the strand of hair that had slipped over her cheek. He glared at his own hand like it had acted without his permission, before dropping it to the bed.

"It means something different." His gaze traced her face. "Anything I do with you will mean something different."

"Like what?"

"All right, naked girl, that's enough."

He carefully bundled her into the blanket and was lifting her from the bed like a burrito when Theodore burst into the room.

"There you are," Theodore grumbled, kicking the door shut, relief written all over his face.

"Here I am," Niko drawled sarcastically. "And I have a naked Sigma. What should I do with her?"

"Feed her!" Isobel whisper-shouted, freeing one of her arms to pump her fist into the air.

"Okay." Niko dropped her back onto the bed. "I'll fetch Kilian to sneak you back into his room then we can go get some breakfast."

She nodded, clutching at the top of the blanket. Theodore gave her a droll look as Niko left. "You gave me a heart attack. Even the string was gone."

"I'm pretty sure it's wrapped around me," she replied, feeling around with the hand that was still stuck inside the blanket. Sure enough, the string had become tangled around her waist. "What should I do with it?"

"Anything but cut it," he answered seriously. "I need to take a picture to show the others."

She struggled to her feet and then wiggled the blanket loose, parting it along her side. Theodore caught her hip and snapped a quick picture of her naked waist before pulling the blanket back around her. Niko returned with Kilian a second later before disappearing into his bathroom. Kilian gave her an amused look, sweeping her into his arms and striding out of the room.

He deposited her in his bathroom, leaning close, his

cheek brushing hers. "You smell amazing. Did you sleep well?"

A smile broke over her face. "I got another soul artefact." She parted the blanket again and his fingers played across the red string, plucking it gently.

"Thread?" he asked. "It wrapped around you?"

"No, it tied me and Theo together by our pinkies."

"Well, that's disgustingly adorable." He reared back, checking to see if she was serious, before he laughed. "How do I get myself a disgustingly adorable soul artefact, now that you're giving them out again?"

She shrugged. "Ask me nicely."

"Cute." His expression grew serious, his pale eyes digging into hers, his face unreadable, before he suddenly backed off.

"The Consolidation Day festival will kick off soon and you still need to pack for the holidays. I'll let you shower." He stepped out but paused in the doorway, tapping his fingers against the frame. "It's nice seeing you happy, Illy. We should have guessed the key to your smile was dancing." He lingered a moment longer, just staring at her, before he forced a smile and disappeared.

She wasn't sure what to make of that comment, but luckily, he hadn't stuck around for a response. She raced through a shower and picked out one of her designer dresses for the day, since she wasn't going to do any training for once. It was a pretty pale yellow—a diagonal panel dress with ladder trims stitching each section together. The neckline was a soft diagonal slash that looped over one shoulder, a loose chiffon sleeve falling down her arm. The other sleeve was attached to the bodice, and it hung from her bicep.

She tucked her phone—which Kilian had put on charge—into her over-the-shoulder bag and added the red string in case any of the others needed to examine it in person. She brushed out her hair and slipped her feet into some tan sandals before planting herself in the living room to wait for the others.

After a minute, she pulled out her phone to sort through the notifications. Theodore had posted the picture of her string-bound waist to the group chat she was in, and it seemed like he had done it without an explanation.

Oscar: The fuck? Are we choosing outfits again?

Kilian: That is not an outfit. That is a piece of string.

Cian: Some outfits are pieces of string.

Moses: No, those outfits are still just string.

Niko: I don't understand. She was naked when she came to me, but you took that while she was still in my room?

Elijah: Rewind. Explain.

Niko: Isobel teleported to my bed half asleep while I was on a video call with my mom.

Niko: And she was naked.

Mikel (admin): A habit of hers, I'm afraid. Although the nakedness is new.

Gabriel: Not as new as you might think.

Oscar is typing ...

Oscar has been muted.

Kalen (admin): Is that a soul artefact?

Kilian: Yes, it is.

Theodore: Sorry, was in the shower.

Gabriel: When did it appear?

Theodore: Last night. Tied around our pinkies.

Moses: Wow. I just vomited in my mouth.

Kilian: You weren't vomiting in your mouth when Isobel was manipulating the shit out of you last night.

Cian: I would kill for tickets to that show.

Kilian: It was highly entertaining.

Oscar has been unmuted.

Kalen (admin): What were you doing when the string appeared?

Theodore: Platonic bonding.

Mikel (admin): Isobel?

The messages stopped there, and she swallowed, typing out a hesitant reply.

Isobel: I'm not sure how much detail I'm supposed to go into.

Kalen (admin): Jesus Christ. Did any of you follow the goddamned rules?

Isobel: What rules?

Oscar: Not a chance.

Moses: No.

Kilian: Yes.

Theodore: No.

Elijah: Obviously.

Gabriel: Don't insult me.

Niko: Of course.

Oscar and Moses were chuckling as they strode into the lounge, both looking her up and down as she quickly pulled to her feet.

"Morning, rich girl," Oscar mumbled, rocking back on his heels, and shoving his hands into his pockets as he surveyed her dress. "Don't you smell nice today."

"So everyone keeps saying." She eyed him, trying to figure out if he was being sarcastic or not.

Moses only nodded at her, his stormy eyes doing another pass over her dress.

"Ready for the festival?" she asked, as Niko walked toward them from the hallway, followed by Elijah and Gabriel.

"Ready as I'll ever be," Moses grumbled, moving to the front door, and shouting over his shoulder, "Hurry up! We're hungry!"

"Wonder why," Cian asked, shouldering past everyone to drop an arm over Isobel's shoulder, his nose brushing along her hairline. He sniffed her but didn't comment on her smell.

She glanced up into his face, noting that his expression was a little drawn. "Any more dreams?"

He shook his head. "I didn't pull your card."

"What do you mean?"

"The moon card." His mouth was tight. "I draw it every morning. This morning I didn't."

"That could mean anything, right?" she asked.

The others were staring at Cian, and she felt a few flashes of worry and panic before they managed to control their reactions. He nodded at her but didn't answer otherwise, steering her toward the door as Theodore and Kilian joined them.

"Mikki and Kalen are going to meet us at the festival," Kilian explained.

Isobel checked her phone again, combing through the rest of her notifications. Nothing from Sophia.

She tapped on their conversation and sent a message.

Isobel: Everything still good?

The reply was almost instant.

Sophia: Yes, and no more dreams.

Sophia: I think whoever it was, the increased security must have messed up their plans.

She resolved herself to keep a close eye on Cian for the rest of the day, but she barely needed to, because he refused to leave her side. He stayed with her as she picked out what to eat for breakfast and sat silently beside her as she ate. As soon as she shifted to leave the booth, he was jumping up, a step behind her as she disposed of her tray.

The others were giving him worried looks, but nobody said anything, even when he looped his arm around her and bent to sniff her hair every now and then, as though reassuring himself that she wasn't hurt in any way.

They loitered along the edges of the festival for most of the morning, lounging in lawn chairs and watching the Hollywood parade as it wound its way around the lake. They chatted quietly, completely ignoring the speeches of the returning guest Icons as they reminisced on their golden days at Ironside, and how winning the game changed their lives forever.

Kalen and Mikel joined them as the top ten Icon contenders took to the stage, saying a few quick words about what Ironside has meant to them and what they were going to do if they won.

"Let's get closer," Mikel suggested, forcing them all to pull themselves together and push through the crowd.

They moved toward the action, the other students giving them plenty of room. The stage had been built out over the lake, leaving enough space for everyone to gather at the front of the academy.

There were snack booths set up along the sides of the paths and lawn chairs scattered around the outskirts for students to relax in. Twinkling strings of lights crisscrossed overhead, strung tightly from wooden pillars, and everyone seemed happy, excited to be going home in the overnight busses later. Some of them would be dropped off at airports with return tickets home, while the rest would travel by bus—depending on how far away their settlements were.

She imagined they would be the superstars of their settlement for as long as they were at Ironside, receiving a hero's welcome home as everyone tried to get them to spill the behind-the-scenes secrets they were contract-bound to keep.

The first Icon-contender stepped forward, holding a microphone up and winking at the audience as his music started. No matter their specialisation, they always performed a song, danced, played an instrument, or did some sort of stand-up routine on Consolidation Day. It was more about entertaining people than showing off their skills.

It was nearing early afternoon when a female official stepped onto the cleared stage to announce the Icon winner.

Isobel squinted at her. "Isn't that the woman from the dining hall the other morning?"

"Looks like it," Elijah replied.

"Frisk," Kalen supplied. "Her name is Olivia Frisk. She's the on-site assistant to the Director of Ironside."

"Welcome, ladies and gentlemen, esteemed faculty members, distinguished guests, and students of Ironside," Frisk boomed into the microphone. "We are gathered here today to celebrate not just the founding of Ironside, but the profound unity it has brought to our world. It is a day of reflection and celebration as we acknowledge the work that Ironside has done to bring the Gifted and the humans together. From its inception, Ironside Academy was intended as a place where we could transcend the boundaries of what everyone thought to be possible. Because of Ironside, we are able to lift the Gifted, one by one, out of the settlements and bring them to this paradise, giving them every little luxury they could ever ask for, with the most skilled cultural experts our world has to offer at their disposal. The Ironside initiative is a testament to the power of unity, compassion, and creativity. So, as we announce this year's Icon, let us remember that only *together* can we achieve the impossible."

She paused as cheers rose through the gathered crowd, before speaking again.

"This year at Ironside has been nothing short of exhilarating, and if there's one specialisation that has consistently captivated our attention over the last year, making us tune into our screens with bated breath, it's the world of dance! Therefore, with no further delay, I have the privilege to present this year's Icon, and it should come as no surprise to you all what her specialisation is! Her dance ability has left us all in awe, and as sad as we are to see her leave Ironside, we're ecstatic to announce that she will be joining the Paris Opera Ballet. We expect big things of her in the future. Please join me in giving an enormous round of applause for the remarkable Astrid Johannson!"

A familiar, petite blonde Beta bounded across the stage. Isobel was sure that she had seen the other girl hanging out with Niko on and off-screen, and she was so distracted by intrusive thoughts about whether or not she was one of the girls he had already seen naked that she didn't hear the sound at first.

The familiar *pop pop pop* that still haunted her dreams.

It wasn't until the screaming started that she realised what was happening, and by then, it was already too late. The crowd surged in an instant panic, all of them trying to push and shove their way to safety. Isobel was toppled over with several other people, and all she could do was hold her arms over her head as a rush of feet threatened to trample her.

Cian managed to fight his way back to her side, and he picked her up by the arms, forcing her up until her head broke the crush of people and she could breathe again. He started forcing his way through the rush, holding her steady with one arm.

"The others!" she shouted, tugging at his arm.

"They can look after themselves," he said. "But you'll get crushed."

Another round of shots rang out, and Cian ducked, the crowd surging again. She was torn away from him, people shoving her backward as they clambered toward the stage.

She strained to keep her head above it all, spotting

Cian with a bloody nose, pushing people out of his way. When his eyes found her again, he pointed behind her. "That way!" he shouted.

She immediately stopped fighting the pushing and shoving of the crowd, allowing them to fight in Cian's direction while she squeezed in the other direction until she could suddenly duck and weave between the panicked students.

She caught sight of the chapel, now running toward it at full speed, her heart threatening to burst out of her chest. She was almost at the door when the first wave of dizziness hit her. Her vision blurred, and her heartbeat slowed to a crawl, dark spots flashing over her vision.

The feeling was accompanied by a sharp flash of memory. A blade cutting into her arm and Eve's scathing voice in her ear.

Eve.

She forced herself to stumble forward, collapsing against the doorjamb to keep herself upright as the screams and gunshots warbled into a strange cloud of sound. The pressure against her head doubled, making her fall forward, a groan catching in the back of her throat as she stumbled into the chapel and caught herself on her hands as her body hit the floor.

She flopped onto her back, trying to force away the dizziness, to pull herself up and lock the door, but Eve was already there, stepping into the opening, her blue eyes clearly shining with smugness, even with Isobel's blurry vision.

"Well, this all turned out rather well, didn't it?" Eve asked. "I've been following you around for *weeks*, waiting for my moment." Her gaze flickered up, focussing on something behind Isobel.

Sophia stalked forward, her short dark hair flopping up and down with how fast she moved, and then suddenly her fist connected with Eve's face.

"Not today, bitch." Sophia shoved against Eve as Maya knelt beside Isobel, pulling her up into a sitting position.

Eve stumbled back, clutching her nose as blood spurted through her fingers. "What the fuck?" she snapped. "Who the fuck even *are* you?"

Sophia shoved her backward and then slammed the door in her face and locked it, before collapsing against the wood, looking pale and sweaty, her hands shaking. She shook her head like she was trying to clear away a fog in her mind—Eve's power somehow working on both of them at once—before she turned to the side and shouted through the door, "A real friend, you psycho!"

"Isobel?" Maya was touching her forehead. "What's going on out there?"

"S-Shooter," Isobel slurred.

"You're going to pay for that!" Eve collided with the other side of the door, her fists pounding against it.

"You're *all* going to pay for that! Shit, he's coming." She suddenly backed away from the door.

Sophia stumbled away, looking at the door in horror. "He's coming? Who's coming?"

"Soph," Maya snapped. "Get away from the door. Luis! Get behind the podium! Is the back door locked?"

"Yes, Mama." Luis' voice trembled like he was crying, and he squeaked when he ran into something, knocking it against the floor.

"Get down on the ground, Luis," Maya ordered over her shoulder, helping Isobel to her feet.

Sophia grabbed Isobel's other arm as the effect of Eve's power began to wear off, and the three of them stumbled toward where Luis was hiding.

"I saw you go in there, Carter!" Heavy fists crashed against the chapel door, and Isobel ducked away from the other two women, pushing them toward the dais when they tried to grab onto her again. She turned to face the door, dread dropping into her stomach.

"Carter!" Fists rained down on the door.

It was Crowe.

Just as she considered darting out through the back door and calling his attention away from the chapel, he fired off a round of shots, breaking apart the lock. She bit back a scream, ducking into one of the vestibules lining the side of the room, pressing up against the thin wall and covering her mouth to muffle her terrified breathing.

She had to do something, or the others were going to get hurt.

But she didn't know what to do.

"I know you're in here." Wood splintered beneath Crowe's boots as he slowly stepped inside. "I'll shoot this whole place up if I have to."

Luis' dream was coming true, and it was all because of her. She had run *straight* to the chapel, thinking they might be in danger. Cian was right. Believing in things did half the work of fate.

She waited until Crowe was almost in line with her vestibule before she slipped out, scooting around him to put his back to the dais. He raised his gun immediately. It was long. Bigger than she expected. He even had ammunition clips strapped to his belt.

He was prepared.

"There you are," he snarled, levelling the gun at her face.

"Get out of here," she said, keeping her eyes on Crowe and hoping the others were smart enough to leave while she was giving them an opportunity to.

She wasn't worth an extra three lives.

"I'm not going anywhere," Crowe spat. "You ruined my life, you little cunt."

She caught the barest glimpse of movement over his shoulder. It looked like Maya, Sophia, and Luis were moving toward the back door. She needed to keep Crowe talking.

"How did I do that?" she asked.

"First, the Track Team told me to ruin your reputation—even promised that Eve would help with her power, then your stupid boyfriend comes after me." He took a step closer, staring at her dress like it personally offended him. "But they never really wanted to recruit me. I was *just* pathetic enough to employ as a tool. They recorded me doing what they *told me to do*, and then used it to blackmail me. They used me to get to you and then tossed me out like garbage as soon as they had you. But you never really escape the Track Team. You know that, don't you? You know they own you now? And I'm going to make sure to sink their precious little investment."

Isobel flinched when the back door opened, a bright shaft of light angling into the room, but Crowe didn't seem to notice it. He was focussed on the slow steps backward she was taking, carefully matching them with steps forward as he kept the gun pointed up.

One of the shadows paused in the doorway and Isobel chanced a quick look up, catching the way Sophia held her fingers up to her head, gesturing a phone.

Isobel yanked her phone out of her pocket and held it up just as Crowe's arm twitched, his heavy brows dragging down in fury.

"Throw it," he ordered. "Or I blast your head off right now."

She flicked it over her shoulder, close enough to the

door to feel where the opening was by the breeze creeping in against her back. She heard it scatter and slide off the chapel steps and Crowe reached around her, wedging the broken doors closed as Sophia finally disappeared from the back door, closing it at the same time.

Hopefully, she would get to Isobel's phone and call one of the Alphas ... because Isobel wasn't sure she would be able to overpower Crowe on her own.

She had tried that once, and there were no candlesticks within reach this time.

"So what should I do?" Crowe asked, his foul, stale-sweat smell washing over her before he backed off. "Give you a few more scars?" He tilted his head, looking her over. "Shoot out your kneecaps? Send them back a cripple? You want to be a cripple, bitch?"

She winced, leaning back against the door, and keeping her mouth shut. He took another step away, planting the barrel of his gun against her cheek. "Or I could shoot a hole through your face? See how much better than me you think you are when you're just as ugly."

He lowered the gun, brushing it across her chest, and pressing it low against her stomach. "Or maybe I'll have a little taste of what you're handing out to all the Alphas first? Maybe if you're a good enough fuck, I'll let you keep one of your legs. What do you say?"

She averted her eyes from his face as his meaty

tongue poked out to lick his lips, her attention zeroing in on the painting hanging above the dais. She had no idea which of the Gifted gods it was, but she was willing to try anything.

So she closed her eyes and begged.

Please. Help me. I'll do anything you want. If you're real, help me.

"Are you *praying*?" Crowe suddenly laughed, backhanding her across the face and forcing her head to whip to the side. Her eyes flew open. "Those gods aren't *real*, you dumb slut!"

Her chest began to tingle as tears tracked down her face, blood filling her mouth. He must have split her lip.

"Please let me go," she rasped, rubbing at the pain in her chest before realising what it was.

She froze, pulling at the neckline of her dress to stare down at the chain. A new gemstone had appeared. Stormy grey and glowing lightly.

She choked on the sudden taste of ash spilling into the back of her throat.

"What's wrong with you?" Crowe lowered his gun, his eyes fixed to the subtle glow shining through her dress. "What is that?" He jerked the gun back up. "Take it off and show me. Now!" He fired a warning shot through the door over her shoulder, and her vision wavered, flashing dark and then suddenly vividly bright.

Her breath was a rasp, pain sluicing through the tips of her fingers.

She ducked as Crowe levelled the gun at her head, his eyes widening in panic, and the second shot punched through the door where her head had been as she dove forward, knocking him off balance, the gun scattering against the ground.

"G-Get off me!" he shouted, but she paid no attention.

Her throat was full of scorching sulphur, her eyes seeing only objects for her to tear her claws into. There was some sort of wiggling prey beneath her, and his whining noises needed to be silenced.

She tore through the gun, breaking off the barrel and using it to hit away at the whining thing until the annoying noises turned into garbles, and then silence. She stood and kicked the lifeless thing aside, enjoying the way the items around her splintered into cracks when she wedged her claws into them.

"Illy." Another prey, though this one didn't smell as foul. She bounded toward it, but a strong grip caught her wrists, trapping her against something hard.

She snarled, but the prey were closing in on her, bodies surrounding her, the hard thing behind her rumbling with a deep voice.

"Time to come back to us, Carter. I need you to listen to my voice very carefully, and try to say these words with me, okay?"

She thrashed, trying to get her claws into the voice box behind her, to silence it.

"Ten," he said. "Try to breathe. Nine. Eight. Seven ..."

She almost managed to dislodge them, but then more hands were holding her, restricting her movement, leaving her to twitch and snarl, biding her time until one of them slipped up.

"Six," the infuriating voice continued. "Five. Four. Three. Two ... One."

And then he started again. And again. And again.

Eventually, the vivid colours started to fade, and she began to blearily recognise the faces. She gave one last desperate tug, but there were so many of them restraining her, and she fell limp against the body behind her as Theodore's face registered in her brain.

His face was bleeding, a short cut along his chin dripping onto his shirt. Moses was beside him, his arms covered in cuts, his stormy eyes focussed. Mikel was behind her, Kalen and Oscar both helping to hold her arms.

She drew in a shuddering breath, her chest keening in pain. "W-What happened?"

"Don't worry about that right now." Elijah appeared in her line of sight. "Just keep breathing. Try to slow it down."

She felt like she was hyperventilating, panic crashing through her in wave after wave. Slowly, they began to release her, but as soon as Moses backed off, she caught sight of Crowe by the entrance.

He wasn't moving.

She stumbled toward him, but Mikel stepped into her path, shaking his head.

She collapsed to her knees, a wail catching in the back of her throat. "I didn't ..." She stared down at her hands, at the blood coating her all the way to her armpits. "I didn't ..."

"Hey." Mikel crouched before her, catching her face, and forcing her eyes to his. "Just focus on me, okay? Everything's fine. You're safe. You couldn't control it."

"Is h-he d-dead?" she hiccupped through her sobs, feeling her chest crack open.

Their fear, fury, and shock poured into her, flooding her as she wavered, Mikel switching his grip to her arms to keep her upright.

"He's gone," he said lowly. "It was the ferality, Isobel, not you. Don't take this on. He was going to kill you. He killed *dozens* of people out there."

"Isobel," Elijah said sharply. "Stop. I can feel that. *Stop*." Alpha voice.

She dragged her walls back up. "W-Wasn't deliberate."

"It's okay." Mikel dragged her against his chest, cupping the back of her head. "It's okay, sweetheart. You're going to be okay."

She thought she could hear sirens in the distance.

"We need to do something about the body," Gabriel said. "And we need to hide her."

Mikel picked her up, drawing her away from Crowe

and keeping her face stuck against his chest. He set her down again on the other side of the room, shrugging out of his jacket and pulling it over her dress, zipping it up so that all the blood was hidden.

"Well ... it worked once." Niko picked up a lighter and one of the decorative lanterns set into one of the little alcoves cut into the wall. He smashed the lantern against the ground, liquid splashing out of it, and the others immediately moved to copy him, smashing the rest of the lanterns before Niko set the lighter against the ground, igniting little fires where the lanterns were soaking the ground.

For a moment, they all just stood there, watching the flames lick at the ground. She couldn't stop crying or shaking, but Niko met her eyes, his expression calm and capable.

"Don't worry," he said gently. "We'll protect you."

"You don't need to watch this," Elijah said. "Go straight to the Guardian's house." He opened the back door, holding it for her. "We'll be there after we make sure this fire takes off. Go *straight* there. No detours." He pulled her phone out of his pocket. "Take this with you. Sophia called us with it."

She nodded, desperate to get away from the sight of flames teasing closer and closer to the bloodied body. She rushed out of the chapel, the sound of sirens growing closer, and was just pushing through the gate when her phone vibrated. She pulled it out, saw her father's name, and accepted the call.

"I'm safe," she said, figuring that was why he was calling.

"Good. Go straight to the front of the academy. Now. Don't stop to talk to anyone or help anyone. Don't try to grab any of your belongings." He barked out the order in Alpha voice, the command already forcing her limbs to move.

"Wait, I—"

He hung up the call and she swore as her body automatically turned in the other direction, pushing back through the gate.

What if he was hurt?

She picked up the pace, making sure Mikel's long sleeves were covering her bloody hands as she ran to the front of the academy, barely able to process the sight of bodies scattered across the grass, groups of terrified people hovering around them. She passed through the gates as the flashing lights of several ambulances and police cars appeared along the road leading toward the first gate into Ironside. Her father appeared in front of her, his hands clasping her arms.

"We're leaving early," he said, his words barely registering.

He didn't *look* hurt.

He began dragging her to a limousine idling at the

curb, and she dug her heels in, trying to yank out of his grip.

"No, I can't—"

"Get in the damn car, Isobel," he snapped, his Alpha voice making her head bow and her blood run cold as he successfully shoved her through the car door. "We're not staying here a second longer. Who knows what could happen."

Cesar Cooper and her father's publicist were already in the car, along with several bags and briefcases. They had been packing up while students were being slaughtered.

"You have to let me out," she tried again. "My surrogates—"

"I don't have to do anything," Braun spoke over her, before barking at the driver—his assistant—to hurry up and leave. "Do you have anything to calm her down?" he turned to Cesar next, who nodded, digging into his briefcase, and pulling out a little bottle of pills, which he tossed to her father.

Braun shook out several pills before grabbing her chin and forcing her mouth open.

"Swallow them," he commanded, snapping her jaw shut.

Her throat obeyed without her permission, and she tried to calm down and think of a plan as her father turned away from her, his voice loud and grating beside her as he launched into a tirade about the dangerous rise of anti-loyalists and how the government wasn't doing anything to cripple them.

Cripple. She shuddered at the word, her eyes closing tightly, panic lacing tight and hot through her body.

You're safe.

You're okay.

Nobody is going to hurt you.

She tried to believe it as her mind rioted, remembering the feel of metal pressing against her face.

You'll find your way back to them.

Her head started to loll, her thoughts turning fuzzy.

"What'd you give me?" she slurred, cracking open an eye.

Braun and Cesar continued the conversation as though she hadn't even spoken.

"What'd you ..." She swallowed, wondering why her mouth was suddenly so dry. "What ..." Her body grew cold and numb, her forehead sagging toward the window, resting there as her mind sank into blackness.

To be continued ...

BONUS SCENE

WHERE IN THE WORLD IS CARTER?

KALEN MADE SURE EVERYONE WAS OUT OF THE CHAPEL AHEAD of him before he paused at the back door, his attention fixed to the body now heavily engulfed in flames. There was a tight ball of fear permanently lodged inside his chest. He saw Isobel go down in the crowd, but after knocking down and injuring at least six people as he fought his way over to her, he realised he had completely lost sight of where she was.

That was when it started.

The fear that refused to budge.

They couldn't lose her again. She was his responsibility now. He promised to protect her.

She had only been out of his sight for a few minutes, but it was a few minutes too long, so he slammed the door and followed the others around to the Guardian's residence. They were going to need to get out of there soon, just in case the fire caught onto the attached house.

Theodore was the first inside after hurriedly knocking on the door, and the rest of them quickly filled the kitchen. Kalen closed the door behind him, peering over the others to the Guardian standing in the opposite doorway.

She was also peering. Searching their faces. *For who?*

"Where is she?" Maya asked, a flicker of horror racing across her expression. "Did you get to her?"

"Where ..." He fell forward a step, that fear growing heavier, making it hard to breathe. "Is Isobel here?"

"No," the Guardian stuttered, "she—"

Oscar shoved through them, shocking Maya into silence. Kalen shoved open the door just as Oscar got to him, and all ten of them rushed out of the house, running back to the chapel. They searched around it as Theodore called her number once, twice, three times.

"She's not answering." He swore, his eyes pulsing black.

"She's fine," Kalen said, keeping Theodore in his sights. "We would feel it like last time, remember? She's okay. We just need to find her."

"I'm going to kill someone." Oscar was pacing, his eyes darting about. "I don't know who, but I'm going to—"

"Her father," Elijah suddenly announced, stalking

off. “There’s no way he’s going to stick around here with shots being fired.”

They followed Elijah to the family centre, all of them squeezing into the elevator as Mikel punched the button for Braun Carter’s floor. Kalen kept his attention on Moses and Theodore the whole time, wary of the way their faces kept twitching.

Mikel didn’t bother knocking on Braun’s door. He kicked it open, splintering the lock, and they immediately split up to search the apartment.

“No brawny motherfucker here to complain about his door being kicked in,” Elijah noted, stopping only a few feet into the room. “That’s not a good sign.”

Kalen waited, having come to the same conclusion, the fear growing and growing.

“Nobody here.” Gabriel strode back into the living room. “Looks like they packed in a rush.”

“Fuck!” Theodore suddenly shoved one of the armchairs, his eyes flashing black so fast that Mikel barely had time to dive over the coffee table and tackle him before the ferality kicked in.

“Shit.” Moses wavered. He was fighting it, but he was going to lose, and everyone knew it.

Elijah and Gabriel moved to help Mikel, freeing up the rest of them to deal with Moses.

“Fuckkk.” Moses gripped the back of a couch, his talons extending and ripping into the material.

Cian ducked as Theodore managed to throw Gabriel at him, the two of them tripping over the coffee table.

"Everyone else help with Theo," Kalen demanded in Alpha voice. "Me and Oscar have Moses."

Kilian and Cian had already jumped in to try and pin Theodore, but Niko was hovering back, waiting to see who would need him more. He helped up Gabriel and Cian, and the three of them moved to surround Theodore.

Moses' eyes exploded with darkness, a growl building up in the back of his throat as Kalen and Oscar drew closer to him.

"Finally," Oscar drawled, rolling up his sleeves. "Let's get this afterparty started."

I HOPE YOU ENJOYED SAUTER!

If you want to chat about this book or catch all the teasers for my next book, scan the code below to check out my reader's group!

If you enjoyed this book, please consider leaving a review. Indie authors rely on the support of our incredible readers, and without you guys, we wouldn't be able to continue publishing. Thank you for everything you do for the indie community!

Thank you!!
Jane xx

CONNECT WITH JANE WASHINGTON

Scan the code to view Jane's website, social media, release announcements and giveaways.

Printed in Great Britain
by Amazon

33030022R00330